If I Only
Had Wings

If I Only Had Wings

—

PAUL DANEMAN

LITTLE, BROWN AND COMPANY

A *Little, Brown* Book

First published in Great Britain in 1995
by Little, Brown and Company

Copyright © Paul Daneman 1995

'If I Only Had Wings' © 1940, reproduced by permission of
Peter Maurice Music Co Ltd, London WC2H 0EA
Lyrics by Sid Corlin
'Long Ago and Far Away' from *Cover Girl*, 1944.
Lyrics by Ira Gershwin

The moral right of the author has been asserted.

A CIP catalogue record for this book
is available from the British Library.

ISBN 0 316 91182 8

Typeset by M Rules
Printed and bound in Great Britain by
Clays Ltd, St Ives plc

Little, Brown and Company (UK)
Brettenham House
Lancaster Place
London WC2E 7EN

To Merry

If I only had wings, one little pair of those elusive things,
You would never hear me complain,
Again,
If I only had wings.

Popular Song, 1940

1

Harry was fond of saying that there was no more sublime sensation in the world than entering a woman's body for the first time. I would nod sagely and add, except of course for the first time you fly solo. Not that I'd entered many women's bodies in those days and, for that matter, I hadn't done much solo flying either. But Harry couldn't argue the point since he'd never flown at all, not even once round the bay for half-a-crown. Actually, that was true of most of His Majesty's Royal Airmen. Eighty per cent of us had our boots firmly on the ground and very few complaints were heard about that. As Harry said: 'I service the bloody things. They're just a load of tin and wire. Only an idiot would trust himself in one.'

I, on the other hand, in the flush of my nineteen-year-old innocence, was a reluctant penguin. The Air Force had hurt me deeply by grounding me. I had offered myself unstintedly on the understanding that I was to be transformed into a dazzling young hero in the uniform that so suited me (the blue, my mother had pointed out, matched my eyes). Nor was it all vanity. I had a passion for flying, and in every specification but one was well qualified for it. What went wrong was not their fault, or mine really, but that didn't make it any less painful to bear.

When I'd packed my kit-bag and departed ignominiously from the little training airfield in the Chilterns, they sent me on leave, which was nice of them. My mother unpicked the white aircrew flash from my cap with remarkably steady fingers while I packed *The Theory and Practice of the Internal Combustion Engine, Air Navigation, Principles of Flight* and three files of laboriously handwritten notes into a cardboard box which I consigned to a damp corner of the cellar. The mice probably ate the lot within a month. And I hope they enjoyed it.

A buff envelope arrived from the Air Ministry to inform me that I had been remustered to something connected with instruments and was posted to a bomber station in Yorkshire to get practical experience before going on the training course. Squatting on my kit in an inky corridor, wedged into a mass of heaving, coughing, anonymous bodies while the train jerked and hissed, halted and crawled through the impenetrable night of a blacked-out nation, I washed my hands of the war. My regrets to Mr Churchill and the people of Britain but now they would have to win it without me. All I required was that it should be over as soon as possible so that I could get on with my life, the life which I now considered to be firmly back in my own hands. I had the wit to see that it might be wiser to keep these feelings to myself, and so I did. And because I did, I found that soon, like flowers in an airless room, they started to wither away.

Until I met Pearl. Then they revived to plague me in a quite different way. Although I suppose what happened did cure me eventually. But it took a long time.

It has to be said that where this passion for things aeronautical was concerned I was not unique (almost, hardly, scarcely unique, as my English master used to say). Born in the twenties, my generation grew up in the air age. Our heroes were Lindbergh, Amy Johnson and Jim Mollison. We read a new

Biggles story every week and knew all about the terror of a jammed Lewis gun in the icy dawn high above the German lines, the scream of the struts in the slipstream as we barrel-rolled out of trouble, and at last the nonchalant stroll across frosty grass to eggs and hot coffee in the mess. We pushed our dads' motoring goggles up onto our foreheads, squinting over the sides of armchairs at the carpet thousands of feet below, and banked steeply into the last leg of the Schneider Trophy. Later we whittled and steamed and glued together real flying replicas of our beloved aeroplanes. Oh, the thrill of the instruction pamphlet that advised: 'Write your name and address on the fuselage of your model in case it flies out of sight and is lost.' Fully fifteen feet it floated before it hit a rose bush and disintegrated. And when, once in a blue moon, we heard the faint but unmistakable throb of an aero-engine, we dashed for the open air and stood motionless, watching the frail machine every second of its path across the sky from horizon to horizon, carrying the lonely leather-clad figure we longed to be.

Some of us grew out of our obsession, but mine got in among the corpuscles and became chronic. The trouble was that for two months of every year I was in mortal danger of serious, long-term, life-threatening addiction. My grandparents had a cottage by the river, next to an hotel, and behind it was a wide water meadow that stretched away, grassy and level, for nearly three-quarters of a mile. Whether it was the convenience of the field or the charm of the hotel I don't know, but the place was a mecca for the weekend fliers from Croydon. My grandfather was sure it was the hotel. It had thrived in Edwardian days because it could only be reached by river and its guests had been able to get back to their own rooms before the King's Proctor could row halfway across. My grandfather was convinced that the fliers were up to the same larks; but adultery didn't mean a thing to me at that age, and even if it had, nothing would have persuaded me that an airman could need any other ecstasy than the onanistic thrill of the joystick.

I spent all my summer holidays in that cottage, and for those long weeks I was in the same danger as an alcoholic in an off-licence. I was unhinged, distracted, ears forever straining for the sound of an engine; and when I heard it, there was a headlong stumbling rush to the garden to see it roar over my head, almost near enough to touch, to see the pilot, helmeted and goggled, peering down from the cockpit, and hear my grandmother, hands clapped over her ears, shouting that they'd have our chimneys off. (They never did; though once one did plough through the telegraph wires into the river and nobody could telephone for a week.) Then there was the interminable wait for the blip of the engine when the roar suddenly dropped to the ragged flutter that meant he was going to land. And I was running into the field, my mother calling, 'Not too near! Wait till the engine stops! Don't touch anything!', just in time to see the plane zig-zagging towards me over the grass, the pilot's head wagging from side to side looking for a place to swing round into the wind and shut off the engine.

In the silence I'd watch from a respectful distance while the gods descended from their machine and disappeared into the hotel. Then I would cautiously approach this beautiful, intricate thing that moments before had come diving and wheeling out of the sky and now stood gravely at rest, dripping oil onto the grass and ticking gently as it cooled. And, emboldened by its passivity, I would reach out a hand and touch its plywood body or the stretched fabric of its wings.

Sometimes the airmen would spend the night in the hotel. Then the planes would be tethered, canvas covers thrown over the cockpits and the wings folded back along the fuselage. In the mornings they would still be there, strange,

4

unlikely shapes rising through the mist, with the cows shuffling around them, tearing at the fresh, wet grass between the guy-ropes. It was a morning just like that when I finally became an incurable, lifelong addict.

A Sunday hush hung over the cottage and over the silent aeroplanes. I slipped through the gate and ran towards them. As I got nearer I could smell the heady scent of engine oil and fresh grass, the aviator's aphrodisiac. Three planes had been parked overnight: a Puss Moth with a single wing and enclosed cabin, and two Tiger Moths. One of the Tiger Moths had already been untethered and had its wings in position. It had a bright-blue body and white wings with the letters G–ADFS painted on the underside in huge black letters. I walked right round it and then slowly approached the cockpit, wondering if I dare climb up and look inside. There was no sign of life anywhere, even the cows had retreated to a far corner of the field. Gingerly I put my foot on the metal plate protecting the wing, grasped the padded edge of the cockpit and hoisted myself up. The smell now was of petrol and leather. And there were the instruments, there was the compass, there the joystick. And at that moment the hotel gate clicked shut and someone walked towards the plane.

I ducked down and crouched on the wing. I daren't jump off or I'd be seen. Whoever it was reached the other side of the fuselage. I heard the hatch behind the rear cockpit open and shut again. There was a long silence. Then I felt the plane move slightly and heard a man's voice say very quietly, 'Christ,' and then again, 'Christ,' and then, 'Oh, Christ,' and there was another silence. Suddenly the whole plane lurched as he climbed onto the other wing. I felt a shadow over me and looked up to see a young man staring at me in astonishment.

It was too late to run and I felt silly squatting on the wing like that, so I stood up.

5

'Hello,' I said feebly.

'What are you up to?' he said.

'Only looking.'

He stared at me for a moment with a puzzled, rather abstracted expression. I recognized him: I'd seen him land the previous evening and go into the hotel with his passenger, a slim young woman with pale gold hair, wearing men's flying overalls. The overalls had seemed to be trying to match her hair, but had failed. They had also failed to convince me she was anything but a girl.

'Like aeroplanes, do you?' he said.

I nodded.

'Know what this is?'

'De Havilland Tiger Moth, 82A,' I said promptly, and added, for effect, 'one hundred and thirty horsepower Gipsy engine.'

'Well, well,' he said, and looked at me again in his abstracted way, as if I wasn't really there. We stood on the wings, face to face across the cockpit, neither of us saying anything. Even to my eyes he seemed very young, although his confident Oxford accent with its connotations of class and money and his air of being preoccupied with graver matters gave him an authority that belied his youth. His eyelids were rather red and swollen. If he hadn't been a pilot one might almost think he'd been crying. He looked back at the hotel and turned to me again, looking straight at me now.

'Could you give me a hand?'

'Oh . . . yes,' I said, anguished to hear myself sound less eager than I was.

'You see those?' He pointed to two small domestic-looking switches on the outside of the cockpit. 'When I say, "Contact", just switch them both on. Don't touch anything else.'

He reached up and opened the petrol cock, then bent over and adjusted something in the cockpit. He jumped down and

6

walked round the wing to the front of the plane. Grasping the blade of the propeller with both hands, he tugged it downwards. It flicked round once and the engine sneezed. Several times he did this, and then he called, 'OK. Contact.'

Almost before he'd said the word I'd pushed the switches down. When he swung the propeller again the engine coughed and fired and I had to narrow my eyes against the sudden blast of air that blew my hair back from my face. He came back round the wing and reached into the cockpit to throttle the engine back. 'Thanks,' he said briefly. He stood on the wing for a long minute, looking back at the hotel. Then he turned back to see me still standing there clutching the cockpit rim, watching him, but alive only to the slipstream in my face and the vibration of the plane under my feet.

'Ever been up?' he said abruptly.

My circulation stopped. My jaw muscles locked. I shook my head.

'Like to?'

I managed to nod.

'Hop in, then.'

I knew I was supposed to ask my parents. The edict against accepting lifts from strangers would certainly seem to apply to this. But just as certainly I knew that if I ran back to the cottage he'd change his mind and roar away across the field and over the hill and my chance would be lost for ever. I was a whim, and whims can't afford to prevaricate. I slung my leg over the side of the cockpit and dropped onto the seat.

It was further down than I expected. He leaned over and clipped the safety harness round me, and when he shut the side flap I could barely see over the edge.

'Don't touch anything,' he shouted. 'And if you're bothered at all just put your hand up. Like this.' He lifted his hand above his head.

I gripped the sides of the seat. No hand of mine would be

seen – whatever happened – although my inside was already tight with apprehension at what might. I felt him climb into the rear cockpit, and I watched the ailerons wag up and down as he opened the throttle and we started to trundle and bump slowly across the field. Absurdly, I caught myself pretending I was in the cockpit of an aeroplane. I'd fantasized about it so often that the habit was in danger of obscuring the real event. I concentrated my attention on the details. The engine burst into a deafening roar and the whole plane shook as I clenched my hands and held my breath. It dropped to a chatter, only to suddenly roar again a second later and this time we were racing back the way we'd come, bouncing and rattling across the grass. As the tail came up I could see ahead at last and it seemed inevitable we'd smash into the hotel, and then in a sudden miraculous moment the bouncing and rattling stopped and I lost sight of the hotel and the trees were underneath us and we seemed high above everything I'd ever known and none of it was recognizable any more. The river wound away into the purple distance like a silver serpent, glinting in the sun, and then astonishingly tipped on its side and slid underneath us while my head and shoulders grew horribly heavy and seemed to want to squash my stomach.

We climbed higher and higher until the river was only a thread and the fields were postage stamps and the air grew colder and colder. My teeth were chattering and my fingers were blue and I was very glad I'd put on my pullover that morning. I was aware of having a rare and privileged experience: nobody I knew had ever done this. But how strange it was. The shattering noise of the engine, the icy wind and the complete lack of any sensation of movement were not at all what I'd imagined. And I wasn't giddy. I knew I had a terrible head for heights; the joke at school was that I got dizzy if I stood on tiptoe. But up here I wasn't connected to the hard, threatening ground; it had become an irrelevant pattern of brown and green. I felt immensely secure in this deafening, vibrating machine. We rose up past a solitary cloud – what an extraordinary thing to be able to do. It was white and fluffy, like a mound of newly fallen snow, soft enough to fall onto, firm enough to sustain one, a dazzling, spotless island of joy. All I'd need would be a harp, I thought, and clutched myself in shivering happiness.

The horizon began to tilt again and went on tilting until the earth was the sky and the sky was underneath us and my behind had left the seat and the straps were crushing my shoulders, and I was praying: 'Please God, don't let me be sick. Please. Please.' But I wasn't sick, not even when the engine roared again, the earth rose above us and then dipped beneath our feet only to reappear long seconds later from above my head, and all while something immensely strong was trying to force me through the bottom of the plane. At one point I realized I was staring straight along the nose at the earth, and it was revolving steadily like a gramophone record. Then we were flying level at last and the air had grown warmer again.

There were a couple of raps on the plywood behind my head. I twisted round to look over my shoulder. He was pointing, so I looked down, to see the river swing into view and start to slide towards us. It grew larger and larger and at the last minute I recognized the hotel rushing to meet us, and then a second later our cottage flashed under the wing, so close I could have touched it. I thought I saw my grandfather in the garden looking up at us.

Half a minute later we were sailing over a hedge and the field was racing beneath our wings. We hit the ground with a lurching bounce and trundled back to the hotel and stopped. My ears were thawing and the air smelt earthy and damp again.

'All right?' I heard him shout.

I twisted round and nodded calmly, as I felt an experienced flier should. He jerked his head to indicate that I should get out. I freed myself from the harness and clambered out onto the wing, shutting the flap carefully behind me. I jumped down. He hadn't moved and was staring back at the hotel.

I craned up and shouted as politely as I could, 'Thank you very much. That was super.'

He smiled briefly and pulled his goggles down over his eyes. The engine opened up again and I backed out of the slipstream. As he taxied away across the field he lifted his arm in salute. Not, I supposed, because he was bothered at all. A moment later the plane tore over my head. I saw the big G-ADFS on the wings and glimpsed his brown helmet, then another second and he had disappeared behind the trees and was gone, the growl of the engine echoing back from the hill and fading into silence.

Everything down here seemed less important than before. I looked up to where I'd been, to the icy blue kingdom whose frontier I had crossed at last. Then I walked slowly back to the cottage. They were all in the kitchen having breakfast.

'Where the hell have you been?' said my father.

'Sorry,' I said. I looked round at my earthbound family and wondered if I should tell them. Perhaps not just yet.

'Did you see that awful aeroplane?' my grandmother asked. 'Roaring about up there, looping-the-loop and I don't know what. It's a wonder they don't kill themselves.'

'Or us,' said my grandfather. 'I thought he'd have the roof off. It ought to be stopped.'

'Where were you?' said my mother. 'You must have seen it. Didn't you, darling?'

My resolve broke. 'I was in it,' I said casually, and crammed a spoonful of cornflakes into my mouth.

10

2

That was my first flight. My last flight was a long time later. And by last flight I mean a flight in a real aeroplane, not a DC10 or a helicopter or a jumbo jet. There have been plenty of those.

When the war came, the sky was full of aeroplanes – aircraft as we learned to call them now. Citizens no longer ran to their doors to catch a glimpse of one; day and night they droned over our heads in swarms, a good few of them intent on killing us. The names Hurricane and Heinkel were as familiar as Bovril and Rinso, and the elegant outline of the Spitfire ousted the lion and the bulldog as the totem of our patriotic pride.

Nations send their youth to fight their wars for them, not because they're the strongest and fittest, but because youth believes itself immortal. Our generation would never admit to such immaturity, but the conviction was still hidden in our hearts. Unlike our fathers who had crossed over to France in blind ignorance, we knew all about death. We'd seen it happen so often in the cinema. Although never to Clark Gable or Errol Flynn or Gary Cooper; only to people who, for all the clutching, spinning and gasping they went in for, didn't seem to suffer all that much. Violent death looked reassuringly clean, tidy and quick. Perhaps that's why, after a battle, so many corpses are found to be wearing an expression of astonishment.

To me the war meant only one thing. I knew in 1940 that we had our backs to the wall, as the wireless kept telling us, and that the nearest help was five thousand miles away and consisted mainly of food parcels and endless Betty Grable movies, but the thrill that in other people's stomachs was fear, in mine was the surge of anticipation. Anyway, we'd never lost a war before, or if we had, I'd not heard about it. Listening to Churchill's broadcasts I was embarrassed by his orotund rhetoric but not at all dismayed to hear that the struggle would be long. I couldn't join up until I was eighteen, when at last I'd be able to learn to fly at the Government's expense and even, who knows, be allowed a plane of my own.

Then, too, there was the matter of sex. Since the Battle of Britain it was quite clear that the quickest way into a girl's heart – or more importantly her bed – was to sport on your tunic the double wings of the RAF pilot. Rank, age, stature or appearance were irrelevant compared to the power of that exclusive piece of embroidery. It's wearer was invested with a glamour that could make even a Hollywood star seem drab, and the transience of his existence only enhanced the magic. I knew that most of the Battle of Britain pilots were already dead, or down in East Grinstead having their faces agonizingly rebuilt, but I didn't care; I had to be a pilot, whatever the price. And anyway, it wouldn't happen to me, would it?

So I waited, watching the fighters tumbling in the sky, hearing the throb of the bombers at night, feeling the walls shiver and seeing the night sky flare, collecting shrapnel and incendiary fins from the streets and Messerschmitt relics from the fields. I learned to shave and to smoke and, in my last terms at school, discovered that I might have a vocation. Not that a vocation was much more than a thing of straw in those days. Aunts and uncles would still ply you with questions about what you were going to be, but carefully avoid your parents' eyes. We all talked ceaselessly about 'when it's over', but the question of who would be around to enjoy that happy day was never discussed, or even thought about except in the clammy hours of the night. My vocation led me briefly to an art school, where I learned a little about drawing, a lot about drinking and was decorously relieved of my virginity by a girl five years my senior. Six months before my call-up was due, I volunteered for the RAF (we all did, to avoid being shovelled into the infantry or down the mines). I applied for aircrew, went through a long and confusing medical at a place in Kingsway, was accepted for pilot training, and twelve days after my eighteenth birthday I was in uniform.

The early humiliations of service life I endured stoically, in the knowledge that soon I would be among the elite. In a sense I already was: I noticed the glances of respect when people saw the white quadrant in my cap; odd looks that could sometimes almost be mistaken for pity. And when I arrived at EFTS (Elementary Flying Training School) and saw those dear, familiar Tiger Moths lined up outside the hangars and inhaled the old bouquet of oil and grass, I knew that my real life had at last begun.

Flying is a strange and subtle business, a complicated balancing act between man and machine. The relationship between a pupil and his instructor is equally subtle and complicated; both of you need to know the sort of person you're dealing with. There were no doubts in my mind about Flight Lieutenant Farrington-Smith. To me he was an awesome figure into whose hands I delivered my life and my fate without a flicker of misgiving. In some ways his appearance was absurd: he was a cartoon ace. His jaw was square, his mouth was firm and his eyes were blue and stern and remote, the eyes of Ulysses returned. He wore his hat at a rakish angle and underneath his wings was a fruit salad of exotic first-war ribbons. And he always flew in white silk gloves, the kind that were really only intended as a lining for the high-altitude gloves issued to aircrew. Whenever I saw them rise to grasp the windscreen in front of him I knew I'd hear that privileged accent in my ears and the momentous words: 'You've got her.' His manner, too, was appropriately cool and reticent, his authority unhesitating, although sometimes unpredictable: as on that grey spring morning when, after an hour of circuits-and-bumps (take off, round the field, land, take off again), he'd suddenly climbed out of his cockpit, stretched and said, 'Better try one on your own. Only one, mind you,' and walked away towards the hangars.

Pilots never forget that unique instant of terror: the first time they're alone a thousand feet above the earth knowing the hard part is yet to come – getting down again. I'd got down, somehow, and without wiping off the undercarriage or tipping the nose into the ground. I'd even done it again, several times, and my confidence was reaching dangerous levels.

The day it all came to an end was, like such days often are, as clear and sunny as an English summer can produce. A gentle breeze carried the smell of clover across the airfield and, before the engines were started, we could hear a skylark rejoicing high above our heads. That morning, luckily, I was not flying alone. We were down for something called Forced Landing Practice: the instructor, without any warning, would switch off the engine, and his pupil would have to find a suitable field and get the plane down into it, in what was called an 'un-engine-assisted landing'. Of course, the instructor knew where the field was: it was set aside specifically for this exercise; it had to be, because at that time any other field in England large enough to land in had been carefully obstructed by dotting it with old sofas or wrecked cars.

14

The white gloves were ostentatiously on show as I brought the tail up and lifted us smoothly over the trees. A climbing turn, a left-hand leg of the airfield and I headed onto the course he'd set me. It had rained the night before and the air was rinsed and sparkling to the horizon. The ground moved imperceptibly below us; up here the engine roared in our ears, the slipstream froze our faces, but the sharp-edged shadows of the struts were motionless on the wings, and my chest filled with the exultation that always came when I felt myself suspended like this between heaven and earth, in control of my destiny. I kept an eye on the compass and repeatedly checked the ground with the map on my knee. I had almost overcome my beginners' tendency to get lost in the air. The moment you're more than a few hundred feet up, the world looks a very different place, and even at a Tiger Moth's chugging eighty-miles-an-hour you can soon be out of sight of anything recognizable; the change of scale and viewpoint means learning a whole new set of visual mnemonics. Although the area round the airfield had become comfortingly familiar in the last weeks, this morning I was taking no chances. And all the time, out of the corner of my eye, I was watching the ignition switches just beyond the edge of his cockpit.

When, swiftly, a white glove reached out and flicked them off, I was ready. In the singing hush after the engine stopped, I dipped the nose into a gliding angle and banked gently while I searched for the field. I knew it must be well within reach: he wouldn't be risking our necks unnecessarily. I tightened the turn. There were a hell of a lot of fields down there. I noticed a large patch of green, no cows or sheep, no main roads or high buildings round it, and very obligingly up-wind of us; it must be the one. A piece of cake.

The sun swung across my eyes and over my shoulder as I turned towards it, losing height carefully, judging my distance

15

precisely. The field floated up towards us at exactly the rate I wanted. This was the cushiest gliding approach I'd ever done. In a few minutes we were skimming the trees and the hedge was slipping underneath us. As I was about to ease the stick back and drop us onto the grass, the engine burst into life with a shattering clamour. The voice in my ear said, 'Better go round again.'

With instinctive obedience I opened the throttle and pulled the stick towards me. As the field dropped away I looked down at it over the side. Across the middle stretched a line of ten-foot stakes at what I judged to be twelve-foot intervals. His voice was expressionless as he said, 'Back to base, I think.'

I seemed to be flying the plane myself, although the gloves were not much in evidence now. Certainly I had the impression I was making the decisions about the landing; and considering the state of shock I was in, I didn't make too bad a job of it. When we'd taxied back to the hangars he switched off and climbed out. I sat in the cockpit, unable to move, desperately trying to rationalize what had happened. Obviously I'd got the wrong field, but how? Why? What was I going to say?

He was standing by the wing, tapping a cigarette on his case. He was waiting for me. I struggled down from the cockpit and clumped towards him, my parachute bouncing on the backs of my thighs. He had one of his oval Turkish cigarettes in his mouth; he reached into his flying suit for an elegant gold lighter and flicked it on. I was astonished to see the white glove shaking slightly. He inhaled deeply and looked at a spot just above my head.

'Didn't you see those stakes?' he said.

I started to bluster. For a long time he listened patiently as I offered up every excuse I could think of; except what I knew was the real one. At last he turned his head in the direction of the Flight Office.

16

'What does it say on that sign?'

I turned to look. The board was only fifty yards away, but there was no hope. Frantically I tried to remember what was written on it – I'd passed it often enough – but panic had wiped my memory clean. In a last mad throw I tried to invent something. His eyebrows went up perceptibly, and I think for a moment even he had difficulty keeping a straight face. He slapped the release of his parachute harness and swung it over his shoulder. The smell of his Turkish tobacco was lacing the crisp morning air.

'I think', he said gently, 'you ought to have a medical.'

Back at the aircrew attestation centre in Kingsway they did everything with my eyes except pull them out onto my cheeks. Then, after interminable hours of waiting, I was paraded in front of a row of middle-aged men, some in uniform, some in civvies and some in white coats. The most senior, an Air Commodore no less, was the spokesman. His uniform was no disguise for the silver hair, smooth cheeks and urbane manner of the Harley Street specialist.

'Well . . . ah, Turner,' he said. 'As you probably are aware, you've developed a not inconsiderable degree of myopia. Short-sight, you'd probably call it.'

Myopia, I'd probably call it, but let it pass.

'Now, the Air Force has spent a lot of money on you, training and so-forth, and we're pretty reluctant to waste it. We could pass you for the Air Transport Auxiliary.' I felt a sudden shock of hope: I hadn't thought of that. 'But the difficulty is that your sort of myopia tends to get worse. Of course, it usually settles down in your twenties. And,' he beamed at me suddenly, 'in your forties it may even improve.'

In my forties? I won't have any forties. I'll be dead by then, if only of a broken heart. The Air Commodore had paused. It looked as if he were about to put the black cap on. Perhaps they'd give me a white stick and send me back to civvy street. I wouldn't mind that.

'So, I'm afraid,' he started up again, 'we're going to have to recommend you for ground duties only. We'll be in touch with your unit right away.' He nodded affably. 'Best of luck to you.'

I managed to keep my voice perfectly steady. 'Thank you, sir,' I said, and saluted.

Outside, in Kingsway, it was another hideously sunny day. I walked as far as Holborn before it occurred to me that I didn't want to be there; so I turned round and came slowly back. I was searching through the newly fallen rubble of my life for a foundation stone on which I could start rebuilding. I sat down on a pile of sandbags, and then remembered I was in uniform: you weren't supposed to loiter in uniform. The misery was too much to bear alone. I set off to find a telephone box.

'Oh, Mum,' I said as soon as she answered. 'Something dreadful has happened.'

There was a pause. I could hardly hear her as she said, 'What has?'

'I've been taken off flying. For good.'

This time the pause went on for ever. I thought we'd been cut off.

'Mum?' I said.

Eventually she spoke again, with her familiar brisk sympathy. 'Oh, darling . . .' There was another silence and then, to her everlasting credit, she said, 'I am so sorry. How awful for you.'

3

Railway stations in the small hours are like antechambers to Hell: sulphurous, yet as chilly as tombs. As I tumbled out onto the platform, lugging my kit-bag after me, the raw air stung my throat, tasting grey and metallic. A straggle of uniformed figures tipped from the train groaned and coughed, the dim blue lights far above their heads carving ghastly caverns in their pallid faces. I shivered. I hadn't spoken to anyone on the journey and misanthropy still gripped my tongue. I didn't relish my companions, my own nonentity, or the prospect of the interminable monotony that seemed to lie ahead. I'd had enough experience already of life at the bottom of the service ladder to know what my future was likely to be.

Near the ticket barrier was a steamy square of light. The WVS were dispensing tea. I dragged my kit-bag over and joined the queue. A white-haired woman with a Mrs Miniver accent handed me a scalding cup of dark-orange liquid. I sipped it, convinced it was staining my teeth brown. I asked the tea-drinker beside me where the buses went from. Piccadilly, he said.

If it hadn't been half-past four in the morning he might have enjoyed a shaft of my native wit, and if I hadn't been so young and untravelled I'd have known that nearly every provincial city in the country boasts its own Piccadilly. To me Piccadilly meant before the war: getting off the bus outside the Café Royal into a press of taxicabs, hanging onto my parents as we were swept towards Shaftesbury Avenue with the other theatre-goers; silk hats, white scarves, long dresses, the smell of cigars and scent and the lights cascading over the Bovril sign. Homesickness rose in my throat at the memory, a lump that even the corrosive tea couldn't dissolve.

In the bus the smell of Woodbines and damp serge rose thickly from the passengers and the windows misted over. I was able to reach one to wipe an arc with my greatcoat sleeve and catch a glimpse of the countryside rattling past. It was flat and featureless, but occasionally a clump of hangars and huts appeared and the bus would stop to let a few people off. It seemed to me that the whole East Riding was one vast airfield and, as I found out later, I wasn't far wrong.

One advantage of the uniformity of service life is that it allays the fear of arriving at new places, the anguish of the first day at the new school. Wherever you're posted it turns out to be deadeningly familiar: the routine is the same, the food's the same, the smell's the same and the language is the same.

When I'd reported to the guardroom I stood outside in the cheerless morning light and looked round this miniature town: main roads, side roads, crossroads, signposts, cinemas, cookhouses, huts for working in, huts for living in. Familiar again, but not quite the same. This was an operational station – the front line. This was what we saw on the newsreels and heard about every day on the wireless: this was where they began, the great thousand-bomber raids on Berlin, Essen, Dortmund, Leipzig; this was the eyrie of the night-flying Halifaxes and Lancasters. The exclusive, dreamed-of citadel. But not for me. Not now. I had no right to be here now, I would never be part of it. I could see this was going to be worse than any dull training depot. I'd been sent here to get practical experience of a new trade and it was like being forced to live in the same house with the mistress who no longer loves you, and having to share the bathroom with all her current lovers.

Crossing the main road again, and in spite of still wearing full kit, mess tin, water bottle, respirator, haversack and carrying my kit-bag on one shoulder, I attempted to salute a very young flying officer. He looked startled, pulled his hands out of his pockets and returned me what was as near a wave as anything else. I found this heartening. I'd heard rumours of the absence of bullshit on operational stations; perhaps they were true. Certainly everyone seemed to be passing everyone else like normal human beings instead of the convulsive semaphores I'd been used to.

After finding my hut – familiar once more with its rows of beds, lino floor and smell of stale socks (although the beds were unfamiliarly unmade and there was enough fluff under them to warrant a court martial where I'd just come from) – I'd been told to report to my section. Relieved of the weight of my kit I felt suddenly committed to this place, no longer a new arrival, being drawn even further into this life I hadn't sought. At each step I felt another gate clang behind me, to remind me that there would be no escape.

Next to the big hangar, they'd said. There was no mistaking the big hangar: it was enormous, twice the size of the other two, and in its shadow was a long, low building sporting a neat sign saying, Instrument Section. Inside, a WAAF in glasses was standing at a lino-covered counter. Over her shoulder a wireless was playing 'This Is The Army, Mr Jones' to a dozen industrious elves in overalls bent over their benches. She looked for my name in her copy of Routine Orders and seemed surprised to find it.

'Oh, yes,' she said wonderingly. She peered at the sheet

again. 'U/t, are you?' she said, a tinge of disgust in her voice. U/t was 'under training', which in this most technical of the Services was to be as nothing, a creature without a trade, a 'useless/type' in the derisory version.

'Compass Section,' she said. 'End hut. Report to Sgt Willoughby.'

The end hut was slightly apart from the others and looked like a child's drawing. It was small and wooden with a door in the middle, a window on either side and a curl of smoke coming out of an iron chimney pipe. Up two brick steps I knocked and went in. There was a desk and two tall cupboards at one end, and at the other the standard cylindrical stove flanked by two NAAFI armchairs with grease-blackened upholstery. Sprawled in the armchairs were two sergeants, one reading the paper, the other staring gloomily at his boots. They had their backs to the door and neither moved when I entered. I cleared my throat.

'Sgt Willoughby?'

The one with the newspaper turned his head. He had a round head and small dark eyes like currants, very close together. He wore a vain, pencil-line moustache and his black hair was Brylcreemed to his scalp. He smiled expectantly at me.

'I'm supposed to report to you, Sergeant,' I said.

He continued to smile. I noticed that the eyes were not currants at all but small black pebbles and had nothing to do with the smile. 'Why?' he said at last.

The smile remained fixed and the eyes examined me while I explained. 'I see,' he said. 'We're another u/t, are we? I hope you're not expecting to get on the course in a hurry. It's full up for months ahead, you know. And you needn't expect me and Sgt Grice to spend hours doing their job for them. We're far too busy for that. You'd best get your nose stuck into the manual and pick up what you can.' He indicated two dusty loose-leaf folders on a shelf. 'In the meanwhile – the Devil

22

finds work for idle hands. You'd better put the kettle on for some tea. Not too grand for that, are we?'

I was used to this. My very average middle-class accent often provoked sarcasm from NCOs, or the occasional your lordship from fellow airmen. To them I was an alien creature and with them I felt myself in an alien world. And I had to admit that even as exalted a person as Sgt Willoughby, with his counterfeit accent, would only have penetrated my modest suburban home to sell something or mend something. I suppose they recognized a snob when they saw one. I wasn't happy with the thought.

Sgt Willoughby leaned back in his chair and raised his paper. 'There's a tap by the Radar Section.'

In the corner was a battered kettle on an improvised electric ring. To reach it I had to step over the other sergeant's legs. He didn't move.

'Excuse me, Sergeant,' I said.

He grunted and looked up from his boots for a moment. I caught a glimpse of a long, colourless face under untidy colourless hair.

Outside the hut, although I'd been in there less than a minute, I felt an immediate sense of relief. I lingered over finding the tap and filling the kettle as long as I could. When I returned neither of them had moved. I climbed over the gloomy one's legs, put the kettle on the ring and switched it on. Nobody spoke.

There was nowhere to sit; only a rickety-looking chair at the desk, and it didn't seem tactful to take that. So I leaned against the wall in an approximation of the at-ease position. I kept my hands out of my pockets because I had experience of the inflammability of sergeants. When the kettle had been boiling for some time, I cleared my throat carefully and asked where the tea was.

'In the cupboard,' Sgt Willoughby murmured behind the

23

Daily Mirror. I went over to the larger of the two cupboards, and tried to open it.

'It's locked, Sergeant.'

There was a sudden bellow behind me. 'Leave that alone!'

I spun round in alarm. He had dropped the paper and was standing, glaring at me, his round face scarlet with fury.

'Not that one, you silly little bastard. The other one.'

He was so clearly beside himself that I murmured, 'Sorry, Sarge,' as I'd learned to with other psychopathic NCOs, and opened the smaller cupboard. He seemed about to attack me again when the hut door opened. Peering round it was a pale, freckled face illuminated by innocent blue eyes.

'Got your wads, Sergeant.'

He was a small, thin airman and he was carrying two lardy cakes on a biscuit-tin lid. 'I reckon they're fresh,' he said enthusiastically as he came in.

'I doubt it, the time you've taken getting them,' Willoughby said, calming down. 'But hope springs eternal.'

The airman pulled off his cap and pushed it through his epaulette. His hair was sandy and curly. 'Shall I get the tea?' he said.

'Of course.' He turned to me. The smile had returned. 'This is Aircraftman Second-Class, Buckley. Another aspirant to the sergeants' mess. What's your name, by the way?'

'AC2 Turner,' I said. He wrote it down in a Stationery Office notebook on the desk, along with my service number, rank and hut number. He indicated the gloomy sergeant, motionless as ever.

'That's Sgt Grice. As you know, this job carries the rank of sergeant and seeing there's only two of us on the station we're pretty well left on our own in this section. Two's company, three's none. But you behave yourself you'll be all right.' His small dark eyes fastened on me. 'You look after us – we'll look after you. Do you get my drift?'

24

I said I did. Although it sounded to me a rather one-sided arrangement.

AC2 Buckley was getting chipped mugs out of the cupboard. 'How many, Sergeant?' he said.

'Two, of course. You don't think we're wasting our best tea on you, do you? You get yours in the NAAFI like other fortunate erks.'

'It's shut now, Sergeant.'

'Then it's time you did some work. The labourer should be worthy of his hire. Those repeaters on S–Sugar want looking at. And take your new mate with you. You can teach him everything you know about compasses, and that shouldn't take more than half a minute.' Then, with his hands in his pockets, he strolled across and stood just behind the boy.

'And don't forget', he said softly, 'to tell him the most important thing you've learned – from your own experience – about the responsibility involved in this job.'

The boy looked up from the teapot and for an instant I saw in his eyes an expression that looked almost like fear and something else too, that I couldn't decipher. Then it was gone and he nodded and lowered his head.

When we were out in the air, Buckley said to me, 'Have you got a bike?'

'No.'

'You're entitled to one if you work out on the flights. You can get it from stores.' There were several ancient roadsters leaning against the side of the hut. 'Take Sgt Grice's for now. He won't be out of that chair till dinner-time.'

He led the way to where the concrete path appeared to end in nothing but sky. For the first time I was at the edge of the airfield, the immense grass arena to which everything else on the camp was an anteroom. It seemed to stretch for miles in every direction, bare and flat, its edges lost in a distant line of grey mist. As we emerged from the shelter of the big hangar the wind, forever combing the wide expanse, caught us, and we tucked our chins in and stood on the pedals as we set off round the concrete perimeter track.

'By the way,' he said, 'my name's Alan.'

He held his right hand out and I, absurdly, tried to shake it with mine, and we wobbled and swerved and nearly locked handlebars, and laughed loudly at our own silly formality.

Now I could see the bombers in the distance, across the eddying sea of grass that lay between the runways. We crossed the end of the main runway. It was a mile long, Alan said. It looked like a giant abandoned highway, wider than any road, straighter than the Romans dreamed of, vast and empty and leading only to the sky beyond.

The perimeter track was nearly three miles round, with every now and then a circular dispersal point off it, and on these stood the great black Halifaxes: not beautiful like fighter planes, but huge and ugly and pustular with gun turrets, perspex astrodomes and observation blisters. We had ridden nearly a mile before we reached S-Sugar's dispersal. Its occupant was waiting, alone and silent, its nose lifted like *Tyrannosaurus rex* scenting the breeze. We dropped our cycles on the grass and walked towards it over the oil-stained concrete. It loomed above us, the undercarriage wheels the height of a man. Alan reached up and opened the hatch in the tail section and we hoisted ourselves up.

Inside it was cramped, ribbed with aluminium and festooned with wires. The air was musty and dominated by the piercingly sweet smell of aircraft dope. We made our way, stooping, up the fuselage, Alan pointing out the black shape of the gyrocompass on one side. Past the mid-upper gun turret and through the flight engineer's compartment we emerged into the cockpit, brightly lit by the perspex all around us. Alan pointed to the pilot's seat.

26

'Climb up there, you'll be able to see the gyro-repeater. It's that one.' He pointed to one of a mass of dials that made the dashboard of a Tiger Moth look like a kitchen clock. 'Give us a shout if it moves. And make a note of the heading, if you can.' He flicked a couple of switches and disappeared down the fuselage again.

I climbed gingerly into the seat and sat, my feet on the rudder-bar, both hands on the control column, looking out along the nose. It was a strange feeling. If things had been different, this is where I would have been, hauling one of these great monsters into the sky, skipper of a crew of seven, master of all I surveyed. I looked down at the concrete quite far below me: farther than the carpet from the armchair. The old excitement invaded me. I imagined the runway rushing beneath my wheels, the whole enormous contraption lifting into the air at my bidding, the steady nerves needed to control it, the firm hands. The keen eyesight. I ground my teeth in an effort to hold back the sickness of disappointment and frustration.

'OK?' Alan was calling from the other end of the plane. The needle had moved.

'OK !'

'And again?'

'And again.'

When we had finished, Alan came and stood beside me in the cockpit.

'Peckish?' he asked.

'Just a bit. Must be nearly dinner.' I had learned not to say lunch.

He took a bar of chocolate out of his tunic pocket, broke it in half and held one half out to me.

'I couldn't,' I said. 'That's your ration.'

'No, go on. Take it.'

'That's all you've got.'

'Go on, it's OK.' I took it and savoured it, piece by piece.

27

I said, 'What's he like – that sergeant?'

'Willoughby? Not bad, I suppose. Got a bit of a temper sometimes.'

'So I've noticed. What's he got in that locked cupboard, gold bars?'

Alan shrugged and said, 'I think that's mostly Grice's stuff.'

'What sort of stuff?'

He shrugged again. 'Dunno. Never seen it.' He looked down at his boots for a moment and then said quietly, 'They need a bit of watching, those two.' He looked up. 'Don't worry, though. I'll give you all the gen you need to keep them out of your hair. I'm supposed to be going on leave in a couple of days, but if you like I'll put it off – till you're properly clued up.'

'Don't be bloody silly. I wouldn't dream of it.'

I knew I shouldn't ask the next question, but my curiosity had been whetted by the events of the day and it got the better of me.

'What was all that about the important thing you've learned from your experience?'

I regretted it at once. I saw the same expression on his face I'd seen in the hut. He turned away and looked out across the airfield to where the control tower stood, small and pale against the grey mist. After a moment he said in a small voice, 'Oh, that . . . that's just . . . just his idea of a joke. He fancies himself as a joker.'

'Strikes me he's more of a bloody lunatic.'

He was still turned away. The tendons in his thin neck were taut like strings. Rain had begun to drum noisily on the metal fuselage.

'Listen,' I said, 'thanks for the chocolate.'

'We'd better get back,' he said, 'or Grice will miss his bike.'

4

Alan spent a day showing me the ropes and various ploys to keep the two sergeants off my back. Then he went on leave, and I was on my own. Not lonely – you could hardly be lonely living in a hut with twenty-three others – but alone, not involved. The first night, as I sat on my bed, knees drawn up to support the letter I was trying to write, I felt as if I were in no-man's-land with a crossfire of repartee and gossip whizzing over my head. I'd been used to spending my evenings with the same people I'd worked with during the day; everyone in this billet seemed to have a different job. As far as I could gather there were fitters, mechanics, clerks, bowser drivers and quite a few trades I'd never heard of. The only thing they did appear to have in common was long service on this station, years some of them; a newcomer could hardly expect instant admission to such a freemasonry of anecdote and legend. So I was content with the occasional nod or wink that came my way when I intercepted a glance or looked up as a pair of boots clumped past the end of my bed. I had caused a small stir of interest earlier by unpacking no less than three books from my kit-bag, and when I was seen actually reading one, my identity had been sealed.

Among the chorus of good-nights when the lights went out, a voice from the next bed had murmured amiably, "Night, Professor.'

At work it was much the same. I had little contact with anyone apart from the sergeants. I swept round their outstretched legs and made countless pots of tea, mainly for Sgt Grice, whose capacity for large mugs of the stuff seemed bottomless. When I was sent off round the camp on one of their inscrutable errands, everyone seemed friendly enough. Since the war stand-offishness had become deeply unfashionable: even the King and Queen in their wellies and duffle-coats (obtained with their own ration books we were told) were occasionally to be seen pretending to queue for a spam sandwich. All the same, most people I met were still preoccupied with the complexities of their own lives and British enough to think it indelicate to enquire into other people's.

Being a naturally gregarious youth, spells of isolation like this had the effect of sharpening my observation: I stopped talking and listened; stopped showing off and watched. What struck me at first about the camp was its normality. It was more like a village than a frontier post of the war, like the village where my grandparents lived: everybody knowing everybody else, calling greetings across the street, gossiping on corners. It was so cosy it was hard to remember what we were all there for, that on the other side of the airfield was enough high explosive to blow a small town to kingdom come.

The only strangers in this fraternity were the aircrew. There had been a hospital near my grandparents' village, and sometimes you would see the convalescents in the high street, pale-faced and still distracted by their recent afflictions. These young men in their flying boots and their casual, unbuttoned uniforms with the silver rescue whistles dangling from their collars had the same air of not belonging, of passing through.

We stayed; they came – and were gone. They walked among us as the elect, honoured yet shunned, our chosen sacrifices.

Although the weather was improving, there seemed to be very little flying. An occasional roar and a black shape would eclipse the daylight, making the windows rattle and the plates dance on the mess tables, but no more; and conversation wasn't interrupted. Then suddenly, on the fourth day, the tempo changed.

I was alone with Sgt Willoughby, silent behind his *Daily Mirror*. Sgt Grice had disappeared off to the village an hour before, balancing an enormous brown paper parcel on his handlebars. A head appeared round the door.

'Ops on tonight.'

Willoughby lowered his paper. 'How many?'

'Twenty at least, they reckon. Briefing's four-thirty.'

The head withdrew. Willoughby rose from his chair and went over to the State of Readiness board on the wall. With a deep, resentful sigh he collected a couple of compass keys off the desk and made for the door.

'Tell Sgt Grice when he gets back I'm over at T-Tommy,' he said. 'You fetch the wads, then come back here and mind the shop.'

Outside, the pace of the camp had changed. Whereas before everyone seemed to have been wandering aimlessly, like ants on a sunny day, now they were propelled in straight lines, as if by a high voltage. Trucks were bouncing up and down the main street and the afternoon was filled with the distant rumble of aero-engines. The NAAFI, normally crammed so near to tea break, was almost deserted. I was even able to get the attention of the tall NAAFI girl with the saucer eyes, usually besieged because the top buttons of her uniform had a tendency to come adrift when she leaned over the counter and you could see down to her bra, which made a heartening change from the collars and ties of the WAAFs.

I sat at an empty table, drinking my tea, while other airmen, mostly in overalls, drifted in and out. Tonight's target was of course secret, but most people were able to make a confident guess at it. Each one had his own bit of evidence to contribute: the bomb load, the amount of petrol, the navigation gear, and the old hands could work out the rest. I tried to imagine how I'd be feeling if I were flying tonight. I supposed I'd be afraid. And excited too. I could imagine the excitement all right, there was enough of it in the air for me to absorb and amplify, but not the fear. Fear is curiously hard to conjure up when you know you're perfectly safe.

No sense of excitement had penetrated the Compass Section. The two sergeants, having presumably made their contribution to the war effort for tonight, were once again supine in their chairs. After a while I propped up the gyro-compass manual and, out of sight behind it, started on a three-quarter rear view of Sergeant Grice. I liked to keep my hand in, and it would have cost half-a-crown an hour to get a model as motionless as this at the art school. Even when Willoughby addressed him he didn't move.

'Fancy a game tonight?'

He grunted.

'Ted and Percy said they'd make a foursome. The mess'll be quiet tonight with all those noisy kids out of the way. With twenty crews going off we might be able to get near the bloody table for once.'

'Twenty-two, I heard.'

'All the better.'

My model had drunk two more pint-mugs of tea before we heard the first engines being run up. There was a brusque rap on the door and a big flight sergeant I recognized from the Instrument Section pushed his way into the hut. He stood looking down at Willoughby.

'Ken,' he said, 'can I borrow one of your lads?'

'Buckley's on leave,' Willoughby said, as if Alan had committed some unspeakable offence. 'But you can have this one.'

The Flight Sergeant looked at me. 'Got a bike, have you?'

'Yes, Flight.'

'Right. Pick the box up from the corporal at the counter and get it over to S-Sugar. Thanks, Ken.' He glanced at Grice, sunk in his perpetual gloom. 'All right, Arnold?' he said and, getting no reply, left.

Silence fell.

'Shall I go now?' I said.

'Well, it won't be much use after they've taken off, will it?' Willoughby said. 'Get your skates on.'

The corporal in the Instrument Section had glasses and a few long hairs that flowed over his bald head like reeds in a stream. He handed me a grey wooden box with a metal handle and WD numbers stencilled on it.

'That's for Sgt Timms, navigator on S-Sugar. And get him to sign for it.' He tore two forms off a grubby pad and passed them to me. 'Here . . . and here,' he said, pointing with the black crescent of a fingernail. 'Know which S-Sugar's dispersal is?'

I said I wasn't sure.

'Turn left on the peri track, it's about the eighth one round. But for Christ's sake be careful if they start taxying. You don't want to finish up like that WAAF last year.'

'What happened to her?'

'Little M/T driver just posted here from a Stirling squadron – nobody told her Halifaxes had lower wings than Stirlings. Drove a jeep straight under B-Beer's starboard outer. Prop took her head right off. 'Orrible mess. Went on driving though, halfway across the field. The blood-wagon had to chase after to stop her.'

He so relished the telling that I could only assume he hadn't actually witnessed the accident.

33

'I'll be careful,' I said.

'Don't take too bloody long, though,' he called after me. 'They'll be off any minute.'

Out on the perimeter track the noise of engines was bellowing from every corner of the airfield, until everything I could see, the sheds, the grass, the trees, seemed to be roaring and vibrating in sympathy. The sun had crept from under the clouds into a streak of turquoise sky just above the hedges and was sending long pencils of light across the grass, but this picture of a gentle summer's evening was absurdly at odds with the deafening racket accompanying it. As I rode one-handed round the track, the other steadying the grey box on the handlebars, two trucks passed me carrying crews out to their aircraft. At most of the dispersals I passed they were already there, many of them aboard and running up the engines.

The crew of S-Sugar were still on the dispersal when I reached them. They were standing around in their Mae Wests and harnesses, carrying their helmets and parachutes and talking quietly. A couple of them were having a surreptitious cigarette, strictly forbidden with all that high-octane fuel in the air. Their skipper was with the ground crew flight sergeant, signing the Form 700. One of the sacred tenets of the RAF was that you signed for everything, even whole aeroplanes. I suppose some of the wilder lads needed reminding that aircraft cost a lot of money, but somehow signing for a four-engined bomber did seem to be twisting the arm of the bloke who had to get it halfway across Europe and – with a lot of luck – back again. I think most people felt the same, and the ceremony was usually accompanied with hoary jokes like, 'If it doesn't work, bring it back and we'll change it.' That one was a particular favourite with parachutes.

I looked for the navigator. They were a non-commissioned crew, all sergeants or flight sergeants, and all, even to my eyes, shockingly young, like a sixth-form eleven waiting for the toss. One of them, who seemed even younger than the others, was carrying a chart bag, so he was probably the chap I was after. I went up to him. He was pale as chalk with untidy eyebrows that met in the middle, giving him a rather perplexed look. He wasn't talking to anyone, just gazing out across the airfield.

'Sgt Timms?'

He jumped as if he hadn't noticed me and swung round. 'Yep?'

'I was told to give you this.'

'Oh, wiz . . . right. Well done.'

'Could you sign for it?'

'Right . . . sure.'

I got the forms and a stub of pencil out of my battledress pocket and held the box up so that he could write on it. He wrote slowly in a large, childish hand. I put the forms back in my pocket and held out the box to him.

'Oh, right . . . yes,' he said, taking it. 'The u/s one's still on board. Do you want it?'

The corporal hadn't mentioned bringing anything back, and it didn't seem the moment to bother with it. 'Oh, no,' I said, 'someone can pick it up—' I was just about to add, 'when you get back,' but I knew there were all sorts of superstitions about saying things like that, so I said rather lamely, 'any time. It doesn't matter.'

He knew of course – knew why I'd hesitated like that. So he grinned at me to show me it was OK by him whatever I said. But it didn't come out like a grin. It came out more like a dog snarling.

The others had started getting into the plane. 'Come on, Tiger,' one of them called.

Suddenly he handed the box back to me. 'Excuse me,' he said politely, and walked swiftly towards the tail, disappearing round the other side of it. I stood holding the box, waiting.

35

After a while I thought I heard a retching noise but at that moment the first engine burst into ear-splitting life and everything around me was blown flat. He reappeared looking even paler but quite jaunty and came towards me, his head tucked down against the slipstream.

'Sorry. Last-minute piss,' he yelled against the noise of the engines. He took the box from me and went towards the hatch. Just before he hoisted himself up he gave me a little wave.

'Good luck!' I shouted. I don't think he heard me. I hope he didn't. I'm sure it was the wrong thing to say.

By now the bombers were starting to leave their dispersals and taxi along the perimeter track towards the runway. I didn't fancy joining them on a bicycle, so I waited. The ground crew had disconnected the accumulators from S-Sugar and pulled the trolley aside. There was a deafening roar as the engines were run at full boost, the whole aircraft shaking and straining against its locked brakes. I backed away from the noise onto the grass. The engines throttled back, two men ran crouching to haul the heavy chocks from under the wheels and the whole huge black edifice rolled slowly out of the dispersal and swung round to join the queue of bombers edging along the perimeter track.

It was an extraordinary sight: twenty-two Halifaxes, strung out nose-to-tail around the airfield, inching past the distant control tower towards the head of the main runway, the ground trembling from the thunder of their eighty-eight Rolls Royce engines. As each one reached the end of the runway it turned, paused for a moment, then came roaring past the little black-and-white-chequered control van towards the distant trees, heaving its great load over them and lumbering up into the sky, wheels folding up into its wings. No sooner had one left the ground than another was racing down the runway after it. I sat on the grass and watched them go, one after another, until the last echo had rumbled away into the distance and the field was silent again; just the faintest ringing in my ears to remind me of the shattering noise of a few moments before.

The sun was large and low now, and yellow, silhouetting the distant figures of the ground crews as they made their way back towards the hangars and casting hundred-foot shadows across the grass. Their chatter and laughter drifted faintly but clearly to me through the soft air. I got on the bike and pedalled slowly back round the perimeter track. The excitement had gone, and I felt enervated and in some odd way abandoned, as I had as a child when my parents had crept down to the front door, leaving me lying upstairs waiting for the slam of the taxi door and for the light to slide across the ceiling into darkness. How remarkable it was that those aircrews could leave the tranquillity of an evening like this for the tumult of a distant battlefield: one minute drinking tea and listening to the starlings chattering in the trees, the next thousands of feet up in the darkening sky, heading towards God only knew what. A thin tendril of fear reached my imagination. I remembered how the navigator had looked when he'd tried to smile at me.

After lights-out I didn't drop straight into sleep the way I usually did; the coarse blankets scratched my chin and I could hear the straw rustling in my pillow. It seemed wrong somehow not to be awake while the whole squadron was on operations. Much later, in the middle of the night, I was jerked out of a deep sleep by the roar of a plane. It had gone right over the huts, so the wind must have changed and they were using the other runway. I heard it land, and then a few minutes later another one thundered over. I lay awake, staring into the dark, counting them as they came in. At first they arrived regularly, one almost every half-minute; then there started to be longer pauses. After I'd reached twenty-one the

37

pause seemed to be interminable. I heard someone moving about in the blackness and the hut door open and close. Then at last, faintly in the distance, came the throb of engines. It grew and grew until there was a woosh over the roof and then silence. After a while the sound of trucks and faraway voices died, and I turned over in my bed and drifted into sleep, my hand cupping the comfort of a dawn erection.

5

At the art school we'd been taught that drawing was the supreme discipline on which all good painting was built, and we were coached in the tradition stretching back through Sickert and Degas to Ingres and David. We were expected never to be without paper and pencil and to be always draw-ing, anywhere, anytime and on anything. There were legends about how Sickert (or was it Degas?) could draw, unobserved, in his pocket, which was a bit beyond me, but the drawing habit had stuck and I usually had a dog-eared pad and a stub of pencil tucked away in my battledress. People were my favourite subjects: the human figure is a thing of infinite vari-ety, and anyway the SPs might have looked askance at anyone making careful elevations of hangars and aircraft. The only trouble with people was that they didn't keep still and they had a tendency to get nosy about what one was doing. I'd already made enough studies of the backs of soporific sergeants to paper a large room, so I needed somewhere else where my subjects would be immobilized long enough for me to do them justice. Since Alan had come back off leave he and I had made a habit of sloping off to the NAAFI; there at least people sat down, and one could be quite unobtrusive at a table in the corner. I took to going there on my own in the evenings and sitting with my sketch book and half a pint of beer, a lonely, dedicated artist in uniform. Dedicated artists in uniform were rather the thing in those days, the pages of *Penguin New Writing* were full of them: poets in Spitfires, pianists in tanks, fireman painters, keeping the torch of culture alight amid the collapse of civilization. I also had hopes that, as well as improving my drawing, this romantic image might help rekindle my sex life, which seemed at the moment on the edge of extinction.

It wasn't that I was all that obsessed with sex, certainly no more than most of the young men around me. To judge by conversation in the hut it was never far from anyone's mind, and on a quiet night the unmistakable sound of an airman seeking relief under his blankets was often heard. In those days it was not a thing that was mentioned, even in the company I was keeping; the daily wank was expected to be kept discreetly out of sight – and sound. Just occasionally, when someone was too desperate or too drunk for caution, the rhythmic creaking would provoke a cry of 'Oh, for fuck's sake, get *on* with it, so we can all get some sleep!' No, that was just a mechanical problem, the age-old dilemma of men on their own; what I was really missing was female company.

The trouble was, I preferred girls. I didn't actually dislike the company of men, although I was often embarrassed by being such a young one and inevitably as uncouth as most young men, but in the end men were so predictable, whereas women seemed to offer all manner of surprises in every department. To me they were creatures of delicacy, wit, sophistication and breathtaking perception, and I missed them badly. At the art school, where fifty of the fifty-two students had been girls, I had been like a puppy with two tails, although sadly too young to know what to do with either of them. Now, quite ready to be a young dog, I had become

40

instead an aircraftman second-class, the bottom of the barrel of any girl's aspirations. And if there was a WAAF likely to be impressed by my lonely sensitivity she didn't seem to frequent the NAAFI in the evenings; or if she did, she wasn't the kind of WAAF I'd want to impress.

I was sitting in my corner one night, drawing a couple of burly M/T drivers on the other side of the room, when I sensed someone over my shoulder.

'That's good,' a voice said. 'That's ever so good.' It was a deep, hoarse voice, but with a slightly pedantic delivery. 'Mind if I join you?'

I looked up, smiling to hide my irritation. 'No, not at all.'

Like me he was an unadorned airman, but a lot older; there was even a hint of grey in his carefully trimmed wavy hair. He was stocky, with a broad, pink face and querulously arched eyebrows. 'Ta,' he said, and sat down next to me. He put down his tea and a plate of beans and chips and leaned across to look at my drawing. 'You've got the big one perfectly. Built like a brick shithouse, isn't he?' He pulled out a large white handkerchief and tucked it over the knot of his tie. I noticed that his uniform had been pressed carefully and so often that the seams were shiny, and when he lifted his tea I saw there was a big gold signet ring on his little finger.

'An artist, are you?' he said. 'In civvy street?'

'I was training to be one.'

'At an art school?'

'Yes.'

He scooped beans onto his fork with his knife. 'That's interesting. What sort of things do they teach you there?'

'Almost everything, in the first couple of years anyway. I was doing design, perspective, history of architecture, life . . .'

'Life?' he said, glancing at me quizzically. 'Teach you life, do they?'

'Life drawing – drawing from life.'

41

'Naked women?'

I was used to this. It was all that interested most people. 'Usually,' I said. 'Sometimes men.'

'Really?' This seemed to cheer him up a good deal.

'Not so often these days. They're in rather short supply.'

'Mmm.' He considered this for a moment. Then, pausing with a chip halfway to his mouth, he said with a faraway expression, 'Do you know . . . on my body . . . there isn't a single blemish . . . not one.'

'Goodness,' I said.

'Not a single blemish.' I could feel him watching me. 'You could draw me, if you liked. Not in the altogether, of course,' he added. 'Not till the weather gets warmer, anyway.'

I laughed nervously and he went back to his plate. He mopped up every ounce of sauce with his last chips and, with his ring-finger carefully lifted, wiped his mouth meticulously on the white handkerchief, which he then replaced up his sleeve.

'Did they teach you scene-painting?' he asked.

'I did some for an amateur society once.'

He nodded. 'Ever see *Up in the Blue*?'

'Er, no . . . what was that?'

'Our last show. At the Station Theatre.'

I explained I'd only been on the camp for a few weeks.

'You missed a treat. We toured it all round the group, you know. We've got quite a talented little cast together here. Mostly amateurs, of course, except for the odd pro like me.'

'Were you a professional?'

'Twenty years, man and boy. You might have seen me – Danny Green, Virtuoso of the Harmonica?'

'I don't think I have . . . I'm afraid.'

'I've been on the bill with all the big names. Played the Moss Empires number-ones for years. Before that I was with the D'Oyly Carte, you know. Chorus and small parts.'

'How exciting.'

'Not much use round here, though. You perform at all, do you? Sing, dance, play anything?'

'God, no,' I said hastily.

'Still, we could do with someone on the scenery. You see, my act—' He leaned forward and grew confidential. 'My act has an oriental flavour. It needs a Chinese background – willow pattern and so forth.'

'Did they have mouth-organs in China?'

I received a stony look. 'Harmonicas,' he said sternly. 'I've got the costume of course,' he went on, dismissing my *faux pas*. 'It goes everywhere with me. But what I need is a set. Just a couple of flats, or a cloth – black and gold and dragons et cetera – you know the sort of thing.' He wrinkled his nose at me intimately, one artist to another.

I nodded.

'Having to work in the Carmen Miranda set last time just killed the act. Presentation is everything in our business, everything.'

'I'm sure it is.' I had a surrealist vision of a pink-faced Chinese mandarin playing a mouth-organ on Copacabana beach and tried to concentrate on my beer.

'I'll tell you what,' he said suddenly. 'You ought to meet Harry.'

'Who's he?'

'Our producer. Brilliant, my dear. Used to be in rep before the war. Now, let's see . . .' He looked at me speculatively again. 'What section are you?'

'Instruments – Compasses, actually. But I'm in here most evenings,' I said quickly. I didn't think Sgt Willoughby would appreciate this veteran of the halls dropping in on us.

'OK, I'll bring Harry over tomorrow and introduce you. You'll love him, he's a real live wire. Always on the go.' He lowered his lids suddenly in an expression of measureless

43

boredom. 'Especially where the WAAFs are concerned, I'm afraid.' He sighed. 'Still, *chacun*, as the French say. Ta-ra, see you tomorrow.'

The signet ring rested for a second on my shoulder and he was gone, carrying himself in a self-consciously erect way, his head tilted back to avoid a double chin, creating a plump little roll over the back of his collar.

He didn't turn up the next evening, or the next. Then there were ops for two nights running, and in the end it was Saturday before I saw him again.

Saturday night on the camp tended to be just like Saturday nights everywhere – crowded and boisterous. Of course, officially weekends didn't exist on active service (which according to King's Regulations was what I was on). The war wasn't intended to stop at lunch-time on Saturday and start up again first thing on Monday; we were supposed to be blowing the blazes out of Germany seven days a week. But, in fact, I can't seem to recall any operations on a Sunday. I imagine there must have been a few, but the Sundays I remember seem all to have been sombre and subdued, the workshops silent, the airmen reading the *News of the World* and nursing hangovers. On Fridays we were paid, and everyone not on duty piled into the bus and rode off singing into York where they were relieved of their three shillings a day and returned by 23.59 hours still singing and sporadically throwing up. By Saturday night the realization that they had spent most of their week's pay the night before inclined them to celebrate the rest of the weekend more frugally on the camp, crowding into the station cinema and the NAAFI.

This Saturday night the noise and the smoke in the NAAFI were so overpowering that I'd given up drawing and was sitting nursing half a pint of mild-and-bitter and a gnawing misanthropy. For all that I loved to hobnob, I'd always been averse to humanity in the mass. Anything bigger than a football team sent me into retreat. I was convinced that a group of a hundred individuals was likely to be a hundred times sillier than any one of the individuals in it. Which was presumably why mobs behaved like lunatics and the ancient sages spent so much time in the desert or on the tops of poles. Being part of an aircrew would have been all right: Halifaxes only carried seven, a nice convivial number, and other planes even fewer. But down here among the hoi polloi I was an ant in an ant-hill, and there was no privacy anywhere.

When I felt sorry for myself like this I usually got homesick and decided to write to my mother, which was cheering for her: she didn't get a lot of letters from me when things were going well. I was just wondering whether to try writing in the billet where the noise and smoke might be a little less, when I caught sight of Danny Green at the counter with a dark-haired man in a baggy battledress. I saw Danny look round the room and then nudge his companion. They came towards me through the tables.

'Well, hello,' Danny said in his ripe, husky voice. 'This is Harry, that I was telling you about.'

'Hello,' Harry said. He had an actor's confident, classless voice, but he didn't look much like an actor. His legs were on the short side, and either his nose was too big for his chin or his chin was too small for his nose. His eyes were lively, though, and shrewd. 'Want a drink?' he asked.

'I'm OK, thanks.'

They sat down on either side of me. Someone was thumping away at a jangling piano, accompanying a grey-haired corporal who was quavering his way through 'The Fishermen of England' while the rest of the room raised their voices to drown him. Harry was saying something.

'Sorry – what?' I said.

'Danny says you're an artist,' he said more loudly.

'Sort of, yes.'

He nodded. I fished a crumpled packet of Players from my breast pocket and offered them round. Harry lit them for us with a perspex lighter of the kind illicitly fabricated in RAF workshops everywhere. Danny immediately told the joke about the King visiting an aircraft factory and asking one of the workers how many fighters they'd produced that week. 'Five hundred, sir,' replies the man. 'Five hundred fighters in one week?' the King says, astonished. 'Oh, sorry, sir,' says the man. 'I thought you said lighters.' I laughed dutifully. Harry's mind seemed elsewhere.

The corporal had now been replaced by a robust baritone who was bellowing his way through 'Deep In The Heart Of Texas' with half of the room assisting him.

Harry said, 'I can't stand this bloody row. You busy tonight?'

'Not at all,' I said.

'Come on then.' He drained his glass, got up and led the way to the door without looking to see if we were following. Outside, he said to Danny, 'We'll go to The Wings. It's quieter.'

'You'll have to manage without me, I'm afraid,' Danny said, as one breaking tragic news. 'I'm off to the billet. Bath night,' he explained, giving me a suggestive glance.

I followed Harry up the main road of the camp.

'What are The Wings?' I asked.

'Just a hut. Where we store scenery and stuff. We call it The Wings because it sounds as if it might be something to do with the RAF. Really it's more the theatrical sort of wings.'

We had gone round the back of one of the workshops and were outside a very small Nissen hut. It was simply a half-cylinder of corrugated iron, not more than fifteen feet long, with the two ends bricked up. There was a single window in one end and a single door in the other. Harry took a large key out of his pocket and let us in. It was Double British Summer Time and there was still daylight about, but not enough to penetrate the narrow window opposite. Harry crossed over and pushed a blackout frame into it.

'Turn on the light,' he said.

I felt about until I found a big metal switch. The tiny room sprang into life. Instead of the usual bare bulb hanging from the roof, two table lamps were alight: both were of ancient design and had seen better days, but both sported warm-coloured shades that bathed everything in a nightclub glow. One lamp was on a trestle-table under the window, illuminating piles of books, magazines, gramophone records, an ostrich-feather hat on a wig block and the chassis of a radio set with the naked speaker dangling from a nail above it. The other lamp was on a plywood imitation of an ultra-modern table, half-moon-shaped, with tubular legs and painted shiny white, like a prop from an Astaire-Rogers film. On either side of this oddity and encircling the rusty iron stove in the middle of the hut, were two old armchairs, even more dilapidated than the ones from which my two sergeants ran the war. In the shadows, under the sloping roof, I could see bits of scenery, paint pots, a portable gramophone and a wicker costume basket. The vertical walls held playbills announcing The Station Theatre Company in *French Without Tears* and *Up in the Blue*, and were smothered in lists, charts, and pictures of stage stars of the last decade: Fay Compton, Owen Nares, John Gielgud, Evelyn Laye, Noël Coward. RAF blankets carpeted the cement floor and there was a smell that I remembered from my childhood visits to pantomimes, the smell that would drift out over the audience when the curtain rose: not of greasepaint but the real scent of the theatre – glue size.

'What do you think?' said Harry.

'It's . . . it's amazing,' I said, which was no more than the truth. It was amazing to find this oasis of everything I thought

47

of as left behind, books, lampshades, Fay Compton, here in the wilds of Yorkshire surrounded by the machinery of war.

'Want a beer?' Harry said.

I nodded. He seemed more relaxed in here, a man under his own roof. He fished two bottles from a crate under the table and flicked off the tops in an opener which was screwed to the door frame. He passed me a bottle and sank into one of the armchairs. I sank into the other and we stretched out our legs towards the stove, empty as it was. He patted the Hollywood table beside him.

'How d'you like that?'

'Marvellous,' I said.

'Made it myself. For the last show.'

I looked round. 'How on earth did you wangle all this?'

'Father.'

'Father?'

'Don't you know him? Old Appleton, Squadron Leader Admin. Everyone calls him Father. Poor old bugger's stage-struck. We gave him one line in a sketch in the last show and he was putty in our hands. He wheedled this place out of Works and Bricks and gave me the key. We're getting it organized gradually.'

'Looks as if you've got it organized.'

'Home from home,' Harry said, and started to fill his pipe. 'You're in the Compass Section then, are you?'

'Yes.'

'With those two sergeants. You want to watch them. Couple of nice ones, they are.'

'How do you mean?'

But now he was lighting it, the flame of his lighter flaring and dipping as he sucked and puffed with great concentration. Before I had time to repeat the question he had snapped the lighter shut and changed the subject.

'I gather Danny's been asking you to design a set for him.'

'Yes.'

'Chinese, I suppose?'

'Yes.'

'Daft bugger. The only oriental number he knows is that terrible arrangement of 'Japanese Sandman'. But to Danny everything east of Suez is Chinese. Anyway, if he will insist on being last on before the finale he'll have to put up with going in front of the tabs, because we're setting up behind.'

'Why does he insist on that?'

'The star spot, isn't it? And he's the pro.'

'You were a pro too though, weren't you?'

'Not for long. Gave it up when I got married.'

'Why?'

'The wife didn't approve.' The lighter came out again and again signalled the end of the subject. 'So, what do you think? Like to do some sets for us?'

'I'd love to.'

'Not exactly Drury Lane, but we do have a bit of money from the PSI Fund.'

'What's that?'

'Supposed to be money for entertainments in general: camp cinema, the band, sports equipment, all that sort of thing. Father's in charge of it, so we get our fair share. Rather more, actually.' He winked at me. 'We'll be starting a new show soon so there'll be plenty to do. We can work together in the evenings, but you can have the run of this place any time you like. I expect Father'll wangle you some time off from your section. Don't suppose you'd mind that?'

'Not a lot, no,' I said, trying to contain my eagerness at these new possibilities.

He puffed away in silence for a moment. 'Do you like the theatre?' he asked suddenly.

'Oh, yes,' I said quickly, adding cautiously, 'I haven't seen a lot, of course.'

Harry got up, took a pile of magazines from the table and dumped them on my lap. They were all called *Theatre World* and seemed to go back some years.

'Have a look at those,' he said. 'There's some great stuff there. Look at that top one. Page seven, I think.'

I turned to page seven. A handsome naval officer was gazing down at a dark-haired beauty hanging in his arms in a rather abandoned way.

'I saw that, you know.' He reached over and tapped the picture. 'Godfrey Tearle and Margaret Rawlings. Sexiest thing I've ever seen. See how she's giving at the waist, and letting her arm hang from her shoulder in that lazy way. Real sex that is, very few English actresses can do it.' His big front teeth chewed his pipe stem avidly, like a stallion on its bit.

We sat there for hours while I turned the pages and he discoursed on the famous faces as they passed. His predilection was clearly for actresses, about whose qualities, usually sexual, he'd expatiate at length. Sometimes he'd jump to his feet to demonstrate, absurd on his short legs and in his baggy battledress, but oddly inspiring in his passion, so different from the wry cynicism he'd affected when we first met.

Then the magazines were put aside and out came the photographs of The Station Theatre Company themselves. After the retouched glamour of *Theatre World* they seemed painfully amateurish, the actors posing awkwardly in ill-fitting costumes, caught in the unflattering glare of a flashbulb. Harry's unabashed pride saw only their remembered triumphs. To him the rows of fat-kneed WAAFs in satin leotards were Cochran's Young Ladies, and the chubby soubrette ablaze with sequins was second only to Jessie Matthews. Warmed by his enthusiasm I had a closer look. For all that there were clearly no Ivor Novellos or Pat Kirkwoods among them and the sight of Danny playing the mouth-organ in his Chinese outfit was just as funny as I'd imagined, I could see that some

50

of the girls weren't bad-looking and the pictures had such an air of eager optimism that it was hard to resist them. I was careful not to criticize the sadly slap-dash scenery of my predecessor, but risked making one or two suggestions about the future. Harry accepted them instantly and, thrusting a pencil and the backs of some old Routine Orders at me, encouraged me to expand them into impossible vistas that would have taxed the facilities of the Covent Garden Opera House.

I don't know what time it was when I groped my way through the blackness to my billet, but the camp was as still as the grave; the rumble of the ventilation from the underground operations room and a thin sliver of light under the guard-room door were the only signs of life. I crept into the hut, counting the ends of the beds until I found my own, cautiously got out of my boots and battledress and slid between the blankets. I pulled them over my ears to shut out the snuffles and groans of my twenty-three room-mates and, after a few moments of semi-consciousness during which a row of bare-legged WAAFS paraded down a flight of silver stairs designed by me, I dropped into a dreamless oblivion. I'd forgotten, of course, to write to my mother.

51

6

The next afternoon I was alone with Sgt Willoughby. Outside it was raining steadily, there was ten-tenths cloud almost down to the ground and ops had been cancelled. Sgt Grice had gone off to the village with another of his mysterious parcels and Alan had been dispatched by Willoughby with a note to the sergeants' mess. I would have resented being sent out in a downpour to run his private errands, but with Willoughby, Alan was like a rabbit with a snake. Or perhaps he preferred the rain to the atmosphere in the hut. The camp had grown very still now, and in here there was no sound but the rain on the roof and the rustle of Willoughby's *Daily Mirror*.

A bicycle banged against the side of the hut and Percy appeared in the doorway, dripping. Percy was the Orderly Room Runner, in which capacity he visited and was known by every section on the station. Because he was tiny, no more than five feet at a guess, with a high squeaky voice and carrot-coloured hair, he had been cast as the camp jester, a rôle he played with gusto, giddy with the awareness of his own celebrity, grinning amiably at epithets like 'the tallest dwarf in the RAF', carrying rumours round the camp with the speed and mischievousness of a podgy Puck. But, like a true jester, his ginger-fringed eyes would gleam with malevolence at moments, a reminder that it might be wise not to lean too heavily on his amiability.

He stumped over to Willoughby, his waterproof cape trailing on the floor, and produced a slip of paper from his haversack. 'Memo from Admin, Sarge,' he said in a Liverpudlian falsetto.

Willoughby lowered his paper. 'Ah, Percy. How's your love life?' he said. 'When's the wedding, then?' This was a well-worn Percy joke. He was known to have been engaged for the last three years and he needed no encouragement to show you photographs of his fiancée, a woman of awe-inspiring plainness called Beryl. Phrasing an acceptable response when homely loved ones were dug out of wallets was an essential art of service life, but even the glibbest experts had been rendered speechless by a sight of Beryl.

Percy took the question quite seriously. 'Next summer, we reckon. If she's better.'

'What's wrong with her?'

'Got a nasty rash.'

'Where?'

'Right up her front, and halfway down her back.'

Willoughby drew in his breath in mock horror. 'You know what that is, don't you?'

'What?'

'The clap.'

Percy gave a shriek, of delight as much as anything, at being the object of such manly ribaldry. 'Ooh, Sarge, you are a dirty bugger!'

'Well, you don't know what she's up to while you're away, do you?'

'She better not try. I'd fucking murder her. And him.' Ludicrous though it was, I couldn't altogether disbelieve him.

Willoughby lost interest in repartee and read the memo. He

glanced up at me and said to Percy, 'They want him right away?'

'Think so, Sarge.'

Willoughby turned to me. 'You're to report to the Admin Office. Get going.'

I got my cap and went to the door. 'Straight back,' he shouted. 'No dawdling.'

Being told to report anywhere was always unnerving. What regulation would I be accused of breaking? Or had they found out about the ones I *had* broken? Perhaps it was a posting: was I to be off tomorrow to the burning Sahara – or the wastes of Iceland? I dashed through the rain, head down, leaping the puddles, my heart in my mouth.

But in the Admin Office all that was waiting for me was Harry, who said, 'Get wet, did you? Father wants to meet you.' He called to a sturdy WAAF corporal with a red face, 'Right, Janet, tell him we're here.'

She led us to a door marked 'Officer i/c Administration, Sqn/Ldr Appleton'. A voice with a Lancashire accent said, 'Come in.'

He rose to greet us. He was tall and stooping, nearly bald, with a grey moustache. There was no brevet on his tunic, only two 1914–18 ribbons. Before we'd had time to salute he said apologetically, 'Hello, Harry, sorry to drag you out in this weather. Is this your friend, then?'

'Sam Turner, sir,' Harry said.

'Nice to meet you,' said Father, startling me by offering to shake hands. 'Sit down, lads, if you've got a minute.'

Sit down? This was unheard of. To say nothing of *if you've got a minute*. I nearly glanced down to see if my cuffs had sprouted a couple of rings.

'I expect you'd like some tea,' he said. 'Tell Janet, will you?'

Harry got up and put his head out of the door. 'Three teas, Janet,' he called. 'One without.' This was obviously routine to him.

Father smiled shyly at me. 'You're going to help us with the scenery, then?'

'I hope so.'

'Grand. Not seen any of our shows, have you?'

'Afraid not, sir.'

'They've been quite a success you know, thanks to Harry here. But the scenery's always been a bit . . . uninspired, you might say. Harry's first-class with the carpentry but it's the painting lets it down. Now, we've got a new show planned.' He leaned back in his chair and rubbed his thin hands enthusiastically. 'And Harry says he wants to get the scenery well under way before we start rehearsing.'

'As soon as I know what's wanted, I could do some designs.'

'*Designs!*' This was obviously an innovation. 'Drawings, you mean? That'd be just the thing, wouldn't it, Harry.'

'Yes,' said Harry uncertainly. I wondered if I'd overdone it.

'That'd be a lot of work for you, I suppose,' Father said.

'Quite a lot, yes.'

'Mmm.' He looked at an open file on his desk. 'You're under training here, are you?'

'Instruments – Compass Section, sir.'

'Who's your officer?'

'There isn't one really, sir. Sgt Willoughby and Sgt Grice are in charge.'

'I don't think I know them,' he said, frowning for a moment as if some memory were eluding him. He turned the pages of his file. 'Mmm, yes. Establishment, two sergeants. No mention of any airmen. Well, you're not vital to the war effort, then.'

Unaccountably, I felt myself go pink. 'Not very, no.'

'Waiting to go on the course, are you?'

'Yes, sir.'

'Mmm.' He spread his fingertips on the edge of his desk as

if about to launch into the Warsaw Concerto. 'How keen are you about it?'

I hesitated. This sounded like one of those trick questions officers were so fond of. I could feel Harry's eyes on me. 'Well, sir,' I said carefully. 'Sergeant Willoughby tells me the course is very full these days, so I haven't allowed myself to get too excited about it.'

'Mmm,' he said again. 'Anyway, I'll have a word with your sergeants and get them to let you off whenever they're not actually instructing you.' I thought it better not to tell him that was all day every day. 'And anything you need – within reason,' he said with a conspiratorial smile to Harry, 'just let me know. The fund's quite flush at the moment.'

There was a knock at the door and Janet came in with three mugs of tea on a battered green tray. She put one down in front of Father and handed us ours, her lips pursed with disapproval at the sight of two airmen lounging in chairs in front of a squadron leader.

When we were outside Harry said to me, 'You can say goodbye to that course.'

'Why?'

'He'll block your posting. He's stopped three of mine. Do you mind?'

'What do you think? Painting scenery's better than bloody compasses. As long as those two sergeants don't make things difficult.'

'Father'll fix them. I doubt if they'll make any trouble. They're not likely to want to draw attention to themselves.'

I wanted to ask him why, but he'd stopped to talk to a WAAF sergeant with a toothy smile who was standing very close to him and fiddling with the buttons on his tunic.

Harry was right about the reaction of the sergeants.

The next day the weather cleared and the squadron put up

twenty-three aircraft as part of some massive operation a long way inside Germany; but the morning after there was an unspoken depression over the camp: two of them hadn't come back and one that had was quite badly shot up. The skipper of G-George had complained that his bowl compass had been playing up, so Alan and I had been sent out to check it.

As we came back into the office Grice was just closing his cupboard door. When he saw us he locked it quickly and slipped the keys into his pocket. I was surprised to see him there as I knew he had the day off because he'd been Duty Sergeant the night before.

'I'll see you later, Ken,' he said, giving the cupboard door a tug to reassure himself it was locked. He made for the door, stopping on the way to drain the mug of tea on top of the stove.

Willoughby looked up from the desk. 'So, it's Van bloody Gogh,' he said, smiling his meaningless smile at me. 'I've had a billy-do about you from Admin. It seems you are required for higher things.'

I tried a smile of my own. 'Hardly, Sarge.'

'That's what it sounds like,' he said, holding up the memo with finger and thumb. 'I'm to let you go off to your theatricals whenever you're not required for essential duties.'

There was a long pause, presumably to keep me in suspense about his decision. 'And,' he said at last, 'why not? No man is indispensable. Aircraftman Buckley and I will continue to prosecute the war without your assistance.' No mention of Sgt Grice I noticed. He turned to Alan. 'What do you say, Buckley? We managed before and we'll manage again, eh?'

Alan looked stricken. Oh Christ, I thought, I've dropped the poor little sod right into it. Perhaps I could get him off too. He might be an amateur tenor or an undiscovered tap-dancer or something. I glanced at him; it seemed unlikely. 'Thanks, Sarge,' I said.

'Just remember please,' Willoughby said, leaning forward and fixing me with his little black eyes, 'your first duty remains here.' He tapped the desk with a yellow finger. 'You still take your orders from me. Understood?'

'Yes, Sarge.'

Harry got hold of a duplicate key for The Wings and presented it to me. I sensed this was a great honour, and something of a sacrifice for him as the hut had clearly been his own private sanctum and, if Danny was to be believed, had been used for some fairly private purposes. The key was iron and enormous, like a medieval gaoler's. It weighed down my battledress and often gave me an agonizing prod in the groin when I sat down. But it was never out of my keeping. Admission to The Wings was by invitation only and Harry advised me to issue invitations discreetly as there were elements on the station that couldn't wait to peg the entertainments people and strip them of their privileges. 'Also,' Harry said, ponderously casual, 'you may find some evenings it's locked on the inside.'

Like Alberich's ring, the key transformed my relationship with the world. Keys were something only officers carried. Other Ranks had no need of them: they had no private property, they were not private people; their lives, like their socks and their underwear, were open to inspection night or day. Whenever my leave was up, the last thing I did before I left home was to take my keys out of my pocket and shut them in a drawer.

I wrote to my mother, asking her to parcel up my paints, brushes, rulers, T-square: all the things I'd not expected to use again until the war was over. Harry briefed me on the new show, which was to be another 'revue' called, for no reason that anyone could sensibly explain, *Over the Moon*. We discussed the various items endlessly, their scenic requirements and the limitations of the Station Theatre, so that when the large cardboard box arrived from home I was ready to start work at once. Every morning I would report to Sgt Willoughby and, with surprising ease, get permission to disappear into the little Nissen hut, where I would spread my equipment on the table by the window, switch on the skeleton radio, tune it to the *Forces Programme* and forget the world outside for hours on end.

Bent over my drawing board, inventing a world of order and symmetry, the neat pencil lines converging on the vanishing points, the creamy paint flowing over the crisp white paper, I felt myself less and less a part of what was going on around me. Perhaps because of my lowly status and the indifference of Willoughby and Grice, I had never become really involved in the operational life of the station; now it seemed more remote than ever. Although I suspected I wasn't entirely alone in this. The work of the squadron was sustained by dozens of different skills, so complicated and demanding that all over the camp, in sheds and huts like this one, there were single-minded experts who had almost forgotten what was the eventual outcome of their efforts – the systematic destruction of people and places. Even the aircrews, juggling innumerable technicalities and clinging desperately to their own survival, were hardly aware of what was happening thousands of feet below them. I was exercising the only skill I had and, if people like Father and Harry thought it important, that was good enough for me.

I did have visitors: Harry of course, and Danny, who would often call with new gossip and suggestions for ever more exotic settings for his act, and occasionally someone who had been commissioned by Harry to make or scrounge something for the show. When the weather turned hot the little tin hut could get like an oven and I would leave the door open, which was why I was startled one morning to hear a voice say,

'Hello,' and when I turned round to see a strange WAAF standing there.

'Oh, sorry,' she said, 'I thought Harry was in here.'

'It's all right. Don't go,' I said, jumping up. She hesitated. She was a little shorter than I was, with curly fair hair and a pinkly healthy complexion. She was barely pretty and she wasn't slim – very few WAAFs stayed slim on all that porridge and potatoes – but neither was she fat. She made me think of my favourite adjective of Huxley's – 'pneumatic'. Other ranks were allowed to abandon their tunics in the summer, and standing there in her pale-blue shirt and trim skirt she looked as fresh and appetizing as newly baked bread.

'Is Harry here?' she said. 'It's about that net curtain he wanted.'

'Can we have it?'

'Yes, but it's a bit old, my auntie says. What's it for?'

'Do you want to see?' I unrolled one of the designs onto the table. 'Here.'

She came and stood beside me. 'Oh,' she said, 'that's lovely. Is that what it's going to look like?'

'I hope so. You see, if we cover that big window with the net and paint The Genie on it, then when the light's behind it you'll see straight through, but if you light it from the front he'll appear as if by magic.'

'Before your very eyes,' she said and giggled. 'That's ever so clever.' She seemed genuinely impressed, although her eyes crinkled naturally, giving her a permanently amused expression.

'Do you want some tea?' I said. 'I've just boiled the kettle.' Which was actually true.

She looked around. 'Do yourselves all right, you lads, don't you?'

'Not bad.'

I got the teapot out and she said with a sigh, 'Come on, I'll

61

do that. Men can't make tea – never heard of letting it mash.'

While she clattered about authoritatively, I went to the door and gently pushed it to. I didn't want the sight of us lounging in armchairs drinking tea to inflame passers-by. By the time she'd found the powdered milk and the sugar in the jam jar and given the brown-stained mugs a wry inspection, the tea was ready.

'I'll be mother,' she said, lifting the pot. 'But not if I'm careful.'

It was nearly half an hour before she jumped up and said, 'I must get back. Our sergeant'll murder me.' By that time I'd discovered that everyone called her Bonny although her real name was Pat Bonham, that she was an M/T driver and usually drove the truck when the shows toured to other airfields. She'd actually been in the last show – but only in the chorus. She was a local girl (which I'd guessed by her accent) and although her home was in Selby, on day passes she usually went into York. Did I go there much? I should, it was a beautiful city, and did I know you could walk right round it on the walls? She knew all the pubs worth knowing and the best fish-and-chip shop this side of the Pennines. Didn't I? Well, she'd have to show me one day, wouldn't she? She waved. 'Thanks for the tea,' she said, and was gone, leaving me holding her mug and squinting at the dazzling oblong of sunlight she'd just vacated.

The hut seemed dim and cramped. I went out and stood in the hot sun, thinking about York and how soon I'd dare to take her up on her offer, and if my savings of two pounds ten would be enough to finance a swift and efficient seduction.

In spite of Harry's hints, I'd never yet found the door locked against me. I was well aware that he and his toothy sergeant were having a pretty active liaison – he spoke glowingly of her enthusiasm and co-operation – but where they conducted it I had no idea. I suppose I assumed that in this weather they were 'hedging and ditching', the airmen's romantic euphemism for love in the fields. On warm evenings at this time of year the half-mile of long grass between the WAAF quarters and the main camp was alive with couplings. (There was an unlikely but firmly believed legend that a bomb-aimer, coming in to land from a daylight raid, had recognized his fiancée spreadeagled under the C-of-E padre.) Harry enjoyed a happy relationship with his bodily functions and made no secret of them to his friends; he was quite liable to greet you by announcing loudly, 'I've just had a beautiful crap!' So when he strode into the hut at half-past nine one morning and said with exactly the same emphasis, 'I've just had a wonderful fuck!' I wasn't all that startled. What intrigued me was how he'd managed it at that time of day and in the middle of a busy aerodrome.

'Where?' I asked him.

'In her office.'

'When?'

He looked at his watch. 'Ten minutes ago, roughly.'

'Suppose somebody had come in?'

'I had my foot against the door,' he said reassuringly.

I was dazzled by his insouciance and longed to know the details. In what position was this achieved? What state of undress did they reach? What would have been the recovery time if someone had knocked? But I couldn't ask, it would have been an admission of shaming naïvety. My limited experiences had always been in – or at the wildest on – beds; and in reasonable security. I couldn't imagine any of the girls I knew tolerating this sort of adventure for a moment. But perhaps when you got older you got more desperate. After all Harry *was* thirty-six, and she was certainly thirty.

By this time, Harry had wangled for me to move into his billet, for convenience as much as anything. The atmosphere in this hut was subtly different from the one I'd left. These were the veterans of the station: they measured their time on the camp in years rather than months. Others came and went, but a posting never arrived for anyone in here. Harry called it The Hut of Forgotten Men. As a result the billet had an air of cosy permanence which was almost homely. Everyone had acquired set habits and learned to live with the habits of the others. In the mornings the younger ones fetched mugs of tea for the older ones, while the older ones reciprocated in the evenings with advice on life, marriage and Air Force Law. The only exceptions were half a dozen Glaswegians, ex-miners most of them, who lived their own lives of passion and violence at the far end of the hut, communicating in some quite incomprehensible language.

Coming in early the next evening I found the place empty except for a small figure sitting on its bed halfway down the room. It was Percy. His ginger head was bent over a sort of invalid table across his lap, beyond which his little legs didn't protrude more than eighteen inches. He looked up and removed a watchmaker's glass from his eye.

'Hello, Sam,' he squeaked. He was a phenomenon; he must have known everyone's name on the station.

'What are you doing?' I said.

'The Wing Co's watch. Lovely job it is – Swiss, fourteen jewel. Look at that.'

I leant over to see. The bed-table was strewn with minute cogs and springs. I stepped back a pace in case I sneezed and blew the Wing Commander's watch all round the billet.

'You're a watch mender?' I said perceptively.

'In civvy street I was.'

'Why aren't you in Instruments, then?'

'Failed the course,' he said with a smirk. 'I make a few bob doing this, though. Keeps me hand in.' He screwed the glass back into his eye and bent over the tray until his chin almost touched it. When he spoke his breath stirred the tiny components. 'How d'you like it up there?'

'All right,' I said. 'I'm not there much at the moment.'

'I know. Good thing too.'

'Why?'

'Dodgy lot that mob. 'Cept for that poor little oppo of yours.'

'Why poor?'

'Well, he was up shit creek over that R-Robert business, wasn't he?'

'What was that?'

'Don't you know?'

'No.' This was news to me. I sat down on the foot of his bed. He gave a piercing squawk.

'Fuckin' look out – I've dropped me balance spring!'

'Sorry,' I said. Gently he lifted it again in his tweezers. I said impatiently, 'So, what happened?'

There was a silence while he slowly lowered the spring into place. Then he let out his breath and said, 'There was a big op about six months ago: Hamburg I think – can't remember. Anyway, R-Robert was an early return.'

'Turned back?'

'Yeah. Compass trouble they said. Must have been bloody bad compass trouble, 'cos they got themselves completely lost and pranged into a mountain in Scotland. Four of 'em bought it; there was only the navigator, the wireless op and the tail-end charlie got out. There was an inquiry and the navigator said the compasses had been so far out they couldn't have been properly checked. But they had been of course – by your little mate, Alan. That Sgt Willoughby took all the blame of course, and got away with a reprimand – Gawd knows how.'

'That was decent of him really.'

'He wasn't going to tell them he'd sent an untrained erk out

65

to do a pre-ops check, was he? He'd have been in the glasshouse for that. Anyway he's made up for it since – persuading that poor little bugger that he was responsible for the whole thing.'

No wonder Alan was so jumpy. I stood up carefully and went over to where Beryl in a Perspex frame graced Percy's bedside cupboard. 'I suppose . . .' I said slowly, 'that in fact Alan *was* responsible.'

'Ah, but he swears blue them compasses was perfectly OK when he left them.' He snapped the back onto the watch. 'Fuckin' fishy, if you ask me.'

'Why?'

'Well . . . early returns and that. That kite was such a mess nobody could tell. Wouldn't be the first crew to have tinkered with the works so as to get home in time for dinner.'

The hut door banged open and two diminutive Glaswegians strode down between the beds. 'Halloo ma wee Percy!' one of them called. When they reached his bed they lifted up the end and shook it until all the cogs and springs and tiny screwdrivers were dancing towards the edge of the tray.

'Stop it you bastards!' Percy screamed. 'Get off you rotten sods. Fuck off youse!'

They dropped his bed with a shuddering crash and swaggered on down the hut, roaring with laughter.

7

Being a member of Harry's intimate circle was my first encounter with theatre people. I'd always assumed them to be monsters of egotism – how else could they get up in public places and do what they did? Harry and his friends did seem flamboyant and pretty self-centred at times, but after the arrogance and insularity of some of the art students I'd been used to, they struck me as surprisingly insecure and dependent on one another. I supposed it was the nature of the job. A painter slaps away at his canvas alone in his studio (or in the middle of a cornfield if he's that way inclined) but, as Harry once pointed out, the biggest star in the world can flop if someone gives him the wrong cues. Their worst trait seemed to be a glutinous sentimentality about their colleagues, living or dead; their eyes would actually fill with tears at the mention of certain performers or theatres, even when they were disparaging them – the theatres, that is, not the performers; performers were never disparaged. It was surely from them that I first heard 'Always be nice to people on your way up the ladder – you'll be meeting them again on the way down.' They could be embarrassing in public, of course, with their loud voices and uninhibited laughter, but their emotions, being their stock-in-trade, were endearingly near the surface. It made them hard to resist, especially when they were being funny – which was most of the time. Listening to the endless stories of the absurdity of their lives, every one polished by years of telling, I could laugh for longer than I'd thought possible, gasping for air, wiping away the tears, always ready for more.

Of course only three of them were real pros: Harry, Danny and a tall, saturnine sergeant called Ernie Tupper who had been the unfunny half of Taylor and Tupper until Taylor had succumbed to DTs in Glasgow. And in a sense, now that we were all professional fitters, clerks, flight mechanics or armourers, they had become amateurs again, and shared with us the amateur's conviction that what he is doing takes precedence over everything else. While the war thundered around us we pursued our cardboard concerns with a single-minded intensity.

By the rest of the camp we were envied but tolerated: envied for our ability to manipulate authority and cross the hierarchical borders of service life, and tolerated because such accomplished skiving was much admired – and anyway we were obviously all daft. It was only the Service Police who couldn't endure us. To them we were idle, subversive and often Improperly Dressed – anathema to any SP. On top of which we were obviously *artistic*, a perversion that had no place in their ideal world of gleaming, identical airmen forming arrow-straight rows across an endless plain of burnished linoleum. The sight of us letting ourselves in and out of The Wings was agony to them. They would stand in lofty pairs, their heads tipped back to watch us from under the peaks of their guardsmen's caps, their smooth blue chins mottling with frustration and fury, ready to pounce the instant we should contravene just one of their beloved King's Regulations.

The idea of a policeman being my enemy was new to me.

68

In my middle-class world they were 'bobbies', kindly and reliable, or at worst, as in plays and films, amiable buffoons intent on taking down your particulars. The 'rozzers' I heard about in the billet seemed a different species, malevolent, violent and corruptible, as liable to beat you up as tell you the time.

In fact, when I listened to the tales of my hut-mates, about their lives or their families or their jobs in civvy street, the whole world they described bore little resemblance to the one I'd left behind. I felt an alien in their company. The truth was that, despite what my parents had intended as a liberal upbringing, the working classes made me nervous. My father read *The New Statesman* and warned me of condescension towards the less fortunate. 'They are,' he insisted, 'just the same as us.' This was patently untrue: their accents, their clothes, their recreations, their whole way of life, were clearly different from ours.

At the art school, of course, we were all fervent Marxists (without a copy of *Das Kapital* between us). The principles seemed unanswerable and the answer to everything. The trouble was that exposure to the oppressed masses in the flesh had begun to have a reactionary effect on me. Most of them seemed boorish, philistine and as prejudiced as I was. And my prejudice, I supposed, had the same root as theirs – ignorance.

Only the week before the bed next to mine had been occupied for a couple of days by a corporal in transit to another group. He'd had thick grey hair, some odd-looking medal ribbons and an incomprehensible guttural accent.

'Dutch, I suppose,' I said knowingly, when he'd gone.

'Dutch?' said Harry incredulously. 'Double Dutch, more like. He was a Geordie. Couldn't you tell?' He roared with laughter and went off, no doubt to recount my gaffe to the first person he met. I didn't even know what a Geordie was.

Then one afternoon I was alone in the billet trying to darn

a sock of which little remained below the ankle. The corporal in charge of the hut emerged from his room by the door.

'Where's everyone?' he asked.

'Dunno, Corp.'

'I'm off on a forty-eight, so I'm making you responsible for telling them there's a CO's inspection Friday morning. OK?'

'Ah . . . OK, Corp.' I didn't fancy this responsibility. I didn't fancy *any* responsibility actually.

'Everyone, mind you. None of your "pass it on" shit.'

So when a large group of Glaswegians banged in at the other end of the hut, I realized it had fallen to me to broach their least favourite subject. If the working classes made me nervous, the Glaswegians frankly terrified me. Apart from only understanding one word in ten they ever said, I was well aware that the aggression pent up in their small, sinewy bodies made them as unstable as nitroglycerine. By common consent the rest of the hut left them to their own devices down there, but they were hard to ignore. Particularly on Fridays. On Friday nights, having drunk every penny of the pay they'd collected that morning, they'd return at midnight, singing, shouting and carrying their unconscious comrades. In spite of having taken on board enough beer to render two normal men insensible, they would be in a mood to fight anything that moved, or anything that didn't, for that matter. Fists, boots and often razors would be wielded in bursts of meaningless anger, until eventually alcoholic stupor brought them to a standstill, overwhelmed by the need to unload their enormous intake of liquid. This was often returned the way it had come, mixed with a half-digested fry-up, over the floor or someone's blankets. The stronger stomachs would confine themselves to pissing. Pissing was directed either at the hot stove to see how much steam they could make or, bare-arsed, out through an open window. The more decorous would even venture out of the door to do it. On a notable occasion

70

one of them tottered outside, lost his bearings, became convinced he was still inside, stuck it through an open window and pissed back into the hut – the really delightful thing being that it was his own bed he pissed on.

I strolled nonchalantly towards them. An urgent argument was going on, of which the only word I could recognize was a repetitive 'fuck!'.

'Excuse me,' I said. There was no response so I tried again with more emphasis. '*Excuse me.*'

They stopped. 'Aye?' said one of them who had skin like white candle grease and huge dark eyes.

'I'm supposed to tell you', I said, shrugging carelessly in an attempt to disassociate myself from the message, 'that there's a hut inspection on Friday.'

A single cry of fury came from six throats. A boot narrowly missed me and rang against the iron stove. The owner shouted, 'Jesus Christ. Not a-fuckin'-gain!'

'Whose idea was that?' said the dark-eyed one.

'Not mine,' I said hastily.

'Fuckin' waste of time.'

'Well . . . orders is orders,' I said with feeble jauntiness.

'Nae bullshit in Russia,' someone murmured.

This was a favourite parrot cry and never failed to irritate me. With unthinking rashness I said, 'How do you know?'

'Because there's not,' came the incontestable answer.

'Because they're too busy winning the fuckin' war,' said the boot owner.

Black Eyes pointed a waxen finger at me. 'And ye ken why?' he said intensely. 'Because they've something tae fight for. They *own* their bloody country. Not like us here. But I'll tell ye what.' He stabbed his finger at me again. 'We fuckin' *will* do. You'll not see us doon those fuckin' mines again till they're ours!' There was a chorus of agreement. 'If they dinna nationalize them, they can dig the stuff oot theyselves.'

'Joe for King and Saturdays off!' someone called. That was another familiar cry. The kindly, moustached Stalin was their idol.

'Joe for King and Saturdays off,' they began to chant in unison. This was obviously not the moment for political dialectics.

'Right,' I said. 'That's the gen, anyway.'

'OK, laddie,' said the dark-eyed one, giving me a sudden and radiant smile.

I made my way back up the hut. At a table midway between the stoves Nozzle was pressing his best blue amid clouds of steam. Nozzle was so called after the legendary size of his prick, an attribute he was not averse to exhibiting to the inmates on a Saturday night, although I'd not yet been accorded the privilege. His appetite appeared as mighty as his equipment. Away from his wife and children (there were five: it was said he'd been on leave five times since he was called up), he played havoc among the local girls. He rarely left the camp without his groundsheet tucked under his arm, a sure sign of serious intent, and the tales of his prowess, mostly from his own lips, had made him a hero of the billet. His delivery was stylish and witty, rather in the manner of the great Max Miller: he had the same roguish eye and cockney assurance. His sexual vocabulary, too, was rich with words I'd never heard of. A favourite was 'gamming': variations with the mouth apparently, by either party. Harry, an encyclopaedia of these matters, assured me that it was a contraction of *gamahuche*, a word much used in the nineteenth century.

' 'Lo, Nozzle,' I said. I felt a bit self-conscious using such a graphic nickname. I wondered if his children called him that.

He nodded, and carefully arranged a trouser leg over the blanket on the table.

'There's a hut inspection on Friday. I've got to tell everyone.'

'Won't bother me, mate. I'll be up the Smoke.'

He dipped a grubby square of cloth in the fire bucket and wrung it out.

'You going on leave?'

'Spot on, my son. First one since fucking D-day.'

'You'll be glad to see them all again.'

'Too right. See the nippers again – and the old woman. Bit of home comfort, eh?'

'I'll bet,' I said, adding daringly, 'Be quite a change for you, doing it in a bed.'

He grinned at me like a Cheshire Cat. 'Nothing like it, old son, I'm telling you.' He spread the damp cloth over the trouser leg.

'Nine days screwing in the warm and dry. You might even get through your whole repertoire.'

He looked up at me, genuinely shocked. 'Bloody hell, no! With the wife? Christ, what sort of bloke you think I am?'

'No, no, of course not,' I said hastily.

Life was very confusing.

A lot more people had filtered into the hut. I went up to the top door and made an announcement as loudly as I could. It was greeted with a few groans and then another chorus of 'No bullshit in Russia!' and 'Joe for King and Saturdays off!'

The next day I said to Alan, 'If they're so fond of Russia, why the hell don't they go there?'

We were in the queue in the cookhouse. He was in front of me and looked wryly at me over his shoulder. 'I thought you were a Communist?'

'A Communist?' I said, taken aback.

Then I remembered him asking me once what my politics were. Not having given the matter much thought and remembering the stirring discussions at college, I'd murmured 'Communist' as casually as I could, and quickly changed the subject. I thought he'd given me a funny look at the time.

73

'Ah, well,' I said, floundering, 'sort of . . . yes . . . in theory.'

He opened his mouth to say something, but there was too much noise. It was a blazing summer's day outside and in here the heat was stifling: for the cooks it must have been unbearable. No doubt Queenie would be wearing nothing under her overalls. This was said to give swifter access to the Flight Sergeant cook with whom she was having a passionate liaison, but in this weather it looked more like common sense. Institutional food seems always to be disliked, whether in schools, hospitals or canteens. The unfortunate Queenie had become the focus of that dislike in our cookhouse: her sex life was seen as symbolic of an unhygienic kitchen. She was said to have been seen coupling with her Flight Sergeant (between meals presumably) in the storeroom, on sacks of potatoes and up against the hot plates. An airman claimed to have found a French letter in his soup and she was rumoured to engage in unnatural practices with carrots, which she afterwards sliced and dropped in the stew. Personally I would have eaten the carrot with relish, because, secretly, I thought of her as an adorable slut.

As we reached the hot plate it was obvious that she was indeed wearing nothing under her white cotton coat. Her blonde hair clung damply to her forehead as she ladled stew onto our plates with one hand and slid us slices of jam tart with the pale pink fingers of the other. We took our food to one of the long trestle-tables and swung our legs over the benches on either side. Alan munched his food silently with a faraway expression.

Suddenly he said, 'It wouldn't work.'

I was watching Queenie over his shoulder, languorously slapping food onto the airmen's plates. 'Sorry?' I said.

'It wouldn't work. Not here.'

'What wouldn't?'

'Communism. Not Russian Communism.' He'd put

74

down his knife and fork and was looking at me intently.

'Oh,' I said vaguely. 'Wouldn't it?'

'Too authoritarian for us.'

'Is it?' I knew Alan took these things very seriously and that I was expected to make a contribution. I dragged my attention away from where Queenie's white neck was rising from her white coat. 'Isn't that what they all want, though? Joe for King, and all that?'

'It's not what they'll get. Not if they vote Labour.'

'Will they vote Labour?'

'They'll have to. You've only got about half a dozen Communists standing.'

I have? I realized that as a representative of the Communist Party I was expected to defend my position. I tried to remember the arguments in the common room but had to admit I was pretty hazy about the policies of any of the parties. I said cannily, 'And what exactly will Labour give them?'

'Not everything they want, or everything they ought to have. But it'll be a beginning.'

'What sort of things?' I said, playing for time. I noticed there was a lull at the hot plate and the queue had disappeared. I saw Queenie push her hair back with a creamy forearm, the ladle still in her hand. Her other hand stole into the waist of her overall and she scratched her crotch with the unselfconsciousness of a cat. My mind wandered off politics. The heat was prickling me with sweat. Alan, uncharacteristically, was talking sixteen to the dozen: nationalization, full employment, health schemes, education – I seemed to have opened the floodgates of all his passionate convictions. Eventually he stopped, and I saw he was looking at me expectantly.

I pushed my plate away and took out my cigarettes. The Flight Sergeant had appeared beside Queenie, his arm behind her back. Her pelvis was undulating almost imperceptibly and she kept glancing at him from under half-closed lids. I lit up and exhaled slowly, tipping my head back. 'Well . . . I don't know,' I said carelessly. 'I mean . . . do we really need all that?'

It was a mistake. Still watching Queenie's gyrations I sensed rather than saw Alan's reaction. I looked at him. His face was bright red.

'You may not,' he said, 'but a lot of people do.'

It was astonishing. I'd never seen him angry before; in such a mild chap the effect was alarming. I retreated quickly. Obviously I'd come up with the wrong quote. I'd certainly blown my communist cover.

'Yes, well,' I said soothingly. 'You're probably right.'

But he wasn't going to let it go. When I got up and collected my plates he trotted after me out of the cookhouse, and while we scraped our leftovers into the swill bins and dipped our irons into the trough of brown, greasy water that was supposed to wash them, he bombarded me with the iniquities of our political system. All the way back to the section he pursued me with story after story: bug-ridden slums, families bankrupted by illness, men out of work for years. It was irritating, but there was no stopping him. Until we were outside the door, when he suddenly paused and took a deep breath.

'Sorry about that,' he said quietly, and gave me an awkward smile.

I seemed to have been forgiven. I felt a little ashamed that my own careless inattention had provoked him to such an outburst. His stories certainly had the ring of reality; a lot of them concerned people I knew on the camp. I began to see why, although some people (my own family among them) looked forward to the end of the war as a return to what they'd had before, most of the country was fervently hoping for something very different.

★

76

In the meanwhile there was Bonny. Political immaturity was no handicap where she was concerned. With her I never felt alien. She teased me sometimes about being an effete southerner, but living in the same conditions and wearing the same uniform we found enough in common to be unselfconscious in each other's company.

I decided it was time to take her up on her offer of a guided tour of York. In case she should think I was initiating a courtship or a seduction, I thought a foursome might be a subtle idea. I knew Harry was wanting to go in himself to buy materials for the scenery. Danny had recently been entrusted with money to get them, and had returned, flushed with pleasure, having spent most of it on junk earrings and brooches for his female impersonation (which Harry was determined to keep out of the show). We decided to go together. Harry would bring his amorous sergeant and I would take Bonny.

There was almost as much air-force blue in York as there was on the airfield. But this was civilization: homes, shops and pubs, peopled by civilians, men and women who wore their own clothes and didn't have to be back behind barbed-wire by 23.59 hours. It was hard not to be in a holiday mood. We dutifully did the shopping first and rewarded ourselves afterwards with glasses of beer and thick slices of pork pie. Harry and his sergeant seemed to have their own plans for the afternoon and Bonny declared that she intended keeping her promise to show me the town, so the two of us climbed onto the ancient walls and set off round the city. The sun burned overhead and the old spires and roofs shimmered in the heat. We took off our tunics and carried them over our arms. Bonny's fair curls glinted in the dazzling light and when she raised her arm to point out the towers of the Minster there was a damp patch under her arm and her breast pushed at the stiff cotton shirt, and I thought how odd it was that a girl in black lace-up shoes and a collar and tie could be so alluring. Apparently oblivious to my desire to ravish her, black tie, collar studs and all, she chattered on about Cripplegate, Stonegate, Clifford's Tower and half the history of medieval England which, although I found it genuinely interesting, was occupying me less than the glimpses of her even white teeth and the moist pink tongue flickering behind them. Then we descended to the streets again and I was shown the old houses, the ancient alleyways and the pub where Dick Turpin was said to have ended his famous ride, and she was impressed that I knew the pub on Hampstead Heath from where he'd started. And when finally we stood in the echoing coolness of the Minster, staring up at the blank glass where the great windows had been before the war, she turned to me and smiled a smile of such warmth and frankness that I was moved to squeeze her hand, as if to reassure her that my unruly lust was at her command and subservient to our friendship. Which, as it happened, was fairly true.

We found the others, as arranged, in a deafening pub; Harry and I ordering pints of beer, Bonny and Harry's sergeant (Brenda, we were now allowed to call her) deciding on rum and orange. The bars were overflowing with airmen, soldiers, several sailors and a lot of Yanks ordering drinks no one else could afford, so down a stone-flagged passage at the back of the pub we found a door labelled Singing Room, behind which were nearly a hundred people sitting round the walls nursing their glasses and bellowing their way through old favourites to the accompaniment of a near-derelict piano. We squeezed into a corner, shoulder to shoulder, and joined in everything, from 'Danny Boy' to 'Chattanooga Choo-Choo'.

There was more singing on the last bus back to camp, but we sat silently, Bonny's hand resting noncommittally in mine. Brenda was on duty that night so we parted at the gates and

Bonny and I set off towards the WAAF site half a mile down the road. With Double British Summer Time adding two hours to the clock, the last glimmer of the sunset was still incredibly on the horizon and the air was warm and still. By common consent we turned off onto a path through the fields. By the black shape of a big tree, I took off my tunic and spread it on the grass. She did the same and we sat side by side lighting our cigarettes. There had been no ops that night and the airfield was dark and silent. All we could hear was a soft rustling as the nocturnal battles of the insect world were fought out all round us.

I leaned across and kissed her. Her mouth was soft and welcoming; I could taste the rum still on her tongue. She didn't say a word, but after a moment she put out her cigarette and lay back on her jacket. I threw my cigarette away and lay over her, kissing her more eagerly. She seemed not averse to this and let me slip my hand inside her shirt and hold her breast, (neither of us was prepared to tackle the collar and tie). When after a while I tried to get a hand inside her skirt it was firmly caught in a surprisingly strong grip, although she went on kissing me with undiminished enthusiasm. We wrestled like this for some time, vigorously but amicably, until I gave up and dropped my head onto her shoulder, panting. She stroked my hair gently as if acknowledging my frustration and asking to be understood. Which, of course, I did. Sex was a dangerous game for girls brought up to believe that if they let you you wouldn't 'respect' them and probably not even see them again, which, in fact, was often the truth. Alternatives to the whole works seemed not to be on offer. It was rumoured that the Yanks had some exotic masturbation rituals that were performed in the backs of cars. In England we didn't have cars, so with us it was mostly all or nothing at all: usually, in my case, nothing at all. Of course, the Nozzles of the world had their techniques but, as he had made clear, they weren't for nice girls. And Bonny was, unquestionably, a nice girl.

We strolled back arm in arm, onto the road to the WAAF site and we embraced again just out of sight of the guardroom. I walked back alone, breathing that curious tang that the English countryside exhales on summer nights. As I neared the airfield the black shape of a single Halifax roared over my head, probably returned from a night cross-country exercise. At that moment the runway suddenly lit up, rows of coloured lights stretching into the darkness. The lights of home. Almost.

8

One of the more boring things about being young is that every-body keeps telling you how wonderful it is. It seemed pretty average hell to me. Harry was particularly given to reminding me how fortunate I was to be seventeen years younger than he was. The first thing I saw, the morning after we'd been to York, was him, sitting on his bed, fully dressed, tying his shoelace. Noticing I was awake he gave me a wolfish grin.

'Shagged out?'

I grunted.

'How'd it go?'

'What?' I said, knowing quite well.

'Get your end away?'

I sat up, rubbing my eyes into focus. He passed me his mug of tea and I took a sip from it: last night's beer had dehy-drated me. When I had recounted my inglorious adventures he shook his head and sighed.

'I wish I was your age again,' he said, looking at me with fond contempt. 'Knowing what I do now.'

That is just the sort of remark guaranteed to make the young rejoice. What was this great wisdom he'd acquired? What would *he* have done last night? And what had I done wrong? And whatever it was, no doubt Bonny was telling all

81

the girls in the M/T Section about it at this very moment. I'd had enough of Harry wobbling his head at me. I grabbed my towel and shaving kit and banged out of the hut. Anyway, how would he have been better off at my age? His legs would still have been short; and his nose too long. He might have had more hair of course.

In the ablutions I had a wide choice of tin bowls, each with a stickier rim of grime than the other, and the water from the hot tap was barely warm. I heaved the full bowl up onto the zinc shelf. The clang echoed along the chilly shed. I had the place to myself; everyone else was up and finished ages ago.

And that was another thing about glorious youth. There was the misery of getting up in the mornings, whereas it was obvious that the older you got, the easier it became. I could remember hearing my grandfather pottering about before dawn sometimes. Harry was inclined to early rising. He was energetic enough at the best of times, but before breakfast he zipped about like a clockwork mouse. He would join me in the cookhouse, where I'd be still in a coma over my bread and marmalade, rubbing his hands with delight, his eyes gleaming with mockery as he told me about the bits of scenery he'd built already that morning.

I propped my shard of mirror on the waterlogged shelf and dipped my shaving brush in the tepid water. And what, I thought, was so wonderful about being young with spots?

Would I have felt differently if I'd been where I should have been, over the other side of the camp in the aircrew quarters, pulling on my officer's tunic over my white roll-neck sweater? Would I have got further with the girls I desired? Or would they have gone further with me? Would I have been less patronized in the officers' mess or the sergeants' mess? Would I have been so impatient to be rid of youth if youth was all there was ever likely to be? I found it harder now to imagine myself one of them, those contemporaries of mine, with their old faces and their schoolboy behaviour. Like everyone else I was excluded from them by the unreality of their existence; although it was we, I suspected, who seemed unreal to them. There was a story current about a pilot officer, on leave after a long tour of ops, who had driven into the back of another car. His defence in court had been that rather than overtake the car he'd pulled the steering wheel back, expecting to go over the top of it. What is more, it was said he'd got off.

On the ground the crews were like fourth-formers out of school, a law unto themselves: and in the air they were still a law unto themselves. Decisions were made between them, thousands of feet in the air and hundreds of miles from home, that no one ever knew the truth about: decisions about priorities and decisions about survival. Aircraft would develop mysterious faults before they reached the coast, necessitating an immediate return to base. Some would get lost, jettisoning their bomb load into the sea. Every squadron had its share of them, ours more than most in recent months, but it was hard to prove anything, and how do you discipline boys whose statistical life-expectancy everyone knows, but nobody mentions?

The wireless kept informing us that squadrons of Bomber Command were active in support of our forces advancing across Northern France, which was presumably why curious hyphenated French names were found chalked up in the briefing room and take-offs were at all sorts of odd hours. Quite a few of these were daylight ops, a novel experience for our station. With the last aircraft back by opening time, the pub in the village did a roaring trade and the noise at night from the aircrew huts could be heard on the other side of the airfield. There seemed to be a sense at last that the end of the war was something one dared to contemplate, however distant it might be: the promise of a life afterwards made the idea of having it cut short now even less attractive.

At the same time, the present seemed more dangerous than ever. Harry and I were in the billet the morning that Nozzle came back off leave. His entrance was uncharacteristically subdued. He pitched his kit onto the floor and flung himself onto his bed, leaning back against his folded blankets and shutting his eyes.

'Have a good leave?' we said.

He groaned. 'Christ almighty, I'm knackered.'

'Been overdoing it?' said Harry suggestively.

'Fuck that. Haven't had a decent night's kip the whole time.'

'I thought that was the idea.'

'It's not fuckin' funny, you know. I mean, I was down 'ome in the blitz – at least you knew where you was. Sirens went, you grabbed your kit and down the shelters. Bit rough but we used to 'ave a bit of fun. Surprising what you could get up to down the dark end, even while the vicar was 'aving a singsong. But these fucking buzz-bombs, you never know when they're coming. You're listening for them all the time, and when you hear one of the buggers chugging along, then you're listening for the sod to stop. 'Cos that's when they land on you. And they make a bloody big 'ole. You can hear it for miles. Like when that kite hit the hill with a full bomb load. I tell you what, it's making people dead jittery.'

He sat up and rubbed his hands across his face. He certainly looked pale and strained, not at all his ebullient self.

'I told the missus to take the kids over to her sister's in Epping. I'm not going down there again in a hurry.'

The progress of the war still intruded occasionally on my absorption with *Over the Moon*. One afternoon I'd actually had to attend to a veteran Halifax out on the far side of the field. It was one of our longest survivors and had two rows of bombs painted on the nose, surmounted by a grotesquely

84

over-developed blonde in a leotard. Like everything else about it, the compasses were nearing the end of their lives, and by the time I'd finished it was late afternoon and the dispersals were deserted. I dropped through the hatch and closed it after me. I was picking up my bike when I saw a jeep bounding round the peri track towards me. I recognized the fair curls that were pushing the driver's cap onto the back of her head. I waved. Bonny turned into the dispersal and stopped.

'Did you hear?' she said, jumping down.

'What?'

'They've liberated Paris. It was on the news.'

Neither of us had ever been there, of course. Not many English people had, and not many of them could speak more than a few words of French; but the city was vivid in our imaginations. It was the place for honeymoons or illicit week-ends: it was the city of love, of pavement cafés, of dancing in the streets on the 14th July; it was the city of Mistinguett, Chevalier and the Moulin Rouge. So unlike our dour pre-war London where the pubs closed at ten and restaurants turned you out at eleven. The day the Nazis had marched up the Champs-Elysées they had shut us out from our fantasies. More perhaps than at any other moment of the war, that had been the day we first felt the chill of the wall at our backs. Now the August sun was warm on our necks as we lay in the grass by the dispersal, out of sight of the camp, chewing the sweet ends of the stalks, listening to the distant sound of a tractor, imagining a new world in which even we would one day go to Paris.

In The Wings that evening Harry, too, was excited by the news, which surprised me, since the war was usually an off-stage drama in his life. I soon discovered the reason.

'How far have we got with the naval number?' he asked.

'I've done the design.'

'But we haven't built anything yet?'

'Not yet.'

'We'll scrap it. I've got an idea for a French number. Paris, you know, apache dancing, Reg singing "Louise" or something, and all the girls doing the cancan. Full stage.'

'Sounds wonderful.'

'Could you do a backdrop?'

'I expect so.'

'What about a view over the rooftops?'

'Why not.' There obviously wasn't going to be time for originality.

'You remember *Sous les toits de Paris?* Great film. Ever see it?'

'I don't think so.'

'Never mind. That's the sort of thing.'

I wangled a pass to York and looked up all the books on Paris I could find in the library, and after three days' concentrated effort produced a design for a view over the city that I was quite proud of. Harry looked at it for a long time.

'Very nice,' he said eventually.

'What's wrong?'

'Nothing.'

'You don't like it.'

He chewed his empty pipe for a few moments, then he said, 'You haven't got an Eiffel Tower.'

'That's the Sacré Coeur.'

'I know, but where's the Eiffel Tower?'

'You can't see it from there.'

'You can see the Eiffel Tower from everywhere.'

'Not at the same time as the Sacré Coeur.'

'You can't have Paris without an Eiffel Tower, they won't know where it is.'

'What'll they think it is – Wigan? With everyone doing cancans and apache dances in front of it they'd have to be pretty dim not to guess.'

86

'Can't you paint the Tower in?'

'No!' I said loudly.

'Why not?'

'Because it's wrong and . . . and because it's a boring bloody cliché.'

'Don't start getting fucking artistic with me. Every film you ever see set in Paris starts with the Eiffel Tower . . .'

'Exactly!' I said triumphantly.

Harry banged his pipe savagely against the stove and went to look morosely out of the window. After a minute he said, 'There's not time to alter it anyway. We've got auditions the day after tomorrow, and rehearsals start next week. You'd better get on with it.'

The dispute was finally settled by Father, who was delighted with the design. He'd actually been to Paris once, although exactly when he wasn't admitting.

'Probably before the bloody Tower was built,' Harry said sourly.

The Station Theatre, where the auditions were to be held, also doubled as the Station Cinema, which dual use had been thought to justify the installation of a raked floor and real plush tip-up seats (retrieved from a bombed cinema in Hull). The place was the apple of Father's eye. He must have spent hours of his life wheedling in the Officers' Mess or the Group Captain's office to get the two dressing-rooms built behind the stage, or the rudimentary orchestra pit dug, ensuring that only the taller bandsmen's heads stuck up over the footlights. The building had originally been a cookhouse and was still a bit like a brick tunnel, with metal rafters and a corrugated-iron roof, which in a downpour could drown out the loudest baritone, but sometimes, when the house was full and the lights were lowered and the curtains pulled back on the brightly lit stage, you could almost believe you were in a real theatre and not in a hut in the middle of the Yorkshire moors. And when the ENSA companies came, sometimes with a star we'd actually heard of, fresh from dressing in charabancs in the middle of muddy fields, and told us how luxurious and professional our theatre was – one of the best in the North, they would say – Father's normally pale face would be rosy with pride and pleasure.

Harry had asked me to help him organize the auditions that evening. A notice had been inserted in Routine Orders, circulated to every mess and section on the camp, asking volunteers to leave their names at the Admin Office, and we'd found we had a surprisingly long list of hopefuls to pick from. We'd rolled up the cinema screen, revealing the huge, dusty loudspeaker which we pushed back out of the way, and we'd dragged an upright piano onto the stage. We positioned ourselves self-importantly in the middle of one of the back rows, with pencils, notebooks and clipboards, while the aspirants filled the front rows: there was no room for them to wait in the wings.

Harry was taking the auditions himself but, as a mere Leading Aircraftman, didn't have the power to control other people's desire to play producers. Father had insisted on being present, and with him had come the C-of-E padre and his wife (who lived in the village) as well as the very formidable WAAF Commandant who was presumably there to ensure that her girls were not required to do anything indecent.

Sgt Muloney, the senior bandsman, with his inky Irish curls and florid complexion, had offered to act as accompanist and my job was to call the performers onto the stage and get rid of them afterwards. The atmosphere was cheerful and expectant. Father's group were looking forward to what they clearly regarded as a sort of home-grown eisteddfod, and the competitors, lacking the professionals' loathing of any sort of audition, seemed impatient to show off their talents.

But after we'd been going for a while our spirits began to sink. It was clear we weren't going to find an undiscovered Crosby or Arthur Askey among this lot: in succession we had a tuneless tenor, a conjuror who took ages getting prepared and then dropped everything, and two dancers with incredibly short fat legs. Looking down my list for the next victim, I was astonished to see Nozzle's name. I called it out and he rose, grinning, from the front row and climbed onto the stage. I heard a hiss of disapproval from the WAAF Commandant behind me. His battledress was filthy and had turned a curious shade of green under a patina of muck and grease. His hands were none too clean either.

'Hello,' I said supportively. 'What are you going to do?'

'Sing.' He stood there awkwardly, looking more as if he'd come to clear the drains.

'OK,' I said. 'Give your music to Sgt Muloney.'

'I haven't got no music.'

'Well perhaps he knows the song anyway.'

'I don't need the piano.'

'Ah, right. Unaccompanied, eh? Jolly good.' I could see Harry watching me from under his eyebrows. He was enjoying this. 'Carry on,' I said.

A hush fell. Nozzle stepped forward and announced gravely: ' "The Sweep Song".' With his right boot he stamped heavily three times and began in a loud, hoarse voice:

> *I'll be up your flue tonight,*
> *I'll be up your flue tonight,*
> *I was up Mrs Higgins' flue last night,*
> *I'll be up your flue tonight.'*

There was a moment of silent, motionless panic. Harry was no longer looking at me. I saw his lips move, and he leaned closer.

'Stop him,' I heard him say through clenched teeth.

I cleared my throat. 'Right. Thank you,' I called.

But Nozzle was in his stride. Verse followed verse, the chimney-sweeping metaphors becoming more obscene in each one. There was shuffling in the row behind as the padre led his beetroot-cheeked wife to safety.

'Stop him,' growled Father, glaring at me as if the whole thing were my fault.

'Thank you,' I called again. But Nozzle was deaf to criticism or direction. At last in desperation I shouted, 'Stop!' and he did. Quite unabashed he strode to the edge of the stage and enquired, 'All right?'

'Yes, right, thank you,' I said. He jumped off the stage, waved cheerfully to his stunned audience and walked confidently out of the theatre. Father was still frowning accusingly at me. I felt paralysed with indecision.

The WAAF Commandant leaned over to Harry and me. 'I think no, don't you?' she murmured.

Harry finished blowing his nose and nudged me. 'Next,' I called faintly.

We had some more singers, including a bald corporal and a stout WAAF who sang 'Fascination' at each other at the tops of their voices, a saxophonist not much bigger than his instrument, and a Physical Training Instructor in his vest who did handsprings and nearly knocked the accompanist off his stool. But the peak of the evening had clearly been passed and soon, to our relief, the Commandant and even Father drifted away, and we had only a few WAAFs left to see.

I think she was the second one; or perhaps the third. She tripped neatly up onto the stage and turned towards us. My eyes are not, as we know, the most reliable of my organs, and at that moment I did find it hard to believe them. We had any number of pretty or good-looking girls in and around the airfield, but even at this distance I could see that this girl was more than that. She was actually beautiful. Beautiful in a way that brooked no argument. It wasn't that she had wonderful hair, or eyes or a ravishing mouth. She had all of them. They were all perfect, and, as I remembered Bob Hope saying in a film once, 'perfectly grouped'. It was the kind of perfection that should have existed only in an idealized advertisement or a Hollywood star. She was small and slim, almost thin, and once again perfectly proportioned. It was absurd to see such an exquisite creature in a collar and tie and a uniform, and yet standing there, one slim hand resting gracefully on her hip, she seemed like nothing less than a ridiculously glamorous recruiting poster for all the women's services.

There wasn't a sound in the theatre. Beauty of that sort has a strange effect on people: it awes them or embarrasses them, sometimes even strikes fear into them. The owner of it is like a freak, you long to stare and know you shouldn't. At that moment at least I had an excuse to stare, and did greedily, my mouth dry with excitement. At last I managed to ask her what she was going to do.

She answered in a small, clear voice, with a strong cockney accent. She asked Sgt Muloney if he knew 'I'll Get By' and sang a couple of refrains in a tiny, shaky soprano and then slipped off her shoes and danced a bit, but for all her natural grace, she was stiff and unco-ordinated. When she'd finished I looked at Harry. He was staring at his notes and frowning.

'Well?' I whispered.

'She can't sing', he said softly, 'and she can't dance.'

I couldn't argue with that. 'I know,' I said as persuasively as I could. 'But . . .'

'But what?'

'She's very pretty.' It sounded as inadequate as it was.

Harry studied my face for a moment. 'All right. We'll give her a try. What section is she?'

I looked up to ask her. She'd gone. She wasn't on the stage or in the audience.

'She just went out,' someone said.

'Go on,' said Harry with a hint of mockery. 'You'd better try to catch her.'

I bounded down between the raked seats and out of the building. I looked round frantically. The sun had set, but the clouds were still rimmed with gold on their undersides and there was enough light to see her walking away from me up the main street. Still clutching my clipboard, I raced after her.

'Excuse me,' I said breathlessly.

She turned. Her hair was dark and I could see that her wide eyes were a curious deep-blue colour. Her nose was short and straight with tiny shell-like nostrils, and her skin was flawless.

'Hello,' she said. 'What's up, then?'

I tried to gather my wits. 'We want to know . . . could you tell me what section you're in?'

'Base Ops.'

'And . . . ah . . . your name?'

'You got it, 'aven't you?'

'Your Christian name, I meant.'

'Pearl.'

'Pearl,' I repeated foolishly, and quite unnecessarily wrote it down.

'What's yours, then?'

'Mine?'

'Your name.'

I told her and she considered it for a moment. Then suddenly she smiled widely, showing me a row of teeth as iridescent as her name.

'I'll have to remember that, won't I?' she said.

9

From that moment my interest in theatricals intensified. So far it had simply been an opportunity to escape from the drudgery of life with the two sergeants and enjoy the privacy and privileges of The Wings. And although I didn't share Harry's passion for the bright lights and the greasepaint, I'd liked the chance to exercise my rusting talent again. But now it all meant only one thing to me – Pearl. I seemed to have acquired an obsession to see her: just to see her, to look at her, at this extraordinary, exquisite creature, to watch her hour upon hour. I wasn't in love with her or anything absurd like that: damn it, I'd barely met her. I didn't even desire her, not really, not like that. It was just an irritant, a constant distraction to me, the thought that she should be anywhere on the same camp, but hidden from my eyes. So when Harry asked me if I'd mind helping out at rehearsals by acting as a sort of general stage manager, I agreed instantly, instead of making excuses as I'd probably have done a week before.

At the first rehearsal she didn't turn up. I ticked everyone else in the exercise book Harry had marked 'Rehearsal

Attendance' (he was very professional about these things, though what we could have done if they hadn't attended I'd no idea – court-martialled them?), I kept my pencil poised over her name for a long time, but she never appeared.

'Where *is* that bloody girl?' Harry muttered. And then, to nobody in particular, 'I knew it.'

The band, of course, were not expected. They were mostly full-time RAF bandsmen and spent their days playing for windswept ceremonial parades and their nights in dance bands touring all the smoke-filled NAAFIs and messes in the locality. Like bandsmen everywhere they affected to be hard-bitten and hard to please and took little interest in anything beyond counting the bars until the next pint. Their substitute during rehearsals was Reg Norris, a small, wispy man, adept at the piano, who was down in the programme for a solo on the accordion in the second half.

The first hour seemed chaotic. Of the twenty-three of us required, nineteen had turned up – not a bad tally for a frontier post in an all-out war. (We'd been lucky: only a small daylight op that morning, and they were all back already.) Every one of the nineteen seemed to have some urgent personal problem, usually when and why they couldn't rehearse, or which part they should be playing that they weren't. I sat on the side of the stage, with my blue Stationery Office exercise book open on a rickety card-table, compiling ever more lists: lists of props, lists of costumes, a list of the lists and recurring versions of the running order. This last was a continual bone of contention. Danny and Ernie Tupper had already locked horns over their positions in the second half, until Harry was forced to announce icily, but loudly enough to be heard by everyone: 'Let's see what the numbers are like first, shall we? Before we decide what order we'll do them in. *If* we do them at all.'

I was impressed by his assumption of authority among all

these unchained egos. In a world as hierarchical as the services it was not easy for a ranker to give orders to his superiors. But in the theatre (even in a converted cookhouse) his unblinking confidence in his own experience made him a natural leader, a Crichton on his island. In spite of being surrounded by corporals and sergeants and even officers (one of the chorus girls was a WAAF Flight Officer), no one thought of questioning his right to command. Perhaps they took their cue from Father, who, as author of a comic monologue ('Anything to keep him off the stage,' Harry said), had been allowed to attend rehearsals and was obviously in awe of him.

While Harry was handing out parts for the sketches and an exquisite sergeant from the photo section, in charge of what the programme called 'ensembles', was selecting his chorus line, there was more activity down in the front rows. The costumes were to be hired from Fox's in London and Molly was measuring people to the accompaniment of much ribaldry about bust sizes and inside leg measurements. Molly I'd already met. She was one of Father's discoveries: a motherly corporal from the parachute section, said to be responsible for a number of brides in the district going to the altar in high-tensile white silk. An obsessive needlewoman, she'd acted as wardrobe mistress on all the previous shows.

Harry addressed his troops briefly and my designs were produced while I was asked to explain them. This was my moment of glory, with a lot of oohs and aahs and some disbelieving smirks from the cast, only dampened by the absence of the person I'd most like to have impressed. The atmosphere was becoming determinedly theatrical: gestures were broadening, endearments growing more frequent. It was clearly some sort of game. We were all pretending to be *real* actors in a *real* theatre, rehearsing a *real* show. Just as I remembered the amateur painters were always the ones with the smocks, the moody looks and the crisp new canvases, so amateur theatricals tended to become more and more like the Theatrical Garden Party. Perhaps that was how Harry held sway over them: in their fantasies he'd become C.B. Cochran.

At the next rehearsal she did show up. Ernie Tupper and Harry had just started plotting a sketch, when she suddenly appeared at the back of the stage. How she'd got there I didn't know, the back doors were supposed to be locked. She hesitated and looked round, then saw me and came straight over, mercifully skirting round the rehearsal. Ernie noticed her and seemed inclined to stop, but Harry continued doggedly. She stood in front of my card-table and I looked up again into that mask of perfection.

'You've started,' she said accusingly.

'Hello,' I whispered. 'It's Pearl, isn't it.' I reached for the attendance book to tick her name.

'What you doin'?' she asked.

'Shh!' Harry said.

She turned and looked at him for a moment with an expression of utter astonishment.

'Better sit down for a minute till this is over,' I murmured, indicating the front row.

She shrugged and picked her way gracefully down the steps. Ignoring the rest of the cast, she sat at the end of the row and crossed her legs.

When they had read the sketch through once, I went over to Harry.

'Pearl's here,' I said. 'What should I do with her?'

Harry appeared to have a suggestion in mind which he then thought better of. 'She should be over with Terry,' he said.

Terry was Sgt Cheadle, our choreographer, who was schooling the dancers in another building. In spite of his obvious personal preferences, he could recognize a pretty girl when he saw one, and had devised a routine for himself in which Pearl was to stand on a pedestal in a green light while he danced himself dizzy all round her. Eventually she was to descend graciously to his level and attempt a few not-too-difficult steps on his arm. 'All she'll really have to do is stand there looking beautiful,' he told Harry. And no one doubted she could manage that.

I went over to her. 'You're supposed to be with Sgt Cheadle, I'm afraid,' I said.

'Where's he?' she said.

'I'll show you,' I said promptly. 'Come on.'

I steered her to the nearest door and opened it for her. Everyone was watching us. At the door she turned and raised her hand to them in a tiny royal gesture. 'Ta-ra,' she said.

Outside I pointed down the road. 'The turning on the right, just before the guardroom. Big building on the left.'

She looked at me blankly. 'The NAAFI, you mean?'

'Yes.'

'I know *that*.'

'Of course,' I said hastily. 'It's just . . . you're new on the camp. I thought . . . I ought to show you.'

Her eyebrows and her mouth re-formed into a dazzling image of mock surprise. 'Service!' she said.

I felt myself turning crimson with foolishness. She rescued me. Almost like an apology she said, with sudden sweetness, 'Thanks, ever so.'

Again I watched her walk away from me down the road. Again I'd lost her.

It was like that for the next week. She was either somewhere else with Sergeant Cheadle or not needed at all. I found excuses to deliver messages to his rehearsals, and once from the middle of the chorus line she winked at me over his shoulder, instantly altering my metabolic balance, but I was never able to exchange more than half a dozen words with her. Until the night that she and Terry had to rehearse in the theatre.

Their 'speciality', as he called it, was the last item that evening, and Harry, being on duty, had left me in charge. I moved down into the stalls to avoid any risk of injury from Terry's *grands battements*, and sat down to watch. He was strutting about in the curious conglomeration of garments he wore for rehearsals, borrowed, from the look of them, from a transvestite tramp. Pearl's only concession to dancing was to remove her jacket. Lacking a pedestal, she'd had to stand on a chair, and I could see she thought she looked silly, which of course she didn't. If you'd hung her upside-down from the roof she'd have looked ravishing. Terry, twirling and cavorting around her, was just a distraction. He puffed and pounded, stopping every now and then with a little stamp of irritation at himself, clicking his fingers at Ted to go back a few bars. His dancing wasn't bad really, only marred by the gentility of his gestures and the solemn moue he affected for serious numbers like this. When at last the moment came for Pearl to step down and join him, it was immediately obvious she had difficulty even with the simple steps he'd arranged for her. She would wrong-foot herself or forget the step entirely, until Terry stopped, rolling his eyes at Ted, and with elaborate patience, more unnerving than any temper, go over it again. But as she grew more confident I noticed that, although she was no dancer, her proportions were so perfect it was almost impossible for her to be anything but graceful. Beside her, Terry began to look almost clumsy. But then – as I was not too far gone to recognize – I may have been partial.

When they'd finished, Terry flung a towel round his neck and, with a fairly abrupt 'good-night', disappeared; Ted gathered up his music and followed. Pearl and I were left. She was tidying her hair in a tiny mirror held in one hand while the fingers of her other hand flickered over the roll of hair at her nape, tucking in the errant strands. They were slim white fingers, only the knuckles coral-tinted by the rigours of camp life. She reached into her respirator case, which obviously had no respirator in it, and brought out her lipstick. She was so absorbed that I don't think she noticed me as she meticulously traced the outline of her Cupid's bow and then the soft cushion of her lower lip. She pressed her mouth together and made a little chewing motion as lipstick-wearers do, then she slipped the lipstick and mirror into the respirator case and turned for her tunic. I was already holding it out for her.

'Oh,' she said as if surprised I was still there. 'Ta.'

She slipped it on. A WAAF uniform was made of lighter material than ours, the sort of worsted officers wore, but on her it seemed stiff and coarse. Her pale neck rose from the shirt like a swan's from a dog's collar. For a moment her smell was in my nostrils. Not any of the sweet, crude scents that the loss of France had forced most girls to wear: it was more the smell of fresh soap, Pears or Lux, a nursery smell, like a child just out of the bath.

She swung her respirator over her shoulder. 'I'm off, then.'

'I'll take you back,' I said as casually as I could.

'Where?'

'WAAF quarters.'

'Why?'

'I'm supposed to.' It was almost true. After ten, WAAFs were meant to have transport back to their billets.

A tiny line appeared at each corner of her mouth as she looked at me. 'OK,' she said. 'Get your white horse and we'll go.'

The SP at the gate all but ground his teeth to powder. It was bad enough that I was known to be associated with 'the concert-party lot', but that I should be escorting such a creature as this, was more than he could bear.

'Twenty-three fifty-nine hours for you, Airman,' he snarled. 'Not a second later.'

Across the main road and into the lane neither of us spoke. I swung between joy and trepidation. I had the thing I'd wanted for days. I was alone with her, in the privacy and comfort of a soft September night, for at least ten minutes – fifteen if I could set a plausibly slow pace. Another opportunity like this might be a long time coming. She'd only been on the camp a few weeks, there might be a chance of staking my claim to some of her attention; she hadn't had much time to socialize, most of the time she must have been rehearsing with us or on duty. *On duty*, I thought suddenly. There were all those bemedalled ex-pilots in the operations section where she worked. And aircrew. Aircrew were known not to waste much time. Panic gripped me. I forced myself to start some sort of conversation – any conversation. I tried a few excruciating gambits of the do-you-come-here-often variety. How long had she been in the WAAF? Just over a year, she said; she'd done her square-bashing at Wilmslow, gone on a teleprinter operators' course and spent the last six months at Command HQ in Wycombe. Did she like it here? A bit out in the wilds, wasn't it; not much life. What about York? She'd never been. Oh, but she should. Shameless in my disloyalty, I gave her the same chat about the city that Bonny had given me, although I sensed the historic walls held rather less fascination for her.

'Aren't there any dances?' she said in an aggrieved tone.

'Yes, but they're usually full of Yanks.'

'What's wrong with that?'

'Gets a bit rough sometimes, if our lot are there too.'

She shrugged. I'd muffed that chance, certainly.

'There's a good theatre,' I said.

'*Theatre?*' I might have been suggesting an evening at the dentist.

'And cinemas,' I added desperately.

100

'Anything good on?'

'This week?' I racked my brains frantically to recall the posters in the NAAFI. 'I'm not sure. Next week there's a Rita Hayworth film, I think.'

In the dark she touched my arm for a moment. 'Oh, I *love* her. Did you see her in that one with Fred Astaire? She's a terrific dancer. I think she's *so* beautiful.'

I had seen the one with Fred Astaire. I'd still been a civilian when I'd watched them dancing along that implausibly moonlit terrace, and like God knows how many millions of men, I'd been ravished by her. I wanted to say: she's no more beautiful than you. But I couldn't. Too many people must have told her, and instinctively I knew that it wasn't what beautiful women wanted to hear. What they *did* want to hear, of course, I hadn't the faintest idea.

It had to be now. 'Would you like to see it?' I said abruptly. 'We could go next week.'

'OK,' she said. Quite casually. It was as easy as that. 'That'd be nice.' She took my arm.

We turned a corner and could see the dim glow from the WAAF guardroom. She stopped. 'What's the time?' she said.

I used my lighter to look at my watch. In the pale flame the message was ominous. 'Three minutes to twelve,' I said.

'Bloody hell,' she said. 'I must run.'

'But . . . next week?'

She was running ahead. 'I'm on duty at the weekend. Leave a message in the ops room.' Suddenly she stopped and let me catch up.

'Thanks for being such a gent,' she said softly, but I wasn't deaf to the edge of mockery. 'Hope you get back in all right.'

There wasn't even a moment to take her hand. 'Bye,' I said and turned away.

'You'd better run,' she called. And I could hear her laughing.

10

She actually kept our date. Making it had been like a juggling act. Would she be on duty that day? Would I? Could she get a pass the same day as mine? And if she couldn't, could I alter my own? Several interruptions of Terry's rehearsals had been needed, and more than one sally into the underground corridors of the Operations Section. And all the time I was expecting her to be snatched from my grasp. There must have been at least fifteen hundred men on the camp and only about three hundred WAAFs (including the Commandant). And this was no ordinary WAAF, this was Aphrodite in brass buttons: and who was I but an aircraftman second-class? The odds were against me, obviously. But what I hadn't had time to notice, what didn't dawn on me until a lot later, was how intimidated most men were by her. Beauty in a woman is like wealth or power in a man, it sets her apart, puts lesser creatures in her thrall. I was certainly in thrall, and quite impressed by my own temerity in pursuing her at all. Looking back, I have an uneasy suspicion that my unusual confidence had its roots in class. A very minor public school and some very ordinary King's English, embarrassing though they were in the billet, had gained me so many advantages with waiters, porters

103

and the occasional warrant officer, that I must have nursed a conviction, hidden even from myself, that this innate superiority would operate anywhere in the great bastion of democracy we were defending, even in the hearts of beautiful girls.

The innate superiority felt distinctly absent as I waited for her in the NAAFI at morning break, the time we'd agreed to meet. But, astonishingly, she came, and not even late. Well, only half an hour. A hole opened in my chest when I saw her, as it always did; she shone like a vivid primary colour in a monochrome world. I swept her through the main gates to the bus stop where the next bus was due in just two minutes. I'd planned the day meticulously, but had no chance to explain my plans as she chattered inconsequentially all the way to York, where, with an unerring instinct for one new to the city, she led me straight to the shops. We stopped at every shop window and quite often went inside. I bought her, at different counters, a *Woman's Own*, a *Lilliput*, twenty Players and some dubious sweets off the ration. She didn't ask for them, she didn't thank me, she just accepted them, as a sort of homage, I supposed. But it was the dress shops that drew her. In a provincial city in the depths of clothes-rationing dress shops were hardly Aladdin's caves. Besides, neither of us had any coupons, or any money for that matter. But still she'd boldly march in, and I would stand watching while she made the assistants empty the racks as she held dresses up against herself and twisted between the mirror and me, making each dowdy wartime garment alive with the possibility of being worn by her, and asking me if it suited her (they all did, of course, however drab or practical or clumsily made). Sometimes I would be given a chair and I would lean back, feeling every inch the sugar daddy (with severely rationed sugar). I longed for it to be like a film where she appears and reappears in creation after creation and he says send the bill to my office and they emerge into the sunlight piled up with enormous boxes all tied with ribbons and great bows.

As it was, we emerged into a light drizzle – and rather hastily, the last shop having realized we had no intention of buying even a pair of stockings. We scurried into a Kardomah and had sausages and chips and fruit flan, the fruit of which defied identification. There was nothing wrong with her appetite and she ate it all, gracefully, as she did everything. Then she lit a cigarette and surveyed the restaurant, apparently oblivious to the eyes that were turned on her. I was torn between a desire to be alone with her and pride at being seen as her companion or perhaps even, dared I hope, her lover. I paid the bill and tried unobtrusively to count the half-crowns left in my pocket.

Another dash through rain that was too fine to fall but hung in the streets like a grey mist, and we were in the warmth and comfort of the cinema. With wild extravagance I bought the best seats: front circle, not the back row in case she thought I might be crass enough to try anything; and in any case I could never see much from so far back. We stretched our legs out towards the plush covered balustrade and leaned back beneath the huge vault of a ceiling studded with a hundred tiny lights. Oh, those cinemas – picture palaces some people still called them, and palaces they were – enormous amphitheatres of luxury: exorbitant decoration, veering between the cathedral and the bordello, thick carpets, soft lights, marble, velvet, and the vast dazzling screen where the tales of love, heroism, morality and reassurance came and went ceaselessly for the price of a packet of cigarettes. They were everybody's refuge from the exhaustion and fear and the sheer unending drabness of life outside. We shared the mildly disgusting off-ration sweets and watched a figure in a white tail-suit flailing about at the organ, producing resonant but barely recognizable popular tunes, until the curtains changed colour yet again and he sank out of sight, all four limbs still going like windmills.

When the lights went down I discreetly drew my glasses out of my pocket and slipped them on. They had been forced on me after the fatal medical in Kingsway and this was the only situation in which I really needed them. They were round and horn-rimmed with a gold bridge and earpieces and I didn't think they did much for my manly image. After a while she nudged me to offer me another sweet and when I turned round she gave a little gasp.

'You're wearing glasses,' she whispered.

'Yes.'

'You short-sighted?'

'A bit. I don't wear them usually.'

'You ought to. They suit you.'

I gave a little snort of disbelief. She was still staring at me.

'I think they're sweet,' she said. A moment later I felt her hand rest on mine, on the arm between us.

By the time we'd sat through the first feature, the cartoon, the news and the trailers, the cinema had started to fill up. It was warm and the air was hazy with smoke. The lights came up again and she turned to me at once.

'Have you always been short-sighted?' she asked.

I hoped she wasn't going to harp on my disability. I liked to think I had other rather more interesting attributes. 'Oh, no. Only about a year.' I decided to tell her about the débâcle of my last flight and the medical and being grounded.

She seemed more interested than she had been all day. 'Did you mind?' she said seriously.

'A bit, yes, I suppose.' I said.

She looked at me for a moment, frowning. 'What's it like, being short-sighted? How much can you see?'

I tried to explain. She pressed for details. Could I see the clock over there, she wanted to know. Of course (not telling her I wasn't too sure what time it said). Could I see her now? Yes, of course I could (oh, yes, indeed I could, thank you very much). Suddenly she snatched the glasses out of my hand.

'Let's try them on.'

Inevitably they looked wonderful on her. The picture in the optician's window. The only girl in glasses in the world that all the men make passes at.

She screwed up her face. 'Ooh, I can't see a thing. You must be *blind*!' At that moment the lights began to go down and she handed the glasses back. I put them on and turned to smile at her with all the confidence of my new-found secret weapon.

The screen flooded with colour as the big picture began, and we were drawn into a world where flawless creatures sang and danced when and where the fancy took them, misunderstandings came and went, but love, once declared, lasted for ever. The plot was ludicrous and at one point seemed to involve Rita Hayworth playing her own grandmother. But then, in a deserted nightclub – so sophisticated, so romantically world-weary – she (herself again) and Gene Kelly, the chairs stacked around them, were alone at last. 'Long ago and far away,' they sang to one another, 'I dreamed a dream one day . . .' Banal words, but the melody had a poignancy that rose above them, stirring the audience's emotions, bringing a thousand lumps to a thousand throats, mine not excepted. We were rudderless on a sea of sentiment; I felt her hand tighten on mine. And because a song like that has a unique power to date-stamp our emotions, I have never heard it since without the feeling of those times embracing me like a tangible ghost, clutching my throat, but leaving me always with a faint and irrational sense of loss.

The next step of my master plan had been to get us straight back to camp so that we could enjoy a little shared privacy in The Wings. But when the trance was lifted and we shuffled out of the cinema, the rain had stopped and Pearl announced that she wanted a drink. I made a feeble attempt to distract her, but all the dress shops were shut and anyway her mind was clearly made up. It wasn't dark yet, and even if it had been, a pub wouldn't have been hard to find, the noise would have been enough to lead us straight to it. She selected a picturesque one up a sidestreet and dragged me towards it. When we pushed through the blackout curtain the smoke and heat stung our eyes and throats; the place was jammed and the din was deafening.

'It's full up,' I said. 'Come on.'

She was standing on tiptoe looking round. 'Hang on,' she said. 'Let's have a look.' She squeezed her way further into the room and signalled for me to follow. Every single table seemed full, even the spaces between them, but when I reached her at last, she was being addressed by a tall GI who had risen from a small table in the corner.

'There's room here, ma'am,' he was saying.

His smile became a little less broad when he saw me, but by that time Pearl had sat down and was beckoning me to sit on the bench beside her. The Yank sat down again on the only chair, on her other side.

'Thanks ever so,' she said, giving him the benefit of her most devastating smile, which I knew could have the impact of a right hook from Joe Louis.

'What do you want?' I asked in her ear, partly to be heard over the din, and partly because I'd noticed the American had a large scotch in front of him and I didn't fancy having to buy him those for the rest of the evening.

'Gin and orange,' she said without hesitation.

I pushed, squeezed and clambered my way to the bar. I noticed the customers were almost entirely American: very smart in their smooth, tailored uniforms, but all, it seemed, either immensely tall or surprisingly overweight. There were a few civilians and the odd soldier or sailor, but virtually no RAF. This was the sort of place one usually avoided. We tended to have our own haunts and they had theirs, and if trouble started it was always better to be in the majority.

Our American had Pearl's undivided attention by the time I got back. I hated him. I didn't hate Yanks on principle as most of the lads did. Although they were just as much creatures from Mars to me as they were to the rest of the population, I could see that it wasn't their fault if they got paid three times what we did and needed the occasional fuck. But this one I hated.

'This is Dan,' Pearl said, as if announcing the star turn.

He rose from his chair and offered me his hand from a great height. I lifted my bottom off the bench and shook the hand briefly. 'Hello,' I said.

'Dan's got a brother who lives in Hollywood,' Pearl said. 'But he doesn't know Rita Hayworth.'

'How extraordinary,' I said.

The American laughed and winked at me over her head. I see, I thought, a chaps' club are we, taking the piss out of Pearl? I hated him even more. I'd show him not everyone in England thought all Americans lived in Hollywood or New York.

'You from there, too?' I asked.

'Nope. Denver's my home town.'

I racked my brain desperately. 'Colorado?' I said, making a wild stab at it. But I was right.

'Right,' he said, and looked quite pleased. 'My folks have a hardware store there. You from round these parts?'

'I'm a Londoner. We both are.' I eyed Pearl, making it sound as proprietorial as I could.

'Gee, that's a great town,' he said beaming.

City, if you please. He had that snub-nosed boy's face and that scrubbed look that is so very American. He did seem quite a nice chap. But I still hated him.

'First time I get me a furlough, I'm gonna take a trip there. That's if I can get your money figured out. Last time, one of your cab-drivers took a week's pay off me.'

'You need someone to look after you,' said Pearl, batting her eyelashes at him. 'When do you think you'll be down there?'

Hang on, I thought, she's going to make an assignation with him right under my bloody nose. What about Mr Myopia, her friend of five minutes ago, who took her to the pictures, and has just bought her a large gin and orange?

I was about to enquire if she had any leave due, when there was a lot of shouting and breaking of glass from the direction of the bar. Our three heads turned together. The atmosphere in the room was suddenly charged. In spite of the row going on over the other side, the noise in the rest of the room had dropped. Everyone was still, staring in the direction of the trouble. We stood up to try to see what was happening. A lot of RAF types seemed to have appeared in the region of the bar and were exchanging taunts with the Yanks. Old-world and new-world obscenities were being flung back and forth, accompanied by short but quite vicious scuffles. As always on these occasions the violence was motiveless and unco-ordinated, but one could feel it spreading out towards the edges of the room. Some people were struggling to get in and support their comrades, others to get to the exits.

Being so tall, our American had a better view than we did. 'Don't look too good,' he said to me. 'Go through the men's room, there's a passage out back there. I'll follow you.'

I grabbed Pearl and we dived into the gents – the door was only a couple of yards away. We dashed past the stalls where a startled PFC was just shaking off the last drops, through a green door and into a half-tiled passage to the rear of the pub. We emerged into a grimy alleyway which led away in either direction. We could hear the noise inside the pub, and beyond that, running feet and shouting in the streets.

'Down here,' said Dan, leading the way round the side of the pub towards the front. In the street a full-scale riot seemed to be in progress. We were just in time to see a bunch of Snowdrops (the US Military Police), in their white helmets and white spats, come trotting into action, white batons at the ready.

''Bout turn,' said Dan quickly, ushering us back the way we'd come. 'Best if you stick with me, I guess. These may help some.' He pointed to the stripes on his arm which presumably meant he was a sergeant, although they appeared to be upside-down. The alleyway ran parallel to the main street and eventually opened into another road several hundred yards away. From the sound of it, the brawling was not confined to the pub, it seemed to be coming from all directions.

I was the first to come out of the alley, and at that moment about a dozen RAF men were running past, shouting and laughing. One of them called, 'Come on, mate, we've just chucked a couple of the buggers in the river!' Then he noticed Pearl and laughed. 'As you were! Carry on, Airman,' he shouted, and ran after the others. Luckily they hadn't seen Dan, who was behind us. I hadn't any stripes to protect him with. After a few more rapid diversions we had nearly reached the bus stop and could pause for breath. The noise now was faint in the distance.

'Guess you'll be OK now,' Dan said. 'I'll leave you, then.'

'What about you?' I said.

'Only going to the train station,' he said. 'Take just a couple of minutes.'

'Yeah, well, be careful,' I said, feeling unaccountably responsible for him. After all, it was my country.

'You too,' he said, giving us – well, Pearl really – a curious right-angled American salute. 'So long.' And with a wave he loped off down the road.

We headed for the bus in silence. Eventually I said, rather grudgingly, 'Nice fellow, really.'

111

'Good-looking, wasn't he?' Pearl said.

God almighty, I thought, I was just getting to like the man.

Suddenly she stopped and clasped her forehead dramatically, a very pretty gesture that entranced me all over again. 'Bloody hell,' she said. 'I meant to give him my address in London.'

'Oh.' I smothered my delight with bogus sympathy. 'Never mind. Perhaps you'll run into him again.'

Her shrug dismissed both the chances of that and my transparently insincere comfort.

Although it was not the last one that night, the bus was fairly full, but we found a pair of seats near the front. As it was about to move off, a stocky WAAF with a red face dropped heavily into the seat across the aisle from me. When she'd finished puffing and mopping herself she spotted Pearl on my other side and, peering round me, waggled her fingers to attract her attention. But Pearl was staring out of the window, so with a brief ''Scuse me,' the WAAF leaned across and tapped her on the arm.

'Doris!' said Pearl, apparently delighted to see her, and they immediately embarked on a conversation which totally excluded me. After about ten minutes I got sick of Doris's khaki teeth snapping two inches from my nose, and sat forward to stem the flow temporarily.

'Would you like to sit here?' I said to Doris pointedly, hoping it might dawn on her that she was intruding on a nascent romance.

But subtleties were lost on Doris. 'Oh, ta,' she said, and stood up. I had no option but to do the same, and we changed places. For the rest of the journey the two girls gossiped and giggled, and across the aisle I stared ahead, stiff with resentment.

They were still talking when the bus arrived at the camp gates and even after it had left us standing by the roadside in the damp night. Somehow I had to get Pearl away from her and up to The Wings.

Before I had a chance to suggest it, I heard Doris say to her, 'Coming back to the billet?'

'That's all right,' I said. 'I'll see her back.'

'No point in us all getting soaked,' Pearl said, avoiding my eye. 'Is there?'

Doris giggled, but there was an unmistakable note of triumph in it. I tried to draw Pearl aside. 'You've got a pass,' I murmured. 'We could go up to the hut for a bit.'

But she was unreachable. 'It's ever so late, and I'm on at seven. 'Nother time, eh?' She pecked my cheek. ''Night.'

'I enjoyed today,' I said desperately.

'Me too. 'Night.'

I stood there while they crossed the road and until their voices had faded into the dark lane that led away to the WAAF quarters.

The camp was strangely silent, although there were still lights in most of the dormitory huts. I couldn't face the ribald interrogations that met anyone returning from a late pass. The rain had gone and the air smelt dry and fresh, so I walked slowly up towards The Wings, busying my mind devising all manner of unspeakable hells to which I might commit the odious Doris, rather than confront the evidence I'd just had of Pearl's indifference to me. There was a thin thread of light under the door when I got there. I hesitated, and then decided to try the handle. It was unlocked. Inside there was a strong smell of glue size from a bucket heating on the stove. Harry was in his overalls priming some newly made canvas flats.

'Hello,' he said without turning. 'Have a good day?'

'Yes thanks,' I said shortly, inviting no further questions. I flung myself into one of the armchairs. Harry took the hint and said no more, just went on dipping his big distemper

113

brush into the mixture and slapping it over the stretched hessian. I kicked open the damper at the bottom of the stove and lit a cigarette with a spill of newspaper. After a few minutes I asked him if he wanted any help.

'You can give me a hand out with some of this stuff,' he said. 'No room to move in here.'

It was true. Now that most of the scenery was finished, the space in the hut was reduced to little more than a passage down the middle. We manhandled the Old Music Hall set, a cut-out of Eros and two completed sections of the rooftops of Paris out through the door and leaned them against the side of the hut. Now there was room for both of us to work. I had my best blue on, but I hung up the jacket carefully, put on my overalls and joined in. I wasn't in the least tired and Harry, as always, was indefatigable, so we worked on, talking very little, absorbed in what we were doing.

It must have been about half-past one when Harry stopped, his brush poised, and said, 'What's that?'

'What?' I said.

'Listen.'

It was an aircraft of some sort. Not a Halifax, certainly: it sounded more like a twin-engined plane. But the note of the engines was completely unfamiliar. It was coming nearer very fast and, from the sound of it, pretty low. Suddenly there was a sort of rattling noise and from the distance what sounded like shouting.

'Bloody hell,' Harry said.

Before I had time to ask him what he meant the roar of the plane drowned out everything, except the rattling which began again and was much louder and unmistakably machine-gun fire. There were several deafening clangs on the corrugated iron of the hut as if someone were hitting it with a hammer and the plane roared over our heads. Harry threw down his brush and dived for the door. I dived after him.

114

'He'll wreck the fucking scenery,' he was shouting. The plane had banked and seemed to be coming in very low over the officers' mess area about two hundred yards to our right. Its guns were chattering again. Harry was capering about and shaking his fists at it, beside himself with fury.

'Fuck off, you bastard!' he yelled. 'Fuck off and leave us alone. For Christ's sake, we open next week!'

'Bloody light out there!' someone shouted.

I tried to drag Harry back inside but he wasn't having any, so I pulled the door shut behind us. The plane had turned and sounded very much as if it were coming in our direction again.

'Harry, get down for God's sake!' I yelled. Quite stupidly I wasn't frightened at all, just tremendously excited, but I did retain enough sense to realize it would be better to present as small a target as possible. I grabbed Harry and we both crouched by the wall as the plane swept over us again. It only fired a short burst but there were a lot of ricocheting noises and sinister splintering sounds.

By now the whole camp was in an uproar. We could hear the anti-aircraft guns starting up on the far side of the field and in the distance what sounded like someone screaming. Finally the air-raid siren began to wail. Of the plane there was no longer a sign.

'*Now* they tell us,' said Harry, getting to his feet. 'Bloody marvellous.' We stood there for a minute listening to the hub-bub all over the camp. Nobody came near us, as presumably nobody knew we were there. 'Better get this lot back inside,' Harry said.

One by one we brought the flats and ground-rows into the hut. Then we shut the door and turned on the light. It was all intact except for the panorama of Paris. Just to the left of the Sacré Coeur was a splintered rip in the sky about six inches long.

'Bastards,' Harry said quietly.

'Can you mend it?'

'Oh yes. Can you repaint it?'

'Easy.'

Suddenly Harry said, 'Look at that.'

Halfway up the side of the hut there was a round hole big enough to put your thumb through, the corrugated iron round it bent back like the petals of a flower. And on the opposite wall there was a dent that hadn't been there before.

Harry looked from one to the other. A line between them would have passed just over the tops of our old armchairs.

'Lucky we weren't taking it easy,' he said.

II

Everything was secret in wartime. No doubt someone somewhere wrote a report on the night's raid which was read by
someone somewhere else, but we never saw it or heard a word
of it. As a result, rumours, those termites in the flimsy walls of
truth, swarmed everywhere. The whole camp next morning
was alive with them: half a dozen airmen dead or wounded,
several Halifaxes blown to smithereens, half the officers' mess
burned to the ground. But one tour of the airfield was enough
to get most of these tales into proportion, and by the end of
the day the tally had been reduced to one unfortunate wire-
less/op killed on his bicycle out by the control tower,
G-George full of holes and in the big hangar, some damage to
the officers' sleeping quarters where an intelligence officer
had been wounded – in his bed, the story went – a fair
amount of minor damage and a physical training instructor
who'd broken his leg running for the shelters. The general
outrage at all this seemed a bit disproportionate if you considered the amount of high explosive we were dumping on
Germany every night, not to mention the crews we'd been
losing recently, but Yorkshire was safe (a lot safer than London
since the new V2 rockets had started arriving) and everyone

was deeply affronted by this intrusion into our rustic peace.

My main interest that morning had been to find out if the WAAF quarters had escaped. It seemed they had, and I was forced to admit that if I'd got my way, and the hole in The Wings was anything to go by, Pearl and I might have been sitting in armchairs holding hands in the small hours with no tops to our heads. The dreadful Doris had probably saved our lives. But I wasn't going to tell Pearl that.

As Harry had pointed out to the marauding German, the first night of *Over the Moon* was only a week away. Nothing, of course, was ready, but according to Harry this was quite normal and authentically professional. So evenings of arduous rehearsal were followed by long nights in The Wings frantically finishing scenery and props. Most of the time I had the impression I was suffering, although in truth it was the pangs of rapture that were taking away my appetite and giving me sudden urges to weep at unexpected moments. I was seeing Pearl every evening and, in spite of our inconclusive day out, she seemed now to regard me as her partner – in this venture at least. It was my advice she consulted, my cigarettes she accepted and I who was allowed to bring her cups of tea (milk, no sugar). The others noticed this and soon began to indulge us as a couple, though sometimes in an oddly guarded way that would give me moments of fathomless insecurity. The only one who ignored the situation altogether was Harry. I got the feeling that in some way he disapproved: not morally, obviously, nor out of jealousy, because I don't think she attracted him in the slightest. Beauty didn't interest Harry, at least not when it came to sex: where women were concerned the gratification of his other senses took priority. So I came to the conclusion that it could only be me he was concerned about. The one time he referred to it directly we were in the ablutions. He had just finished shaving and I suppose I'd been talking about her as usual, when he looked round at me and said solemnly, 'You want to be careful there.' Before I had time to ask him why, he'd disappeared into one of the bogs. I never did get round to asking him what he meant. It seemed unlikely that he'd suspect her of being riddled with disease; or did he think she was a gold-digger? If she was, she was showing a pathetic lack of ambition attaching herself to me.

Then, of course, there was the matter of my conscience about Bonny. I had hardly seen her since the day of the auditions, but I'd had recurring twinges of dread at the prospect of meeting her at rehearsals and explaining my hopeless preference for Pearl. I told myself that most Romeos were lumbered with a Rosalind (although Shakespeare had never revealed what *she* thought of that whole affair). A rumour that Bonny had been seen in the company of a good-looking flight sergeant was brought to my attention by Percy, grinning puckishly and not yet aware that true love had already struck from another direction altogether. My cheerful reception of his news must have disappointed him sadly. But in the end I was rescued by the RAF's callous system of postings. However long one had been on a station a telex from the Air Ministry could mean that within days or even hours any one of us could be in transit to any corner of the globe, and all friendships and relationships were amputated on the spot. It was brutal for the romantically vulnerable but a godsend for the Casanova. Bonny's telex came just a few days after the start of rehearsals. Her corner of the globe was only Norfolk and there was talk of meeting on leave perhaps, and writing, and in fact after a few weeks I did get a postcard from Cambridge, but when she had gone, all I could really feel was a shameful sensation of relief.

Not all postings were so welcome. Four days before the dress rehearsal, Harry burst into the hut, where I was bent over a poster for the show.

'Ever acted?' he asked abruptly.

119

'Only at school,' I said, delicately outlining the second O of Moon.

'Colin's been posted,' he said.

'Christ. When?'

'Friday.'

'Can't Father fix it?'

'Too late. It's overseas I think. I can cover him in most of the numbers but not in the adjutant sketch or the opening and the finale.' He knocked his pipe against the stove. 'Think you could do it? You must know the show pretty well and there's not time to find anyone else.'

This flattering offer sent me into a panic. I dropped my brush and turned round. 'But I only played Hortensio in *The Taming of the Shrew*,' I said. 'I mean, I can't *act*.'

'You don't have to. You've only got a couple of solo lines in the opening chorus and a couple in the finale. The steps are easy. Terry'll show you.'

That wasn't an attractive prospect either. 'But what about the sketch?'

'Just say the lines. Ernie does the jokes. You're behind a desk, so you can have it written down if you can't learn it in time. You're about Colin's size so the costumes should be OK. We could always scrounge you another uniform for the sketch.'

Colin had played an adjutant, and the idea of masquerading as an officer, even on the stage, was quite appealing: Pearl might see me in a new light, if only for five minutes every night. And, of course, I'd be one of the company, on the stage with her, singing with her, perhaps even dancing with her. I fought down my terror at the thought of performing in public.

'OK,' I said.

My instant panic at having to learn lines, songs and dance routines in a few days was relieved by the quite unexpected

120

postponement of the first night. The whole airfield was suddenly put on alert, and for a week every available plane and crew was in the air ferrying petrol. It seemed that a parachute division had been cut off at one of the Rhine bridges and massive attempts were being made to reach them. Quite a few ground crew were being flown to Brussels to service the turn-rounds, including two of our cast, and the whole station was engrossed in keeping the planes flying day and night. Convoys of giant bowsers rolled into the camp every morning, jerry-cans were stacked in every available corner of every aircraft and special tanks fitted in the bomb bays. One of the regular bowser boys in the billet reckoned we must be transporting nearly twenty thousand gallons a day. Everyone and everything stank of petrol, until one was almost afraid to light a cigarette in case the whole place went up with a giant bang. Harry, needless to say, saw the entire enterprise as an unwarranted disruption of his rehearsal schedule, particularly as he was having to spend whole days out on the flights actually working on the aircraft. I, on the other hand, was hardly affected. Compasses were not much needed to find Brussels. 'Straight down the East Coast, you can't miss it,' as one wit remarked. 'And if you get lost follow another kite – they're all going the same way.'

By the next Tuesday it was over. The squadron, still intact, was stood down and the ground crews on detachment came back, most of them with hair-raising tales of the shambles at Arnhem. For a moment events in Europe, so remote from us on the ground up here, came uncomfortably near.

It was raining that night. Summer had faded and the air was chill and damp. As I walked down the muddy path between the dripping huts I looked up at the dim outline of the water tower against the threatening sky. That gaunt shape looming over the huddle of corrugated iron and concrete, over the rusting piles of scrap, the sour smells and the miles of barbed

121

wire, was depressingly reminiscent of a prison camp; and suddenly, for one moment, I didn't care that I couldn't fly any more or that I'd never be commissioned and drink pink gins in the officers' mess, and that after all I wasn't going to be expected to die for my country. All I wanted at that instant was for the whole sordid, meaningless business to be over so that we could all go home where we belonged.

The show was re-scheduled for the following week, so rehearsals continued, with me being put through my paces by Harry, Reg and Terry, and the rest of the cast being helpful to the new recruit with a mass of conflicting advice and suggestions. In the opening number, set in Piccadilly (for which I'd painted a plywood cut-out of Eros – whom none of us had seen since 1939), we were all passers-by in the shape of toffs, tarts, policemen, a flower-girl (Pearl) and for some reason her mother, played by Harry in the Old Mother Riley tradition. I was to be a newsboy with a placard and a bundle of papers and had to shout, 'Read all about it!' at specified intervals. We all launched into an encouraging chorus (encouraging to the audience, we hoped) with words by Danny to faintly familiar original music by Reg. Each of us had a mercifully short solo verse. My other two musical appearances were the finale, which took place in a sort of nightclub where I had little to do except sit at a table clapping and saying things like, 'Jolly good show!', and the famous French number where I was to sing *and* dance. Dancing, as I'd feared, proved not to be my strong point. Terry's sighing and tutting didn't help either. I couldn't memorize one step, let alone a whole sequence of them, and felt a complete fool, particularly in front of so many nimble-footed girls. Pearl told me my trouble was that I was Terryfied which cheered me enormously as not only was it indisputably a joke, but direct from her native wit.

It was the sketch that I feared most. I was an adjutant with a motley collection of airmen in front of him on various charges. The star turn was Ernie Tupper who had been apprehended with a sack containing 543 washbasin plugs. This, I was assured, would bring the house down, as it was a celebrated fact of service life that washbasin plugs, even if chained, always went missing with uncanny speed.

I asked Harry how he thought I should tackle the rôle. He looked nonplussed.

'I don't know. Just pretend you're a posh sort of officer – rather daft.'

'How?'

'How?' he said with touch of exasperation. 'Well, you pretend. When you were a kid, didn't you pretend to be other people sometimes?'

'Yes.'

'Well, then.'

'But not in front of people.'

'How d'you mean?'

'Not when other people were watching. Only on my own.'

He sighed. 'Yes . . . that could be a handicap.' He thrust his hands in his pockets and examined the floor for a moment. 'I suppose', he said, 'what you'd better do is pretend you're alone, and *then* pretend you're a rather daft officer.'

I could see that this was not the sort of direction he was used to giving. All the others, even the amateurs, had lots of experience and were keen as mustard – they must have been, or they wouldn't have volunteered for this lunacy. I, on the other hand, was not only an amateur but a reluctant amateur, an unheard-of thing. I decided I'd have to grit my teeth and go solo.

At the next rehearsal all seemed to be going well, when Ernie Tupper leaned towards me and murmured, 'Wait for the laugh there, son, won't you.'

'What laugh?' I said.

'There'll be a laugh there. You don't want to tread on it, do you?' he said ominously.

'No, no,' I said quickly. I hesitated. 'How long do I wait?'

'Till they've finished, of course.'

'And what do I do?'

'When?'

'While they're laughing.'

Harry interrupted swiftly. 'Nothing. Just stay looking at Ernie.'

Ernie said, 'Of course, on the other hand you mustn't let it die, must you?'

'Oh, no.'

'Come in just before the laugh ends, that's the moment.'

I didn't dare ask how you were supposed to know when it was going to end while it was still going on. Ernie was looking at me like a zoologist at an unknown species.

'Done this sort of thing before, have you?' he asked.

'Not really . . . no.'

He nodded slowly and glanced at Harry.

But in spite of my private terrors, I found I was beginning to enjoy the rehearsals. When I wasn't actually being called on to sing, dance or act – which mercifully was most of the time – I found the atmosphere of enthusiasm, concentration and excitement hard to resist. And whenever my performance had been more than usually inept, Pearl always seemed most eager to encourage me.

The night before the dress rehearsal Harry and I carried the last of the scenery down to the theatre where, with the help of Freddy Pearce our stage manager, we tried putting it up and then taking it down again; and when Tiny Hopkins, the electrician, had hung the extra lamps from Strand Electric, we tried lighting it. We were there until the small hours. Freddy, an energetic little man with a sandy moustache, was a perfectionist, and Tiny (who needless to say was enormous) was the sort of peculiarly British technician who loves to shake his head sadly and tell you categorically a thing can't be done, and then half an hour later sidle up to you and mention casually that he's done it. This all took a long time, and wasn't made any quicker by some of my scenery not fitting quite as snugly as I'd hoped.

The night ended with mugs of tea in The Wings, and when the others had gone Harry said, 'You got any make-up?'

'Make-up?'

'For tomorrow night?'

I said I hadn't thought about it.

'Better give you some of mine.' He pulled what looked like a wooden instrument box from under the table. He'd lovingly converted the inside with all manner of trays and compartments, and the greasepaints were lying in neat rows. The pre-war Leichner sticks had a uniquely sweet scent which was set off by the tang of spirit gum.

'What a marvellous smell,' I said.

'Aha,' he said, bending over them. 'Don't let it get into the bloodstream. Look what it's done to Danny.'

I laughed. He had taken out one or two of the sticks and was cutting a couple of inches off each of them with a razor blade.

'There's a Five there, and a Nine. And a Thirteen. Personally I prefer Thirteen, makes you look less nancified. You can have these old liners, I've got plenty. And I'll put some powder in a spare tin for you. You'll need some liquid paraffin and a bit of old towel to get it off with.' He was expertly trimming the gold wrapping from the ends of the stubs. I emptied the biscuit tin that held my paints and shovelled in the bits of make-up. I didn't like to tell him I hadn't the remotest idea how to use them. As Hortensio I'd been made up by one of the boy's mothers, and my only contribution had been to powder my nose in the interval.

So the next night I found myself staring at my bare face in the mirror, holding a stick of Number Five and wondering what to do next. We had two dressing-rooms, a great luxury for a wartime airfield like this, one for the girls and one for the boys, with a narrow passage between. Neither room was very large and the walls were thin enough for shouted messages to be heard, as well as the occasional indiscretion. Whenever the girls' door opened, heady glimpses could be caught of exotic kimonos, naked shoulders and stockinged legs, and also a smell that was part make-up and scent and part something subtler and more disturbing. And, of course, Pearl was in there.

Our room was more crowded since there were ten of us to only six girls. We were elbow to elbow at a narrow wooden shelf round the walls. Next to me was Hubby Mills — Hubert to his mother. He was a plump LAC of about twenty-eight with receding straight hair of which he seemed surprisingly vain, because, he explained, his hairline resembled Noël Coward's. In civvy street he'd been a solicitor's clerk and the star of his local dramatic society. His talent was severely limited but he was incurably stage-struck which in these circumstances, Harry said, was worth more than talent. He never missed a rehearsal, was prepared to do anything to help; and if you could endure the earnest interrogations about his 'performance', he was worth his weight in gold.

I swallowed my pride and asked him what to do. He sprang to life. Nobody can resist being asked for their advice, least of all an amateur.

'What've you got there?' he asked, peering into my biscuit tin. I showed him.

'Oh, not Thirteen,' he said. 'Makes you look too sallow.' He demonstrated how to spread the Number Five and then the Number Nine and how to put a little Carmine III on the cheeks and the lips. 'And what colour are your eyes?' I muttered that they were probably blue. 'Blue eyeshadow, then. Haven't you got a blue eyeliner?' I searched through Harry's stubs. 'Here, use mine,' offered Hubby.

Under his instruction I achieved what he considered a near-perfect make-up. I was not so sure. Caught in the street, I felt, I'd be lucky to get away with three months.

The dress rehearsal went on half the night. We had the band with us for the first time so all the music sounded unfamiliar and people kept missing what Terry referred to as their entries. Mick the conductor wasn't too sure of his cues either, and sketches would end in a resounding silence while the band put out their cigarettes and found the place. Props were lost and, in two cases, disintegrated, while the scenery, which I began to realize was perhaps a bit over-ambitious, seemed to take for ever to get on and off. Harry was leaping on and off the stage, half-dressed in a variety of costumes, to see what it looked like from the front, and I was leaping about backstage trying to supervise the scene-shifting. I hardly had time to admire myself in my flight lieutenant's uniform, except to notice that it seemed on the big side, but Pearl gave me a gratifying 'Ooh!' and rolled her eyes when she saw me in the wings. She, of course, looked more astonishing in every costume she wore: from the straw boater and shawl of the opening (with an artful dab of dirt on the peach of her cheek), to the finale when she emerged in a pink off-the-shoulder evening dress, her hair piled up on top of her head, sporting paste earrings and looking as if she'd stepped straight down from the very silver screen that was now rolled above our heads.

When it was all over and we were locking the theatre, I said to Harry, 'What the hell's going to happen tomorrow?'

'It'll be all right,' he said calmly.

'But it was a disaster.'

127

He shook his head. 'Not bad, for a dress rehearsal. I'll have to go over those cues with Mick.' He looked at me. 'Take your time in the sketch and use more voice.' He put the keys in his pocket. 'And for God's sake use the Number Thirteen. You looked like Jeanette MacDonald.'

12

The next day people began to buttonhole us on our way through the camp and ask if it was going to be a good show. Harry would reply politely, 'Wait and see,' and mutter as we walked off, 'Bloody silly question. What do they think I'll say – it's a pile of crap but I hope you enjoy it?' It wasn't until I was in the dressing-room making up again that the nerves started. Everyone had assumed a noisy and cheerful indifference, but it was obvious that the pits of all our stomachs had been seized by the same clammy hand.

For me, nerves changed to real fear when we heard that the queue for the doors had stretched as far as the cookhouse. Suddenly the audience was a reality, it had an identity. In less than an hour I would have to walk out in front of them. I was afraid of them because I knew them: I'd sat among them, seen them destroy well-meaning ENSA shows, heard the obscene advice offered to any actor fool enough to attempt a sentimental love scene, watched a comedian disintegrate as they listed his shortcomings at the tops of their voices. These were not the polite, postprandial audiences of Shaftesbury Avenue – most of them had never been inside a theatre before, except perhaps the sort of music hall where the brutality of the audience was a byword among old pros like Danny and Ernie.

Now Freddy put his head into the room and called 'Five minutes!' and I could hear them, a muffled growl beyond the curtain. Another face appeared round the door – Father, in his best blue, beaming nervously, his bald head glittering with excitement.

'Good luck to everyone,' he said. 'Make it a good show. They're all out there: the CO and his wife, and the AOC Base, too.' We were meant to appreciate the honour. The Base Commander was something of a legend. He'd been a celebrated cricketer before the war, played for England more than once, been a Battle-of-Britain ace, got shot down, lost an eye, and was now said to be the youngest Air Commodore in the RAF. His presence gave the evening the status of a major event, and did nothing to soothe our nerves.

Father looked longingly at us all, trying hard to find something to say that would identify him with us rather than the other side of the curtain. Then one of the girls burst in, wearing little more than bra and pants, to borrow Terry's mascara, and Father flushed pink and retired. We all laughed, louder than we meant to, and drew closer together.

The cast of a show, I realized, could be as exclusive as the crew of a bomber, united by a mutual fear of their enemy, the audience. Hardly comparable, one might think, to the fear of death or disfiguration; but public humiliation is a very real terror, and the sad truth was that many an aircrew preferred to face death rather than the shame of being branded with Lack of Moral Fibre, the RAF's euphemism for cowardice.

Now it was time. I put on my flat cap, tied the spotted scarf round my neck, picked up my newspapers and joined the others on the stage. I checked to see if Eros was on his mark and safely braced. The band were pinging and tootling in the pit, the most tantalizing sound in the world, and from behind

130

the curtain the murmur of the audience had grown to a roar. I peeped at them. The sight of all those faces was shocking. The place was packed from the back to the front, where a row of armchairs had been brought from the officers' mess for the brass hats. There was the CO beside his tweedy wife and next to her the AOC, sprawled in his chair and laughing, a smart black patch over his missing eye.

I relinquished the peephole to Tiny who was waiting for the signal from Father, and took up my position. I looked across at Pearl. She smiled nervously over her flower basket and I gave her what I hoped was an insouciant grin, which only seemed to alarm her. Tiny sprang suddenly to the dimmers and there was a loud cheer from in front as the lights went down and the overture began.

Harry murmured, 'Good luck, everyone,' and darted into the wings. I tried clearing my throat but an outsize frog had taken up residence there, and the stage lights were making me sweat. As the overture ended I saw Freddy heave at the rope that opened the curtains. Abruptly our protective wall was whisked away and we were exposed. I couldn't see the audience – the lights in my eyes were too bright – but the thick, warm smell of them came over the footlights at me. I could feel their restless breathing. There was a burst of applause, whether for Eros or us or because the thing had started at last, I couldn't tell. At that instant I became aware that my limbs and voice and brain were quite numb, but oddly enough I found I was still performing automatically. Everyone around me seemed wildly energized, eyes bright in their painted faces, teeth flashing in their reddened mouths, concentrated entirely on placating the unpredictable darkness. It was all happening very fast, the music pushing us on mercilessly. Suddenly we reached the solo verses: first Danny, then Brenda, then Hubby. I stepped forward, the fourth Christian in the arena, and managed to croak mine out in roughly the same key as the others. When it got to Pearl's turn her tiny voice was instantly drowned by appreciative whistling. I was horrified, but she seemed not to mind. Her mouth went on moving, and at the end she grinned and shrugged at them which precipitated another fusillade of whistling.

Before I could decide if it was going well or not, the number was over and Tiny had plunged us into darkness. Freddy closed the second set of curtains. Behind them we had to remove Piccadilly and replace it with a Turkish harem while sketches were going on in front. As soon as the harem looked as if it might stay up unsupported, I dashed for the dressing-room to get into my flight lieutenant's uniform. Everyone was changing frantically to the accompaniment of *sotto voce* humming and la-la-ing from Danny. I did up the belt and grabbed the hat. The sight of myself in the mirror thrust a spear of terror into me at the thought of what was to come. I squeezed back into the wings. The harem girls were already wriggling robustly in front of the giant Ali-Baba jar (painted on the net donated by Bonny's aunt). On cue a brilliant green light came up behind the net to reveal Terry, apparently inside the jar, in a turban, a lot of body make-up and, I think, hoop earrings. There was a gratifying round of applause for this and I moved away, leaving Terry to emerge and fling himself into his Dance of the Genie, alternating athletic scorn with acrobatic humility. I grasped the chair I had to take on with me and silently tried out my first line. To my horror I found I didn't know it. At that moment Terry finished his dance and the lights went out. I groped my way onto the stage, found my table and sat on my chair. My mouth was as parched as the Sahara and my lips felt twice their normal size.

The lights came up again, dazzling me, the applause died and to my amazement I spoke the line I'd forgotten. The sketch had begun. Hubby and Fred were the first two miscreants. The lines seemed to be coming out of me in the right order, and they managed to raise some polite laughter. Then it was Ernie's turn. My heart was thudding under my officer's tunic. Doing or saying the simplest thing seemed unbelievably difficult out here in front of all these people. A huge laugh greeted Ernie's entrance in a uniform five times too small for him. I gripped the edge of the table with damp fingers and forced myself to look up at him.

'Name, rank and number?' I asked.

'Thwee-thix-thwee A-Thee Thethil Thykesth,' he said, spraying spit in all directions. Another huge laugh, throwing me into complete confusion. I saw that he'd removed his false teeth, collapsing his mouth into a rubber hole and making him splutter on all his S's. He'd never done that in rehearsals. In fact, I could see that rehearsals meant very little to Ernie. This was a love affair between him and the audience. And I was the spare prick at the wedding. I had an overwhelming desire to run into the wings. The laughter was going on and on and I felt completely naked sitting there saying nothing. Several times I tried to start the next line, but although his face was expressionless I could *feel* him glaring at me. Eventually I managed to say, 'Three-six-three AC Sykes, you are charged with being in possession of a sack containing (I remembered to pause), seven hundred and seventy-six wash-basin . . .' I stopped. I had to, nobody could possibly have heard 'washbasin plugs' over the laughter. I looked at Ernie. With his new hideously elastic mouth he was silently mouthing 'theven hundred and theventy-thixth' to the accompaniment of a showerbath of saliva. I wanted to die. I hadn't waited for the laugh and now the whole point of the sketch had been lost. What the hell could I do?

Ernie knew. As the laugh began to fade he stepped up to my table and saluted. 'Thir,' he said. Some spit landed on my cheek. Without thinking I discreetly wiped it off. To my

133

surprise there was another huge laugh, under cover of which he hissed at me, 'Say it again!'

All Harry's careful coaching went out of the window. I waited until I thought I could be heard and repeated the line as loudly as I could. The laugh came, but I could tell from Ernie's face that it was a shadow of what it should have been.

But he was undaunted. He took the audience to his breast and spoke of his love of the common washbasin plug. They laughed and laughed and his panegyric to the plug grew more and more fantastic and further and further from the script we'd rehearsed. I sat behind my desk, sweat melting my collar, listening desperately for any line I might recognize as a cue.

Eventually, with me dazedly following, he led us back to the end of the sketch. I was supposed to have the last line, but when I said, 'Case dismissed, march him out,' Ernie, without warning and in a positive cloudburst, replied, 'Oh, *thsank* you, thir,' and strode off to deafening laughter and applause. I tried to get my line in but Tiny, who obviously thought the sketch was over, blacked out and left me to grab my chair and scuttle for the wings. I felt the bitterness of anyone denied the last word, not to say the last joke. But soon the relief of having the worst part of the evening over flooded through me, and I was able to apologize graciously to Ernie for having nearly wrecked the sketch, to which he replied, equally graciously, 'All right, son. You're getting the hang of it.'

My memory of the rest of the evening is of being in a sort of daze. One minute I'm wriggling into a striped jersey and beret to be a spare Parisian, then Brenda and Reg seem to be singing 'Fold Your Wings of Love Around Me', while I'm trying to lug Pearl's pedestal onto its marks. She climbs onto it, a heartbreakingly demure Galatea in her long Greek dress and curly gold wig, while I stand, a statue myself, watching her from the wings. In the dressing-room I struggle into my

134

tail-suit (hired from Fox's in London and a trifle full in the waist) before the others come pouring in again. Then while another sketch finishes in front and Reg gets through his baritone repertoire, Harry and I are hauling the Night Club set together. Everyone is on and it's the last scene. Pearl and I are sitting at a rickety card-table that's disguised with a white tablecloth. All we have to do is pretend to be drinking champagne from what are plainly NAAFI beer glasses (a last-minute slip-up), while Ernie delivers his favourite jokes, most of them old and blue but much loved by the audience. The audience doesn't alarm me any more, my responsibilities to the show are at an end, and as a mere extra I no longer feel self-conscious in front of them. I relax, waiting now for the high point of my evening. As Danny appears, in an extraordinary satin suit, and begins to play his harmonica, Pearl and I get up to dance. Her cool hand is in mine, my arm is around her slender waist, her bare shoulder is pressed against me. This is the sort of dancing I *can* manage: with a partner like this, who couldn't? I feel her breath on my neck. 'You look ever so handsome in your tails,' she whispers.

Then it's over. The audience erupt in a cacophony of clapping, cheers and whistling. We line up, clutching each others hands, grinning and bowing. We've done it. They like us. We've survived. It's not the applause – that's just a noise in the dark – it's the surviving. We built a house of cards under their very noses and it didn't fall down; it flickered, it glittered, once or twice it sagged, but it stayed up. We did it. Pearl, lovely beyond words in her pink evening dress, is holding my hand. Even Harry is beaming. As soon as the curtain is down the brass hats are pushing their way through it to congratulate us, led by the proud Father, his face matching Pearl's dress. I'm introduced to the CO's wife. 'I say,' she says, 'was it you who painted that scene of Paris? Simply gorgeous. Gosh, it took me back. Leonard and I used to go there a lot.' Leonard! The

AOC is beside himself. With a fine contempt for the spirit of King's Regulations he's slapping Father and Harry on the back at the same time. 'Bloody marvellous. We could have been in the West End. Bloody marvellous.' 'Could've been in the West End,' he repeats to everyone as he goes round shaking their hands, his one eye twinkling with delight. In the dressing-room at long last we hug each other and open the beer Father's thoughtfully had sent up from the NAAFI. We tell each other how clever we are, laugh over the moments we nearly weren't, and, in front of everyone, Pearl throws her arms round my neck and kisses me smack on the lips.

The next day Harry was still beaming. He'd been to see Father and been told that a grand tour of the whole group was to be arranged, which would mean about twenty-five dates between now and the end of the year. I was beaming too, but for a different reason. Pearl and I had finished up in The Wings the night before, drinking mugs of tea with Harry and Brenda. After a while, realizing that I was expected to bow to Harry's seniority, I'd left them to it and walked Pearl back to the WAAF site where there had been a lot more kissing, until eventually we'd both run out of steam from sheer exhaustion. This morning the possibilities of life seemed infinite.

The squadron was still on stand-down after the petrol ferryings, so we gave two more performances on the station; not quite as ecstatically received as the first night, but unquestionably successful. Discreet adjustments were made: Reg and his piano-accordion changed places with Vera Piper's tap dancing to allow him more time to change, (his collar had burst open under the stress of Ravel's *Bolero*), and one of the less successful blackout sketches was removed. Danny and Ernie made helpful suggestions about shortening each other's acts, but neither gave way. Harry, Freddy and I spent most of the time adapting the scenery for unknown places.

Then the real life of the station began again in earnest. We lost two aircraft on two operations on two successive nights. And then, one morning, a brand-new replacement crew crashed while doing their first circuits-and-bumps on a Halifax. They overshot coming in to land, skidded off the end of the runway, straight across the main road and into a field where the Halifax burst into flames, incinerating all seven of them. I could hear the fire tenders and the blood-wagon screaming round the perimeter track, and an immense number of people and trucks seemed to be heading in the direction of the crash. A huge pall of smoke hung over the field all day and everyone was plunged into deep gloom. To lose a whole crew right here on our own station seemed somehow much worse than in some distant action over Germany, although no doubt it was all one to the crew.

I'd never met them, of course, and I never saw the crash. A few days later I was cycling round the field and passed the gaping hole in the barbed wire and the great swathe of churned earth where the bomber had ploughed its way across the road. Over in the field I could see a tail fin and part of a wing, but most of the plane had been removed. The incident seemed as remote from my life as if I'd read about it in a newspaper. I tried to talk to Sgt Willoughby about it, but he seemed to take little interest. All I got were the usual grunts from behind the *Daily Mirror*. I could only assume his unconcern was because neither he nor his section were involved. But then I felt reproached by my own detachment: my preoccupation with Pearl and the show probably made me no better than he was. Or were we all the same? Was familiarity breeding indifference?

With no more rehearsals to escape to, I was having to spend whole days in Willoughby's company, days of stultifying boredom, only relieved two or three afternoons a week when Harry, Freddy, Tiny and I would load the scenery, lights, costume baskets and props onto a lorry, and with Joy (who'd replaced Bonny as our driver and spare chorine) at the wheel and the rest of US squeezed beside her on the front seat or reclining on the prop sofa in the back, set off through the lanes to another airfield. Sometimes it would be only four or five miles away, sometimes as much as forty. Usually it would bear the name of the tiny village that had been engulfed by its creation, a name with origins buried under the centuries: Rufforth, Acaster Malbis, Full Sutton, Skipton-on-Swale, Holme-on-Spalding Moor; and on the way, tucked beside the narrow, lonely roads, we'd pass other villages, incognito in a land without signposts. If the journey was a long one, we'd often stop to eat on the way. Our favourite was a ramshackle lorry drivers' café in the middle of nowhere on a long, straight road across a deserted moor. Harry called it The Petrified Forest because it reminded him of the gas station where Leslie Howard and Humphrey Bogart had been holed up with Bette Davis. The couple who ran it certainly had a sinister air about them, and sometimes very strange noises would emanate from the back room, but they appeared to have an unlimited supply of fried eggs and sausages, and as we nearly always had the place to ourselves, we would sit there as long as we dared, drinking cups of dark, sweet tea and allowing ourselves the brief illusion that we were free men and women in a free world.

The camps we came to were always bomber stations like the one we'd left, but always in their own way different. Some were peacetime stations with brick-built hangars and ivy growing up the cookhouse walls; others not much more than a runway, a huddle of tin huts and acres of mud. We judged them all by their theatres, of course, which varied between bare platforms with one set of dusty curtains and elaborate prosceniums with gilded pillars and sunken foot-lights. We would unload and struggle to make the scenery fit while Tiny folded his arms and insisted that our lighting couldn't possibly be run from their switchboard. By the time we'd succeeded and Tiny's lights were working, as we always knew they would, the band and the rest of the cast would have arrived in the coach. While the costumes and make-up boxes were unpacked, Molly would be ironing frantically, and the local Entertainments Officer sent after chairs, buckets, mirrors for the dressing-room or Elliman's Rub for Terry's back.

But it was after the performance that things really got interesting. It was traditional for visiting ENSA shows to be entertained in the officers' mess or, at the very least, the sergeants'. But we presented a problem, as most of us weren't even corporals. Nevertheless, we did have an ace card – Sarah Cross. Sarah was from the home counties, fair, very tall, very posh, acutely shy, hopelessly stage-struck and, most important of all, a Flight Officer. As there seemed to be a rule (written or unwritten we never knew) that an officer could only be entertained in an officers' mess, having Sarah with us meant that we all had to be invited along with her. On our own station it would never have been contemplated, but as visiting performers our lowly status could apparently be overlooked. This meant unparalleled luxury, foods rare in wartime, and even rarer drinks like wine or whisky. These usually broke down the initial social awkwardness, although we did get some sideways looks from the mess orderlies who were handing round the sandwiches. The girls were all right, of course: being chatted up by bewinged officers was nothing new to them, but some of the men found it uncomfortable and felt they were being patronized. For me, such was the power of snobbery, once my accent was heard I was immediately accepted as an equal – equal but eccentric, as I was obviously wearing the wrong uniform. I tried not to take advantage of this, but I was ashamed to have to admit to myself, how much more at home I felt among these people, and how comforting it was to be readmitted to the world I had grown up in.

One night we'd been playing at one of the smaller airfields, thirty-five miles from our own. The mess was small and shared (WAAF and RAF) but well stocked. Pearl had been swept away by several grizzled squadron leaders and I was on my own, leaning against the bar. A slim, rather elegant WAAF officer came and stood beside me.

'Potter,' she called to the barman, then turned to me. 'What are you drinking?'

'I'm all right, thanks.' I showed her my glass of whisky.

'I'll have my usual, Potter,' she said, and then to me, 'Jolly super show.'

'Thanks.'

'Pretty lavish. For a concert party, I mean.'

I was glad Harry wasn't in earshot. 'Concert party' made him see red. A revue was more how we liked to think of ourselves. But she had bright-gold hair and was rather good-looking, so she was forgiven.

'But I must say,' she went on, 'I thought your comic was a bit off. Rather hot-making, some of his jokes.'

I smiled. 'And rather old.'

'Oh, I don't mind them old. Come to that, I don't really mind them hot-making. But I do like them funny. I mean, look at Douglas Byng. He's filthy but he's frightfully funny.'

I laughed. 'He's certainly filthy. He did a concert in our local hall for Battle of Britain Week . . . some of the locals nearly had apoplexy.'

'Whereabouts is that?'

When I told her it was where I went for my holidays, she said, 'Oh, yes. It's super there, by the river. I had a chap who used to take me down sometimes.'

'From London?'

'Yes.'

140

'Well, it's no distance. Straight down the Great West Road.'

She bent her head and swirled the drink in her glass. 'We used to fly, actually.'

I looked at her quickly. 'In a Tiger Moth?' I said.

'Yes. There was a funny little hotel we used to stay at.'

'On the river?'

'Yes.'

'With no road to it?'

'That's the one. Casanova's Castle the boys used to call it.'

I looked at her again. She must have been about thirty and although the eyes were clear enough, the skin round them looked a bit crashed. But I remembered a slim girl, her hair bright gold in the evening sun, climbing down from the cockpit of a Tiger Moth.

'Did you by any chance,' I said carefully, 'have a yellow flying suit?'

She was startled. 'Well . . . as a matter of fact, I think I did. How the hell did you know?'

'I saw you.'

'Saw me? How?'

I told her about the big field and how I used to watch for the planes and how that evening I'd seen them land and how I'd seen them walk across the grass to the hotel arm-in-arm. She listened attentively, frowning slightly. When I'd finished she shrugged and laughed sceptically.

'It was probably Bunny Mason you saw. She was always dropping in there with Hugh.'

But I was sure. And I told her about the next morning and how he'd taken me up and flung the plane all over the sky, and then flown away, alone. She was sure too, I could see; but she wouldn't say anything. She just kept looking down into her glass. I said, 'What was the registration number of the plane?'

'Christ, how do I know?'

'Was it G-ADFS?'

She stared at me in silence, and then at last, almost in a whisper, she said, 'How could you remember that? You were only a kid.'

I swallowed a big mouthful of scotch. 'I remember everything about that day. Probably always will.'

And then she believed me. She told me they'd gone down there quite a few times. They were 'sort of' engaged, she said, but used to have terrible bust-ups. In the end it just fizzled out. I remembered how he'd walked out on his own the next morning, and how he'd kept looking back at the hotel. I asked her what had happened to him. He'd joined up in '39, she told me. The RAF of course – on fighters. And did she ever hear from him?

'Not any more,' she said and emptied her glass. 'He bought it in 1941. Over Kent somewhere.'

'Ah . . . well . . .' I said uselessly. I thought of him spiralling down in a Spitfire. His hand lifted above his head perhaps. As she put her glass down I noticed the wedding ring on her hand. 'But you married someone else,' I said.

She looked at me with an extraordinary expression I couldn't fathom. 'Yes, well,' she said eventually. 'He's gone too. Last year. Berlin. Still, we never learn, do we? Brave boys in blue. Fucking silly war. Come on, for God's sake, let me top you up.'

13

I'd been in love before. More than once, in fact. There'd been the sister of my schoolfriend, a hilarious episode for her family, excruciatingly painful for me; and the brown-eyed art student (not the one I'd slept with), over whom I'd agonized and wept for nearly a year. Each time I'd been well aware that my behaviour was archetypically adolescent, but that had only made the pain harder to bear. Love for me had meant sex with girls I was barely fond of, alternating with passionate adoration of unattainable goddesses. My adoration of Pearl was certainly passionate, but this time I had hopes that Olympus wouldn't be beyond my reach.

In the company of this curious group of strolling players in uniform, she seemed happy to accept me as her escort. She liked to share what she saw as my privileged position and was always eager to travel with the advanced guard in the truck. I think, like us, she enjoyed the sense of truancy in those stolen meals at roadside cafés. She would sit, her elbows either side of her mug of tea, a cigarette motionless between the tips of two slim fingers, listening while we talked. Her face was almost always expressionless, she rarely spoke, and sometimes I suspected she was miles away, but because that kind of beauty can't be ignored for long, our eyes would always come back to her, and out of politeness someone would ask her opinion. Then she would just exhale, smile and shrug; but occasionally, when she'd actually been listening, she'd treat us to a succinct comment in her direct cockney way. 'I wouldn't cross the road for a tanner's worth of that'; 'My Mum'd soon see him off'; 'We could all do with a bit more of what she's got.' Everyone would laugh appreciatively and I would feel immensely proud of her; because now it must surely be obvious that it wasn't just beauty I'd fallen for so abjectly.

But the real advantage of Pearl's joining us in the lorry was that it then became perfectly legitimate for her to travel back the same way, instead of in the coach with all the others. The prop sofa was always the last thing to be loaded before we left, and she and I would climb over the tailboard and huddle on it side by side in our greatcoats, breathing the night air that was chilly but still sharp with the tang of grass and hedgerows, while the truck lurched and rattled through the inky darkness. When it was very cold we would pull one of the heavy stage curtains over our laps, and with our hands under each other's coats we would turn our heads to find the other's mouth in the blackness and fasten on it endlessly and insatiably. On moonlit nights on the long straight stretches Joy would put her foot down and the truck would bounce over the potholes like a tennis ball and our teeth would crash together and we would laugh and pull apart until she slowed down again. And on other nights autumn fogs would close round us like a blindfold and the truck would have to crawl forward yard by yard, and the journey would take hours and in the back our tongues would find new dexterities and our hands new intimacies.

I did my best in front of Harry to keep my passion within proper manly bounds. I could sense that any hint of a sentimental rhapsody would only embarrass and even, I suspected, puzzle him. Because, for all his obsession with women and his genuine liking for them, I'd never heard Harry mention the word love. (Unless, of course, he was putting up the same front as I was. But I don't think so, somehow.) As far as I could see, romantic love didn't feature in his scheme of things, any more than beauty, or moonlight or soft music or any of our other justifications for the animal act. Harry enjoyed being an animal, and liked to claim that most women were as animal as he was.

'Of course they are,' he would say. 'Look at their biology – walking wombs, aren't they?'

I said that most of the girls I'd met appeared to have the animal well under control, and seemed a lot subtler and more fastidious than the men I knew.'

He laughed. 'That's all for our benefit. To get us going. We're the fastidious ones – not them. They can't be very fastidious, can they, otherwise how could they put up with great hairy things like us crawling all over them?'

We both laughed. I didn't really believe it, and I wasn't too sure he did either. In spite of his appetite for women he wasn't really promiscuous, and I'd never seen him treat them with anything but respect. Maybe it wasn't so much their animal appetites that made women respond to him as his own transparent enthusiasm for their whole sex. But when I thought of him bending Sgt Brenda over her desk, his foot jammed against the door, I did wonder if perhaps he might not be missing something. Certainly I was in a very different case. Sex seemed almost inadequate to express my feelings about Pearl. What I wanted from her I didn't really know, but whatever it was I was desperate for it. Knowledge, perhaps? To be privy to every detail of her life, her past, her present, her wants and fears? For her to share mine? To make her a present of every pleasure I'd ever experienced? The fact that she seemed indifferent to so much that gave me pleasure was only a spur. All her shortcomings (and I was by no means blind to them) served only as a challenge to my all-conquering love.

I began to lose weight. Sleep, something I'd never had any problem with, began to evade me. I would lie awake for hours in my narrow bed, the hairy blankets scratching my chin, listening to the sighing, mumbling and burbling in the darkness, considering ways of capturing the part of her attention that always seemed beyond my reach. As I hadn't now for months, I began to long again for the prestige of a being a pilot. Even a navigator or a wireless/op would do. How else could I compete with the commissioned and the bewinged surrounding her on all sides.

When maximum-effort operations were planned, our visits to other stations were often postponed or cancelled. Then days would go by without my catching a glimpse of her, and I would find excuses to venture into the underground operations block where she worked, on the off-chance of meeting her in a corridor. Being mainly staffed by senior ranks, it was the cleanest, driest and warmest place on the station, humming with air-conditioning and electric light. And to tell the truth, it wasn't only Pearl that drew me there. I'd discovered a small, tucked-away lavatory, with handbasins, a mirror and two warm and spotless cubicles where one could sit with a good book, undisturbed for a surprisingly long time. With winter on the way it was infinitely preferable to the windswept airmen's latrines, and I took to visiting it almost every day.

I returned from there one morning, my book hidden in my battledress top, to be greeted by Sgt Willoughby, on his feet for once, and in his brusque mode.

'Absence makes the face grow longer,' he barked. 'And where've *you* been?'

'Only to the bog, Sarge,' I said.

146

'Bloody long shit.' He eyed me suspiciously. 'Well, time and tide wait for no man. You're flying tonight.'

I was dumbfounded. 'Flying?'

'You heard. Brand-new crew on K-Kitty, doing a training cross-country tonight. Give us a chance to check that dicey gyro.'

Occasional flying duties were required in this job, I knew, which was why it carried the rank of sergeant: sometimes the only way to check a rogue compass was to test it in flight. But it was always Willoughby who did it, never Sgt Grice (who was said to be terrified of flying) and certainly never us erks.

'Sgt Grice is duty sergeant tonight. And I'm off on a forty-eight.'

So that explained it.

'You *were* mustered aircrew, weren't you?'

'Yes, Sarge.'

'And you can use a sextant?'

'Well . . . yes, I suppose so.'

'The navigator'll help you. You'll need to check as many bearings as you can. Take-off's seven-thirty. Briefing at six.' He stared at me in silence for a moment. Then the meaningless smile stretched across his face. 'Of course, you're not supposed to be going on a trip like this, so don't go shouting about it too much.'

Because you're not supposed to be sending me, I thought.

'You'll need a blood chit,' he said. 'The Flight Office will give you one.'

A blood chit was a permit for non-aircrew personnel to fly, in case something went wrong and you came back in pieces – or not at all. Then no one would have to carry the can. It was the old service rule: get a signature for everything.

'I won't be here, but make sure you get Sgt Grice to sign all your stuff in the morning.'

And then you'll be in the clear, I thought. 'Right, Sarge.'

Alan was green with envy when I told him.

'You jammy bugger. Ever been up in a Halibag?'

'No.'

'Me neither. Mind you, it's just as well it's not me. I was up in a Wimpey once,' he said, 'and I was sick as a dog.' But I could tell he was lying.

There were no ops that night, and the camp was unusually quiet. K-Kitty was the only plane scheduled to fly. I got my chit and drew some flying kit and at five-thirty, as I'd been told to, I went over to the aircrew mess. As I opened the door I had a sudden sensation of walking out of one world and into another. Here was the real life of the station, the life I'd never penetrated to before. This was my first glimpse of what might have been.

The new crew were sitting at a table at the other end of the room. All the other tables were empty. I hesitated, stricken with shyness and a paralysing sense of inferiority. One of them turned and saw me.

'You the compass bloke?' he called.

I nodded.

'Get yourself some grub and come and sit down.'

I collected a plate from the hatch and took it to the table. I wasn't very hungry, which was a pity as the food was rather better than I'd been used to. I sat myself opposite the one who'd spoken. He had a square face and dark hair low over his forehead. He stretched his hand across the table.

'I'm Greg, the navigator. And this is our skipper, Alex,' he said, nodding to a grave, skinny young man sitting next to me who had blond hair but very dark eyes, which gave him an oddly artificial look. The dark eyes were restless and only stayed on mine a moment as he gave me a thin hand and a sudden warm smile.

'Nice to have you with us,' he murmured diffidently. He introduced the other five, pointing his fork at each of them in

148

turn, and I nodded, trying hopelessly to remember their names. They were all sergeants and their stripes looked a good deal newer than their uniforms. None of them was more than a couple of years older than I was. The skipper turned to me again. 'You been on the squadron long?'

'About five months.' On the station, though. Not the squadron. The squadron was this side of the door. And I'd only been here for ten minutes.

'What's it like?'

How did I know? How did I know what it was like in the aircrew quarters, in the briefing room, out on the flights waiting for take-off? What could I tell them – the NAAFI's OK – we put on good shows in the theatre? 'It's all right,' I said.

'Lot of ops?' someone asked.

'Average, I suppose.'

Someone else said, 'Not a new kite, K-Kitty, is it?'

'Oh, no. It's been here as long as I have, I think.'

They smiled at that. It was a good omen.

'The last crew were posted. They'd finished their tour. Their second, I think.'

The smiles broadened. A lucky kite. So I told them about the quiet New Zealand crew who had been famous on the station for taking such care of K-Kitty, always checking every detail before they flew, and surviving when so many hadn't.

Greg, the navigator, nodded seriously. 'Yeah, that's what they say. It's the careful ones get through. Eh, Alex?' He looked across at the skipper.

'And the sober ones,' someone said.

Everybody laughed. The skipper got to his feet. He was taller than I'd thought. 'Come on, chaps,' he said. 'Briefing.'

'Where're we going?' asked a little air gunner.

'Grand tour of the British Isles again.'

There was a groan. As we filed out of the mess I noticed a bowl of caffeine tablets on the table for the aircrew to take on long night ops. I pocketed a handful. They'd be popular when we were engaged on late scenery-painting sessions – or other nocturnal activities.

I had been in the briefing room before. I'd sneaked in there one morning and been mesmerized by the atmosphere of the place. Much more than our converted cookhouse, this was the true theatre of the camp. No stage drama could ever compete with the moment when the grey curtains rolled back to reveal the great backcloth of Europe filling the entire end wall and the anxious crews leaned forward to see where the coloured tapes were reaching to tonight. That morning the room had still been redolent of the night before: cigarette ends and sweet papers under the rows of chairs, the aircraft and crews still chalked on the boards, the tapes still pinned across the North Sea and halfway into Germany. I'd gone closer to the huge map. With my eyes about level with Frankfurt, my out-stretched left hand could reach into France and my right could just touch Leipzig. Yorkshire was far above my head to the left. The scale was extraordinary. Every village, every lane, every church spire from the Bay of Biscay to Poland, was there on the map. I'd stared at the names in front of me: Bad König, Obermoschel, Mespelbrunn, Hirschorn-am-Neckar, seen the streams tumbling down the contour lines and the roads zig-zagging up them – forbidden territory. Each village no bigger on the map than the ones dotted around the airfield. And in all of them, people eating, working, sleeping, listening for the sound of our bombers going over, praying that the tape didn't end at them. And I thought how frightening it would be to be falling silently towards them in the night, swinging under a parachute, cold and alone and a long, long way from home.

This evening the atmosphere was more mundane. The floor was swept, the boards wiped clean and there was nothing on the walls but the usual dusty aircraft-recognition

150

silhouettes and 'Careless Talk' posters. There were no tapes on the map – obviously we didn't rate them. The eight of us sat along the front row while a bored flight lieutenant tapped the map with an old billiard cue.

'Heading one-one-six to Gloucester, then Holyhead,' tap, 'Belfast,' tap, 'Dundee,' tap, 'and home. Right? The weather's a bit murky but you should get a fix over Belfast, and probably Dundee. Pretty simple. But don't go to sleep. There's always a chance you might run into the odd Jerry stooging about. Especially on the leg down from Dundee. ETA back here should be about midnight. Any questions?'

There were one or two, some of which I didn't understand, and then a corporal from the met. section intoned a brief weather report. Ten-tenths cloud everywhere it seemed, so it wouldn't be a sightseeing trip; not that it mattered as it would be pitch-dark anyway.

In the crew room the little air gunner said, 'Four and a half fucking hours. I better have a crap.'

The stores had lent me an outsize pair of flying boots. God knows whose they'd been. I struggled into my Mae West. I'd never worn one before – they hadn't been thought necessary over the Berkshire Downs – but I made an effort to look knowledgeable as I wrestled with the inflation tubes, zips and tapes. I tried on my helmet with its microphone and oxygen mask, but took it off again when I saw that nobody else was wearing his. We collected our parachutes from the parachute section. Molly, our wardrobe mistress, saw me and came over. 'And where are you off to?' she said with a wink. 'Here you are, a special for you. Packed by my own fair hand.' I hoped there wasn't a hole the shape of a wedding dress in it.

Cigarettes were lit and everyone smoked hungrily while we waited for the transport. Dressed like this I had the same feeling of a masquerade that I'd had wearing the flight lieutenant's uniform in the show. Still, I would have liked Pearl to see me in flying kit, ready for action. But she must have gone off duty ages ago.

There was the faintest chink of light along the horizon as the truck drove us out to the dispersal, but the low ceiling of cloud had plunged the rest of the world into darkness. K–Kitty loomed over us, barely discernible in the blackness, just the glow from her cabin floating over our heads. After the crew were aboard I chucked in my flight bag and my parachute and hoisted myself through the hatch. For all its great size the Halifax was designed to carry bombs, not passengers. There were seven cramped spaces allotted: two turrets for the air gunners, cubby holes for the navigator, wireless operator, engineer and bomb-aimer, and a high, narrow seat for the pilot; the only other space was the optimistically named 'rest position', two metal ledges along the sides of the fuselage between the mid-upper turret and the tail. Members of the crew not immediately involved were supposed to sit there during take-off and landing, so I squeezed myself onto one of them while the engines started up one after another and the plane lurched and shook as they were run up. The noise was mind-splitting and I put on my helmet to protect my ears as I noticed the others had done.

After what seemed a very long time, two or three of the others joined me on the benches and we began to trundle along the perimeter track. There was a tiny scratched perspex porthole near me and I could just see the occasional runway light as it slid past. We seemed to be swinging this way and that and intermittently stopping dead, and then, without warning, the engines were roaring again and we were racing down the runway into that sudden creamy, floating feeling that means you're airborne.

Greg, the navigator, gestured to me to bring my bag and led the way down to the nose. Emerging into the cockpit I stopped, entranced. We had just climbed through the thick layers of rain cloud into a crystal-clear night sky. We were skimming across a great white plain like polar tundra stretching away to a horizon that was as sharp as the edge of a knife. Here and there in the distance huge piles of cumulus rose out of the plain, gleaming in the starlight like ice-cream mountains.

Alex turned his head and nodded to me. As I stepped down into the navigation section I noticed his haversack by his feet with a Thermos flask sticking out of it. Greg saw me looking. 'Fancy a coffee?' he said with a broad grin. 'He'll probably give you some later, if you ask him nicely.'

He drew the curtain across his porthole and switched on the light over his desk. He unfolded his charts and showed me the headings he'd plotted. I unpacked the sextant and the almanac and squatted on the floor, making notes. There was plenty of time. I only had half a dozen headings to check before we landed again. It was getting very cold. I'd put on both my sweaters before we left but I felt frozen to the marrow, and we'd only been flying for half an hour. I stood up and tried to move about, but there wasn't much room for gymnastics in a cabin only the width of a pair of outstretched arms. I took the sextant and made my way up to the astrodome, a clear bubble of perspex in the roof of the cockpit just behind the pilot. It was really the engineer's position, but when he saw the sextant he climbed down to make way for me and signalled that he was off to the Elsan. I plugged into his intercom socket and told Alex what I was doing so that he could hold the course steady for me. I hadn't done this since Initial Training and never in a moving aircraft, but I was helped by the astonishing clarity of the stars at this altitude. I had to take off my gloves to use the sextant and could feel my fingers growing stiff with the cold. Through the perspex I could see there was a film of ice already over the wings.

Five more times I climbed back up to the astrodome. I

probably didn't need to, but it was better than staring at the aluminium ribs of the fuselage and listening in to the desultory chat on the intercom. Hour after hour the engines throbbed on either side of us and the cold penetrated deeper and deeper into our bones. Whenever one looked out there were the same galaxies of unwinking stars and beneath us the endless carpet of white cloud. We never caught a glimpse of the earth. Occasionally, in the wireless operator's cabin, just behind the navigator, the rotating arm on the radar screen would trace in its wake the green ghost of a shape I could recognize from the map. 'Derby?' I would say; or 'Gloucester?' and the wireless op would nod. By ten o'clock we had reached Belfast and turned north-east, back across the sea. I was standing behind Alex once again, under the astrodome, when I glanced down over his shoulder. The control column was nodding gently under the influence of the automatic pilot. Alex had his Thermos flask in one hand and with the other he was fumbling in his flying suit. He produced a long flaccid penis and pointed it at the flask. His piss steamed in the freezing air.

It was after midnight when at last we began the descent to the airfield. Back in the rest position with the others I tucked my flight bag between my legs and waited. After four and a half hours of cold and boredom I'd had more than enough of this trip. I could see nothing through the tiny porthole except some drops of rain blowing across it, but I felt the shudder as the flaps went down. The engines were throttled back and for an instant a couple of lights sped past in the blackness. We were bracing ourselves for the bump, when suddenly the engines roared, the floor tilted upwards and we were climbing again. We banked sharply. Then banked again. A long pause and we banked a third time. And a fourth time. We were coming down again. Again the engines were throttled back. Again we were dropping towards the runway and again we braced ourselves for the landing. And again, at the last moment, the engines roared and we were climbing away from the field.

This time the pauses between the turns were longer. I looked across at the tail gunner. In the dim light from the bulb in the roof I saw him shrug. Greg, next to him, made a gesture, flapping both hands from the wrist, which I didn't understand. Then at last we were coming down once more. Let's get it right this time, shall we, I thought waggishly, to stem the feeling of nervousness that was spreading through me like ink across blotting paper. It seemed to be taking for ever. I was sure we must be only a few feet from the deck by now. Suddenly the ground hit us with a wallop that nearly threw me off the bench. The plane lurched and rose again, groaning. A second later there was another boneshaking crunch and this time the engines raced madly and we clawed our way up at an angle I didn't think a Halifax was capable of.

I wasn't nervous now, I was scared: unnaturally calm but thoroughly scared. Something was seriously wrong. You shouldn't need more than three goes to land a Halifax. The crew were hanging onto the aluminium struts and avoiding each other's eyes. As we'd climbed the last time I'd slid down the bench, and now I noticed there was an intercom socket just by my elbow. I found the plug trailing from my helmet and pushed it home.

Someone was saying, 'Wipe the sweat out of my eyes for Christ's sake, Fred. I can't see a fucking thing.' It was Alex's voice, talking to the engineer. Then I heard Fred say, 'Take it easy. We've got enough juice for a few more tries.'

'What about the bloody undercart?'

'It must be down now. The light's off.'

'If it's still there.'

I don't remember how many times we went round the airfield that night. I lost count. The undercarriage seemed to be holding up, miraculously: the problem appeared to be getting it to stick to the ground. The weather wasn't helping. I heard Alex say, 'This bloody rain! Where's the runway? I can't see the end of the bleeding runway.'

Accidents usually happen suddenly and swiftly, before one has time to get properly frightened. This was more like being in a flying condemned cell. There was plenty of time to contemplate the outcome. I was quite sure that my chances of getting out in one piece were pretty slim. I kept remembering that column of black smoke rising over the camp. There was nothing I could do: just sit there and wait. Part of me persisted in believing I'd be all right, and part of me knew there was no particular reason why I should be. I still felt quite calm and kept thinking of silly things like who'd play my part next Saturday and whether they'd send my paints and brushes back to my mother. Curiously, I never once thought about Pearl. By now Alex's voice was hoarse with strain. My last shred of confidence disappeared when I heard him say, 'Oh, Jesus. I've never landed one of these things at night before.' But, astonishingly, that was the moment we hit the ground with an impact that must have loosened every rivet in the plane – and stayed there, slithering along the runway, the old Halifax wagging its tail like a dog greeting its master.

When we finally stopped moving, the relief was like warm oil pouring through my veins. A babble of voices from the control tower filled my ears and I pulled out the intercom plug. We all looked at one another and laughed – to show we hadn't really been frightened. Perhaps they hadn't been? Well I certainly had, and I had a split second's grateful communion with an Almighty I didn't really believe in. The interminable trundle round to the dispersal began. I realized I was wet with sweat and that my legs were shaking. When the engines stopped at last I pulled off my helmet and in the singing silence could hear the rain drumming on the metal fuselage.

Someone opened the hatch and one by one we dropped onto the soaking tarmac and dashed through the downpour to the transport that was waiting for us. Out of the corner of my eye I saw the fire truck and the ambulance making their way back along the perimeter track.

We followed them in the truck, rattling comfortably over the solid ground. Cigarettes were passed round. Matches flared. Nobody mentioned the landing. In the darkness I heard Fred say, 'Debriefing in Base Ops?'

Alex said, 'That's right.'

'Ah,' said a voice – Greg's I thought. 'Perhaps your crumpet'll be on.'

'What crumpet?' Alex's voice. Very casual.

'The one this afternoon. Little dark one – gorgeous.'

'Don't remember.'

'You bloody do,' said a voice. 'You bet Brian a fiver you'd fuck her before Christmas.'

'Get in there, Alex,' said the tail gunner. 'What's her name?'

'Pearl, isn't it?' said another voice. 'Passionate Pearl, is what I heard.'

There was a lot of laughter.

'Get stuffed,' Alex said. 'I only spoke three words to her.'

'I *lurve* you,' groaned someone in a Charles Boyer accent.

In the darkness my face was flaming with anger, shock and jealousy.

And this was the man who'd just nearly killed me.

14

The one I most wanted to recount my adventure to was Pearl, but by the time I found her, at lunch-time, she'd already heard all about it. Most people had, it seemed. I asked her if she'd ever met the crew. Yes, she had seen them, she thought. I didn't tell her that they certainly remembered her. Or why. When I mentioned Alex – Sgt Puddifoot (not a name you'd forget), she looked vague and said she didn't know which one he was. The pilot, I told her. She thought for a moment, a delectable process that involved a slight lifting of both porcelain nostrils, and then shook her head. I was satisfied.

On my way out of the operations warren I was stopped by a tall squadron leader with a moustache that reached towards his ears. I recognized him from the debriefing after we'd landed.

'Weren't you in K-Kitty last night?' he said.

There was no point in denying it. 'Yes, sir,' I said.

'Ropey do, that landing. I was up at flying control last night. We thought your undercart was jammed. Your skipper was sure it hadn't locked. Been a nasty mess if it hadn't, eh?'

'Yes, sir.'

'Still, you got her down.'

'Yes, sir.'

'Bloody good show.'

I emerged into the daylight, hands in pockets, the last of the few, the man who'd brought K-Kitty safely to the ground – and ran straight into an enormous Flight Sergeant SP.

'Stand still, Airman,' he said in a voice sandpapered by a thousand parade-grounds. 'Take your hands from your pockets.'

'Sorry, Flight.'

'And where is your hat?'

It was stuffed under my epaulette.

'Put it on your head.' He looked me up and down slowly, making me feel rumpled and soiled. The buttons on his own tunic scintillated like a dozen suns, his boots gleamed and the creases in his trousers were sharp enough to draw blood. He raised a huge red finger and pointed to where I'd just come from. 'Is that your place of work?'

'No, Flight.'

'What is your place of work, then?'

'Compass Section.'

'Flight Sergeant.'

'Flight Sergeant.'

I hadn't encountered this sort of bullshit since I'd arrived here. He leaned towards me and narrowed his eyes.

'Aren't you one of that concert-party lot?'

Ah. That was it. 'Yes, Flight.'

'So you don't really have a place of work. Because you don't do any work, do you?' He beamed in appreciation of his own wit.

It seemed wiser not to comment.

'But you do make a lot of noise, don't you? Especially late at night. When honest airmen are trying to get a good night's kip.' He leaned even closer and spoke softly and hoarsely. 'In that little peed-ah-terr of yours. What do you get up to in there, eh? Till all hours? We can hear you, you know. Right

160

down at the guardroom, we can.' The red finger jabbed at me. 'We're watching you. So watch yourself. Right?'

'Yes, Flight.'

'Right. Carry on.'

Abruptly he turned on his heel and marched away, his steel-tipped boots striking sparks from the concrete path.

When I told Harry about this encounter he seemed unimpressed, but I wasn't so confident. I said I had a feeling the SPs were closing in on us. He laughed a good deal at that and told me not to be melodramatic. But I knew they were itching to get their hands on us. The trouble was that most of what went on in The Wings was, by service standards, illegal if not plain criminal. All our comforts: the armchairs, the table, bed, blankets, pots and pans had been sneaked in, usually under cover of darkness, from other corners of the camp. Because it was officially only a storeroom, we were allowed no coal ration for the stove and fuel had to be smuggled in sacks from the operations boiler room. Things like bread, milk and sugar were lifted too, in night raids on the back of the cookhouse.

The SPs were also convinced that fornication, actual or attempted, was going on behind our tantalizing green door. In that, they weren't entirely wrong: the actual being Harry's and the attempted inevitably mine. Luckily for us there was one particular night when nothing of that sort was in progress.

We'd been doing the show at a nearby airfield and had got back quite early – just after midnight. We'd brought back a few beers from our hosts' mess, and Danny and Freddy had helped us to finish them before going off to bed. Harry and I had just poured ourselves our ritual mugs of cocoa when there was a sudden knock at the door. We always kept the door locked so, thinking it was one of the others having forgotten something, I got up to open it. I held it ajar a few inches and peered out.

A rather posh voice said, 'Mind if I come in?'

161

I opened it wider. A stocky figure with a sizeable fruit salad under its wings was leaning with one hand against the door-post. It had a black patch over one eye.

Shock reduced my voice to a hoarse whisper. I managed to say, 'Yes, sir,' as I heard Harry leap to attention behind me.

'Thanks,' said the AOC, strolling in and looking round. 'Better shut the door, though.'

I sprang to shut it. I'd expected him to be followed by half a dozen slavering SPs, but he appeared to be quite alone.

'Sorry to butt in on you like this,' he said, 'but I've always wondered what went on in this hut.'

He wasn't the only one.

'It's the Station Theatre Company, sir,' Harry said, rather self-importantly I thought.

'Ah, yes. Thought I recognized you chaps.' He looked at the two of us, both playing sentries. 'Look, do relax . . . I mean, stand easy . . . or whatever.' He took a few steps into the hut, looking round. 'I don't want to disturb you or any-thing, if you were busy.'

'We were just having some cocoa, sir,' Harry said. And then, good old Harry, never at a loss: 'Would you like some?'

'Really? You got enough?' He sounded quite pleased. He stood there, smiling, hands in pockets, while Harry tried to find a clean mug and I swept a pair of underpants off the least dilapidated chair and pushed it forward.

'Would you like to sit down, sir?'

He would, and settled himself in his characteristic sprawl in front of the stove. Harry brazenly shovelled some illicit coal into the top and then handed him his mug. Emboldened by his extraordinary complaisance we drew up our chairs and joined him.

'Bloody smashing, that show of yours,' he said, sipping his cocoa. 'I get a lot of compliments when I'm going round the group, you know. Of course, I take all the credit.'

162

We laughed. He started to ply us with questions and was fascinated to hear that Harry had actually been a professional. I'd already discovered that almost everyone turned out to be insatiably curious about the theatre, but it was odd to find that this famous young man, a fighter ace and a celebrated cricketer before the war, was so stage-struck and such an eager audience for Harry's anecdotes. He led Harry through his repertoire, laughing uproariously at every story, and Harry brought them all out: the rep stories, the touring stories, the star stories. Harry hadn't actually worked with any real stars but he knew all the tales, the rumours and witticisms. By the time we'd reached the one about the actor whose toupee had fallen into the scrambled egg we were all helpless with laughter.

Without any warning the door crashed open, the lights were snapped off and a blinding torch was shone into our faces.

A voice shouted, 'All right! On your feet!'

Obediently we stood up. Including the AOC. The torch-beam must have caught the fruit salad and the single broad ring on the cuff, because there was a sudden intake of breath. The torch went out and the lights came back on. In the doorway stood two SPs, rigidly at attention, thumbs glued to the seams of their trousers, eyes focused in mid-air, their faces suffused with the horror of the situation.

'What's the trouble, Corporal?' the AOC said amiably.

'Sorry, sir. Nothing, sir. Sorry to trouble you, sir.'

'Thought we heard a noise, sir,' said the other one.

'You probably did,' said the AOC. 'We were laughing. A bit loudly, I'm afraid.'

The corporal looked as if he'd never laugh again – if he ever had. 'Sorry we disturbed you, sir,' he said through clenched teeth. Then, with elaborate decorum and heavily aspirated: 'Have we your permission to retire?'

This was too much for Harry. I heard a faint snort from his direction. The AOC nodded at them and they gave a brief drill demonstration, stamping and swivelling until a little cloud of dust rose from the concrete floor. Then they disappeared into the night.

We all avoided each other's eyes. The AOC said, 'I'd better let you chaps get to bed. I enjoyed our chat. And thanks for the cocoa.'

When he'd gone and the door was safely shut, Harry and I laughed with sheer glee until the tears ran down our faces. I said, 'Well, either they'll leave us alone now, or our lives will be hell on earth.'

'I think they'll leave us alone. They'll be too scared. That bloke's a legend round the group. They won't dare touch us.'

When we were leaving I said to Harry, 'What do you think he was doing, wandering about the camp on his own in the middle of the night?'

Harry slipped the keys into his pocket. 'Doing his Henry the Fifth, I expect,' he said.

If there'd ever been any truth in the Flight Sergeant's jibe about not working, there certainly wasn't now. Not for me, anyway. As well as being one of Messrs Grice and Willoughby's domestic staff and spending nights travelling to far-flung aerodromes, I now had new duties. Harry had become obsessed with thoughts of the next production: Father, aglow with the success of *Over the Moon* and all the pink gins he was being treated to in the mess, was pressing for another triumph after Christmas. It was to be a straight play this time, a thriller or a comedy, nothing too esoteric. And an already proven success. Amateurs, Harry said, find it hard enough to do a good play, there's no point in sending them to sea in a leaky ship. There were other factors to be considered too. The play had to have only one set, there hadn't to be too

164

many female parts, as choice on the station was limited, and above all, there must be no rôle in which, by any stretch of imagination, Father could envisage himself.

Every spare moment Harry was poring over his catalogue of *French's Acting Editions*. He and Father changed their minds daily. One minute it was *George and Margaret*, the next, *Night Must Fall* or *French Without Tears* or perhaps *Ten-Minute Alibi*. And each time, Harry expected designs for the set, ground plans and even lists of furniture. Night after night the T-square would be sliding up and down my drawing board, while Harry's pipe bubbled and reeked as he mulled over the casting.

Casting, with Harry, was almost entirely a sexual matter. Not the casting couch: Harry took his theatre far too seriously to let his own appetites interfere with his judgement. But when he was contemplating the idea of a particular actor in a particular part, he would narrow his eyes and look down his long nose at the smoke rising from his pipe, and murmur, with a sort of sensual relish, things like: 'There's a little girl in the Orderly Room I'd like to try out. She's only a tiny thing but she's got this deep, husky voice – like a schoolgirl who's escaped from a brothel.' Or: 'No, he won't do. He's good-looking enough, but they'll never believe he could fuck a fly, let alone that big blonde in accounts.' At first I was rather shocked by his attitude to the art of acting, but after a while I began to see the sense behind the sensuality. Harry loved being in an audience almost as much as being on the stage. He knew what audiences needed and how they felt. Most of the plays we were considering were, in essence, love stories, and for the audiences the actors would be their surrogates, acting out their sexual and romantic fantasies. 'It's no good playing Juliet unless all the men want to be in Romeo's tights,' he would say. 'And not much good playing Romeo unless the audience believes you've got something considerable in there yourself.'

With winter fast approaching, contacts between RAF and WAAF were having to return indoors, and dances in the messes or the NAAFI were on the increase. There was to be one on a Saturday when I knew we'd not be playing away, and I immediately offered to escort Pearl. In spite of the informality and camaraderie of camp life it was still not done for a girl to attend a dance on her own. Whom she left with was often open to speculation, but she always arrived either with a prearranged male or with her girl friends. In Pearl's case I was pretty sure it wouldn't be girl friends. So I stepped in smartly.

We arranged to meet in The Wings, to give me a chance to be alone with her and for her to put the finishing touches to her appearance. Congenitally unpunctual as I was, I managed to be there only half an hour before the time we'd agreed, having completed a long and exacting toilet. My hair shone with a powerful new brilliantine bought for the occasion and even my toenails were trimmed. I was wearing my best blue and in the right-hand breast pocket was a brand-new French letter. Well, you never know your luck. The old one had finally been abandoned after being carried unavailingly for many months. The pink-and-purple packet had disintegrated and for the sake of hygiene I'd been forced to part with my old companion. Mind you, I wasn't short of replacements. The packets-of-three were ostentatiously displayed in the camp barber's shop, and one couldn't have one's hair cut month after month and always say no to the coded question, 'Anything *else* you need, sir?' It could create the impression that you were a celibate, or, even worse, unlucky in love. I drew a new one from the store at the bottom of my kit-bag.

I'd smoked several cigarettes and read most of Harry's latest *Theatre World* before I started to worry. I'd never known her to be less than half an hour late for our meetings, but when the half became a whole, anxiety began to knot my insides and I found I couldn't concentrate on Fay Compton's latest triumph at the Vaudeville Theatre. I got up and paced about, peering out of the window again and again. I lit another cigarette and had almost finished it before it occurred to me, with a lurch of horror, that she might have thought we were meeting at the dance. I grabbed my greatcoat and made for the NAAFI.

In spite of the blackout there were chinks of light all over the building and the noise was tremendous. The chinks hadn't improved the ventilation unfortunately: when I went in I was met with a wall of hot air from which all the oxygen seemed to have been extracted. The place was packed, and up on the platform Sgt Muloney and his men were blasting their way through 'I'll Get By', while the couples, elbow-to-elbow, foxtrotted their way anti-clockwise round the room like a great revolving blue-grey wheel. I pushed my way round the edge, side-stepping the beer drinkers and tripping over the wallflowers. At the bar I found Harry with Brenda, who, out of deference to the lower ranks surrounding her, had removed her tunic to hide her stripes.

'Seen Pearl?' I asked Harry.

'What?'

I shouted. 'Have you seen Pearl?'

He shrugged and shook his head. I continued round the other side of the room. At a table in the corner I saw Pearl's friend, Doris, sitting with two other girls and what looked like six bottles of Tizer. I elbowed my way across. I was still wearing my greatcoat and my face was burning with the heat. I was no match for Doris, though: her normally red face was scarlet. She flashed her dreadful teeth at me.

'Hello,' she said coyly.

'Where's Pearl? Do you know?' I asked.

The coyness disappeared. A rather different smile appeared. 'She went out, I think.' One of the girls nudged her and whispered something. 'Yes, well, I think she might have had a headache,' Doris said, turning back to me. And then, as if to a backward child: 'She's probably on duty, you know.'

I knew she wasn't. Not unless she'd got extra duty at the last minute. Anyway, she obviously wasn't in here. I tried to look as if it was of no consequence to me and shoved my way out into the cool night air.

I stood, irresolute between anger and fear: anger at being stood up so callously and a gnawing fear that it was all a terrible misunderstanding and probably my fault. Not knowing was a pain like toothache seething through me and blurring my judgement. I had actually started to walk towards the main gate with the intention of going on to the WAAF quarters, before I realised how futile that would be. The only thing that could relieve the pain would be to find that she was, after all, on duty. I turned and made my way to the operations block. There'd been no ops that night and the place was almost deserted. I went quickly along the empty, humming corridors to the office where I knew she worked. The door was shut. I braced myself and opened it. A WAAF I'd never seen was sitting in Pearl's chair; she was the only one in the room.

'Oh, sorry,' I said, as casually as I could, and quickly shut the door before she could ask me what the hell I was doing there.

Now I knew for sure that I'd either been ditched or just simply forgotten, and the pain became an unrelieved misery. I walked slowly, looking down at my immaculately shined shoes following one another along the tarmac road towards the billet, until the thought of my welcome from the stay-at-homes in there brought me to a halt. I anticipated the relish with which little Percy, peering up from the entrails of his watches, would quiz me about why I was back so soon. I turned away towards the NAAFI and quickened my pace.

Sod the beautiful, exquisite, bloody bitch. I could enjoy myself without her, couldn't I?

This time I took off my coat and went straight to the bar. Harry and Brenda were still there, beginning to show signs of lechery towards each other. Harry endeared himself to me by not asking where I'd been or if I'd found Pearl, but ordering me a large drink and pushing it towards me. I gulped it down at a speed which in other circumstances would have drawn a round of applause. My empty stomach in no way impeded its journey to my brain, where after a few minutes it began its mercy mission, softening the edge of my misery. But not enough. I banged my empty glass on the counter and turned to Harry and Brenda.

'Want another?'

They glanced at each other. Harry said, 'Not now. We're just off.' Brenda slung her tunic over her arm and her bag over her shoulder. Harry leaned towards me. 'Presume you won't be using the key tonight?' he said quietly; more an order than a question.

I gave him an eloquent Bogartian shrug and exhaled smoke from my cigarette. 'Hardly.'

'OK . See you later.'

I watched him walk away, his stubby fingers on Brenda's shoulder, steering her between the dancers. I felt bitterly envious of the simplicity of Harry's sex life. I envied him in the way one envies a dog sleeping carelessly in a patch of sunlight, its mind undisturbed by the complexities of human existence. He knew what he wanted from Brenda and she knew what she wanted from him. They needed none of the frills of romantic love. Of course, when you came down to it, the truth was that she was no beauty. It was beauty that was the trouble. Why was it? What was it really? Like whoever it was said about Helen of Troy's nose. Such a little difference: an eighth of an inch here or there. But Christ, what it could do.

The thought of Pearl's beauty was like lead in my lungs. I pushed my glass across the counter.

'Same again?'

Nancy was behind the bar tonight. Her arms, bare above her elbows in her blue overall, gleamed as she pulled the pint. Now, she wasn't beautiful; no one would call her that. But she was attractive. In a directly sexual way, of course. Not obviously, but directly. I remembered Harry eulogizing her attractions once, though in a purely suppositional way. She had possibilities, was what he'd said: praise indeed from Harry. And yet she wasn't beautiful – which was very interesting. Of course, she had a good figure. You could see that, even under the overall. But her face would never launch ships. Perhaps it was her mouth? Her lips were full, with a sort of bruised look that was undeniably suggestive. By the time I was nearing the bottom of my glass I was in complete agreement with Harry; and I suppose with a good few others too – Nancy was never short of admirers. Nor, one heard, was she mean with her favours: as sexy as she looked, the word was. I drained the glass and looked across to where she was laughing with two airmen at the other end of the bar. Ah, but, I wondered, did she look like that because she was sexy? Or was she sexy because she looked like that? I wasn't too sure what I meant by that. I propped my elbows on the bar and tried to concentrate. What I thought I meant was, was she really sexy, or did we just assume she was because she made us feel sexy? I seemed unable get this any clearer. It was very confusing. But interesting. Life was interesting. Very, very interesting. And what was more the pain seemed to have receded: it was little more than a distant ache now. I began to feel an overwhelming desire to rejoin the human race. I called to Nancy.

She came down the bar at once, still laughing. Ever since I'd been in the show I'd always had flatteringly prompt service from Nancy. I think perhaps she harboured a secret ambition for the stage herself.

'Again? You got a thirst on, 'nt you?' And as she was filling the glass she said, 'Not dancing?'

'Nobody to dance with.'

'Oh, go on.' She put the full glass in front of me, and gave me a teasing smile.

'Would you like a drink, Nancy?'

'Not allowed, love.' She glanced at the clock. 'Tell you what. I'm off in a few minutes. You look after a gin and orange for me and I'll be round and drink it over your side.'

Five minutes later she had ducked under the bar and was beside me, reaching for her glass. The blue NAAFI overall had been discarded and she was wearing a flowered rayon dress that clung to her hips, giving her an infinite advantage over the unfortunate WAAFs in their shirts and ties. She gulped the drink and leaned back on the counter, watching the dancers. She was wriggling impatiently like a child at a party. When she'd emptied her glass she reached behind her and put it on the bar. 'Give us a dance,' she said abruptly, and pulled me onto the crowded floor.

We danced the next number, and the next. Then we had another drink, and then we danced again. Nancy was a committed dancer – committed to her partner. None of your fancy Victor Sylvester stuff: with her it didn't matter much what your feet were doing as long as the rest of you was having a good time. Her left arm was round my shoulder and her fingers on the nape of my neck and her hips never lost contact with mine even when I attempted a reverse. Under my right hand I could feel through the thin dress the beautiful long muscles of her back, flexing and unflexing as I steered her backwards through the crowd, her thighs sliding across mine. To dance with her was to be plunged into an instant intimacy – lovers for the duration of a foxtrot.

171

She was quite tall and her mouth was near my ear. 'Where's your little WAAF tonight, then?' she murmured.

'Dunno,' I said, as carelessly as I could.

She leaned back to look into my face for a moment. Then she smiled and squeezed me. 'Lucky us, then.'

The band played 'I'll Walk Alone', 'It Can't Be Wrong', 'I'll Get By' – plangent love songs, their lyrics wrestling with the moral anarchy of wartime. We danced them all. Dancing on concrete floors was never easy going, but with Nancy it was a good deal easier than with some of the potato-fed WAAFs that I'd squired in the past in their brass buttons and solid lace-ups. Only when we attempted a quick-step did Nancy's nightclub style make things difficult. When we'd spun to a halt I said – in all innocence, I swear – 'Hot, isn't it?'

She stood back, one hand still on my shoulder. Sweat gleamed in the hollow at the base of her throat. 'See you by the back door in a couple of minutes,' she said, and disappeared into the crowd.

Obviously, to those who knew the ritual, the exchanges one would have expected to follow – 'Yes, isn't it', 'Perhaps we should get some air', 'Perhaps we should' – were all superfluous. And I hadn't even meant *that*.

I found my greatcoat and made my way to the back of the building. The night was black as pitch but surprisingly warm for November. Alone in the dark I tried to think about Pearl, but drink and the memory of Nancy's body against mine made it difficult. A slit of light appeared and I heard Nancy's voice calling good-night to someone; then the light vanished. I whispered, 'Nancy?'

'Here,' came a whisper back. I put out a hand and went towards the voice. She found my hand and guided me to her side, by the wall. I put an arm round her waist and she turned to me, unresistingly. She was wearing a coat but hadn't bothered to button it.

172

'Wasn't long, was I?' she said.

'Hours.'

She laughed softly. Her lips were warm and her tongue was like a soft, busy ferret in my mouth. We stood a long time like that, leaning against the wall, her arms round my neck, my arms inside her coat. Over her shoulder I saw light spill from the door again. Two sets of footsteps clattered up the path to the main gate. As they passed us a girl's voice called, ' 'Night, Nancy!' followed by a gale of giggles. Nancy buried her nose in my coat collar to muffle her own laughter.

We could still hear the band playing, but people were beginning to leave. There was a crash of dustbin lids near us and a voice groaned, 'Ow, fuck!', then the sound of someone being sick. Nancy took my hand. 'Come on,' she said. Parallel to the side of the NAAFI block there was an air-raid shelter, a long grass mound with brick entrances at either end. I hoped she wasn't planning to go in there: it was flooded half the time and stank of urine. But she had a much better idea; she had run ahead and was clambering agilely up the grass sides and whispering for me to follow. Once on top we were a dozen or more feet above the ground, almost level with the NAAFI roof. Below us I could hear voices and see the gleam of torches, but if we lay down nobody would be able to see us.

As soon as I took off my greatcoat and spread it on the grass she sat down on it, and when I'd sat beside her she lay back and held out her arms.

'Not a bad idea, this,' I said.

'All right, isn't it?'

I wondered how often she'd been up here, and with whom, and if she was the only one who knew about it. I'd remember to glance up here next time I passed it in the evening. But just now the sensation of lying wrapped in this girl's arms, within a few feet of everyone, and yet as secret as in a locked and shuttered room, was too deliriously exciting to allow a thought of anything else. I kissed her mouth, her eyes, her ears, her throat. She let me unbutton her dress and cup the breasts that had been tantalizing me all night. Their roundness and firmness drove everything from my mind but the desire to have her, here and at once. When, at last, I dared to reach down and slip my hand under her skirt she murmured thickly, "'Ere, what are you up to?' but made no serious effort to stop me; and when, after another respectful pause, my hand found its way under the hem of her knickers, her mandatory groan of 'No!' was denied by the moist welcome my fingers found there. And then suddenly the rain began: or perhaps we'd not noticed it until then. But by the time we did, it was a steady downpour.

Nancy said, 'Bloody hell,' and sat up, nearly crippling me in my amorous condition. I staggered to my feet and helped her up. The rain had the ominous feel of being here to stay. We buttoned our coats and slid back down to earth. The dance was over now and the camp dark and quiet. We collected her bicycle from behind the NAAFI and, to prove I wasn't only after one thing, I walked her as far as No.3 Dispersal, where there was a gap in the wire and less far for her to ride to the village.

On my way back, the rain, running into my eyes and under my collar, completed the sobering process that had begun when it started to fall. As I came past the Guard Room on my way to the billet, I saw that the last bus from York had stopped outside the gates and a dozen or more people were getting out. I couldn't see who they were, it was much too dark, but for a moment I thought I'd heard the sound of Pearl's voice. But, of course, I hadn't. I couldn't have. And it was the beer I'd drunk that brought on the sudden wave of nausea.

15

It was still raining and still pitch-dark when I was woken the next morning by the scrape of matches and the acrid smell of sulphur and Woodbines. Above the shuffling and coughing that followed I could hear the rain drumming on the hut roof. I pulled the hairy blanket over my ears. I could smell scent on my hand and a darker odour of sex. Tears stung my eyes. I remembered the night before and, in this sober, shivering hour before dawn, I was stricken with self-pity and self-disgust. Pearl had failed me, or so I supposed; and then, without a moment's compunction, I had failed her. Without hesitation I had looked for the first solace I could find. Only the rain had saved me from being more ashamed this morning than I already was. Last night, cheated and frustrated, I had cursed it; now, in my hung over detumescence, it sounded, as it dripped from the eaves and swirled in the gutters, like the soft voice of circumspection.

All I wanted was to see Pearl: I was in an agony of suspense until I could find out what had happened. I dreaded knowing; but not knowing was worse. By breaktime the rain had at last stopped and I ran through the brimming puddles straight to the NAAFI. She wasn't there, of course. Not many people were.

The place had been swept and restored to normal, but the beer and smoke of the night before were still heavy in the air. There was no sign of Nancy, either, for which I was grateful.

As lunch-time approached I was getting desperate. As soon as the sergeants had disappeared I slipped away, leaving Alan in charge, and hurried towards the operations block. I hung around as unostentatiously as I could, for what seemed ages, never taking my eye off the entrance. At last she emerged with two other WAAFs and they walked off in the direction of the main gate. I caught her up.

'Pearl,' I said.

She turned. 'Oh . . . hello,' she said, apparently surprised to see me. She looked at me enquiringly, as if she had no idea what I might want with her.

'Can I talk to you?'

She hesitated and then to the other two who were waiting, all attention, she said, 'I'll catch you up.' When they were out of earshot she turned back to me. But before I could ask her the question I'd been phrasing and rephrasing all the morning, she suddenly said, with as severe an expression as those exquisite features would allow, 'And where were you last night?'

I was too astonished to answer.

'You never turned up,' she said, and then, with a tiny flicker of doubt, 'Did you?'

I was too distraught to notice the uncertainty. 'What d'you mean? Where?'

'By the WAAF gate.'

'But . . . we said we'd meet over here – at The Wings.'

'No.' She shook her head stubbornly. 'Down the WAAF site.'

Even if I was right, which I knew I was, it still seemed like my fault. 'Oh, Pearl, I'm sorry,' I said miserably. 'What a balls-up.'

She shrugged. 'Was a bit, wasn't it?'

'Pearl!' one of the girls called.

'Coming!' she answered; and then to me with a generous smile, 'Don't worry.'

'Listen—' I started to say.

'Must go,' she said quickly. 'See you soon.' And she ran after the other two.

All the way to the cookhouse I went over and over the arrangements we'd made; I couldn't think of a single phrase – word even – that could have given her such an idea. And here I was, still stretched on my rack of doubt, not even knowing when I'd see her again. It might be days before I got any sort of comfortable explanation. I queued up for a plate of fatty mutton, sodden cabbage and a floury potato. In my other hand I collected a plate of pallid duff, a neat cube, like a rubber sponge, standing in a puddle of watery jam. I took them over to a table and sat looking at them for a while. Then I went outside and scraped them into the pig swill.

I had no desire for any company but my own. I was the only companion I was fit for. Anxiety had so distracted me that I couldn't concentrate on anything. Fortunately, life with the sergeants was normally monosyllabic so my inattention wasn't noticed; but I dreaded the gossip in the billet or a tête-à-tête with Harry. So, as our theatre was operating that night as a cinema, my best hope of privacy would seem to be in the dark with everyone else.

Going to the pictures just for the sake of going can introduce one to some unlikely films. Whose decision it was to show this one on an RAF operational station I can't imagine, but it wasn't a wise choice. It concerned the fortunes of a Flying Fortress and its crew of Hollywood stars as they triumphed over adversity and the Japanese. It was greeted with groans at the sentimental heroics and roars of laughter at the wild technical inaccuracies: crews departing on missions with

177

no apparent briefing, engines never run up before take-off, and the bomber itself executing manoeuvres that would have pulled the wings off a Spitfire. I wondered if the Yanks in their airfields in East Anglia were as embarrassed by films like this as we were, and if anyone in Hollywood ever realized how unhelpful they were to the uneasy relations between their lot and ours.

When the Boeing had flown off into the sunset followed by the ironic cheers of the audience and the lights had come up, everyone began to stumble down the steeply raked rows to the exit, their belief in the inferiority of the US Air Force satisfyingly confirmed. In front of me were two WAAFs. I heard one of them say, 'You going into York tomorrow?'

'No,' said the other. 'We went last night.'

'Who's we?'

'Me and Vera – and Dixie and Kaye of course. Pearl was on the bus, but she went off with some sergeant. Joyce came, though.'

At that moment two large airmen moved out of a row and between me and the girls. I couldn't hear any more.

Of course, it might not have been her. There were probably other Pearls on the station I knew nothing about, although short of breaking into the orderly room and going through all the WAAFs' documents there was no way of being sure. I told myself that must be it. But I wasn't convinced.

I began to suffer a serious character deterioration. I mooched about, hands in pockets, and in a state of unrelieved apathy. The weather had turned very cold and I spent hours huddled over any stove I could find, reading or just daydreaming, my mind more and more fuddled by the coke fumes. I told the sergeants I was working in The Wings, and Harry that I was working in the section, and hid myself in any corner I could find. I spent hours in my lavatory in the operations block. It

178

was warm and dry; and there was always the chance I'd run into Pearl on my way in or out. But I never did.

She'd once mentioned that she rather liked the pub in the village, so I took to trudging over there in the evenings, along the lane between the dripping trees. A couple of times I took Alan with me: he wasn't interested in girls, or if he was he never talked about them. He didn't talk much anyway, and then it was usually about the mechanism of the gyrocompass, which was blissfully boring and allowed me to pursue my own thoughts undisturbed.

The pub was generally packed, particularly the public bar where other ranks were expected to confine themselves so as not to cause offence to the officers and NCOs in the private bar. One evening it must have been rather less full and we actually managed to get seats on the bench by the fire. Ops had been on for that night, but after briefing they'd been suddenly cancelled, probably by the met people as the weather did look rather unpromising. The crews still had to stand by, of course, in case the situation changed, which was no doubt why the pub was not so crowded, and also why I was surprised to see the fair-headed skipper of K-Kitty shouldering his way towards the private bar. He noticed me and gave a nod but pressed on into the other room. A minute later he reappeared and this time came straight over to Alan and me.

'Hello,' I said.

He bent down to my ear. 'Can I talk to you for a minute?'

Privately was obviously what he meant, and I wondered what the hell he could want to confide in me about: I hadn't exchanged a word with him since the night of a thousand landings. 'Sure,' I said, and left my pint on the bench in Alan's care.

He drew me to a corner of the bar and said in a low voice, 'Ops are on again. And Len's in there,' he indicated the other bar, 'pissed out of his skull.'

179

'Christ,' was all I could say.

'I've got to get him into the kite without anyone finding out. Can you give me a hand with him?'

'Oh. Right,' I said.

At first glance the little rear gunner appeared perfectly normal. He was sitting at a table in the corner with several empty shorts glasses in front of him. He was still in his flying boots and polo-necked sweater, but not the rest of his gear. He looked up at Alex and took a moment getting him in focus.

''Lo, Skipper,' he said cheerfully. 'Back again?' Alex leaned over him and said quietly, 'Come on, Len. Time we were going.'

'Going? Going where?'

'Ops. Take-off's twenty-thirty.'

'No,' Len said. And with the quiet reasonableness of the serious drunk, added, 'I really don't want to go.'

'Come on, Len,' Alex said, taking his arm.

Len shook himself free. 'No . . . don't want to go. S'too fucking far.' His voice rose in protest. 'Fucking Bremen!'

Alex grabbed him and we both looked round quickly. Announcing tonight's target to a crowded public house probably qualified Len for the firing squad. Luckily no one seemed to have heard.

'S'too bloody far, you know. And it's too fucking cold.' Len's voice sank to a whisper. 'I'm staying here . . . like it here.' He looked up at us again, and suddenly a happy smile spread across his face. 'You fellers have a drink?'

Alex said fiercely, 'Come on, you stupid bugger.'

We grabbed an arm each and got him on his feet. He peered into my face. 'Who's 'is?' he said. Then he shook his head solemnly. 'Not going, you know.'

I saw an officer at the bar eyeing me, looking a bit askance at this erk who appeared to be arm-in-arm with a sergeant air gunner. I gave the officer a reassuring smile, at which he

180

turned away and, I'm almost certain, tossed his head.

We got Len outside and started to frogmarch him back to camp. We hoped that the night air might sober him up a bit but it seemed to make no impression at all. Alex said it might be better if he could bring his grog up and suggested the fingers-down-the-throat technique. I didn't much fancy that job and allowed Alex to exercise his seniority by doing it himself. But it wasn't any good, Len seemed determined to hang on to his surfeit of alcohol. At one point he announced that he wanted to piss, so we propped him against a tree and stepped back cautiously while he sprayed an unsteady stream all round him.

I asked Alex tentatively if he thought it was really a very good idea, Len flying in his condition.

'He's got to, hasn't he?'

'He could go sick.'

'Sick! Are you kidding? That's drunk on duty, isn't it? Or LMF, which is worse.'

I knew what he meant. Lack of Moral Fibre was the most hideous stigma the RAF could attach to you. Aircrews lived in constant fear of it. All too often some poor bastard would give way under the strain of living day after day with the terror of death; and then, unless some kindly psychiatrist had him shoved in the bin, his documents would be stamped LMF. After that he'd be stripped of his rank and aircrew status and probably remustered as Aircraftman Second-Class General Duties, which was an elaborate title for a shithouse cleaner. There'd been one on the camp where I'd done my square-bashing: a little pale fellow who never spoke to anyone. We all knew, though, because you could still see the pale shape on his tunic where his wings had been. I remembered someone saying that there are only two things a man can't stand having said about him: that he has a tiny prick, or that he's a coward.

Nevertheless, I felt I should have pointed out to Alex that

he and his crew were putting all their lives at risk for the sake of one man's reputation, but I knew it would be useless; aircrew loyalty, forged in the heat of battle and the ice of fear, made any other solution unacceptable. So we staggered along the puddle-pocked lane towards the airfield; Len, his arms round our necks, slung between us like a wounded comrade.

The plan was to get onto the airfield through a gap in the wire, smuggle Len round to K–Kitty and get him aboard ahead of the others. Getting him on board was the tricky part. There were a couple of fitters doing something on the starboard wing who took no notice of us, but it was heaving him up through the hatch that nearly defeated us. When we'd at last managed it, it was already time for Alex to get back to collect his gear and Len's and join the others on the transport. Len was stretched out in the rest position, snoring.

'If he wakes up, see if you can get him into the turret,' Alex said, and slid out onto the tarmac.

I sat opposite Len in the darkness, listening to his snores, remembering the last time I'd sat here with him, circling the airfield, stiff with cold and fright. And I thought of them tonight, alone in this fragile machine, high over Germany with their rear gunner probably asleep over his guns, a sitting target for every night fighter in the sky. Their chances of survival weren't worth a lot at the best of times, but tonight I wouldn't give tuppence for them. I knew what I ought to do. I ought to go straight to the Flight Office and tell the duty officer that K–Kitty's rear gunner was too drunk to fly. That's what their fathers and mothers, wives and kids (if they had any) would want me to do: save their lives, if only for one more night. That's what I should do. But I knew perfectly well I wouldn't. The idea was unthinkable. Not only the crew of K–Kitty, but the whole camp, would despise me to a man. And I knew I hadn't got that sort of courage. And that, I supposed, was how wars got themselves fought.

I sat in the dark, dying for a cigarette, but that was forbidden, and anyway the bowsers had not long been gone, leaving the air heavy with the reek of high-octane petrol. The plane lurched as someone climbed aboard and groped past us in the direction of the cockpit. The lights came on and as he came back I could see in the dim glow that it was one of the ground crew. He fell over Len's outstretched leg and called, 'Sorry, mate,' as he disappeared into the darkness.

That brought Len round. He sat up groggily and peered across at me.

'Who's zat?'

'Me . . . er, Sam.'

'Oh? Oh . . . yeah.' He seemed to remember where he was and how he'd got there. 'Where's the Skipper?'

'He'll be back in a minute.'

There was a long silence and then he said, 'I jus' nipped down for a quick one, thass all. Jus' the one.' He paused. 'But I'm OK, you know. I'm OK.' He stood up suddenly and hit his head on a strut. He subsided again. 'Oh, fuck,' he said and rubbed his head.

I wondered if I ought to suggest getting into the turret but decided I couldn't cope with him on my own.

He leaned forward and pointed a wavering finger at me. 'They said it was scrubbed, din' they. Din' they?' His voice rose. 'So what the fuck're we doin' in 'ere?' He looked round suspiciously. 'And where's the others?'

'They're coming.'

'Ah.' He nodded solemnly. 'I expec', you see,' he said, suddenly confidential, 'the Skipper's gone to find her.'

'Who?'

He leaned so far towards me I was afraid he'd fall off the bench. 'Skipper's very super . . . superstitious, you know. I s'pose we all are.' He fumbled in his breast pocket and pulled out a large medallion which he thrust under my nose. It was a rather beautiful St Christopher. 'My Auntie Kath give me that. Solid gold it is. Never fly without it.' He put it back in his pocket. 'And the Skipper 'as to see this little WAAF before take-off, you see, or it's bad luck. Greg says . . .' He giggled. 'Greg says, he ought to give her one . . . so's we'd be sure to be OK. But Fred said then he'd be too shagged to get us off the ground.' He laughed a good deal at this.

'Who is she?' I said.

He stopped laughing. 'Who?'

'The WAAF.'

'Oh, she . . . she's a gorgeous little thing . . . really gorgeous. Dark hair, she's got . . . and beautiful blue eyes. You mussa seen her . . . in the ops block . . . she's gorgeous. I tell you what . . .'

I was cold with fear. 'What's her name?'

'Name? Name . . .' He frowned. 'I know her name . . .'

At that moment the transport roared up with a screech of brakes and feet clattered across the tarmac. Alex hoisted himself in through the hatch, followed by Greg, the navigator.

'Here y'are, Len,' Alex called. 'Here's your gear.'

As the rest of them climbed in, Greg and the mid-upper gunner heaved Len to his feet and started to get him into his parachute harness.

Alex put his hand on my shoulder. 'Is he OK?'

I shrugged and nodded.

'Thanks a lot, kid,' he said. 'You'd better scarper now, if you don't want a free trip to Bremen.'

As I dropped out of the hatch I could hear Len shouting. 'It's too bleedin' far, I'm tellin' yer. And it's too fuckin' cold.'

The air was filled with the roar of engines from all round the field. Puddles reflected the runway lights, but the clouds had gone and the stars were bright and sharp. As I watched I could just see a dim shape being bundled into the rear turret. The engines started up and I stepped back out of the slip-

184

stream. I waited until the accs were disconnected and the chocks pulled away and the huge plane rumbled out to join the thundering queue edging round the perimeter track. I lost count of the take-offs, so I didn't know which one was K-Kitty, but I waited until they'd all gone, my hands in my pockets, shivering in the cold night air. Then I walked slowly back round the empty field.

I lost count again, at three in the morning, when they started to return. I'd been half-awake all night, tense with the confusion in my mind. I was sick with jealousy and hatred of Alex. I knew I had no concrete reason to be, but since when had reason anything to do with jealousy. I was well aware that the only cure for me would be if K-Kitty didn't come back. But I'd just helped to make that a likelihood: I would be a sort of murderer. I didn't know what to pray for. I was desperate for some outcome or other, I knew. I suppose it was not so much that they should get back safely, as that I should *want* them to.

In the morning I was out of bed as soon as the hut lights were switched on. The airmen who'd been on night duty were still huddled in their blankets, so I grabbed my washbag and towel and dived through the icy darkness to the ablutions. Inside there were clouds of steam and a cacophony of tin bowls and groaning pipes. I filled a bowl with water, which at this hour was still miraculously hot, and found a place, standing on a slimy duck-board in a lake of soapy water. Across from me were several wireless-ops who had obviously just come off duty. I called through the steam and the cavernous clatter.

'All back last night, were they?'

'Yeah, I think so.' One turned to the other. 'All back, weren't they, Jock?'

'Aye, every one. Nae a scratch on 'em.'

My moral confusion must have resolved itself in my sleep,

185

for I felt an instant flood of relief. Of course, by the time I'd collected my mug and irons and was on my way to the cook-house, the knives of jealousy were turning in my stomach again. But in the cold light of the dawn which was at last breaking, I was able to persuade myself that my fears were probably imaginary.

I was spreading some transparent marmalade on my snow-white square of bread – which was all I could face so early in the morning – when someone slid along the bench towards me and a plate loaded with sausages, bubble-and-squeak and powdered egg landed next to mine.

'Morning, Brian,' I said, rather proud to be seen at break-fast at such a spartan hour. Brian was in the show, in a minor capacity, and only because he was the boyfriend of Vera Piper, the skinny dancer with the buck teeth. He was a hearty, rather dull young man; but he was also a corporal medical orderly and wonderfully indiscreet about who on the camp had got piles or the clap, or both.

I drained my mug and went to refill it at the tea urn. When I got back Brian said, 'You want to go easy on that stuff, or you'll finish up like your Sgt Grice.'

'What's up with him?'

'Tannin depression.'

'What's that?'

'Depression from drinking too much tea, the MO says.'

'You're kidding.'

'Well he drinks a lot of tea, doesn't he?'

'Never stops.'

'And he's pretty depressed?'

'Suicidal, from the look of him.'

'Well, there you are. The MO says it's quite common.'

'I don't believe it.'

'Listen, we see funnier things than that down at sick quar-ters.' He pushed his empty plate away and picked a slice of bread off the stack he'd brought from the counter. 'Last night, for instance. They brought this aircrew bloke in from ops; not a mark on him – dead as a doornail. Seems he'd thrown up in his oxygen mask and it had frozen and blocked the supply. He was in the rear turret so no one noticed. Silly way to go, though.'

I asked him which crew it had been. But, of course, I already knew the answer.

16

Where moral fibre was concerned it began to seem as if my own wasn't up to much. Twice in the next few days I behaved like an arrant coward. The first time was when I saw Alex walking towards me from the direction of the sergeants' mess. He was a hundred yards away and alone; and I dived between two huts and hid. I knew I wouldn't be able to look him in the eyes: I dreaded what we would have to say to each other – co-conspirators in Len's death. So I pressed myself against the wall like a fugitive in a cowboy film and watched him walk by. His head was down and I wondered if I was imagining that his face looked paler and more drawn than I'd seen it before. Was he weighed down by what had happened? Did he have dreams like the one I'd had the night before of Len drowning alone in a sea of vomit? Or to him and the crew was it just another death among so many, just someone to be replaced and swiftly forgotten? Or was he simply grateful that the rest of them had survived?

My next act of cowardice was with Pearl. We met again, at last, at a rehearsal. After two weeks without a performance Harry had decided to see how much we remembered before our next date. She was late, of course. I was sitting at the back watching Harry and Ernie racing through the words of a sketch when she came sidling gracefully along the row and sat down beside me.

She slipped an arm through mine and whispered, 'Hello, stranger.'

'Hello,' I said.

She squeezed my arm. 'Miss me?' she said softly.

'You bet,' I said. Which was true, but craven.

No mention was made of the last time we'd met. Or hadn't met. Not on that evening or any other evening. She was as light-hearted, as teasing and as affectionate as she'd always been. And, of course, as dazzlingly beautiful as ever. And I couldn't – didn't dare to – say what I so much wanted to; or ask the questions that had been torturing me for so long. Where *were* you that night? You were seen, you know. Who was he? Do you see him all the time? When you're not with me, is it him you think of? Are you like this with him, too? Or more? Do you give him more? More of yourself? But here she was beside me again, her small pale, coral-tipped hand in mine, and I drove all thoughts of him, and what he might do with her, out of my mind. I looked into those candid blue eyes, blameless as a Mediterranean sky, and I dismissed him, or the likelihood of him, from my life. Without a little self-deception life is unbearable. And with too much it is, too.

Restored once more to the land of the living, I could give up skulking in corners and devote myself to designing a set for *Ten-Minute Alibi* which was Harry and Father's choice for the next offering. The last performance of our 'musical extravaganza', as it was described on the posters, was due in mid-December, but at the last minute we were told that 'by special request' there was to be one more date, just before Christmas.

190

Harry was in a fury, as with great difficulty he had wangled himself ten days' leave over Christmas.

'I thought you didn't like going on leave.'

'I don't,' he said. 'But the wife's kicking up.'

'You could postpone it.'

'I'll have to. But getting leave at Christmas scores me more marks, you see. And I've already told her I'm coming, so she'll have organized all the relatives. They'll all be sitting round waiting for me to come down the chimney like Santa bloody Claus.'

I knew very little about Harry's home life: he rarely talked about it. I knew he'd been married for about eight years and that there were no children. Her family owned a dairy, and from what I gathered, she'd made Harry give up the theatre and work for her father. The old boy had started him off on a milk round. I must say, knowing Harry's predilections, the idea of him as a milkman seemed richly appropriate. Of course, he'd finished up as some sort of branch manager, but I don't think anything could compensate him for the loss of his beloved theatre. God knows how she'd done it, but I once caught a glimpse of her photograph in Harry's wallet, and she did have a pretty steely look about her.

'What is this special request, anyway? Where are we going?'

'The Free French place. They're having a big night apparently.'

This was a nearby airfield that had been taken over a few months before by a squadron of the French Air Force from North Africa. It was entirely manned by French, even down to the cooks, so rumour had it. Rumour also had it that there was wine with every meal, but all that most people knew about the camp was that, there being no French WAAFs, ours had to be ferried over there in busloads every time they had a dance. Volunteers, one could only hope.

'Do they have a theatre?' I asked.

'Of sorts, apparently. Of course, they won't understand a word. It'll be the bloody Poles all over again.'

We'd been stunned one night to have all the sketches received in stony silence. It was only afterwards we'd discovered our audience was entirely Polish.

'And what are they going to think of the French number?' I said apprehensively.

'Christ knows. They'll probably tear the place apart.'

But we were wrong. It was we who brought the house down. They hadn't had much in the way of entertainment, not being on ENSA's itinerary and French movies being in short supply, so we were greeted with wild enthusiasm. Particularly the French number; they seemed to take it as a personal compliment (perhaps they thought we'd knocked it up just for them) and cheered each item to the echo – even Danny's shaky rendering of 'Louise'. By the curtain call we were nearly as emotional as they were and sang the 'Marseillaise', which the band had mugged up that morning, so lustily that we reduced ourselves to tears. But, of course, the 'Marseillaise' could make a Warrant-Officer cry.

And afterwards rumour was triumphantly vindicated. The food was succulent in a way we'd forgotten was possible (if we'd ever known) and everywhere you looked there were indeed great jugs of red wine. It was a pretty rough Algerian, but it was *wine*, and the more cosmopolitan among us raised our glasses to the entente cordiale and tipped incautious amounts of it down our unaccustomed throats. As a result we rapidly caught up with our hosts in conviviality, and one or two of us overtook them. England was not a wine-drinking country and I'd rarely had more than one glass at a time. Now, after rather more than one, I was vaguely aware that I was becoming dangerously amiable. The only cure for that seemed to be more wine, so I held out my glass for a refill.

Pearl was enjoying her share too. Her colour was a good

deal higher than usual and her eyes more brilliant, which of course only made her more ravishing than ever. The French airmen had seen nothing like her for a very long time and crowded round her like starving wolves round a doe. I think even she, so used to male homage, was a little alarmed by their naked hunger, and whenever she was dragged away to dance she returned firmly to my side.

As her partner I was the centre of a very different sort of attention, part respect and part envy. I attempted to air the little I remembered of my fifth-form French, which at once provoked an incomprehensible stream of slang and colloquialisms bearing no resemblance to anything I'd ever heard in the classroom. Some of their English was a lot better than my French, so I managed to discover that the squadron was non-operational this week while they converted to a new mark of Halifax, and so they'd grabbed the opportunity to celebrate Christmas and especially the Liberation. With the Germans all but out of their country they were confidently expecting to be back there in the New Year.

'*On va bientôt rentrer au pays,*' said one of them emotionally, raising his glass. '*Ça s'arrose, pas vrai?*'

But first, what was really occupying them this evening, was women. Here in England they had taken to playing up to the popular conception that all Frenchmen were expert and passionate lovers. This idea, dating probably from the Second Empire, was firmly planted in Anglo-Saxon minds and confirmed by every sighting of Maurice Chevalier or Charles Boyer. Our imported WAAFs certainly subscribed to it. They were enraptured by these exotic young men with their dark-blue uniforms and their dark-brown eyes, kissing their hands and murmuring passionate things that, mercifully, they couldn't understand a word of.

My companions at the bar were more direct. The English, I was told, knew nothing of making love. They should learn from the French who understood it all, from the cradle apparently. My instructors became increasingly excited and wine was spilled everywhere as graphic practical advice was offered. At this point Pearl returned again, looking very pink, with a thickset Frenchman in hot pursuit. I held out her glass which I'd been guarding. She took a gulp and handed it back.

'Come on,' she said. 'Come and dance with me.'

'Right,' I said, nothing loath.

The thickset Frenchman barred our way. '*Non. C'est mon tour*,' he said abruptly and took Pearl's arm.

'Now, hang on,' I said.

He turned a very nasty glare in my direction. '*Écrase! Fiche le camp, petit merdeux!*'

Oh God, I thought, a confrontation.

Pearl withdrew her arm from him in a sublimely aristocratic gesture: firm, but giving no offence. 'I beg your pardon,' she said carefully, and I suspected she might be a little less sober than she looked. 'You've 'ad lots of goes, and so now I'm going to dance' – she turned to me with a radiant smile – 'with my fiancé.'

In spite of her rhyming it with finance the word was instantly recognized and stopped them in their tracks. My sex instructor said, 'You shall be married?'

'Er . . . yes,' Pearl said.

'*Ça y est*,' he said delightedly. 'When?'

'Oh,' she said coyly, but without a moment's hesitation, 'we 'aven't got *that* far yet. We've only just got engaged, 'aven't we?' She turned to me fondly.

Her insouciance was so infectious and the idea of being her betrothed so heady that I found no difficulty in saying, with a suitably bashful grin, 'This morning, actually.'

'*Ce matin!*' exclaimed my friend, and turned to the others. '*Ça alors – chapeau!*'

They all cheered except the thickset one, who muttered something obviously unpleasant.

'*La ferme, Jean,*' said the other. '*Tu piges pas? Ils se sont fiancés ce matin même.*'

'*Alors, va-t-en, t'es con ou quoi?*' someone called.

Jean growled something that sounded like '*Va te faire foutre,*' and strode off in a sulk.

There were a lot of handshakes and *félicitations* and refilled glasses. Then Pearl grabbed my hand and said again, 'Come on'. A path was opened for us onto the dance floor. The band was playing a slow waltz and she put her arms round my neck and her warm cheek against mine and whispered, 'Cor, thanks for rescuing me.'

I was under the impression that it was she who'd rescued me, but I just giggled and murmured, 'Lucky no one wanted to see the ring.'

'S'all right,' she said, 'I swapped it over while they was talking.' She wiggled her left hand briefly in front of my eyes and I caught sight of a thin gold band and a tiny eponymous pearl. I laughed and held her tightly and we danced across the concrete as if it were the glittering black expanse of a Hollywood musical. The wine had gone to our heads, and most of the other parts of our bodies, and we were warmly secure in the conviction that we were creatures of superhuman grace and style. And if the Astaire and Rogers of the East Riding did sometimes stumble or bump into other couples, for me the illusion was indestructible because, as well as being disgracefully drunk, I was as absurdly and hilariously happy as I'd ever been in my life.

And that was about the last moment of that night that I could remember afterwards with any degree of clarity.

The next morning I lay under my blankets, only able to groan, while the rest of the hut stamped and shouted and crashed around me until all I wanted was to die. When at last they'd all gone I slipped back into an aching coma, and it wasn't until after ten that I felt strong enough to stagger out of bed, to find that I was still in my shirt and socks and my uniform was in a heap on the floor. I managed to make myself presentable in time for NAAFI break and tottered over there in the hope that a cup of tea with a lot of sugar might bring me back from the brink.

The place was quite full and I got an unusual number of smiles and waves as I made my way to the counter. I thought I heard someone say 'Congratulations' as I passed but I felt too frail to stop and ask him what for. I saw Alan sitting by himself, so I took my tea over and joined him. The cup rattled in the saucer as I put it down.

'Hello,' he said. 'How'd it go last night?'

'OK.'

'I hear congratulations are in order.'

'What?' I said, spooning sugar into my cup.

'You got engaged, didn't you?'

I looked up. The wire round my head tightened like a tourniquet. 'Who says?'

'Well . . . everybody. Actually, I think it was Percy mentioned it.'

'Percy! Oh, Christ . . . that means the whole camp. Where did he get it from?'

'I don't know. Isn't it true, then?'

'Ah . . . not entirely.' My tea was like syrup and tasted disgusting.

Alan said, 'Oh,' quietly, and looked embarrassed.

'I think it's a sort of misunderstanding,' I said to console him. I felt even sicker than when I'd woken up: it had just dawned on me that I couldn't remember getting back to camp last night or even leaving the party. 'I think', I said, pushing the cup away, 'I'd better get this sorted out.' I made for the door, ignoring the winks and thumbs-up from well-wishers, and headed for The Wings.

Harry was at the table in front of the window, cutting pages out of a copy of *Ten-Minute Alibi* and pasting them into a big exercise book. There was a lingering smell of what I recognized as Brenda's scent, and I noticed that, on our recently acquired camp bed, the 'biscuits' (three square sections of mattress) had been stacked at one end with ostentatious neatness.

'Harry,' I said, 'what happened last night?'

'Show went well,' he said, smoothing a page with his handkerchief.

'I mean after that.'

'We got pissed. Well, you certainly did.'

'Yes, but . . . ah . . .' I didn't know how to broach this, not to a man for whom getting engaged was on a par with morris dancing. 'There seems to be an impression going around that I'm . . . engaged.'

'Really? Can't say I'm surprised.'

Harry, too. 'Why?'

He looked at me with amusement. 'Don't you remember?'

'Well, Pearl did tell this French bloke that we were, just to get rid of him. But . . .'

'But you made an announcement, didn't you.'

'I *what*?'

'You got up on a table and made a speech. Very moving it was, too.'

'Oh, Christ, no.' My insides, already in trouble, recoiled in horror. 'What's Pearl going to say.'

'Shouldn't worry. She was on the table with you.' He gave me his wolfish smile. 'She probably won't remember, either.'

But she did. I'd managed to get a note to her, suggesting we met at the pub and, amazingly, she got there just after I did. I was stricken with embarrassment at first, and so was she: but then we caught each other's eyes and both started to giggle.

The unfair thing was that while I still felt like the walking dead, she was as fresh as a daisy, her eyes sparkling, her hair, even in its regulation roll, soft and gleaming. I bought us drinks, extra-large for me as a kill-or-cure hair of the dog, and we took them into the darkest corner we could find for a council of war.

'You were a bit far gone last night,' she said.

'I know,' I said shamefacedly. 'I'm sorry.'

'S'OK. So was I.'

'I'm afraid I made a bit of a fool of myself . . . and of you, too.'

'Don't worry. I've told everyone it was only a joke – we was just pissed.'

For an instant, quite foolishly, it felt like the sting of a slap where one had expected – what? That she'd meant it? Surely not. Dear God, I should hope not. I took a deep breath and another gulp of my drink, which was beginning to make me feel better at last. 'I've done the same,' I said.

There was a silence between us. Her delicate hand moved her glass slowly across the table until it was touching mine. Still looking down at it, she said, 'That was awfully nice, what you said last night.'

'When?'

'When you made that speech.'

Suddenly she lifted her head and looked straight at me. Her beauty, when it stared me in the face like that, always took my breath away; but now, wiped clean, as I'd never seen it before, of any trace of pretence or caution or mockery, it sang in my veins and in my head, drowning every other thought than that I would steal for her, lie for her, die for her, just to have her go on looking at me like that.

But what *was* it I'd said last night?

I was never going to know, was I.

★

Nevertheless, whatever it was, it seemed to have initiated a new phase in our relationship. Perhaps it was just the Christmas spirit, but she was unusually tender and undemanding and seemed to want nothing more than to be in my company. Not that being in my company was all that easy to arrange. The promotion of the war made no concessions to the Season of Goodwill; flying seemed to be going on day and night. Admittedly there were no operations on Christmas Day, but we suspected this was due more to the weather than any resurgence of the football-in-no-man's-land impulse. Anyway, the quaint rituals of the RAF served to segregate us for most of the day; one of these being that the airmen had their Christmas Dinner served to them by their officers. This created an atmosphere of such false jocularity and embarrassment that it almost put one off one's turkey and plum pudding. Was Pearl at this very moment, I wondered, being offered another helping of custard by our commissioned chorine, Flight Officer Cross? The whole business was a perfectly contrived reminder of the subservience expected from us for the other three hundred and sixty-four days. After the dinner there was a lot of organized jollity and it wasn't until the next day that Pearl and I were alone long enough for me to present her with the tortoiseshell cigarette case with a silver 'P' on it and her to give me a record of 'Rhapsody in Blue' by the Paul Whiteman Orchestra.

That evening an ENSA show managed to reach us through the icy fog that had blanketed the airfield, and she and I, together with Harry, Brenda, Terry and Danny, went along, as amateurs are fond of doing, to criticize the professionals. We may have gone to mock, but we stayed to pity. The station theatre was freezing and the little troupe, particularly the girls in their skimpy satin costumes, were blue with cold. The casts of ENSA shows were usually under eighteen or over fifty, but the conjuror in this one seemed unlikely to see seventy again. His poor arthritic hands shook so much with the cold that the empty boxes he proudly displayed to us could be heard rattling with their concealed surprises. A swarthy contralto in black velvet was racked with bronchitis, and the girl with the piano-accordion was so tiny that her instrument threatened to topple her onto her face at any moment. Her bare arms were thin as matchsticks, and with her left hand she kept grabbing at the enormous accordion as it slid from her narrow chest towards her knees, while the frozen fingers of her right tried frantically to keep up with the demands of the 'Sabre Dance'. As I watched their exhausted attempts to entertain a sparse and apathetic audience, and I thought of the grisly lodgings and rationed meals they'd be going back to, I was astonished at their lunatic devotion to their cruel profession.

It was a depressing evening, and when we'd finished off a few light ales in The Wings and listened to 'Rhapsody in Blue' half a dozen times, we all gave up and decided to head for our beds. I offered to walk Pearl over to the WAAF site, but she was going to the sergeants' quarters – to get a lift, she said, from the cooks who'd be coming off duty. She didn't seem to want to be escorted there either, so I kissed her freezing cheek, pulled the collar of her greatcoat up over her ears for her, and waved her goodnight.

The next morning the fog had gone, swept away by an icy north wind that was to blow cruelly for the rest of the week. The cold gripped us as if trying to squeeze the life from our veins. Anything that could freeze froze: the pipes in the ablutions, the milk in the cookhouse, Percy's teeth in the mug beside his bed. You could have skated, if you'd felt so inclined, on the static water tanks, and damp boots discarded at bedtime were solid blocks the next morning and had to be prised off the hut floor. Everyone developed a roly-poly look from wearing two lots of underwear and several sweaters at the same time; except, inevitably, Pearl, who had acquired a chunky aircrew roll-neck and managed to look adorably cuddly in it, its bulkiness giving her that deliciously *louche* look that certain men's garments give to certain girls.

In spite of having to take off and land on runways like ice rinks, operations went on, culminating in a massive raid on Cologne on Saturday night when the stars, brilliant in the icy sky, were almost obliterated by the shadows of hundreds of bombers from all the airfields in Yorkshire as they rumbled and roared over our heads on their way to the coast. Our planes all returned safely that night, and we woke on the last day of the year to find that the wind had dropped and snow was falling thickly and silently over the camp. The snow-ploughs tried to clear the runways, but it was falling faster than they could shift it, and by lunch-time the squadron was stood down until the next day.

Pearl had wanted to see in the New Year at the pub in the village, but I'd persuaded her to come to the celebrations in the NAAFI as I had other plans for the early hours of 1st January. Harry had at last gone on leave and the key of The Wings was mine, and mine alone. I had filled the coal bin to overflowing with the best stuff I could steal, and torn two old blankets into strips to stuff in all the draughty crevices. I'd spent my last few bob on a bottle of gin and a bottle of Kia-Ora orange squash, and was ready for an intensely romantic evening.

We drank quite a lot in the NAAFI, and danced quite a lot too; and at midnight we all yelled with joy and kissed the girls fervently. This New Year's Eve, for the first time, there was a feeling that perhaps, just *perhaps*, by the next one it would all be over and we'd be released from purgatory. I managed to kiss Pearl several times, in between others, and then we all sang 'Auld Lang Syne' and embraced each other again, and when the Scots took over, as they always do on these occasions, instigating all manner of reels and square dances, I whispered to Pearl, 'Come on, let's start the year our own way.' Rather to my surprise she agreed at once.

201

The top layer of snow crackled under our feet as we made for The Wings. Inside, I was relieved to find, it was as warm as anywhere on that bleak encampment. I topped up the stove and opened the bottom flap until it roared like a blast furnace. I could scarcely breathe with the excitement of what might happen. As I turned the big iron key to lock us in and the world out, I felt like Bluebeard, and expected at any second to hear what I'd so often heard from her before: 'Here! What're you up to?'

But nothing happened. When I turned from the door she had taken off her greatcoat and was sitting in one of the armchairs, leaning forward to warm her hands at the stove. My preparations for tonight had included reducing the lighting to one table lamp, draped with a red silk square I'd found in a basket. The dim ruby light was kinder to the inside of this tin hut, and quite unnecessarily benevolent to Pearl. Only a single ray of pale light, escaping from the silk, fell across the perfection of her cheek and lit a deep magenta glitter in her eyes. She gave me a wickedly conspiratorial smile that ran like brandy in my arteries. I laughed with relief, and she laughed back. I showed her the bottle of gin and the bottle of squash and she laughed again and said, 'Yes, please.'

We sat side by side and drank our gin and orange. It was her favourite, I knew. It wasn't mine, but I drank it, because I wanted our mouths to taste the same. And when, after a while, she put her glass down and sat in my lap and her mouth opened on mine, our tongues found no other alien flavours, only the secret taste of each other. It was warm enough now to take off our tunics. I poured some more gin and put a record on the gramophone, stuffing two old paint rags into the horn to muffle the noise. She held out her arms and we danced, clasped in each other's arms, shuffling round that tiny space, kissing as we went. In fact it wasn't dancing at all, more what the drill manual might describe as Kissing On The

Move. As we bumped into boxes and benches I felt her lips smile, and when we reached the bed I swayed and sat down on it, pulling her after me. Whatever I attempted met with no resistance and, dizzy with gratitude, I grew bolder; but the narrow iron frame of that bed was designed for single airmen, and thin ones at that. I stood up. She looked up at me with wide, unfathomable eyes, her hair falling across her forehead, her lipstick blurring the outline of her mouth. Without daring to speak I took the biscuits, one by one, and laid them on the floor. Also without a word she stood up and started to unbutton her skirt. The stove was red-hot now, and the top and sides of it glowed in the dim light as brightly as the shrouded lamp. It gleamed on her narrow thighs as she slid the skirt down to her ankles and stepped out of it. She sat on the mattresses, and while I struggled out of my trousers and shoes, she pulled her shirt over her head and undid her bra. Then she lay back and looked at me. It was an odd look: a smile, welcoming enough but uncertain, almost apprehensive, completely unlike her. I knelt beside her, ready to gather the most longed-for prize of my life, and as I looked down at her my desire began to ebb away.

I loved her, I wanted her, she was the most exquisite creature I'd ever seen, but, nearly naked as she was, she suddenly seemed to me like a child. She was so beautiful, so graceful and slim, but somehow the slimness had become skinniness, the body I had coveted for so long appeared almost meagre, pale and unfledged in the dim light, as she lay supine and still as if ready for some expected violation. In her smudged make-up and black suspenders she might have just raided her mother's wardrobe. A paedophile's idea of heaven I supposed, but not mine.

I lay beside her and caressed her and told her how I loved her, and told myself how miraculously lucky I was, but it was no use, her passivity undid me. Perhaps if her hands had been more inventive, done more than stroke my hair or trace my spine, perhaps if they'd even been warmer, she might have kindled a fire in both our loins, but neither of us was experienced enough to provoke that in each other or in ourselves.

Eventually she whispered, 'What is it? Is it me?'

'No, no,' I lied valiantly. 'I'm sorry . . . I'm so sorry.'

'It's all right,' she said. 'Really it is. It doesn't matter, honestly.' And her fingers brushed my cheek.

After a while she murmured hesitantly, 'I'm a bit cold.'

We dressed wordlessly, not looking at one another. I wanted to run a thousand miles away and be alone with my shameful unmanliness, but to leave her now would surely be even less manly; and dimly I suspected that she was feeling as much of a failure as I was, although why she should I couldn't really imagine. So I stoked the fire and made us cocoa and we talked determinedly about anything except what had just happened. Back in our clothes the shell of confidence we showed to the world began to grow again. Her imperious little shrug returned, and I was able to mask my humiliation with a few fragile witticisms. But when I'd left her at the WAAF gate and I was plodding back through the snow towards the silent camp, I knew by the stone I was carrying in my heart, that tonight wouldn't just go away – it would always be there, shadowing our future. If any future was on offer, of course.

Later that same day the war resumed in earnest. Operations were announced at lunch-time and a largely hungover squadron set about putting them into action. It was a massive effort and planes seemed to be coming and going all night. Two of them, S-Sugar and Alex's crew in K-Kitty, were early returns, landing before midnight after turning back over the sea with mechanical troubles. About two in the morning the entire camp was rocked by an almighty bang which proved to be G-George overshooting the runway, wiping the roof off a farmhouse and landing in the fields beyond. The crew got out alive and so did the farmer and his wife, although it seemed that her aged mother in the attic hadn't. Not a lot of sympathy was felt for the farmer who had sat tight throughout the war without sowing a seed or milking a cow, living off the compensation he was paid every time another Halifax ploughed into one of his fields.

After two nights without much sleep, a fatigue-induced depression descended on me in the afternoon as I made my way over to the Compass Section to make a routine appearance. Coming round the corner of the hangar I was astonished to see the section door open and Pearl come down the two steps. She walked quickly away in the opposite direction without seeing me. I suppose I should have called out or run after her – she'd obviously come looking for me, something she'd never done before – but feeling as I did I wasn't ready yet to face her again. I let her go and hurried over to the door.

Willoughby was on his own, sitting at the desk. 'Afternoon, Sarge,' I said.

He acknowledged me with a grunt. I waited for him to make some sarcastic remark about my WAAF following, but none came.

At last I said, 'Any messages for me, Sarge?'

'No,' he said.

How he loved to savour even the tiniest crumb of power. 'None at all?' I said.

His head came up. 'Why? Should there be?'

'It's just . . . I saw someone – a friend of mine – come out of here just now.'

I waited for the culmination of the great joke he was obviously cherishing, but the little black eyes went on staring at me. Finally he said, 'You *thought* you saw, is what you mean.'

'No, honestly, Sarge. I saw —'

'Your eyes deceived you. As we know they have a tendency to do,' he added brutally. Then he leaned towards me across the desk with an expression in which there was not even the smallest glint of humour.

'Nobody,' he said slowly, 'nobody has been in or out of this hut in the last hour. Got it?'

17

My feelings towards Pearl were in complete confusion, like a game of patience that's just about to come out when a door blows open and the cards scatter in all directions. My feelings were still there, but I could make no sense of them. To myself I made all the available excuses for my incapacity that night: too much to drink, too tired, too uncongenial a situation, (for ten whole minutes I actually persuaded myself I'd been in a *draught*); but I did know enough about sex to be well aware that the problem was more likely to be between my ears than between my legs. So – didn't I love her after all? Of course I did. How else would you describe the joy and agony she could arouse in me with a single word or glance? Did I not desire her, perhaps? But if what I'd been feeling for months wasn't desire then what the hell was it? Of course, I didn't have quite the same fantasies about her that I'd had about other girls: Susan Hayward, for example, in that suggestively post-coital photograph in the billet, or – I had to admit – Nancy, since that night when rain had stopped play. But that was because I *loved* Pearl. Wasn't it? Surely. And any doubts I might have had about loving her had been extinguished by the torture I'd been in since her mysterious visit to Willoughby.

He and Pearl? The idea was grotesque. It was unthinkable and absurd. But if she'd gone there to find me, why would Willoughby deny it so categorically? Why would he deny it anyway? I could only think of one explanation, but that one I couldn't bring myself to believe. Several times since then I'd tried to edge his conversation round to the subject, but failed completely. I supposed I would have to ask Pearl directly, but I shrank from doing it. And my fears were hardly allayed by an encounter I had with Percy.

I was just turning into the operations block in the hope of finding Pearl when I met him coming out.

'No good, matey,' he said looking up at me with a satanic grin. 'She's not in there.'

'Who?'

'Your intended.'

'Percy, she is *not* my intended.'

'All off, is it?' he said in his squeaky falsetto.

'It was only a joke.'

'Just as well, I'd say.' He set off up the road. I walked beside him, trying to sound casual.

'What d'you mean?'

'Well, what I hear, she's goin' about with this sergeant, i'nt she?'

'What sergeant?'

'I dunno. Just some sergeant.'

'But who?'

'Don't ask me. How would I know?'

How would he *not* know? There was nothing on the camp that escaped Percy. But he wasn't telling me.

'Ta-ra,' he said abruptly and turned off towards the photographic hut, his heavy satchel bouncing against his little legs.

I stood there, my heart hammering, angry at having

revealed my desperation to him. I had to see her. Harry was still on leave and I'd been nursing a hope of luring her back into the hut where I could reaffirm my manhood and so live happily ever after. I'd got a pass for Thursday; I could take her into York to the cinema. Or the shops – she could never resist that.

I waylaid her eventually at the main gate. She seemed friendly enough.

'Pearl,' I said.

'Yes?'

'Could you get a pass for tomorrow?'

'Oh,' she said, 'I've already got one.'

'Have you? Good. I thought we might . . . go into York.'

She looked uncertain. 'Well . . . I'm already going, really.'

'I see.' This was it. I braced myself. 'With anyone?'

'Got to meet me Auntie Vi,' she said apologetically. 'She's ATS, you know. Been posted to Scotland, so she's dropping off to see me for the day.'

I thought she might suggest that I went with her. I had no objection to sharing her with Auntie Vi; I could be quite effective with mothers and aunts. But nothing was said, and I didn't dare offer.

She put her hand on my arm. 'Sorry, love,' she said, her eyes on my face. ''Nother time, eh?' She kissed me quickly on the cheek. 'Got to rush.'

I wanted to make another time there and then, but I was too late. She was out of the gate with the other girls and climbing onto the lunch-time transport.

So I had a pass for the next day but nothing to do with it. I'd use it of course, one didn't throw away a chance to get out of the camp for a whole day; but I didn't like the idea of trailing over to York in Pearl's footsteps. Then I thought of Leeds. It was further away than York and a good deal less attractive, but there were things I could do there that would make me feel useful. I went across to Father's office and asked if I could see him.

'I've got a pass tomorrow, sir,' I told him. 'I thought I might go over to Leeds and get the canvas for the new flats. If I could have the money for it.'

'On your day off? That's very good of you.'

I looked down modestly.

'I tell you what,' he said. 'We've got some sports gear waiting to be collected in Leeds. If you wouldn't mind picking it up, I'd arrange some transport for you.'

This man was a miracle. I'd pick up half a Halifax for him if he supplied the transport. He reached for his telephone.

'Any particular driver you'd fancy?'

I don't think he quite meant that, but for a moment I toyed with the idea of Big Bertha, the six-foot blonde, built, in Harry's words, like a brick shithouse, and the object of all our bedtime fantasies, but I resisted the temptation. 'ACW Watson usually drives for us, sir.'

'Little Joy. Yes, of course. I'll see if she's available.'

The next morning she and I set off in a light truck across the frozen East Riding. Here in the North, January was a serious business. Snow didn't mean the few festive days of my childhood: snowballs on Hampstead Heath or toboggans on the Downs. Here it lay for weeks, hard and immovable, virgin acres of it untouched even by the zig-zag patterns of rabbits or the deeper perforations of a fox. And more was threatened. Over our heads as we drove between the piled white hedges stretched a heavy ochre sky, its wintery light draining the colour from everything: the skeletal trees were black, the farmhouses grey, even the pillar box on the hill was a dull brown. Joy, her head hardly higher than the steering wheel, found her way unerringly through this buried landscape. There were no signposts of course, but so many airfields, all familiar to her, that we'd hardly left one huddle of Nissen huts behind when another water tower would appear in the distance.

In Leeds the snow was grey. Smoke was pouring in great columns from the hundreds of factory chimneys and hung, trapped by the clouds. From it a fine veil of soot fell through the air, sprinkling the hard snow on shed roofs and front gardens, and when we reached the black Gothic centre of the city we were driving through brown slush. With the truck the shopping didn't take long and by lunch-time Joy had the distributor arm in her bag (immobilizing her vehicle as regulations demanded) and we were deciding on a cinema. We settled (or rather Joy did – it seemed churlish to argue when she was doing the driving) on Deanna Durbin singing her way across the Wild West in a covered wagon. The plot held as many surprises as the Flopsy Bunnies but the Californian sun on the screen thawed the December in our bones, and made Leeds seem even less hospitable when we emerged into the darkening afternoon.

We had collected the truck and were on our way out of the city when we stopped at some traffic lights. On the other side of the road I saw a tall, fair sergeant come through the swing doors of a hotel and stand on the top of the steps looking round. I recognized Alex Puddifoot, the captain of K-Kitty. I slid the truck window back and was trying to attract his attention when the hotel door swung again and another figure joined him. It was Pearl. Unmistakably. She took his arm and I had just time to see her expression as she smiled up at him before Joy let in the clutch and they were jerked out of my vision.

The trouble with being in love, as a man, is that you are a member of a despised minority – where other men are concerned, that is. You're not supposed to fall in love; it's an aberration, a disease, a weakness, like being an alcoholic (no,

211

worse than being an alcoholic – 'heavy drinker' is usually intended as a compliment). The best the lover can hope for is that masculine mockery may be tinged with a modicum of sympathy. On the other hand my observation of women had led me to believe that perhaps it was different for them. Girls in love appeared to be the elite of their sex, objects of awe and unfailing interest. But I was a man, and had to hide my wounds until I could crawl off and lick them in secret. Fortunately, with Harry still away, the little corrugated-iron haven was still mine, and I spent the whole night there as any jilted lover would, sobbing, writing letters, tearing them up, searching through dog-eared anthologies for crumbs of literary comfort.

The next day, of course, I had to rejoin the human race: a largely male and vociferously insensitive one. I longed to escape, but at the same time I envied them their cheerfully obscene chatter. I'd almost stopped noticing – because I did it so much myself – how we expressed almost everything in terms of copulation or parts of the female body. By this, and our unending stream of dirty jokes, we exorcised our need for the opposite sex. But it was a vocabulary that didn't contain the word 'love'; and love was what I wanted to talk about. I longed for female company: for those dear girls at the art school, the ones you didn't fancy, who for the price of a warm beer and a sandwich would listen endlessly to your troubles and offer you sisterly advice with brimming eyes and a gentle hand in yours.

In the end I did turn to female company, but not for sisterly advice. More snow had fallen all day, so a trip to the pub would have needed a dog team, and besides, the thought of finding her there with Alex was more than I could face, so I made for the NAAFI to drown my sorrows in beer. The place was half-empty and Nancy was on duty.

'On your own?' she said, reaching for a glass with her

smooth bare arm. Even in this weather she seemed to be wearing nothing under her short-sleeved uniform. 'Where's your mate? The one with the bedroom eyes.'

I assumed she meant Harry. It would hardly be Alan, or Danny. 'He's on leave,' I said.

'Not rehearsing, then?' She pushed my pint towards me. 'Aren't you doing a new show?'

'Yes, we are. But it's a play this time.'

'No music, you mean?' She sounded disappointed. 'I love a show with a band. And singing. I sing a bit myself, you know.'

That was it, of course. The lure of the footlights. She had designs on us. Not to disappoint her I said, 'We'll probably do another revue — after the play.'

'That last one you did was ever so good.' She folded her arms on the bar and leaned over towards me, hunching her shoulders intimately. 'I've done quite a bit of dancing, as well.'

'Yes,' I said, remembering the supple body pressed against mine.

'Not like that,' she said, as if reading my thoughts. 'Show dancing, I mean.' Those strange inflamed lips were parted in the suggestion of a pout, but her dark eyes were alight with interest. I noticed how round her eyes were, fringed with thick black lashes. I know she wasn't beautiful, but she was extraordinarily attractive. I could never decide quite what it was. Her skin, smooth and firm and faintly dusky? Or was it the sort of languorous vitality she had? She never behaved in a conventionally sexy way, flapping her eyelids, thrusting her tits out or wiggling her hips; but her movements had a candour, an openness and unselfconsciousness, quite unlike the closed way so many girls carried themselves, as if clenched against intrusion. Contemplating her for more than a minute, one's senses tended to riot, provoking an insistent desire to touch, taste, inhale, stroke, clasp and invade her, all at once.

The dancing had given me an idea. On the wall behind her was a poster announcing a Twelfth Night Dance in the NAAFI. I pointed to it.

'You going tomorrow night?'

'The dance? No thanks, bit like a busman's bloody holiday, in't it?'

'What're you doing then?'

'Nowt, I reckon. With this snow you can't move round here. Anyway, I'm on duty till eight.'

'How about coming up to our hut after? I've got some booze up there.'

She knew all about The Wings. Her eyes were alive with speculation. She let me see that she knew quite well what *I* had in mind, but her own desire to penetrate our inner sanctum was even stronger. 'That little place where you do the scenery . . . and things like that?'

'It's quite civilized,' I said. 'Very comfy, in fact.'

'Sounds lovely.'

'I'll pick you up at eight.' The power of the casting couch. All I needed was a cigar and a bald head and the part was mine.

I slept in the billet that night, staving off my misery over Pearl with lustful thoughts of Nancy, and all the next day I went on concentrating on her, until by evening I was an erotic volcano, a sex-starved satyr. Even setting the scene, just as I had a few nights before – draping the lamp, stoking the stove – I was able to stifle painful memories of New Year's Eve and think only of what might happen in a few hours.

We had a couple of drinks at the bar for appearance's sake, and danced a couple of dances; but Nancy's cheek-to-cheek style was too much for me in my state. 'Come on,' I whispered.

The stove glowed in the darkness of the hut. I locked the door carefully before I switched on the light.

214

'Ooh,' she said. 'This is all right.' She looked round swiftly and then turned to me teasingly. 'I see you've got a bed too.'

'We work at nights sometimes,' I said, trying to keep a straight face.

She laughed. 'I'll bet you do.' She pushed her hair off her face. 'God, it's hot in here.' She took her coat off and threw it over a chair.

'Would you like a drink?'

'What you got?'

'Gin and orange?'

'My Lord, it's the Ritz here, in't it?'

I grinned. 'Nothing's too good for you.'

Or Pearl.

'Well, go easy on the gin. Or I might get carried away.' But she didn't complain when I handed her a glass with a good deal more gin than orange. While I poured my own she inspected the hut, examining everything closely.

I carried my glass over to her. 'Well . . . happy Twelfth Night.'

'Ta, love. And you.' She clinked her glass against mine and we both drank. She gave a little shudder as the gin went down. We were so close I hardly had to lean forward to kiss her. The result was instantaneous. She ground herself against me and we swayed to and fro in our desperation to get at each other. Ever practical, but still kissing, she took my glass out of my hand and put it down with hers. Her dress unbuttoned down the front and I pulled up her bra to release her breasts into my hands. After a moment I felt her kick off her shoes and wriggle her pants down her legs, still with her mouth on mine. Then we were on the bed and I had a glimpse of thick dark bush, damp with welcome, before I was in her, and home at last. I strove manfully to survive as long as I could, and managed pretty well, but eventually her own enthusiasm was my undoing and I had to grope frantically on the floor for

215

the back pocket of my trousers before I could re-engage and ride safely to an ecstatic climax.

After a breathless moment or two it became obvious that the bed could only accommodate two people in the missionary position, and not too safely at that. Nancy's knickers were still round one ankle, and as she tried to kick them away we both nearly fell off. So I got up, and she dragged the biscuits onto the floor. The stove was red-hot and so were we. She pulled off her dress and everything else, and I followed suit. She stood, naked and unaffected, and pointed down at the makeshift pallet. 'Come on, then,' she said. I lay down obediently and looked up at her. She was like an Ingres model, or one of Etty's erotic fantasies, her body firm and rosy in the light from the shrouded lamp; her gleaming skin seemed to be stretched tightly over the roundness of her young girl's body, the bafflingly subtle roundness that has obsessed painters for hundreds of years – and lovers for thousands.

She dropped to her knees and kissed me. Then, stretching out beside me, she pulled a blanket over us. We lay like that for a while, arms round each other, whispering inanities. After a time her clever fingers roused my enthusiasm again and she flung back the blanket and straddled me, leaning down to offer her nipples to my mouth like grapes at a Roman orgy. Now I felt amazingly strong and tireless, and when she suddenly got up on all fours I knelt behind her and mounted her easily while she watched me over her shoulder with an expression of impish lechery that I'd never seen on a woman's face before. And when at last she lay back again and welcomed me into her and we were hurtling towards the end, she suddenly clutched me violently and whispered hoarsely, 'Don't stop . . . don't stop . . . I'm coming.' And she cried out and shuddered and held me fast in her arms, panting and whimpering almost as though she were crying.

216

I was astonished. I'd heard tell of this phenomenon but never experienced it. Some of my older and more worldly friends had told me categorically that it was a myth. Tarts, they said, sometimes pretended to do it, but it was always a fake. Somehow I didn't believe that Nancy had been pretending. I was still inside her and I could feel her fluttering deep in there.

By the time we'd at last finished with one another the fire had burned down and we realized we were getting chilly. We climbed into our clothes again and I collected the empty purple-and-pink packets from the floor. A visit to the barber was clearly called for. I felt light-limbed and wonderfully clear-headed, capable of some superhuman intellectual achievement or act of creation, but at the same time the spark of desire, temporarily extinguished, had been replaced by that odd, unfocused post-coital melancholy. I would have liked to have taken a great canvas and attacked it until dawn with a palette loaded with wild and unlikely colours. But I couldn't: the girl was still here, hanging on my arm, my responsibility now. I wanted to get rid of her, and I was so ashamed of wanting to that I over-compensated, boiled a kettle, made us cocoa, pulled the chairs towards the cooling stove and listened patiently for a long time while she listed her theatrical ambitions.

She couldn't get home through the snow, but there were beds in the NAAFI apparently. 'My gran'll think I was on duty,' she said with a wink. So outside the staff door I kissed her affectionately and with a flood of gratitude for her generous spirit. And then I was alone. I turned towards my billet through the thick snow; and without warning guilt poured into my mind. I told myself it was irrational – what I'd done was probably no worse than what Pearl had been doing – and the thought of that was an icy shock, an unexpectedly graphic image. I looked across in the direction of the WAAF quarters as I'd done so often, imagining her asleep, anticipating the addictive pain that would follow; but the moment failed me — after all, she probably wasn't even there — and I turned, dry-eyed and oddly dissatisfied, towards my bed.

18

I had never seen so much snow. There seemed to be a blizzard every other day and no sign of a thaw, so that the familiar outlines of the camp began to disappear behind huge drifts and the roads round the airfield became impassable. As a schoolboy I had often read in the papers about Yorkshire villages being cut off for days at a time, and I'd rather envied the inhabitants surviving on tins of baked beans and not having to go to school. I think the feeling on the station was much the same, certainly for the aircrews; no doubt their headmaster, Bomber Harris down at Command HQ, was prowling around his empty classrooms whacking the desks in frustration, but there was nothing he could do. The aircraft were frozen solid, the snowploughs couldn't cope with the buried runways, the petrol tankers couldn't get through. Millions of weightless snowflakes, each one a fragile, perfect, hexagonal crystal, had combined to bring the great killing machine to a halt.

The only thing lacking was the baked beans. The cookhouse cuisine was never of the highest, but with the raw materials in seriously short supply hardly anything eatable was being produced. Harry, in high spirits now that his leave was over, announced that he and I would have to live off the land. This turned out to mean night raids on the cookhouse stores, preferably when it was snowing so that our tracks were covered. We would creep back to The Wings loaded with bread, milk, tubs of margarine, jam, cheese and once a whole string of sausages. The bread and cheese were necessary for innumerable Welsh rarebits which we lived on for days, toasting them over a glowing stove on a massive wire fork, made by Harry, which could do two pieces at a time. Harry also made a rat-proof box where we stored the perishables, deep frozen and hidden under the snow outside the door.

The biggest problem was keeping the stove going. Coal on the camp was dwindling fast and severe rationing had been imposed on huts and workplaces, with the result that so much was being nicked from the main dump that guards had to be posted day and night. But a stove needs to be red-hot to make a decent rarebit. And anyway, we liked to be warm. We noticed that the only place that never seemed to run out of coal was Base Operations. It had a boiler room at the back which supplied the air-conditioning system and was fed by giant hoppers. The snag was that the coal was fine-ground to allow it to feed into the boilers automatically. In our stove this tended to form giant clinkers which had to be attacked through the top with an iron rod. Harry cursed and swore and threatened to stop stealing the stuff, but for several weeks we were undoubtedly the only really warm place on the camp. How we were never caught lurching through the snow with sacks of the stuff on our backs I'll never know.

Among those in the know The Wings became a popular retreat. Rumours of warmth and Welsh rarebits spread rapidly and visitors would tap hopefully on our door at all hours. The nights, at first, were largely booked for Harry's reunions with Brenda, and I hardly saw Nancy, as the NAAFI seemed to be operating with only the few girls who lived in. It was much the same with Pearl. As the snow got thicker the WAAFs couldn't make their own way across and were brought on and off duty in trucks. I got to talk to her once or twice but she seemed rather preoccupied. Once she actually wrote me a note; I carried the single page, with its neat, unformed but feminine hooks and loops, in my pocket for months. I couldn't tell if anyone was seeing more of her than I was, but somehow, in the state of frozen suspension we all found ourselves, it didn't seem likely. It was a curiously peaceful time, uncomfortable but pleasantly irresponsible. It seemed to go on for ages, until at last, after several false starts, the thaw set in, and in the Sleeping Beauty's castle life began to stir once more.

In a dripping, chilly landscape, along sodden runways, between mountains of greying snow, operations got under way again: day after day now – the Air Ministry was anxious to make up for lost time. One particular morning the atmosphere on the station was unmistakable and by lunch-time the secret was out: it was a distant and dangerous target, probably Berlin. The tension spread quickly through the camp. Over twenty aircraft were to be operational, which meant that even Alan and I were involved, out on the flights, checking compasses; but not so involved that I didn't feel the need to have a book with me. My girl friend from the art school had sent me a book of poetry for Christmas, a small volume that I could get into a pocket, short poems that could be read in short bursts. The author had been captured in Norway at the beginning of the war, and there were a lot of poems beginning 'Oh –' about being separated from loved ones, which I suppose was why she'd given it to me. But she'd written in the flyleaf and I felt it was something from my real life which often felt so remote these days; so I was upset to find, when I got back to my billet, that I'd left it in one of the aircraft.

There was still an hour to take-off: I grabbed a bicycle and pedalled round the slushy perimeter track to the last plane I'd left. It was bombed-up and probably out of bounds to me, but nobody seemed to notice as I climbed aboard. Then I realized it was K-Kitty, Alex's plane, and I stood for a moment thinking about him and the others who'd be flying in it that night. I'd heard someone say they were getting jumpy these days, but that had been before Christmas – they'd had an easier time since then. The Halifax creaked as I moved: sometimes, big as they were, these contraptions seemed too fragile for what they were expected to do. I climbed down into the navigator's position. There was my book, lying on the chart table. I was just slipping it into my battledress when I felt the aircraft lurch as someone climbed through the rear hatch, and when I came up into the cockpit I came face to face with Sgt Willoughby.

The little black eyes snapped at me. 'What'you doin 'ere?' he said.

'Left something behind, Sarge.'

'What?'

I showed him.

'A book? What d'you want with books in here? It's not a bloody library, you know.'

'Yes, Sarge.'

'And this aircraft is now out of bounds to non-essential personnel.'

Including sergeants? I wondered. 'Everything OK, Sarge?' I said supportively.

He looked at me sharply for a moment, then said, 'Shouldn't it be? We'll have to see, won't we? Have to check on you buggers all the time. On your way, then.' He squeezed back into the flight engineer's position to let me pass.

Must really be a big do tonight, I thought as I rode back towards the hangars. It took a lot to get Willoughby off his arse and out on the flights.

★

Harry shook me awake in the morning and pushed a mug of tea into my hand. 'Come on you little sod, stop playing with yourself or you won't get any breakfast.' He'd been up for hours no doubt, building flats or making furniture or something depressingly useful.

I felt as if I'd hardly slept, but then I remembered the coming and going and the roar of engines that had seemed to go on all night. I swallowed a mouthful of the dark-brown tea. 'They all back?' I asked.

'All but two.'

'Which two?'

'A-Apple and K-Kitty, I think.'

I felt a shock of what I was horrified to recognize as exhilaration. I'd never knowingly wished for anything like this, but I suppose my subconscious must have been hard at it all the time. A rival is a rival, after all, and earns no concessions. Then I thought of the others, the crew I'd been a part of, however briefly, and I began to feel a bit sick. When aircrews had been lost before they'd always been strangers to me; this time they were faces to me, and voices, and people.

Over at the section I found Alan on his own with more up-to-date news.

'A-Apple bought it over the target, it seems. They don't know if anyone baled out. Probably not.'

'What about K-Kitty?' I said.

'They're OK. Diverted, that's all. Somewhere in Lincolnshire, I think. It was an early return apparently.'

So that was that, after all. My conscience felt relieved, if nothing else. 'Why were they diverted?'

'Lost their way, they said. Skipper says the compasses were u/s.'

'They were all right when I checked them.'

Alan didn't answer. After a moment he said, 'At least they got down all right.'

223

I remembered the story Percy had told me in the billet. This situation must seem uncomfortably familiar to Alan. I said tentatively, 'History repeating itself, do you think?'

He looked at me quickly, his pale-blue eyes anxious and uncertain. 'You heard about that?'

I nodded.

He turned away and stood by the stove, hands in pockets. 'Not quite the same, this. Still, lucky it wasn't me working on K-Kitty last night.'

'No, it was me, actually.'

'Oh, God, I didn't mean . . . but after last time . . .'

'Sure.'

He picked up the poker in a thin hand and prodded the stove for a few moments. Then he straightened up and looked at me. 'I was *absolutely* positive those compasses were OK that time. So . . .'

I wanted to hear more, but at that moment Willoughby appeared, clearly in a foul temper. He ignored us and went straight to his desk where he sat, opening drawers and moving things about. Suddenly he slammed a drawer shut and banged his fist on the desk. We both looked up. Willoughby was staring straight at me.

'Defective gyrocompass,' he said heavily. 'That's what they said. K-Kitty had a defective gyrocompass last night.' He paused for effect and then flashed his empty smile. 'And who did the final check on K-Kitty last night?'

I knew it was probably not the height of tact, but somehow I couldn't resist it. 'You did, Sarge,' I said.

'I *beg* your pardon?'

'You told me you were going to.'

The smile had completely disappeared. 'I don't recall doing so,' he said softly. I could see it might be dangerous to press the point. 'However,' he continued, 'you personally have no cause to be apprehensive. If there is any blame to be laid at our

224

doorstep, I shall no doubt shoulder it.' His gaze transferred itself to Alan. 'As I have on previous occasions.' He sighed. '*Noblesse oblige.*' He made for the door. 'If required, I shall be in the mess.'

For all his gangster pretensions, it was hard not to laugh at him. But when I looked at Alan I saw he'd gone very pale indeed.

Willoughby didn't come back after lunch, and at about three o'clock the phone on the desk rang. I picked it up.

A voice said, 'That the officer in charge?'

'No, this is AC Turner. It's Sgt Willoughby you want, but he's not here at the moment.'

'Ah.' There was a pause. 'Can you give him a message? It's RAF Market Hareby here. Tell him we've stripped down the gyro on that diverted Halifax of yours, and it looks as if it's been got at. Somebody's nobbled it. I'm putting in a report. Tell him to ring me when he gets in. Sgt Tooley, Compass Section.'

It was nearly a week later that we heard about the court martial. I arrived at work that morning to find Willoughby and Grice in their armchairs and Alan doing his best to be invisible in a corner. Willoughby rose to his feet.

'No doubt you will have heard the news,' he said to me.

'What news, Sarge?'

'The skipper of K–Kitty is to be court-martialled for monkeying with the gyro in order to abort his mission. I shall be required to give evidence.' At the thought of this he lost himself for a second in a trance of self-importance. Then he said, 'I'm told that he denies having done it, which implies, of course, that the equipment was not in a serviceable condition when it left our hands.' Neither Grice nor Alan had stirred but I could tell they weren't missing a word. 'That, you realize, would reflect on the work of this section. I shall, of course, defend our position to my utmost. But,' with his hands behind his back, he thrust his head towards me, 'in the process I may be forced to inform the court that the final inspection was carried out by you.'

'But . . .'

'Yes?'

'You checked the compasses after me.'

He shook his head. 'Ah, no.'

'But you said—'

'Said – *said*!' He held up a finger. 'Even if this story of yours were true, it doesn't mean that I *did* inspect the compasses on that aircraft, does it? And I think you'll find that your signature is the last one in the book.' The dreaded smile spread across his face. 'So you'd better hope that the captain of K-Kitty is found guilty, or you may find yourself a fair distance up shit creek without a paddle. Or even a boat.' His laugh matched his smile exactly.

When we had escaped to the NAAFI at breaktime, Alan said to me, 'I don't think he'd really dare. I mean, he won't want to admit he'd let an under-training aircraftman do the final check; or let him sign the book.'

'I suppose it depends which is worse.'

'What is?'

'Which drops him further in it – letting an erk do his job for him, or cocking up the job himself. What do you think?'

'I don't know. All I do know is he'll use this to put the frighteners on you for as long as he can.' Alan peered into his coffee for a while. Then he said, 'Still . . . at least K-Kitty got down in one piece. He tried to make me feel responsible, you know, for all those bods in R-Robert going for a burton.' He rubbed a thin hand over his face. 'I was new here then, and I believed everything I was told. But not any more. I don't know what did go wrong, but I do know it wasn't my fault.' He lifted his chin and gave me a weak smile. 'They're a dodgy

226

couple, those two, but if you need any help . . . you know . . . OK?'

'OK,' I said.

The trouble with life in the service was that none of us led a totally blameless life – it would have been an impossibility. The regulations contradicted each other to such an extent that many of them simply had to be ignored. The result was that we all skulked about expecting the hand of authority to descend on our shoulders at any moment; and then it wouldn't be so much a matter of what crime we had committed, as which crime. I was no exception, and in spite of Alan's reassurances I could see that Willoughby was quite capable of dragging me into an area where even Father's protection couldn't save me. And from time to time this thought gave me a chilly feeling in and around the stomach.

I did talk to Harry about it, but preparations for the play now absorbed him completely and he seemed unimpressed by my worries. I think he noticed my downcast looks, and assuming, as he always did, that the problem must be sexual, he offered to find a job for Pearl in the new production. I was rather touched by his offer, although I doubted if she'd accept. The play only had a small cast so there was no question of her getting a part (in any case, ravishing as she was, even I could see she was no actress). But the set of *Ten-Minute Alibi* had to be dominated by a large clock, which Harry was in the process of making. It couldn't be a real clock as it had to keep time not with Greenwich but with the action on the stage, which involved the complicated timing of a murder. This meant that an unfortunate assistant had to stand behind the scenery right through the play, moving the hands on minute by minute. I was a bit apprehensive about offering such an incredibly boring job to Pearl, but after Harry's magnanimous offer it seemed churlish not to try. In any case, the thought of being in another show with her relit the hope, never quite extinguished, that we might get together again. I'd been missing her badly, in spite of Nancy, and perhaps because of Nancy I felt now that Pearl and I were on a more equal footing.

So I persuaded her to come up to The Wings one night when she came off duty. I fed her tea and toast and jam, and to my surprise, when I put the proposition to her she accepted at once. I think it was the thought of the officers' mess parties that was the attraction rather than me, but she did smile sweetly and say what fun it'd be to be together again.

Her cockney cheek was less aggressive these days and her face, although just as beautiful, had a thoughtful look about it – in fact, in my opinion, it was more beautiful than ever. Her decision raised my spirits instantly and I managed to infect her with my own cheerfulness by talking about the last tour. Reminiscence is the life-blood of all performers, and soon we were like two old pros in a green room, reminding each other of when Terry had split his tights or when Danny had lost his mouth-organ down the lining of his kimono. We were both laughing about the night when Sarah, our home-counties Flight Officer had been carried insensible from the officers' mess to the coach, when the door opened and Harry walked in.

'Hello, you two,' he said, rubbing his hands and advancing on the stove. 'Any tea going?'

'I think there's one in the pot,' I said, getting up to look. Harry immediately took my chair.

'Big carry-on up at SHQ today,' he said. 'That skipper of K-Kitty's up in front of the brass hats.'

I had my back to Pearl and didn't dare to look round. I'd never told Harry of my suspicions about her and Alex, and it was certainly too late now. I edged myself further behind Pearl so that I could catch his eye over her head, but his feet were up on the hearth-stone and he was in full flight.

'Apparently he's saying that neither he nor any of the crew touched the compass. But if they didn't, who did? I mean it's quite obvious they didn't fancy a trip to Berlin, and who could blame them? Wouldn't be the first time. I'm afraid he'll be for the chop.' He swung round and grinned at me over his shoulder. 'Anyway, it'll put some people in the clear.'

I shook my head violently.

'What?' he said, puzzled. But the damage was done. Pearl was on her feet, her eyes narrowed like an angry kitten's and her lips pulled back from her perfect teeth.

'Don't talk bloody silly,' she said. 'Course he didn't do it. None of them did. He . . . they wouldn't do nothing like that – never!'

Harry was looking at her in astonishment. 'Well . . who would, then?' he said reasonably.

'I don't know.' She looked at me and the colour flooded back into her white face. 'I don't know. But it wasn't him. It wasn't him!' She snatched her bag off the table and rushed out of the door, slamming it behind her.

'What the bloody hell?' Harry said.

I dashed for the door and out of the hut. But it was dark and I couldn't see which way she'd gone. I called her name, but there was no answer.

19

The rumour started to circulate the very next morning, but it wasn't until the day after that we heard it confirmed from a reliable source. Sgt A. Puddifoot had been found guilty of Lack of Moral Fibre and sentenced to be severely reprimanded and reduced to the ranks. Nobody I knew saw him leave the camp and none of us ever caught sight of him again.

Alan was convinced that he wasn't guilty. As always with Alan it was a feeling he had rather than a rational opinion. But for me Alex was a rival and, sorry as I was for him, I was happy to believe anything disparaging about him. And so, I hoped, was Pearl. With him disgraced and out of the way my prospects with her must surely be brighter. So I argued with Alan that Alex must have done it: the rest of the crew didn't have the opportunity and, other than them, nobody else would *want* to do it, would they? Curiously enough, the only person who seemed inclined to agree with Alan was Willoughby. For all that the verdict had put him in the clear, he still liked to imply that the whole affair was really my fault, and that some sort of threat still hung over my head. All his conversations with me were now punctuated with innuendoes and I recognized the technique as the same he'd used on Alan. Only in my case no loss of life was involved and, anyway, he was dealing with someone a lot less sensitive than Alan. All the same it was as much as I could do sometimes not to punch the silly smirk right off his face.

After Alex's departure, Pearl was not much in evidence and I thought it more politic to let her get over whatever she had to get over. There was Nancy of course. I hung around the NAAFI for several evenings, but it was clear that the night with her was a non-repeatable event. She had been on holiday and returned to duty flushed and sparkling and informed me that she was engaged. Her Ted had come back from North Africa with a bit of shrapnel in his leg, she said, and as soon as it was out they were going to be married. She said she'd have loved to ask me to the wedding but she hoped I'd understand if she didn't. I certainly did. The numbers of her admirers might well have overflowed the church, and the sight of all those proprietorial airmen beaming at his bride would surely have been unsettling for poor Ted. Actually, not poor Ted at all; I thought he was a very lucky man, and I told Nancy so, and wished her every happiness I could think of. And then I decided to give up women and concentrate on creating a lifelike flat in Bloomsbury for Harry's production of *Ten-Minute Alibi*. One night I was absorbed in painting long lines of fake moulding on the canvas walls when there was a timid tap on the door. I drew the brush steadily to the edge of the flat and propped it on the paint pot before I went to the door. It was Alan.

'What's up?' I said. 'Come in.'

He'd only been inside the hut once before. He seemed nervous of it as if he were expecting it to be booby-trapped. I had a feeling he'd been brought up to believe that anything theatrical was the work of the Devil. I sat him by the stove and tried to get on with my mouldings before the paint dried.

'Sorry to barge in,' he said, rubbing his knees nervously, 'but something funny's happened. I've just been talking to Percy. You know that cupboard that Grice keeps locked all the

232

time? Apparently it used to be in the Orderly Room ages ago. They've just had a big clear-out and found another key for it. Percy said we might find it useful.'

'We who? Willoughby and Grice or you and me?' I could see at once what Alan had in mind and my moulding was beginning to develop a wobble.

'He can't be bothered to bring it up to the section. He says you're in his hut, so he'll give it to you tonight.'

I tried to straighten the moulding but only made it worse. 'Do you think he's told Willoughby or Grice about the key?'

'Shouldn't think so.'

'But he might, mightn't he?' I gave up trying and wiped off the last three feet of moulding with a rag. 'It's a bit risky, isn't it?'

'What is?'

I put down the brush and the rag. 'Oh, come on, Alan. I know what you're thinking. Same as me. We can have a look in that bloody cupboard. See what's in it that's so secret.'

'D'you think we should?'

'Course we shouldn't. But we'd be fools not to.'

'We'll be fools if we do.'

'Why did you come up here to tell me, then? D'you want me to double straight over to Grice and say, "Please Sarge, here's a lovely second key for your lovely cupboard – the one that none of us are interested in?"'

Alan shook his head.

I washed the brush in a bucket and banged the lid onto the paint. 'Well, if we're going to do it, the sooner the better. Just in case Percy does mention it to them.' I looked at the time. 'He's probably mending his watches by now. I'll nip down to the billet and get the key off him. What hut number are you?'

'One-one-four.'

'I'll pick you up there in a quarter of an hour.'

I was quite surprised at my own forcefulness. I'd always

233

tended to be the led rather than the leader. Perhaps it was Alan's submissive conformity that brought out the renegade in me.

Percy was where I'd expected him to be, sitting on his bed, his little legs sticking out from under his bed-table. As soon as he saw me he squeaked, "Ere! Got somethin' for you.'

He dived into his top pocket and pulled out the key.

'Thanks,' I said; then, carefully, as I took it: 'Am I supposed to give this to the sergeants?'

'Suit yourself. Hang on to it if you like. Might come in 'andy one day.' He took the watchmaker's glass out of his eye and winked at me.

There was never a way of being sure how much Percy knew about anything. Usually a great deal; but he wasn't telling. I felt fairly sure, all the same, that he wasn't going to mention the key to Grice or Willoughby.

'How's Beryl?' I said.

'We fixed the date.'

'For the wedding? Oh, wizard.' It was getting harder to produce the proper enthusiasm, there'd been so many dates and so many postponements.

'May the ninth. Definite.'

'It's a lovely time of year for it.' It was the best I could manage, but it seemed to satisfy him.

I collected Alan from his billet and we made our way over to the section. We let ourselves in and I closed the door behind us and switched on the light. Alan had been nervous about doing that and wanted to use a torch, but I'd pointed out that the WD blackouts were pretty efficient and if anyone did find us there we'd look a lot less shifty with the lights on.

Alan stood motionless by the door while I crossed over to the cupboard and put the key in the lock. The sooner we got this over and were out of here the better I'd feel. It turned easily and I opened both the doors widely.

'Christ,' I said. 'Look at this.'

234

Alan darted over to my side.

It was a big cupboard and it was packed full. There were radios, bottles of whisky, civilian clothes, suitcases, binoculars, a cricket bat, even a set of golf clubs, all jammed in any old way.

'What on earth . . .?' Alan said.

On one shelf there seemed to be a collection of watches, fountain pens, razors and things like that. Something vaguely familiar caught my eye. I reached in and picked it up. It was a round, gold medallion, a St Christopher. As I held it in my hand I remembered the night in K-Kitty when Len had showed it to me, and I realized at once what Grice had been up to.

'What *is* all this?' Alan whispered.

I didn't answer because I was listening to the crunch of footsteps which seemed to be heading towards the hut.

'Quick!' I said, shutting and bolting the left-hand cupboard door. I'd just slammed the other one shut and leapt well away from it when the hut door opened and Grice came in, followed by Willoughby.

Grice's long jaw fell open, he blinked at us. 'Here,' he said, 'what're you doing here?'

I could have asked him the same question, but my mouth was too dry.

Willoughby closed the door and stepped in front of Grice. He looked from me to Alan and then back to me. 'Right, what's going on, then?'

'Nothing, Sarge,' I said.

'You're not usually so keen on attending your place of work. What're you up to at this time of night?'

In all the contingency plans that had gone through my head that evening, this was the one question I hadn't an answer for.

'I left my book here,' I said.

235

Willoughby groaned. 'Oh, not *again*. Can't you think of a new one? Where is it, then?'

'It wasn't here after all,' I said lamely, knowing I wouldn't have convinced a two-year-old.

I didn't convince Willoughby either. 'You're a bloody liar!' he said loudly. 'You were snooping, weren't you? What were you after?' He glared at Alan and me.

We were snooping of course; but what made him so sure we were? There were a dozen other perfectly sound reasons for us to be there; though I had to admit that none of them would come to mind at that moment. Grice moved closer to Willoughby and murmured something in his ear. I froze, fighting a desire to glance at the cupboard. The only word I could catch was 'report' but it seemed enough to make Willoughby hurry round the desk and jerk open a drawer. He pulled out a black folder and looked quickly at Grice. I saw a flicker of relief on both their faces. Then Willoughby must have realized that he'd just drawn our attention to the folder. He held it for a moment uncertainly, while an expression of doubt crept into his eyes. Had we already seen it perhaps? I saw him decide to brazen it out.

'This what you were after, was it? Was it?'

Grice cleared his throat. We all turned to look at him. 'I think,' he said in his slow way, 'these two lads are getting a bit too clever for their own good, Ken.'

'They're not clever, Arnold,' Willoughby said. 'Clever Dicks, that's all they are. They don't know nothing.'

'All the same, I reckon steps should be taken.' The lethargic delivery somehow made the remark all the more sinister.

Willoughby leaned over the desk and thrust the file towards me. 'Have a good look at it, did you? Have a good read?' I tried to see the label but it was waving about too much. I managed to glimpse the date, and a large K, which was enough to tell me what the folder was about. Not that

236

Willoughby seemed inclined to make any secret of it. 'Well, it won't do you any good,' he was saying. 'So you'd better keep your nose clean, and your mouth shut, or you'll be in big trouble – because it's you, you know, you're the one the shit'll fall on!'

I was looking at him, but I was still seeing the inside of that cupboard and the mute indictment of its contents, and my anger was growing harder to control by the second. Something warned me to keep my counsel about it now, so with a huge effort I directed all my fury towards Willoughby and what he was saying. And then, before I could stop myself, I found I was shouting at him.

'Why don't you shut up, you stupid bastard!' I heard myself yell. 'You've been bullying Alan for months, but you're not going to bully me. I don't know what you're up to – either of you – but you can't shove any of it onto us, and you bloody well know it!' There were only a couple of feet between us now, and I was shouting into his face. 'So you just leave us alone, or by Christ, if you don't, I'll knock your teeth down your fucking throat !'

There was what seemed like an interminable silence. I realized that I'd done for myself, although I'd certainly succeeded in distracting attention from the cupboard. What is more it quickly dawned on me that I'd made Willoughby a very happy man; Grice, of course, was never happy, but Willoughby was clearly elated. He hadn't moved and was standing stock-still with his head tilted back in triumph and his black eyes glinting.

'Right,' he said, and his voice was almost a whisper. 'You're on a charge. And a very serious charge I think you'll find. Two very serious charges probably: insubordination and threatening to strike a superior officer. Sergeant Grice here is a witness.' He inhaled deeply and ecstatically. 'Report to the guardroom tomorrow morning at oh-eight-hundred hours.'

He paused dramatically and, Harry would have said, a fraction too long. 'Now get out.'

We did, like rabbits. My bravado had suddenly deserted me and I was shaking, no longer with anger, but with fright. I led the way as fast as I could towards The Wings, with Alan trotting behind. Neither of us spoke. I'd been on charges before, of course; it was almost impossible for an airman to avoid them altogether. But they'd all been trivial: late on parade, improperly dressed, things like that. But this was more serious; I didn't know what the punishment was for offering to punch a sergeant, but fearful images came into my mind of the dreaded 'glasshouse', the legendary service prisons where everything was done at the double and life was stripped down to its brutal essentials.

Once inside the hut I locked the door behind us and poured myself two fingers of courage from the remains of the seducer's gin bottle. I offered some to Alan but he shook his head vehemently as if I'd suggested he ate a live toad. The gin warmed my insides and made things appear slightly less melodramatic, and when Alan asked me, with the sublime lack of tact of the deeply concerned, what sentence I thought I'd get for insubordination and intimidation, I even managed a smile and a limp joke about being out in time for my twenty-first.

Alan picked up the poker and swung it gently in his fingers. 'How do you suppose', he said, 'they knew we were in there?'

'I don't think they did. It was just our bad luck they came barging in at that time of night.'

'Yes, but why *did* they?' Alan insisted. 'I mean, what were *they* up to?'

'Exactly.'

'They seemed very worried about that file in the drawer. What was it? Could you see?'

'Some sort of report on the K-Kitty business, I think.

238

There must be something in it they don't want us to see.'

'But reports like that get circulated to everybody, don't they?'

'To officers and gentlemen – even NCOs – but not to us.' I took another swig of gin. A new boldness crept along my veins. 'I'd love to have a look at it.'

Alan gripped the poker and pointed it at me. 'No you don't. No, thanks very much. You can count me out.' He lowered the poker. 'Just because you want company in the glasshouse.'

His tactlessness was almost endearing. Especially when he realized what he'd said and went rather pink. After a moment he went on, 'And all that stuff in the cupboard, what was that?'

I looked at him in surprise. 'Don't you know?' It hadn't occurred to me that he didn't.

'No. Was it stolen?'

'You might say that. It's aircrew gear – dead aircrew. Their personal property. It's supposed to be returned to their families, I think.'

'That whole cupboardful?'

'Well, he's been here a long time.'

'Grice?'

'Yes. It's been his personal cottage industry, I'd say. No wonder he's always volunteering for duty sergeant. It's the duty sergeant who collects the kit of missing aircrews.'

'If the other crews haven't got there first.' True as it was, the cynicism was rather shocking coming from Alan.

'Well, I'd rather they had it than bloody Grice,' I said. 'I suppose he sends off their socks and underwear and letters and stuff, and then flogs the rest.'

'That must be all those big parcels he keeps lugging around.'

'Must be.'

239

Alan leaned forward to put down the poker, then he sat rubbing his shins. 'Are you going to tell them?' he said.

'Me?'

'When you're up on your charge tomorrow. You could tell the CO about it.'

I'd already considered that. 'I don't think I will – not yet. I don't want to alert Willoughby; I want to find out what he's up to first. Anyway, they wouldn't believe me.'

'Just give them the key and tell them to look for themselves.'

The mention of the key jolted me like a high-tension shock. I leapt up. 'Oh, God!'

'What?'

'The key. The bloody key. I left it in the door. They'll know we've opened it. Grice'll have shifted all that stuff out by now.'

'No, he won't,' Alan said quietly.

'Why not?'

With what, for him, was a theatrical gesture, he pulled the key out of his pocket and held it up.

I laughed with relief. 'You're a genius,' I said. 'How did you manage that?'

'While you were getting yourself put on a charge. I turned the key and got it into my pocket.'

'You crafty sod.'

He threw it across to me. 'You better look after it. And good luck tomorrow.'

After he'd gone I put the key into my pocket. It clinked against something metal and I pulled out Len's medallion. I must have shoved it in there as they came through the door. It gleamed on my hand and felt quite heavy. 'Solid gold,' Len had boasted. A good few carats anyway. It shouldn't be hard to get hold of his home address. His Auntie Kath might be glad to have it back.

240

20

It's possible I was imagining the sense of suppressed joy in the guardroom, but I don't think so. The SPs were scrupulous in their efforts not to show it; they went about their business with their usual demeanour of rigid disdain and kept their mottled profiles averted, only glancing at me occasionally from under the visors of their caps. But I knew. And they knew that I knew. At last they had a genuine renegade theatrical in their net, and their stony hearts were gladdened.

I stood against the wall, hands behind my back in the at-ease position, breathing in the service smell – stronger here than anywhere else on the camp – of disinfectant and floor polish, until I was joined by two other criminal types. We weren't allowed to talk, and so eyed each other cautiously, speculating about what depravities had brought us together. Eventually an enormous corporal appeared, accompanied by two embarrassed airmen who were to be our escort. 'Caps on!' the corporal shouted. 'Attention!'

We were marched through the camp in the direction of Station Headquarters. I looked straight ahead, praying that we wouldn't pass anyone I knew. Being on a charge was not regarded as in any way a disgrace by one's fellow erks, but the details, like being paraded about under escort, could be humiliating – they were designed to be. Mercifully the camp was quiet this morning and I reached SHQ unnoticed and with a sigh of relief. I mean, suppose we'd run into Pearl? My entire skin turned scarlet at the thought.

SHQ was in the farmhouse, all that was left of the farm the War Department had acquired to create the airfield, and the only pre-war structure on the camp. It didn't seem much like a farmhouse now, just offices and corridors like most RAF buildings. Whitewash, green paint and brown lino can eradicate the soul of any house. We waited in a damp corridor at the back until the Adjutant, a stocky, red-faced flight lieutenant with a handlebar moustache, hurried past us and disappeared into his office. A few minutes later the corporal SP started to shout and stamp about and the first miscreant was marched in.

I was the last, but I didn't have to wait long. Whatever the verdict on the other two, the proceedings were obviously summary, and before I'd had time to rehearse my defence, the corporal was yelling, 'Prisoner and escort, attention! Left turn, quick march! Right wheel! Halt! Prisoner, one step forward, march!' and I was standing, thumbs along the seams of my trousers, looking down at the Adjutant behind his desk which was piled with cardboard files, ashtrays and brown-rimmed mugs.

Without looking at me he read out the charge in a bored, upper-class voice, which sounded to me acquired rather than inherited. When he'd finished he glanced up for the first time and said wearily, 'Anything to say?'

I'd met this kind of officer before and I knew what impressed them. 'Well, sir,' I said in my best public-school accent, 'there is something I should like to say.'

This time his head jerked up and he inspected me carefully. He looked down at the charge sheet again and then said, 'All right, Corporal. I'd like to talk to this man alone. Wait outside, will you?'

When the corporal had barked enough directions to turn the escort round and head it out of the door, the Adjutant leaned back in his chair.

'Stand easy,' he said and eyed me again for a moment. 'Now, look here.' His drawl became noticeably more pronounced. 'What's a chap like you doing, coming up on a charge like this? You've been properly brought up. You know the rules. You can't go about threatening to hit superior officers. Even if they *are* non-commissioned.' He raised his eyebrows in a small gesture of disdain. 'You're letting the side down, aren't you?'

I tried to look as clean-limbed and blue-eyed as I could. He leaned forward. 'Where did you go to school?'

This was what I was waiting for. I'd known this do the trick on other occasions. Since the start of the war I'd been at a grammar school, but before that I'd been to a minor public school for a couple of years. I brought out the name with a casual flourish.

'Really?' he said, brightening visibly. 'I had a navigator once who'd been there. Decent chap. Before your time, of course. They used to have a bloody good first fifteen. Beat Merchant Taylors' one year, didn't they?'

'I believe so, sir,' I said, having no idea.

'Not playing yourself by any chance, were you?'

'Afraid not, sir,' I said, with a sort of rueful smile.

'Bad luck, eh?' He laughed at that, a near perfect sixth-form bray. Then, rather more sharply, 'You do play, do you?'

'Oh, yes, sir.'

'What position?'

'Scrum half, sir.' I hoped that sounded plausible.

He seemed satisfied. I'd passed the test. I was no longer one of them, but one of us. His manner was almost affable now.

But he was still curious about me. He stared at me, fingering the end of his moustache.

'What I don't understand about you, Turner,' he said, using my name for the first time, 'is why you haven't taken a commission.'

Taken a commission. I loved that – the idea that somehow I'd been modestly refusing to become an officer all this time. I explained to him that I'd been training for aircrew and been grounded for medical reasons. This raised my stock even further.

'What rotten luck,' he said, shaking his head sympathetically. He pulled at his moustache. 'Look here, a chap like you shouldn't be wasting his time frigging about in the ranks. I'm going to have a word with the CO about recommending you for a commission.'

'Oh, thank you, sir,' I said. I'd heard all this before. The only jobs left that carried a commission at this stage of the war were in aircrew. And anyway, Father would block anything that involved me leaving the station. But I gave him a grateful smile, the smile of an eager fifth-former for his kindly housemaster.

'In the meanwhile,' he said, leaning forward and tapping the charge sheet with a yellow forefinger, 'what are we going to do about this?' He looked up at me. 'Bloody silly way to behave. What was it all about?'

I suspected the man was no lover of NCOs. He probably even preferred the lower ranks, honest sons of the soil, pulling away at their forelocks. Nobody hates the tradesman class like someone who's just hauled himself clear of it. I didn't think Sgt Willoughby would carry much weight with him, not against an ex-public schoolboy, brimming with eagerness. There was no accusation I could really bring against Willoughby – I only knew he was up to something, and I'd decided to stick to my decision not to mention Grice's game

244

yet, so I simply explained that Alan and I, as airmen under training, were being expected to do work for which we weren't yet qualified, and being blamed afterwards if things went wrong.

The Adjutant listened gravely, nodding from time to time. When I'd finished he said, 'I understand how you feel, Turner. Must be very frustrating for you here on an operational station and not being able to fly. But you're going to have to stick this out.' He clasped his hands behind his head and sighed. 'God, you do miss it – the flying. I remember when I was grounded, I nearly went bonkers. Still miss it, you know. Taking up one of those old kites and stooging around over Germany blasting hell out of Jerry – Christ, there's nothing like it.'

I wasn't entirely sure I agreed with him, which rather surprised me when I thought about it. His attention seemed to be elsewhere for a moment. I noticed the red of his nose was tinged with purple and his eyes had a yellowish tinge; I could guess why he'd been grounded. His uniform needed pressing too, and his pilot's wings were coming unstitched.

He sat up and cleared his throat. 'Now, I can't let you off scot-free, you realize that. You admit to being guilty of this – ah – offence. So, you'll do seven days Confined to Camp. All right?'

'Thank you, sir.'

'Now, for God's sake keep your bloody nose clean. And if there's anything bothering you, just come and tell me.'

I could see he was relishing this paternal relationship he'd invented for us. I gave him an immaculate salute. It was the least I could do. I'd arrived expecting a trip to the glasshouse and was leaving with a recommendation for a commission.

'Right-ho,' he said. 'Carry on.'

Confined to Camp, CC, or jankers as it was called by those who suffered it, consisted of reporting to the guardroom at an

245

unearthly hour every morning, being employed all day on the most disgusting jobs that could be found, and, of course, not leaving the confines of the barbed wire for the duration of the sentence. In practice it usually meant being farmed out as a cleaner to one of the sections: the ablutions being the least popular and the most sought after being the radar section which was always dust-free and warm. Harry did suggest that he might apply for me to clean The Wings, but we didn't think they'd wear that.

It was a long week, and I was introduced to aspects of camp life that would have turned the strongest stomach. By the end of each day I only had enough strength left to climb out of my evil-smelling overalls and fall into bed. Oddly enough the SPs, whom I expected to wreak a terrible revenge, behaved with perfect decorum towards me. I think it was enough for them to have me in their clutches, as it must have been to see me, mop and bucket in hand, covered in every variety of filth. The one humiliation I really feared – Pearl stepping over me as I polished the floor at her feet – I was spared.

On my first evening of liberty Harry took me down to the pub to celebrate, along with Danny, Freddy and Tiny Hopkins, the electrician. Ops had been scrubbed that day, and the bars were jammed to the doors, but we took our drinks over to where two old couples from the village were sitting at a table, and stood round them swapping obscene stories about Churchill and the King until they got up in disgust and left, and we could sit down in comfort and take the weight off our pints. I was repeatedly congratulated on having survived a week of jankers and my health was drunk so often that everyone became very convivial and a lot of refills were demanded. On his second trip to the bar, Tiny fell over Harry's outstretched legs.

'You ain't 'arf got fuckin' big feet, 'Arry,' he said.

'It is said that feet are often an indication of the size of other organs of the body,' Harry said complacently. 'You'll notice I also have a big nose. You may draw your own conclusions.'

'Are big feet an advantage?' asked Freddy, always a practical man.

'What for?'

'For standing on, and that.' He rubbed his balding head. 'I mean, they might distribute the weight of the body more evenly, mightn't they?'

'I don't know about that, but they used to ache a bit at work.'

'My feet are only size seven,' Danny announced. 'They're small, but as unmarked as a child's,' he said, glancing at Tiny.

The others laughed.

When it was my round I struggled up to the bar and waited for a chance to order. The counter was awash with beer and the girl was swilling glasses in water that looked darker than anything coming up from the barrels. I got the barman's attention at last, and while he was drawing the four pints I looked round the room. Instantly, because that was the kind of effect she had, my eye was drawn to Pearl. She was standing in the far corner by the door and talking heatedly to someone who was out of sight. When the crowd shifted slightly I could see through the haze of smoke that it was Willoughby. He was smiling his hideous grin at her, which I knew could imply anything from lust to anger. I watched them, riveted, trying desperately to decipher the movement of their lips. Then the barman said, 'I'll need paying for these, lad.' I turned back and reached in my pocket for the money. He pushed the brimming glass tankards towards me and I gathered them up, two in each hand, and turned back towards the door. They'd both gone.

Without thinking I started towards where they'd been, but realizing I was carrying four pints, I gave up and went back to the table.

247

Tiny jumped up to take the beer. 'Come on,' he said. 'Where've you been? We're dyin' of thirst here.'

Willoughby was furious that I'd got away with such a light sentence. I would catch him sometimes staring morosely at me over his *Daily Mirror*, hatching some new attempt to make life a misery for me. For my part I watched him closely for any sign of a connection with Pearl, but never saw a flicker of one. And as the weeks went by he fell back on his accustomed sneers and taunts, and I persuaded myself I was imagining things: there was no reason why she shouldn't have met him in the line of duty; they could have been discussing anything – the weather, or even politics (well, perhaps not in Pearl's case). And why didn't I do the obvious thing – ask her outright? Because I was a coward. I was afraid of what she might decide to tell me in her direct, insouciant way. So I said nothing, and contented myself with our occasional meetings which were still few and far between.

The new play had only one set, and no scene -changing would be needed during the show, so to justify my presence on the tour, Harry had appointed me as prompter. This meant attending all the rehearsals, sitting in a corner, following the script with my finger on the line and glancing up nervously to see if a pause was intentional or not. I discovered that the prompter is the most abused man in the theatre. If he doesn't give the prompt quickly enough, the actor, on the edge of a breakdown from having crammed his head with inane lines, stamps his foot, clicks his fingers and snaps, 'Come on! *Come on!*' If he gives the prompt too soon the actor glares at him and says loudly, 'I *know* that! I was *pausing*!' The only thing that stopped me hurling the book at them and walking out was that in a few days' time Pearl would be joining us to take up her duties with the dummy clock.

We propped it up on a chair, roughly where it would be on

the set, and she sat beside it on another chair, one leg crossed over the other, one slim hand on the script on her knee, the other on the handle of the clock, her face a beautiful mask of expressionless boredom. The others were fairly sure of their lines by now, so I was able to keep my eye on Pearl, ready to get her attention if she missed one of her cues. Then she would flash me a grateful smile and duck her dark head towards the book to check the time; and I would want nothing more from life than it was offering at that moment.

Ten-Minute Alibi had been a huge success in the West End twelve years before, but it might as well have been thirty. The men in it called each other 'old chap' or in moments of passion, 'you swine!' and the implication was that for girls a visit to Paris was simply the first step to South America and the white slave traffic. But the wooden characters suited the woodenness of amateur actors and the plot was undeniably ingenious, and with Harry being engagingly odious and Hubby over-acting outrageously as the police inspector, the play seemed to satisfy everyone at its first performance. The audience appeared to accept without question that bachelors in Bloomsbury flats still had their own butlers and that anyone over fifty had a title: I supposed they assumed such things to be the commonplaces of life in the upper classes. There was occasional gratuitous sexual advice offered from the back rows during the love scenes, but as these were few and very staid, it didn't diminish the general appreciation. As a result, Father had enough requests from other stations to justify the PSI money he'd lavished on the set, and we were able to set off round the countryside again, rogues and vagabonds once more.

This time there were less than a dozen of us, so no coaches were needed, only one medium-sized truck. The cast either squeezed themselves in front with the driver or draped themselves over the furniture in the back. Returning from the first date, I climbed over the tailboard in the darkness, to hear

Pearl whisper my name and feel a soft hand grope for mine and pull me onto the sofa beside her. And as the truck rolled forward and we sat there, watching our breath freezing against the dim square of night sky, I found the courage to pull her to me so that I could feel her cheek against mine and turn her face towards me once again. It was like old times, and as always with old times revisited, it wasn't quite the same. But, as before, it became a routine, and one that she seemed prepared to accept.

And then things started to happen that distracted me even from Pearl.

The war, which had dragged on for so long – the whole of my adolescent life in fact – so that peace had become a fading memory or a distant promise, was at last showing signs of hurrying towards a climax. We were done with strategic withdrawals and glorious retreats; now the news came ringingly triumphant in the headlines and over the radio. German cities were falling day by day, the Russians were nearing Berlin and, most significantly, all over the world countries were bravely declaring war on Germany: Uruguay, Turkey, Syria, Chile, every few days another one. Britain was exhausted, but buoyed up like a marathon runner in sight of the finishing line. The excitement made us stagger, but the world was cheering us on, and the Americans and the Russians were on our side. The latest news was that no rockets had landed on London for several days, the Germans had at last evacuated the launching sites – no more unannounced horror falling at random out of a midday sky; and for the ground staff up here on the airfields, no more guilt that our families were in greater danger than we were.

Operations had become chaotic: we were mounting daylight sorties over the battle areas or the lines of communication, and at the same time night raids into Germany, sometimes long ones, even as far as Berlin. It was the morning after one of these that Alan grabbed me as I arrived at the section.

'You know O–Orange was an early return last night?'

'No, I didn't,' I said.

'Compass failure.'

'Again? Who checked them last night?'

'Willoughby.'

'Well, he can't blame us this time.'

'No.' Alan hesitated. He seemed agitated – more, I thought, than the situation warranted. Abruptly he said, 'Anyone in that place of yours?'

'Don't think so.'

'Listen. Willoughby's just rung and told me to go out to the dispersal and bring the gyrocompass back here.'

'What for?'

'So's he can check it over, he says. Apparently he and Grice can't get in. They're caught up in some bullshit at the sergeants' mess. He sounded a bit frantic. He says he doesn't want the instrument blokes tinkering with it.'

'I'll bet he doesn't. What the hell's he up to?'

'That's what I want to find out.'

Alan's normally pale face was pink, clashing quaintly with his freckles. I could see he'd got one of his bright ideas, and I thought a little caution might be timely. 'But how are you going to do that?' I said carefully.

'All we've got to do is get the gyro back to that hut of yours and have a look at it before we bring it in here.'

'Have a look at it?' I said, disbelievingly. 'Where will that get us? I don't even know how the bloody thing works.'

'I do,' Alan said.

I looked at him in surprise. He clearly meant it.

'I've been through the manual a couple of times,' he said. 'And last month I helped old Jimmy in Instruments strip one down.'

251

I'd forgotten how keen he was. While I had escaped into the privileged world of The Wings, he'd been sweating his way through the handbooks, preparing himself for his chosen trade. I said, 'Look, I'm in deep enough shit already with that bastard.'

'Don't you want to know what's going on?'

'Not particularly.'

But he knew that wasn't true. I did want to know. In fact, there were lots of things about Willoughby I wanted to know. Alan was looking at me anxiously. I could see he wasn't going to give up as easily as that. 'Oh, all right,' I said, 'but we'd better get a move on.'

There was a cold wind cutting across the great, treeless plain of the airfield that turned our knuckles blue on our handlebars. Fortunately O-Orange's dispersal was only about five minutes round the peri track, and we brought our hands back to life by blowing on them and tucking them into our armpits while we waited for the Flight Sergeant in charge of the ground crew to deign to notice us.

'Come for the gyro, Chiefie,' Alan said when at last he came over.

'You from Instruments?' he said. He looked tired, and his mind seemed to be on more important things.

'No. From Sgt Willoughby. It's to go to him.'

The Flight Sergeant shot him a quick look. Then he nodded. 'OK. One of the lads is getting it off for you. Sign here, will you?'

Alan glanced at me in alarm. I grimaced behind the flight sergeant's back and shrugged to indicate that he had no choice. Reluctantly Alan took the proffered stub of pencil and signed the sheet on the clipboard.

'You got transport?' the flight sergeant asked.

We hadn't thought of that. 'No, Flight,' I said.

'You can use the trolley.' He pointed to a two-wheeled

252

barrow up-ended on the grass. 'But bring it back.' He walked away and stopped by the undercarriage, the great wheels as tall as he was, and gazed up into the open bomb doors.

'You'd have had to sign for it anyway,' I said to Alan.

'That's OK,' he said coolly. 'Actually, I signed it Willoughby.'

The master compass wasn't big, no bigger than a narrow bucket, round and black; but it was too heavy to balance on a crossbar. Pushing it on the trolley was easy, but took longer than cycling. We got it inside The Wings without being seen, and I cleared a space on the table.

'Buck up, for God's sake,' I said.

Alan had brought a few tools and a copy of the service manual in his haversack. He laid them out next to the compass and, with what seemed to me amazing confidence, started to remove screw after screw, while I hovered nervously behind him. After a little persuasion the casing came off, uncovering an exquisite complexity of brass, steel and fine multicoloured wires. Alan gazed at it as rapturously as if it had been a girl he had just undressed. I could see how he felt: there was something aesthetically seductive about all those beautifully crafted levers, cogs, pivots and tiny springs, gleaming in their unsullied golden brass. But this wasn't the moment for contemplation. Willoughby might already be waiting for us in the section.

'What now?' I said, wishing I'd taken the trouble to glance at the manual once or twice myself.

Alan shook his head and turned a couple of pages. Then, six more screws, and a whole section came loose, connected by only half a dozen wires. He peered into the mechanism that was now revealed, turning the compass to catch the light from the window. 'Ah!' he said suddenly. 'There it is.'

'What?' I said, looking over his shoulder. 'Where?'

'There.' He pointed the screwdriver at a wire that was

253

hanging loose. It was bent back, but was obviously intended to be attached to a tiny brass terminal just above it. What even I could see at once was that the end of the wire had been soldered to form an eyelet, but the nut was still on the terminal, so it hadn't come loose by accident, someone had removed it deliberately and screwed the nut back on.

'That'd be enough to do it,' Alan said. 'It'd still go, and work the indicators in the cockpit, but the readings would be all to cock.'

'You sure?'

'Absolutely. Somebody made sure of that.'

'Willoughby?'

'Must be.'

'But, why?'

'You tell me,' Alan said. 'Come on, we'd better get this back.'

Neither of us spoke as he screwed the casing in place or as we pushed the trolley towards the section as fast as we could, but the same thoughts must have been going through both our heads. It seemed incredible. I found myself thinking of all those posters, yellowing on the cookhouse walls, about secrecy, sabotage and fifth-columnists, and those stiffly acted War Office films we'd yawned through when we first joined. It *was* incredible. I mean – right here on our airfield and right under our noses. It couldn't be. But, if it wasn't sabotage – what was it?

Alan was the first to break the silence as we bounced the trolley up the path towards the section. 'I always thought', he said, 'spies were supposed to be smooth and charming.'

21

We agreed that there was no question about what we'd seen. Alan explained in more detail the implication of the disconnected wire; the technicalities passed through my understanding leaving no trace, but his own conviction convinced me. What *was* in question was what we should do about it – and when we should do it. Presumably Willoughby would restore the compass, report that he could find nothing wrong with it, and then, as before, there'd be an inquiry into why the crew had turned tail. Alan said he thought that might be the moment to spill the beans, before another poor sod was reduced to the ranks.

So we awaited events. In spite of the solid evidence, Willoughby's motivation in all this seemed hard to imagine. To go to the lengths and run the risks that he had, simply to incapacitate one plane in all the hundreds taking off from all the airfields that night, seemed scarcely worth it. Or was that how spies (or agents or saboteurs, or whatever he was) went about it? Did every success count, however small, on the principle that for the want of a nail the battle was lost? It was difficult to believe in Willoughby as a creature of such selfless dedication. But then didn't they say that it always turned out to be the last person you'd suspect?

The days went by and became a week, the week became a fortnight, and still nothing happened. The crew of O-Orange were seen to be at liberty and there was no whisper of an enquiry.

'He must have reported that there really was a fault in the compass,' Alan said.

'But then Instruments would have had to repair it.'

'Not if he said it was only out of alignment in some way. He could have pretended to fix that himself.'

'So what do we do now?'

Alan rubbed his head. 'Tell someone, I suppose.'

'Who?'

'Well, what about your friend, the Adjutant?'

He was known as my friend the Adjutant ever since I'd got away with my week's jankers. In fact, I think it had been Willoughby who had first called him that. I didn't relish going there with my story. I didn't relish going anywhere for that matter. With each day that passed the evidence seemed flimsier – in fact non-existent. All we had was my word and Alan's. I was horribly nervous of what the consequences might be for us; and so, I was sure, was Alan. But his eyes were fixed on me with an irritatingly trustful expression. I think he felt he'd done his part with the manual and the screwdriver, and that now it was my turn to bat for England. So rather than be thought LMF myself, I took a deep breath and strode over to the orderly room to request an audience with the Adjutant.

'What about?' the clerk said.

'A personal matter.'

He looked at me suspiciously, as if doubting already that my mother was dying or that my wife was having it away with the lodger, and gave me an appointment for the next morning.

I'd told Harry what Alan and I had discovered and he'd been disappointingly calm about it. It seemed that everyone on the camp had smelt something fishy about Willoughby for a long time. 'Although this does take a bit of swallowing,' Harry said. 'I guessed the bugger was devious, but not *that* devious.'

This gave me no comfort. I was sure now that nobody would believe our story. To Pearl I had said nothing. If her relationship with Willoughby was anything like I feared, I didn't want her alerting him to what was going on. Anyway, perhaps she was in it with him. Could she be? Dear God, the idea seemed ludicrously melodramatic. Well, if she was a Mata Hari she'd picked an odd victim in me, who couldn't tell you where the squadron had gone last night, let alone where it was going tomorrow.

The following morning I presented myself to the Adjutant with shining boots and glowing buttons and a painfully close shave. He was not as affable as the last time and looked oppressively hung over.

'Right. What can I do for you, Turner?'

'Can I speak to you privately, sir?'

He squinted up at me as if the light was too strong for his eyes. It probably was. Then he sighed. 'All right, Corporal. Piss off for a moment, would you?' When the corporal had gone he said, 'Well?'

'Well, sir,' I said. And I told him the whole story, starting with Alan's experience before I'd arrived on the station, then our suspicions about the K-Kitty business, and finally our discovery of the broken connection. While I was talking he slowly put down his pen, leaned back in his chair and watched me attentively.

When I'd finished there was a long pause. Then he said, 'Have you told anyone else about this?'

'No, sir. Buckley and I are the only ones who know.' I thought it better not to mention Harry.

'You realize this is a very serious accusation you're making?'

'Yes, sir.'

'Very serious indeed.' There was a pause while he rubbed his eyes with the backs of his hands. Then he leaned forward and rested his chin on his interlaced fingers. A platoon of the RAF Regiment marched past the window behind him, their sergeant bellowing orders. The Adjutant winced slightly; his head was obviously bothering him. With a visible effort he said, 'You have no actual evidence? Just what you and this . . . ah . . .'

'Buckley, sir.'

'You and Buckley observed?'

'Yes, sir.'

'And is this AC Buckley prepared to stand up and swear to it?'

'Yes, sir.'

He nodded carefully. 'A bit flimsy though, isn't it, this story about a wire coming loose?'

'It didn't come loose, sir. It was disconnected.'

'Yes, yes. So you say.'

'It's true, sir.'

'My dear chap,' he said hastily, 'I'm sure you're right. But . . .' He spread his hands. 'As evidence it's pretty slight. You must see that.'

'But it's not just that, sir. I told you. There were those other incidents.'

He gave me a rueful smile. 'Speculation, mostly.'

'All the same, they do add up.'

'Yes, but to what?' He massaged his moustache with his finger for a moment and then adopted a severe expression. 'I have to say, Turner, that you want to be careful about this. I don't have to remind you that this NCO you're accusing of . . . of God knows what, had you on a charge not so long ago – a pretty serious charge as I recall. This,' he made a gesture embracing me and all my accusations, 'might begin to look like vindictiveness, mightn't it?'

He leaned back in his chair again and assumed his favourite role of the paternal housemaster. 'Now, look here. What you've done is absolutely correct. You were quite right to come to me – very responsible. But what you've told me doesn't really amount to a case.' He held up a hand to stop me interrupting. 'You may be right; perhaps something ropey is going on. All the more reason to go carefully.' He lowered his voice confidentially. 'You see, Turner, we have to think of the reputation of the squadron. There have been rather a lot of early returns recently. Not a good show at all. The AOC is pretty cheesed off about it – he's got Command on his back. And rumours of something like this getting around aren't going to help, are they?'

'I still think it should be reported, sir,' I said stubbornly.

'Oh, it will be, it will be. Once it's been investigated properly – by the right people.'

What right people? And when? Never, if he had anything to do with it. I could see he had no intention of getting himself involved in anything that might cloud his true blue horizons. I felt a sudden surge of fury at having to stand there listening to this boozy old time-server. I felt in my pocket. Yes, I'd got it.

'Well, while they're at it, sir,' I said, 'they might like to investigate this.' I pulled out the key to Grice's cupboard, stepped forward and laid it on the desk, directly under the Adjutant's nose.

'What's this?' he said, startled.

'It's a key to a cupboard in our section, sir.'

'What cupboard? What're you talking about? What's in it?'

'I'd rather not say, sir.'

'Why the bloody hell not?'

'I think it should be investigated by the right people, sir,' I said, looking him straight in the eye. 'For the reputation of the squadron.'

259

It seemed to have been my fate always to miss the great moments in my life. When the England captain was bowled for a duck, I was buying an ice-cream; when the house opposite went up in flames and burned all night, I was away at school camp, and whenever anything really dramatic happened at a party, it was always just after I'd left. So it was no surprise to me to realize that if there was to be any outcome of my report to the Adjutant, it would inevitably happen while I was away on leave.

Over the months, I had accumulated an entitlement to nearly a fortnight's freedom and I'd arranged to take it as soon as possible after we'd played the last date of *Ten-Minute Alibi*. Pearl, I discovered, was also going on leave, several days before me. She only had a week, but it did mean that there would be four days at the end of her leave and the beginning of mine when we'd both be in London at the same time. I pointed out this happy coincidence to her and suggested we might meet.

'What, up West?'

'Yes.'

'Go to a show?'

'If you like.'

She thought about this, frowning slightly. Then she said, 'In our civvies?' She was already deciding what to wear. Then she eyed me speculatively, probably wondering what I might appear in. The first date in civilian clothes was always a dangerous moment: romances had been known to shrivel at the sight of the loved one's Sunday best.

'Of course.'

'Lovely,' she said. My heart bounded.

She seemed not to have a telephone, but I made her promise faithfully to ring me somehow, the very day I arrived home.

So she went off and I stayed behind, helping Harry to store

260

the scenery and return bits of furniture to shops and well-wishers in the district. And still nothing happened. Willoughby and Grice remained, silent and immune, on either side of the stove; the cupboard stayed locked. I told Alan to drop me a card if there was any news, and at the end of the week, wearing my best blue, with my green railway warrant in one pocket and seventeen pounds twelve shillings of my carefully hoarded pay in the other, I was on my way to London, home and beauty.

22

For nice boys from nice homes, leave, that longed-for, dreamed-of fragment of paradise, held one particular terror. A cold sweat broke out all over us at the thought of letting slip one of those short, everyday Anglo-Saxon expletives in front of our innocent families. In those days the BBC could scarcely let a 'damn' through its clenched teeth, 'bloody' could still rock a theatre audience almost as much as it had on the first night of *Pygmalion*, and before I'd joined up I'd hardly ever heard the other words except in the murkier moments of school; I'd never seen them written down, only up – on lavatory walls and with variable spelling. I couldn't really believe that my mother even knew what they meant, and I was anxious not to give her the opportunity of finding out.

The trouble was that where I was now coming from the words had become like mortar between the bricks of our everyday exchanges: no two words could be spoken without a four-letter one in between, together they formed a sort of lingua franca without which our speech sounded oddly bereft. We were well aware of it, of course. In fact, one of the favourite jokes going the rounds was about the airman

263

who told his mate, 'Last night I met this fucking gorgeous girl in the fucking pub and she took me back to her fucking flat and when we fucking got there she locked the fucking door and took me into the fucking bedroom and turned down the fucking lights and then she took off all her fucking clothes and pulled me onto the fucking bed.' 'And then what happened?' asks his mate, excited beyond endurance. 'What do you think?' retorts the airman. 'We had sexual intercourse.'

But, by some miracle, I seemed to shed the habit along with my uniform. Once home and in my three-year-old sports jacket and grey flannels, the danger receded. My old life invaded me and relaxed me along with the infinite easiness of my civilian clothes. The airfield seemed another country entirely; even Pearl was hard to imagine in this world.

All the same, almost the first question I asked my mother was, 'Have there been any phone calls for me?'

'No, dear. Should there have been?'

Of course it was too soon. She'd probably ring tonight. Or tomorrow morning.

With no more fear of air-raids, my mother had moved back into our house in West London, trying to restore some sort of comfort to it in the hope that my father might soon be back from the Middle East. Some rooms were still shrouded and dusty, and on the top floor wallpaper hung in festoons, while across the ceilings spread great brown stains like the coastlines of uncharted seas where rain had come through the disintegrating roof. The house had actually been officially condemned after the bomb had dropped on the house opposite. But that had been conveniently forgotten: if every condemned house were to be abandoned, London would be a ghost town. I peered through the new, finger-marked glass in the drawing-room window, smelling the fresh putty. The house whose garden backed onto ours was an empty shell,

264

open to the sky. I wondered where the little girl with the red hair was, the one who used to come to the fence and call my name when we were both ten.

London's war was over now: no more bombs, no more doodlebugs, no more rockets. It seemed strange to be able to move about without one ear cocked for a siren or the thump-thump of an alien engine. The blackout was lifted, which at least meant that we could breathe at night instead of being sealed behind those cumbersome screens jammed in the window frames, but in the streets it was still dark; even if the lampposts and neon signs had survived the bombs, there still wouldn't have been enough electricity to light them. By daylight the city was indescribably scruffy, the plywood nailed over empty windows peeling and splitting, dirty sand dribbling from rotting sandbags. Not a lick of paint on anything for five years, and of course everywhere, round every corner, the gaps, the bombsites. Some had been cleared and held huge, scummy static water tanks. On others all that remained was a chimney or sometimes a solitary lift shaft, twisted by the heat, corkscrewing like a gaunt double helix through a vanished building. And the more recent ruins, where no one had got round to any sort of tidying up, were like dolls'-houses split open with an unfeeling axe. Half a house would have been blown away leaving the interior naked to the world. What had once been so private was now shockingly public: pictures still on the walls, unmade beds hanging in mid-air, people's odd choice of wallpapers. In one house, not far from us, dresses still hung in a doorless cupboard on the third floor. No one could reach them: there was no staircase. It seemed indecent somehow, like catching one's neighbours in the street in their underwear. And as one hurried past, the thought sometimes came: how many undiscovered corpses were there still under the mounds of rubble?

In the West End some attempt had been made to persuade us that London was still a capital of empire. The theatres and cinemas were packed, encircled with queues, and at Rainbow Corner by Piccadilly Circus, fresh-faced, well-laundered GIs leaned against the hoardings, chewing and watching with disbelieving eyes the passing show of under-nourished British eccentrics.

And now the spring had come – for me, almost overnight. In the first week of April, to travel two hundred miles south is to find a transformation in the landscape. Round the airfield only a few crocuses had shown their heads above ground. Here in London the daffodils were almost over and the tulips bursting into bloom. The displays in the parks were a bit patchy, but they still came up, year after year. And on the bombsites, sprinklings of blue and purple were poking from all the rotting nooks and crannies. London looked like an old, dirty tramp with an incongruous crown of flowers.

Pearl didn't ring the next day, or the next evening. My mother couldn't understand my reluctance to leave the house. But by lunch time the following day I was beginning to wonder myself if it wasn't silly to spend so much of my precious leave at home. So when at last the phone did ring I was already on my way to the front door.

'Hello,' I said breathlessly. I heard a cascade of pennies at the other end.

''Lo,' said a voice. 'It's me.'

'I thought you weren't going to ring. How wonderful. How's your leave going?'

'Oh, wizard.' There was a pause.

'So . . . are we going out?'

'Yeah, sure.'

'Tonight?'

'I'm busy tonight.'

266

'Tomorrow night, then?'

'Can't do tomorrow night, neither.'

'But that only leaves Wednesday. You go back on Thursday, don't you?'

'That's right.'

'Wednesday, then?' I presumed she could manage Wednesday. Otherwise why the hell had she rung up?

'OK.'

'Go to a show, shall we, and then have dinner? What would you like to see?'

'Oh . . . I don't mind.'

'All right. I'll surprise you.' Silence again. 'Well . . . Wednesday evening, then. OK?'

'Where shall I meet you?'

The one thing I'd completely forgotten. My mind sped across the possibilities and came up with nothing. All I could think of was my mother's favourite trysting place, along with half the rest of London. 'Outside the front of Swan and Edgar's. Half-past five. That all right?'

'OK.'

'See you then. Bye.'

'Be good.' And she'd rung off.

I didn't know whether I was elated or depressed: elated because she'd rung, or depressed because Wednesday was the only night I'd see her. I had somehow imagined the first part of my leave being devoted to her, dreamed of squiring her round London, lavishing my hoarded pay on her, walking her home through moonlit streets night after night. Now, all that would have to be condensed into one evening.

The weather at least was on my side. Wednesday arrived bright and clear and astonishingly warm. I was outside Swan and Edgar's far too early and stood there in the sunshine watching the crowds milling round the boarded-up base of Eros. My preparations had all been made the day before. I'd remembered Harry saying that the revue at the Ambassadors was the smartest and funniest thing in town; and now the tickets were in my pocket and there was a table reserved for us at a restaurant in Dean Street. I was wearing a dazzling white shirt and my best jacket, and one way and another I felt I was equipped to give even the most demanding girl a good time.

I didn't mind waiting. It was much too early to expect Pearl and the spring weather seemed to have given everyone a jaunty look, just as it had given me a feeling of rising elation. I watched the girls hurrying past in their skimpy Utility dresses, revealing parts of themselves that had been obscured in wool and serge all through the winter, and I thought how many desirable women there were in the world and how sad it was that even the greediest boy in the shop couldn't taste all the cakes. Mildly ashamed of such fifth-form thoughts, I addressed myself to the human race in general. I watched them benignly. How much less inhibited everyone seemed than before the war. Perhaps it was only the effect of the spring weather, but several people engaged me in conversation while I stood there, which would have been unheard of a few years before. Perhaps the British character was changing after all. I had just returned to speculating about the sex lives of two tall Wrens who were holding hands on the edge of the pavement, when I saw Pearl crossing Regent Street towards me.

It was extraordinary to see her here, in this setting, out of uniform. She hadn't noticed me yet and, resisting the urge to run towards her, I kept my eyes on her as she advanced confidently through the crowds, walking with that perfect, natural grace it was always so entrancing to watch. She was hatless, her hair loose, almost to her shoulders, and wearing a dark-blue coat open over a flowered dress. Even here her beauty was enough to make people turn and look, and I felt over-weeningly proud that it was me she was coming to meet.

She was late, of course. Not late for *her*, but late enough for us to have to hurry to the theatre, which started at a quarter past six, as most shows had since the war. When we got to our seats she took off her coat and I held it for her while she smoothed her dress under her and sat down. She took my hand at once but then, uncertain perhaps of the etiquette of the theatre, squeezed it and relinquished it. She looked round the little auditorium.

'Ooh,' she said. 'Posh seats.'

The box-office had done me proud, we were sitting slap in the middle of the stalls, and surrounded by the sort of people that, in uniform, we wouldn't have been allowed in the same room with. When the lights went down and the tiny band in the pit, all tinkle and drums, struck up the sprightly overture and the curtain rose on the first number, my attention was more on Pearl than on the stage. We weren't touching, but I kept glancing at her like a fond parent at a party to see if she was enjoying herself. She was sitting upright, her perfect profile rimmed by the light from the stage, her lips slightly apart, gleaming faintly. She laughed a lot at Hermione Gingold's parody of a lady cellist, but could only manage a frown of concentration at some of the sketches which seemed to rely on the audience having seen every other show in town. I felt as obtuse as she did, and wished I'd been briefed by Harry, who would have understood every innuendo. But in the interval she told me she was loving it, and when it came to the duchess taking the GI to the pantomime and explaining to him why the dame was a man and the principal boy was a girl, she laughed so much that I had to lend her my perfectly ironed handkerchief which was really only for show.

The restaurant was supposed to be Hungarian, although rationing had made the goulash indistinguishable from Irish stew, but it tasted good, there was plenty of it, and thanks to the new law I was sure of being able to pay the bill. Faced with the impossibility of rationing restaurants, the Government had decreed that none of them, however celebrated, could charge more than five shillings for a meal. Even with the cover charge that the grander ones were allowed to add, it meant that we impoverished men–about–town could dine our girlfriends at the Savoy or the Café Royal and still be sure of change from a pound note. Unless, of course, they drank. Then the bill could suddenly rocket out of sight. Teetotal partners were very popular at this time, but Pearl not being one of them, I had chosen a place I knew had a cheapish house wine. And after the waiter had finished performing with corks and napkins, we downed it happily and uncritically. To be individuals again, wearing our own clothes, sitting in freedom and comfort, having our food set before us, was luxury enough for us. In my jacket pocket was something I'd made up my mind to show Pearl, but my courage kept failing me. Even now the moment was too perfect to risk. All I wanted was to go on watching her face in the redundant flattery of the candlelight while, with her reticence dissolved by the wine, she chattered on about her family and the legion of her aunts and uncles spread, it seemed, across the whole of East London.

When we came out into the warm night, the pubs were closing and Shaftesbury Avenue was full of people. We turned towards Piccadilly with no thought of where we were going. We'd stopped for a moment to look at the photographs outside a theatre, when I felt a heavy hand on my shoulder.

A big man in the uniform of a Flying Officer was grinning at me. 'It is Sam, isn't it?' he said. 'I thought it was.'

'Hello, Douggie,' I said. I remembered him from Elementary Flying Training.

'Wonderful to see you again,' he said. 'This is Prue.' He pushed forward a thin, fair girl with round eyes and rabbit teeth who offered us a limp hand.

I introduced Pearl. 'How do you *do*?' Douggie said,

pumping her hand enthusiastically and staring at her. He could hardly be blamed: I'd often seen her beauty shock people into forgetting their manners. 'Look here,' he said, 'are you going anywhere?'

'Not really,' I said. Which was true.

'We're off to my club for a drink. Why don't you come along?' he said, to Pearl as much as anyone.

The word 'club' was enough for her. 'Lovely,' she said, not waiting for me to agree.

Taxis were still as rare as gold. The Yanks used them like buses and paid extortionate sums for the privilege, so the cabbies weren't much interested in any other sort of passenger. But within a minute Douggie had one at the kerb. I suppose the old pilot's wings still had their magic. His club turned out to be one I already knew, just off Shepherd Market, a drinking club for RAF aircrew (commissioned, of course).

'You a member?' he asked.

'No.'

'Better sign you in, then.' Which he did with a flourish, then led the way up the narrow stairs to the bar. It was crammed and the noise was deafening.

'What's it to be?' Douggie shouted as we struggled towards the bar.

'No, let me,' I insisted, getting there first.

My round was quickly gone and Douggie ordered another. Not till after the third did we slow down a little.

'So,' Douggie said to me, 'on leave, are you?'

'Yes.'

'What are you on these days?'

I knew what he meant. Not what drugs was I taking or what alcohol was I addicted to, but what aircraft was I flying. 'I'm not,' I said. 'I'm not flying.'

'Tough luck,' Douggie said sympathetically. 'Have a prang, did you? Or have you finished your tours?'

271

'I'm not aircrew.'

'What?'

'I'm not aircrew,' I said loudly.

'Not aircrew?' he repeated, as if I'd announced I was on a visit from the moon.

'No. I never was. I was grounded, you know. I was a bit browned off about it,' I added as cheerfully as I could.

A slow smile spread across Douggie's face. 'You crafty sod,' he said conspiratorially. 'How did you pull that one? Develop a nervous tic, did you? Couldn't read the letters off the card? Jammy bugger. Felt safer on the ground, eh?' He winked at the girls and turned back to me. 'So what are you now? A Whitehall warrior, I suppose. Air Ministry, or something cushy?'

I could feel Pearl looking at me. My face was very hot. 'I'm an AC2, actually,' I said.

Douggie lowered his glass onto the bar as if he were afraid of dropping it. 'You're joking,' he said. 'A plonk? You mean you're still a plonk? Bloody hell's teeth. You poor little sod.' He contemplated me for a moment, shaking his head in disbelief. Then he said, 'Mind you, you're still here to tell the tale, aren't you? Most of our lot bought it, you know. Little Reg, remember him? And that thin bloke, Mervyn what's-his-name. And Barry Staines . . .'

I gripped my glass tightly and stared at the knot of his officer-quality tie and wondered whether I should try to explain or whether, in a noisy bar, after so many drinks, it might be better just to shut up and hope he'd soon stop.

He did stop, almost at once, because suddenly, over my shoulder, he caught someone's eye. 'Tommy!' he shouted. 'You old bastard! How are you? Hang on a minute.' He turned away abruptly and began to push his way along the bar.

There was an uncomfortable pause. Prue said awkwardly,

272

'Douggie doesn't fly now, either, you know. He's at Command HQ, at Stanmore.'

Douggie's voice called down the bar. 'Come on, Prue. Over here. Old Tommy wants to meet the popsie.'

''Scuse me,' she said quickly, and backed into the crowd.

Pearl pulled at my sleeve. It was difficult to look at her. 'Do you want to go?' she said.

'Go?' I said defensively. 'No. Why?'

'I thought you might,' she said, looking at me warily. I suppose my feelings must have been more obvious than I'd hoped.

The noise seemed to have become worse in the small room. We were having to shout to make ourselves heard. 'I wouldn't mind some air, would you?' I said. She nodded. 'Come on, then,' I said. 'Bring your glass.' I grabbed her free hand. I'd remembered from a previous visit that there was a flat roof you could reach from a window on the landing. We found a blackout curtain still over it, but pulled it aside and climbed out into the warm, clear night. The roof was the area of a small room and was surrounded by a waist-high parapet. We had it to ourselves; nobody seemed to have discovered it that night. We leaned against the empty parapet, our glasses in our hands. Breathing in the fresh air I realized I'd drunk quite a lot. I wasn't drunk, but I felt a comforting alcoholic insouciance about everything I said or did.

We listened to the rumble of the traffic and looked at the chinks of light from the windows across the way, something we'd not seen for years. Pearl put her hand on my arm. 'Will your friend wonder where we've gone?'

'Shouldn't think so,' I said as carelessly as I could. 'Anyway, he's not really my friend.'

Pearl's hand tightened on mine. 'No,' she said thoughtfully. A second later I felt her lips on my cheek. I put my arm round her shoulder.

I would have liked to take advantage of the moment, to scoop her up and devour her with the pent-up hunger of months, but I knew I'd already prevaricated for too long. The doubts and questions in my mind had grown like a thorny hedge between us; if I didn't resolve them now I never would. I dropped my arm and pulled out of my pocket the postcard that had arrived that morning from Alan. I'd wanted to hand it to her and watch her face while she read it, but it was too dark for that; I'd have to read it to her. Of course, it was too dark for that too, but, as the short-sighted often do, I put on my glasses in the fond hope of seeing it better.

'What's that?' she said.

'It's a card from Alan . . . chap in my section.'

I heard her sigh. 'What's he say?' she said, leaning over to look down into the mews.

'It seems,' I said carefully, 'Sergeant Grice is being court-martialled.'

It was a second before she said, 'Good God! What for?'

'Pinching kit from missing aircrew.'

'What a bastard,' she said quietly. I waited. The pause seemed endless. Then at last she said, so softly that I could hardly hear her, 'Is Ken Willoughby still there?'

This was what I'd been expecting. This was the moment I might at last discover the truth, or a part of it. With my throat tight with apprehension I said, 'He's been posted.'

I heard her intake of breath. Then she said steadily, 'Posted? Where?'

'I don't know.'

'Away from the station?'

'Out of the group, Alan says.'

In the darkness I could just see that she'd turned away and was looking towards the end of the mews. If only there'd been at least a glimmer of moon so that I could have seen her expression. Just then there was a lull in the traffic. In the sudden

274

silence I thought I heard what could have been a sob. My heart froze. This was the reaction I'd dreaded. 'Pearl?' I said tentatively.

She turned back to me. Her voice sounded stifled. 'Are you sure? Is it true? Is it really true?'

I tried to be gentle. 'They've both gone already, Alan says.'

Now the tears were unmistakable. She was rummaging in her bag, so I pulled out my handkerchief, stained already by tears of laughter. She wiped her eyes and blew her nose decorously.

'I'm sorry,' she said, sniffing. 'Too many gins I expect. It's just that . . . Oh, Sam,' she said with a sudden rush of emotion, 'it's just so wonderful.'

Perhaps if I'd drunk a little less myself my responses might have been sharper. As it was I had my arm round her and was half through 'never mind' before I realized that consolation was not what was required. It was joy that had provoked the tears. But why?

'Why?' I said.

She wiped her eyes again and pushed the handkerchief into her bag. 'I'll wash this for you,' she said.

'Why is it wonderful?' I insisted.

She was hesitating. Then she said solemnly, 'Promise you won't tell anyone?'

' 'Course not.'

'Not anyone? Not a word?'

'Not a syllable.'

'Well . . .' I could sense that it was her turn now to try to see my face in the darkness. 'You know what that Ken Willoughby was up to.'

'Not . . . not entirely,' I said cautiously. 'Was he fifth column or something?'

'Fifth column?' The tears had gone now. Relief had lifted her spirits. She gave an uninhibited laugh. 'A spy! That little twerp! Don't make me laugh.'

My relief was as great as hers. To hear her talk about him like that was so intoxicating I could hardly concentrate on the details of the plot.

'No, no,' she said, eager to tell me, now that she'd taken the plunge. 'He was on a fiddle, that one. Know what he did?'

I shook my head.

'When there was a big op on, and a crew asked him to, he'd take money off them to fix their compasses so they'd have to turn back.'

I could see at once he'd been on to a good thing: a compass was a lot less risky to nobble than other parts of the plane. And the next day he would have put in a report that the compass had been faulty but that he'd readjusted it. 'Where did you hear this?' I said.

'When I was on briefings. The boys used to joke about it sometimes – Ken's Cure they called it. I don't think many of them took it seriously, though.'

'One or two did.'

'Yes . . . oh, yes. One or two.' She hesitated again. 'You remember that skipper of K–Kitty?'

So here came part two. Now what was I going to hear? I gripped the edge of the parapet hard.

'That was one of Ken's jobs. Only it went wrong, didn't it? Went wrong for Alex. And went wrong for me.' She gave a little snort of disgust. 'My own silly fault though, you know.'

I kept my voice very calm. 'What happened?'

'Well, this Alex sort of adopted me as his mascot. You know how superstitious those aircrew blokes are. It started with his very first op. He came over to me after briefing and just stood there, looking down at me – he was ever so tall, you know. Then he said, quite ordinary, "You look just like an angel." A bit cheeky I thought, but quite nice all the same. 'Course, he didn't know me very well.' She paused and emptied her glass, putting it carefully on the parapet. 'After that he'd always come looking for me whenever he was flying. He'd stroll over and just say, "Hello, Angel," and then shove off. One of the boys told me that he reckoned it was good luck for him to see me at the briefing.' She sighed. 'That's all very nice, you know, but it wasn't half a worry. It got so that if I was off duty when he was flying, I'd have to go over specially so's he could see me. Well, you would, wouldn't you?'

'I suppose you would.'

'And he was ever so nervy, that boy. Used to get in a terrible state before ops. And it got worse after he lost his tail gunner that time. Anyway, on this particular day it was a very dicey target – Berlin, I think – and when he came across to me he was shaking all over, really shaking I mean. He was a bit of a funny colour too. "Oh, shit, Angel," he said, "I don't think I can do it." Well, I tried to cheer him up a bit – you know – but it wasn't no good. Then he said did I know a Sergeant Willoughby, and was it true he could fix early returns. I told him I'd heard rumours but I couldn't swear to it. "Ask him, Angel," he said. "For God's sake ask him. I'll pay him whatever he wants."'

'Why didn't he ask him himself?'

'He was afraid he'd be seen. He wanted to keep it secret – even from his own crew.'

'So you did it for him?'

'I had to, didn't I? I mean that boy was half off his head. I was ever so nervous, mind you, and your Ken Willoughby was dead suspicious. I told him why Alex had sent me, and after a bit he said yes he'd do it but he had to have the money first. I said there was no way I could do that and we had quite an argument. In the end he said, "By next week then, either you or him had better bring it me, or there'll be trouble."'

'What could he have done, though?'

'I don't know. But you know what he's like.'

Did I not.

'And then the next day I hear Alex is in the clink. I'm really upset about that, so I don't think too much about the money, until up comes that little sod and says where is it. "Why don't you go over to the Guard Room and ask him yourself," I says. Then he tells me, very nasty, "I'm holding you responsible." After that he started following me around and going on and on at me. I found out where Alex had been posted and I wrote to him. I got a letter back saying he was sorry he couldn't help because he was now on an erk's pay, and his dad was so disgusted with him he'd stopped sending his allowance.'

Allowances from dad indeed. 'Some of us manage to save on an erk's pay,' I said stiffly.

'Not that sort of money. Anyway, the bugger left me holding the baby. In a manner of speaking. And that Ken's been after me ever since. He's kept threatening all sorts of things.' She turned her head away and said in a low voice, 'I think he fancied me a bit, too. He didn't have the nerve to ask me straight out of course, but I think he was hoping I'd suggest that if he forgot the money he could . . . you know.' Her voice choked. 'It was horrible . . . really creepy.'

'Why didn't you tell me?'

'I was too scared. Oh . . . I wish I had. I wish I had.' She put her arms round me and pressed her forehead against me. I felt desperately sorry for her; and at the same time gratifyingly protective. Not to mention triumphant. Willoughby had clearly never been a rival; and as for Alex, although I wasn't too sure about her real feelings towards him – all that mascot business sounded a bit dubious – at least he'd left the arena in disgrace. And hadn't I just heard her call him a bugger?

She was crying again; relieved now, I supposed, to have got the story off her chest. I held her very tightly and suddenly, to my alarm, my own feelings of relief welled up inside me in a great bubble of love and pity for her, and absurdly I felt tears start in my own eyes. I tried desperately to hold them in but I couldn't, they started to run down my face.

She raised her head. 'Sam?' she said, and lifted her hand to touch my cheek. 'Here . . . you silly bugger. What the hell are *you* crying for?'

I suppose to be called a *silly* bugger is all right, really. It's quite different, isn't it.

Eventually we went back inside. We'd wiped our eyes and blown our noses and laughed at ourselves for being silly, and my handkerchief, the receptacle of so much human emotion, was now unrecognizable. Douggie and Prue seemed to have gone, so we went straight to the bar and ordered ourselves drinks. We toasted Pearl's freedom from the wicked Willoughby, and privately I toasted my own release from doubt and jealousy. I didn't even mind when she started to say how sorry she felt for Alex. He'd joined the wingless wonders and was no longer to be feared as a rival. After that we had another drink, and then, if I remember rightly, another. By this time the crowd had thinned out and it was clear the club was trying to close. God knows what time it was, but when we came out into the street, everywhere was still and silent.

We were both more than a little drunk. Arms round each other, we wandered through a deserted Shepherd Market, stopping every other yard to kiss with a new-found abandon. After a while we found ourselves in a dark, empty Piccadilly. A solitary taxi emerged from a sidestreet, ground its gears and disappeared in the direction of Knightsbridge. We were alone in the centre of London: it was like the day after the apocalypse – the world was ours – only the occasional survivor skulked along by the walls. The night air was crisp with the scent of renewal. Across the other side of the road we could just see the glimmer of the trees in Green Park.

'Let's go over,' Pearl said, in an unnecessary whisper.

We ran across the road. There was no traffic, but we ran because we were gripped by a heady feeling of delinquency: the guardians were all in their beds behind their locked doors, but we had escaped, we alone, and the city was wide open and ours for the taking.

The park railings had long since gone, melted into tanks or Halifax bombers. We ran down the bank and across the path onto the grass. There was no moon and it was very dark under the trees. After the warm day the earth was exhaling the tang of spring. The lights of a car passed on the road, but no one could see us here, no one knew we were here, no one cared. We clung to each other, kissing frantically, swaying like wrestlers in a lock. My desire for her became suddenly ungovernable. Every longing I had ever felt had narrowed itself down to this single need to thrust myself into her. I took her coat and spread it on the grass and we fell onto it, clawing at each other's clothes, until with surprising ease I was inside her. I could feel nothing but an overwhelming desire to possess her. It was too dark to see her face, her beauty was hidden from me, she was anonymous; she lay under me, hardly moving, making no sound, just panting in rhythm with me. But when I tried to withdraw for safety, she grabbed me tightly and murmured impatiently, 'No, no. Go on. Go on.'

We lay, exhausted, for a few moments, her rapid breath warm in my ear, her hand stroking the back of my head. After a minute I felt her shiver and realized I was cold myself: the night was not quite as warm as it had seemed a few moments before. We got up and straightened our clothes and I shook Pearl's coat and helped her into it. Then we walked slowly back towards Piccadilly.

She lived in the opposite direction from me. I wanted to see her home but she said it was bloody miles and she wouldn't hear of it, so I persuaded her to wait for a taxi.

'But it might be hours,' she said.

I didn't mind if it was. Pearl was rather quiet but I had a thousand things I wanted to tell her — it would take until dawn to say them all. Before I could utter one of them, a lone taxi appeared. Pearl leaped into the road and waved it down, and while she got in, I pressed a pound note into the driver's hand and said grandly, 'Take this young lady wherever she wants to go.'

Pearl giggled and said, 'Home'll do.' She slammed the door and put her head out to give me a quick peck. 'See you next week,' she said. The driver pushed his flag down.

'Oh . . . yes.' I tried to formulate the right words, any words, to express at least something of what I was feeling, but the cab jerked away from the kerb and turned in the road to go the other way. All I could do was wave.

'Bye!' she called from the other side of the road. 'Thanks for a lovely evening!' And the taxi rattled away into the darkness.

I pulled up my jacket collar and set off for home. I felt tireless and ready to walk from one side of London to the other. By the time I'd crossed Hyde Park, the moon had risen and the big houses in the squares were bathed in its ghostly, colourless light. My footsteps rang in the silence. I saw no one; the few cars in London were garaged for the night and the moonlight disguised the scars of wartime: I might have been walking these streets a hundred years before, they would have looked no different. I remembered my grandfather telling me that when he had lived here as a boy, he would look out of his bedroom window at dawn and see the lines of carts, loaded with hay for the thousands of stables in London, coming down the Bayswater Road from the country. And the drivers, he always loved telling me, were asleep, because the horses all knew the way. And strangely, the one thing I heard that night was the sound of a horse's hooves as an early milk cart passed in the distance. The only other sign of life was on the street corners where a gleam of light through a grating would reveal that a baker was working, and as I passed, the mouthwatering smell of freshly baked bread would drift up into my nostrils. I realized how hungry I was, and wondered what time it was.

23

Just in case a glimpse of civilian life should have stirred any individuality or rebelliousness in the returning airman, our CO had devised an instant reminder of his place in the scheme of things: anyone below the rank of corporal coming off leave had to spend his first day back delivering coal. This meant humping man-size sacks of the stuff to every bunker on the station, and by the time he staggered into the billet that evening, exhausted and black from head to foot, any memories of clean sheets, pillows and the armchair by the fire had shrunk back into a remote past.

So it wasn't until the next day that I could make contact with anyone. I was greeted in the section by a mild-looking sergeant with grey hair called Tenby, who introduced himself as Willoughby's successor. There was no sign of a successor for Grice – perhaps they actually thought he might be acquitted. Alan told me at breaktime that Tenby seemed to be as mild as he looked, and what was more he read the *News Chronicle*, which was a very good sign, Alan said. I'd half-expected to see Pearl in the NAAFI that morning, she must have known I was back, but she never appeared. I left a note for her in Base Operations, but that produced no response. Then the next day, in the main street, I ran into her friend, Doris.

'Hello,' she said, flashing her dreadful teeth at me.

I had never liked to use her as a go-between, she was always grudging about it and managed to give the impression that she would only deliver her own version of any message entrusted to her. But at that moment it seemed the only way.

'Will you be seeing Pearl?' I asked.

'Shouldn't think so,' she said in a voice heavy with sarcasm.

'Why not?'

'Haven't you heard?' Her eyebrows shot up with astonishment to remind me how excluded I was from Pearl's intimate circle.

'Heard what?'

'She's been posted.'

I felt as if I were falling through space towards a wild and icy sea. She must be lying. She was quite capable of it, the bitch. I couldn't breathe. Only single words would come out. 'Posted? When?'

'Last week. It came through while she was on leave.' Then, with a sort of malicious sympathy she added, 'Bit sudden, wasn't it.'

'But where to?'

Doris pursed her lips and looked affronted. 'I'm not supposed to say.'

'Oh, for God's sake, Doris,' I snapped, my temper suddenly beyond control. 'It's not D-day any more and she's not Winston bloody Churchill. Every other bugger on the camp probably knows. You do, for a start.'

Her red face became two tones redder, but she had the grace to look a bit scared – as well she might be – the messenger's life was hanging in the balance. 'Well,' she said, lowering her voice to show that as far as she was concerned it was still a state secret, 'I think it was St Merryn.'

'Where the hell's that?'

'Cornwall, I think.'

Which was about as far as you could post anyone without sending them overseas. I turned away to avoid the look of triumph in her eyes. 'Thanks,' I said shortly.

Like a sick animal I wanted to hide myself away from the world's view. I wanted to shut myself up and weep and rail against fate, the RAF, the war and life itself. I fled to my bolt-hole in Base Operations, but extraordinarily the door was locked, someone was actually in there. I got out as quickly as I could. The operations block had been a mistake anyway, it was too reminiscent of her. There was nowhere, nowhere on this damn camp I could be alone. I could have gone out onto the flights and communed with nature, but it had started to rain and I wasn't so unhinged by grief that I wanted to get soaked to the skin into the bargain. I made for The Wings and, of course, Harry was already there.

He was by now deeply engrossed in plans for yet another musical extravaganza and could hardly be distracted, even by my account of the shows I'd seen in London. When I finally gathered enough courage to tell him about Pearl, he did stop what he was doing for a moment and regarded me with a fatherly eye. But when he heard where she'd been posted there was no disguising the amusement he was trying to control. In the end he had to say it.

'Well, you won't be nipping down there on a forty-eight, will you?'

'I could get there on my next leave.'

'You've just been on leave. You're not due any more for months. By then she'll probably be posted to Inverness.' He saw the look on my face and had a shot at being more supportive. 'Look, it's life in the service, isn't it. It's not a matrimonial agency, you know.' He smiled grimly to himself. 'Quite the reverse, in fact. It doesn't do to go around getting

285

sentimental. We're all on the move. One night you're up to your bollocks in some little girl and the next day she and her kit-bag are on the train to God knows where. Or you are.' He smiled again, knowingly this time. 'Sometimes it can be an advantage.'

I thought of Bonny, and knew that he had a point. But I always found his farmyard view of sex rather unappetizing. Today it seemed unbearably callous.

'It'll pass, you know,' he said airily. 'Everything does.' He pushed several pages of scribbled notes at me. 'Get your great brain going on these. I want to have a big shipboard number to close the first half. We should have about seven minutes to set it behind the tabs.'

It didn't pass, not as easily as that, but other things happened that began to diminish its significance. A week later I took myself off on my own – I was a loner now, wrapped in a lover's self-pity – to a cinema in York. Before the main film began it was announced that there would be an extended newsreel of a concentration camp at Belsen, liberated a few days before.

When the first pictures came on the screen I was suddenly scalded with horror, trapped in a nightmare, I wanted to look away but I couldn't. I'd never seen anything like this before. I had once been made aware of what the war was really about when I'd had to watch bits of aircrew being brought out of a shot-up aircraft. But they'd been hastily bagged and removed, not left in mounds in the open air. Our newspapers and magazines had always hidden from us any of the really unacceptable nastiness that was going on all over the world. I had seen one picture, a private photograph passed round in the hut, which I'd never forgotten. It was of an execution in what looked like the compound of a Japanese prison camp. The prisoner was kneeling, his hands behind his back, and a soldier had just sliced off his head with an enormous sword, the weight of which had twisted him away like a golfer following through. The head was a blur on its way to the ground, but the startling thing about the picture had been the two spouts of blood arcing high into the air from the severed arteries. I had handed the picture on at once, but the image had never left me. It kept returning, and I would wonder who had photographed it and who the victim had been and what he'd been feeling a few seconds before it had been taken. But that had been an old thumbed snapshot taken with a box-camera; its impact was nothing to the sharp-focus reality I was seeing now.

The packed cinema was as hushed as a tomb. We'd seen dead bodies before – in a war like this it would have been hard not to – but these things were alive. They lay in rows, moving feebly; some of them, unbelievably, were on their feet, stepping slowly and jerkily towards us, their lips pulled back from their teeth in an animal grin, their eyes, huge and staring in their emaciated faces, looking out at us uncomprehendingly. Their faces were expressionless: there was nothing left underneath the stretched skin that could register a recognizable expression. And these were people – still, incredibly, people. Mostly Jews, the commentator was saying, because Hitler wanted to exterminate them. Like this? All of them? It was an inconceivable lunacy. A woman two rows in front of me moaned out loud.

As a child I'd had a terror of skeletons. A single glimpse of one in a book and there'd be nightmares for a week. I'd been carried sobbing from a Disney cartoon in which skeletons were dancing happily by the light of the moon. At art school, of course, I'd handled skulls and bones and drawn them exhaustively and become carelessly familiar with them, but the spectres of childhood still lurked beneath my consciousness. And here they were, in twenty-foot-high detail on the screen, not dancing now, but staggering, swaying, dragging themselves towards me, living skeletons, the creatures of my darkest dreams, telling me that my worst nightmares could indeed become reality.

Then they showed us the corpses. The camera moved slowly along an endless mound of them: eighty yards long this one was, apparently, and thirty yards wide, hundreds and hundreds of them, all little more than bones and skin, and all naked. The only parts of them that seemed not to have shrunk away were their genitals; a grotesque reminder of Nature's determination to go on reproducing itself to the last. This mound was of men's bodies, the women's bodies were on yet another vast pile. Flung helter-skelter, one upon another, naked women's bodies sprawled in an indecent final abandon. Many of them were young girls and some of the faces, in spite of starvation and the rictus of death, were still beautiful. I was horrified to find the naked shamelessness of some of them sickeningly erotic. What at last turned revulsion and horror into pity were the final pictures: heap after huge heap, carefully separated by the efficient camp staff, of shoes, spectacles, wigs, shaving brushes, false teeth. Somehow the sight of these pathetic relics returned the corpses to the status of human beings, the human beings who had carried these heartbreakingly personal possessions to the very end of their terrible journey.

When the film finished I couldn't move. I was unable to understand what I was feeling. I seemed to be sick with fear, with horror, with anger and with anguish all at the same time. I do remember being intensely grateful for a brief moment that I hadn't had to be one of the soldiers who'd discovered the place. When the curtains opened again and the main picture began, I realized it would be utterly impossible to sit through it, and I got up and shuffled along the row to the exit. Quite a lot of other people, I think, were feeling the same, and as we all made our silent way towards the street we avoided one another's eyes.

In the time before the bus was due to leave I wandered through the narrow, erratic streets, trying to reconcile what I'd seen with what was around me. These people, hurrying discreetly along their ancient pavements, were no different from Germans, I knew. We'd been reminded so often that our quarrel was with the Nazis, not with the German people (though how many Germans *were* Nazis no one seemed able to tell us). But that place, they'd said, was only fifty miles from Hamburg. Did none of them know it was there? None of them? Some of them did, obviously, because they ran the place. I tried to imagine the mentality of people who could actually operate a human slaughterhouse like that. If I was honest I knew that in the last couple of years I'd come across quite a few people who wouldn't have needed much conditioning to become enthusiastic concentration-camp guards. And if they had set up business in the English countryside, a few miles from a town like this, would we too have been unaware, deaf to any rumours, ignoring the columns of evil-smelling smoke that rose from behind the distant barbed wire? I turned a corner and saw above the crowded roofs the sublime bell towers of the Minster, serene in the evening sunlight. The Germans had created things every bit as beautiful; I'd seen photographs of German towns hardly different from this one. We'd nearly won the war, but when we'd won it, what were we going to find? How were we going to look them in the face? They weren't wild Turks or headhunters from Borneo, they'd produced Goethe and Beethoven and Bach, and were more akin to us, they always claimed, even than the French. What in God's name were we going to do with them?

My sleep that night was dreamless, but in the morning the nightmare was still with me. In the grey early light the naked figures in the ablutions seemed to be miming the gestures of those other bodies, the lines of wooden huts in the mist could have been the lines of huts in that other place; the bodies too plump, of course, and the huts too comfortable. But how hard would it have been to lock the gates, to stop feeding us, just to let us die – if the order had come from the right place? Later I tried to describe my confused thoughts to Alan. But even his well-informed liberal mind couldn't cope with the implications of this news. Eventually he shook his head slowly and said, 'At least, I suppose, it shows we're on the right side.'

It had never really occurred to me that there was any other side, but I could see that to someone like Alan, struggling with a pacifist heart, barely concealed beneath his uniform, these nightmare revelations had actually come as a sort of reassurance, redressing his balance of guilt.

I had intended to write to Pearl that evening, a witty, gossipy, newsy letter about life on the camp: I would disarm her with laughter. But other camps were still on my mind. How could I explain to her about them? I took out the only photograph I had of her and stared at it, seeing only the flesh falling away from that exquisite skull, the skin shrivelling, the radiant blue eyes glazed and staring. I gave up. I was like a romantic poet, obsessed with death and worms. Not till two days later did I finally manage a long, involved letter, rewritten half a dozen times, trying to convey my feelings about her absence, to convince her that this separation would only be temporary. After all, both our homes were in London, weren't they? And the war would soon be over, so we'd be sure to see each other again, wouldn't we? Anyway, the first leave I had I'd come down and see her: I'd worked it all out (hours spent in the orderly room poring over the railway timetables, calculating all the possible permutations of main lines, branch lines, departures, arrivals and connections until I knew them by heart). I posted it with a beating heart and waited for an answer. The days went by but nothing came.

Time seemed to be moving at two different speeds. My own days were interminable, strung between one parsimonious postbag and another, but for the rest of the world there were not enough hours to accommodate the dramatic events that were crowding in on us. On the day the Americans and the Russians met on the Elbe, our squadron flew what turned out to be its last sortie. After that a curious peace, still but tense, hung over the airfield. It was as if we were at the motionless centre of a maelstrom of history. City after city fell to the Allies, Mussolini was found hanging beside his mistress from a petrol station in Milan, Berlin fell and Hitler killed himself, while from the cracks in the runways fresh grass appeared and the birds perched fearlessly on the wings of the bombers. And then suddenly it was all over, the Germans surrendered and for twenty-four glorious hours the pubs stayed open all day. Bonfires were lit, strangers were kissed, vicars leaped to ring Grandsire Triples on bells that hadn't been touched for years – in a church two villages away a tenor bell fell eighty feet from the belfry, narrowly missing the verger. On the camp all pretence of discipline was abandoned as hundreds of airmen, hatless, their tunics unbuttoned, their arms linked in victorious camaraderie, poured out into the countryside to consume every last drop of alcohol they could find.

In the days that followed, a series of non-operational routines was hastily concocted to re-establish some sense of purpose: aircraft were stripped and reassembled, stores were inventoried and aircrews sent on extended training flights. It was one of these that broke the monotony for me. Crossing the camp one morning I ran into Greg, the navigator from K-Kitty. He was a flight sergeant now and a veteran of the squadron, flying with the same crew, although only four of the original seven were still together. I asked him how he was finding life as a peacetime navigator.

'Cushy. We haven't left the ground since VE Day. Tomorrow'll be the first time, actually. We've got some photo recce over North Germany to do. Fancy a trip, do you?'

'Tomorrow?' I said, startled.

'Yeah. We don't carry air gunners any more so there'll be plenty of room. Get yourself a chit.'

'I will. Thanks.' I was thrilled; it would be my first flight since the night cross-country.

He hadn't forgotten that either. His smile was slightly sardonic. 'That's if you trust yourself with us, of course. But our new skipper's very keen, flight lieutenant, DFC no less. So we should be all right.'

I wanted to ask about Alex but was afraid he might think that as part of the compass section I'd been involved in the whole affair. 'You heard from Alex at all?' I said tentatively.

'No. Not a word,' he said, and looked down at his shoes, frowning. 'Poor bastard. Rotten luck, that.' Then he dismissed it and slapped me on the shoulder as if to show he knew I wasn't implicated. 'See you tomorrow, then. Briefing's at ten-thirty, I think.'

We took off at midday in cloudless spring weather. I was in the mid-upper turret which I could spin through a hundred and eighty degrees, giving me a perfect view in every direction. We flew over Hull, across the Wash and past the tip of Norfolk. At a bare thousand feet I could see the hardy early bathers sprinkling the beach at Lowestoft like a rash of measles. Out of sight of land I clambered down to find Greg, who showed me the flight plan, pointing with a stubby finger to the towns we were to fly over. He tapped his compass repeater like a barometer and pulled a face of mock astonishment that it was working. We both laughed. Back in the turret, Europe had appeared: a slender yellow line stretching from horizon to horizon, which grew and broke into islands and then became the Zuider Zee. Vast areas of Holland were under water, flooded by the retreating Germans, only occasional roofs and spires protruding from great lakes of silent water.

As we approached Hamburg, the daredevil DFC said, 'Going down to five hundred feet, chaps. Tuck your feet up.' Five hundred feet is low – less than half the height of the Empire State Building, I remembered being told in training – you feel you could reach down and touch the chimney pots. The suburbs of the city were green and orderly and close enough to see the faces of the people looking up in astonishment at a British bomber just above their heads. One or two of them, perhaps forgetting the war was over, started to run for cover. Then, suddenly, the green disappeared, and with the green, the roofs. We were racing across mile after mile of deserted, roofless ruins, not a sign of life anywhere. I twisted the turret: in every direction it was the same, a huge city, stretching to the horizon, obliterated and abandoned. The sun shone down into the empty stumps of buildings, and nothing stirred, not a man, not a woman, not a creature, not even a cat. To be set down in the middle of this would be to find yourself on the other side of the moon, alone, with nothing left to sustain life. Now the streets had become just rows of rubble, and still we flew on for what seemed like hours until the streets themselves disappeared into one huge scorched and desolate rubbish heap. The industrial centre was a giant scrapyard: blackened girders twisted into monstrous shapes, half-melted cranes stooped over them like leafless iron willows. And in the docks, a great ship lying on its side like a toy in a bath.

The chatter on the intercom had stopped. No one spoke. Occasionally a voice would whisper, 'Bloody hell, look at that!' or just, 'Jesus Christ!' None of the crew had seen this before, not as close as this and in broad daylight. Night after night they'd emptied their bombs from high in the night sky, desperate only to dodge the flak and get home in one piece. It had never occurred to them that thousands of bombers were doing the same thing, over and over again, and that this was the inevitable result. They couldn't have imagined it. Nobody could. Even now, skimming across it in the glare of the afternoon sun, it was hard to believe what we were seeing.

After Hamburg we flew north to Kiel where the devastation was the same and the *Admiral Scheer* lay bottom-up in the ruined dock. We turned for home and out over the island of Heligoland, barren and bare, pockmarked with craters like a sponge. Hardly anyone spoke on the way back across the sea, or when we landed, or even in the transport back from the dispersal. We smoked and looked at the floor or out of the back of the truck. I suppose the same questions were revolving in all our minds. Were all the German cities like the ones we'd seen? And where were all the people? Were they dead, or hiding, or wandering in the country? How did you stay alive in such conditions? Who was going to clear up the mess? Could a whole nation be rebuilt from this? And what did they think about us now? What did we think of ourselves? The truck jerked to a stop. We handed in our parachutes and our Mae Wests and wished each other a muted good-night.

In fact, it was only seven o'clock, and I realized I was starving. I went to the NAAFI and bought myself a pint of beer and a plate of spam and chips. There was no one I knew in the place, and I was grateful: there was far too much to think about. I walked slowly back to the billet, roofless ruins still spinning past behind my lowered eyes. On my bed was a highly coloured postcard of a rocky shore and a bright-blue sea. I stared at it for a moment before I realized what it was. I

snatched it up and turned it over. With my heart in my mouth
I deciphered her small, schoolgirl handwriting.

Dear Sam,

*Thank you for your long letter. Sorry not to have answered
before but we don't have much time here. It is very nice here. The
other girls are very nice. We are quite close to the sea here and we
might be able to go swimming soon only there might still be mines.
It would be nice if you could come down here. Sorry there's no room
in my billet, ha ha! Well I must close now. Kind regards to all up
in Yorkshire.*

Love Pearl.

PS Thanks again for a lovely day in London.

24

24

How odd it was to find the war was over. Only, of course, it wasn't over. On the other side of the world, like a creeping weed, the Japanese were still spread across half a dozen countries. They were retreating, it was true, but still fighting ferociously and suicidally every yard of the way: through those labyrinthine jungles and lethal swamps and across the innumerable islands it looked like being a long and agonizing campaign. And a lot of us were going to be part of it. Some plans for early demobilization had already been announced: we were all to be given a number, calculated on our age and length of service, the smaller your number, the sooner you'd be out. The old sweats would be the first to go (Harry reckoned that Father's number was probably 1). But for people like me, young, and with less than two years' service, the Far East loomed ominously. The horror stories of the snakes, the insects and the Japanese way with their prisoners were vivid in all our minds. The snapshot of the beheading was not far from mine. I began to realize what a lucky war I'd had so far. A grizzled LAC in the billet was inclined to agree with me. 'Do you good, son, a bit of overseas. Get your knees brown.'

And, amazingly, not everyone was reluctant to go. My

friend the Adjutant for one. I was summoned to his office one afternoon and found him rubbing his hands with glee at the prospect of chasing the Japs out of the jungle. It being after lunch there was a distinct whiff of whisky in the air and he was in expansive mood.

'Ah, Turner,' he said in response to my immaculate salute. 'Stand easy.' He leaned back in his chair, lifting one leg as if about to rest his foot on the edge of his desk. He saw me looking and lowered it again. 'We've had a signal from records about you. It seems that your chosen trade is now redundant, so you'll be required to remuster.' He shook a cigarette from its thin paper packet. 'Now, I know' – he lit it with a perspex desk lighter – 'that I said I'd look into the chances of a commission for you. But I'm afraid, with the end of hostilities in Europe' – he actually sounded depressed about that – 'they're not commissioning anybody at the moment. Unless, of course, you were contemplating becoming a regular.' He inhaled deeply and blew two plumes of smoke from his nostrils like a mythical bull. 'How would you feel about that? Great career for a youngster from a good school like yours. I've been in the service all my life. Never regretted a moment. And there'll be plenty to do, believe me. The Japs are going to need a pretty long hammering, and by the time we've sorted them out we're going to have to deal with the bloody Russians – you mark my words. Bloody good show, eh?' He was so exhilarated by the thought of all this that he jumped to his feet and started pacing about, dragging fiercely at his cigarette.

The man was clearly deranged and needed careful handling. Rather than try to explain that nothing on God's earth – not even an instant pair of wings on my tunic – would persuade me to join the regular Air Force, I told him soberly that I'd think about it.

'Good man,' he said, stopping his pacing and sitting down

298

again. 'Good man. Anyway there'll be no more Compass Section for you. Don't suppose you'll mind that too much.' He looked down, slightly embarrassed suddenly. 'Rotten business. Very grateful for your discretion over that. All sorted out now without too much parley-vous.' He lowered his voice. 'Sergeant Willoughby, I think you have a right to know, was posted to a non-operational unit where there'll be no opportunity for him to get up to . . . ah . . . whatever it was he was up to. Grice, of course, is in the glasshouse.' He cleared his throat loudly and stubbed out his cigarette in the lid of a cocoa tin. 'Now . . .' He peered at my documents on the desk in front of him. 'There's a note pinned to your fifteen-eighty here to the effect that any records communication is to be referred to Squadron Leader Appleton for some reason. I'd better pass you on.' He picked up his phone.

It took me a moment to realize he was talking about Father, we so seldom called him anything else. I was despatched along the corridor to the Admin Office.

Father came round his desk and shook my hand. 'Sit down, Sam.' He lowered his tall frame into a chair opposite me. 'Now. The Adj tells me you've got to remuster. Is that right?'

I relayed what I'd just been told. He nodded and rubbed the top of his bald head briskly. 'Well, Sam, I've got a bit of news for you. I was having a natter with the CO in the mess last night and it seems that with everybody at a bit of a loose end, the AOC is very keen to have a full-time entertainments unit covering the entire group. Based here, of course.' He beamed proudly. 'I've already spoken to Harry, and he told me he'd like you and Corporal Pearce to work with him full-time.'

This seemed too good to be true: I waited for the snag, which wasn't long in coming.

'Of course, if we're going to keep you on the strength here, you'll have to have an official job. At the moment we've an

299

establishment for one more Clerk GD, so if you remustered to clerk, we could hang on to you indefinitely – certainly as long as I'm around.'

To the bottom of the ladder in one bound. Goodbye the officer's rings, the sergeant's stripes, even the LAC's modest little propeller; I'd be an aircraftman for the rest of my RAF career. I didn't hesitate.

'It's all right by me, sir.'

Father smiled fondly at me. 'That's very nice of you, Sam. I realize it'll mean a bit of a sacrifice for you, financially.' (Financially seemed a grandiose way of describing an extra sixpence a day.) 'But I expect you enjoy working with the Theatre Company, don't you?' He loved calling it that.

'Of course I do, sir,' I said genuinely. Then I remembered Harry's assessment of Father's demob number. 'But will you be here much longer yourself, sir?'

He scratched his moustache and looked sly. 'Oh . . . I shouldn't be surprised. I've got a few strings I can pull to stop them putting me out to grass just yet.' He gave me a wink.

Another madman. But as long as he was around I knew that I would be, too. Unless, of course, an overseas posting came through. A faint chill cooled my enthusiasm for a moment. But then perhaps, in the jungle, being a clerk might be as safe a job as any.

Father seemed to want to shake hands on the deal. 'You don't have to rush off, do you?' he said. 'I asked Janet to bring us some tea.'

Harry was in high good humour when I met him that night. So, for that matter, was I, and when Freddy Pearce came over to share the news with us he was beaming under his moustache like a satiated walrus. The three of us sat round eating my grandmother's cake which had arrived the day before, a bagful of crumbs in one of her disintegrating parcels. Freddy was a temperate soul and liked an early night, but when he'd gone Harry unearthed a half-bottle of whisky from his make-up box and we toasted our new-found autonomy. Harry was already full of plans and timetables. As soon as the new revue was on we'd start rehearsing another play during the day and planning yet another revue to follow that. He seemed to see a limitless future for this personal repertory company he'd acquired, and I had to point out that perhaps his own demob number wouldn't be all that high.

'That won't be for a long time yet,' he said dismissively. 'Anyway, Father could probably get it postponed for me.'

Another one. I was surrounded by lunatics. 'For God's sake, Harry,' I said, 'don't you *want* to get out?'

'Of course I do. It's just . . .' He poured some more scotch into his glass. 'I need some time to think about what I'm going to do.'

'What *are* you going to do?'

'Well . . .' He took a large swig from his glass. 'I thought I'd go back into the theatre.'

'That's wonderful, Harry. Of course you should.'

'Mind you, I'd have to start at the bottom again.' He rubbed the tip of his big nose with the back of his hand. 'I thought I might get a job as a stage manager in a small rep somewhere, and then perhaps work up to being a producer.'

'You'd be brilliant.' I was relieved he wasn't thinking of acting again. Those short legs were not effective from the front.

He peered into his glass and looked gloomy. 'The trouble, you see,' he said slowly, 'is Betty. She wants me to go back to the dairy.'

I said nothing. It was very rare for him to talk about his wife, or even refer to her by name. He usually discouraged any mention of her.

301

'If I won't,' he went on, still staring into his glass, 'she says she wants a divorce.'

This was extraordinary. Divorce, in my family, was confined to very distant relatives and spoken of in muted tones, and never in front of the younger members. Now here I was discussing it man-to-man with someone who was actively contemplating it. I listened gravely.

Suddenly he startled me by looking straight at me and saying, 'What do you think I should do?'

He clearly expected an answer. But what on earth could I say? I'd never even met her. I knew Harry, of course, but only in a man's world where his relations with women were a knee-trembler, as he called it, behind a door or trousers down over a desk top. Was that how he and Betty had started? Probably not. I imagined a genteel suburban courtship, both holding hands on the sofa. Did that give her more rights over him, or less? Did it entitle her to expect him to live his life her way? How the hell did I know? For God's sake, he was the one who handed out the advice, not me. He was still looking at me. I felt myself blush as I said, 'I think you should leave her.'

He nodded. 'You're right,' he said sagely, apparently completely satisfied. Was it as easy as that to seal a man's fate for him?

The wisdom of my advice being so instantly recognized, I felt justified in justifying it, and did, at some length, pointing out Harry's great love of the theatre and the fact that, since they had no children, they were the only ones who could be hurt by the separation (a sentiment I'd overheard my mother expressing more than once). But Harry wasn't really listening, and it dawned on me that he'd made up his mind about this a long time ago. I'd only been a sort of witness to his signature. All the same, having his decision confirmed seemed to have inclined him to unburden himself about his now defunct marriage. He lit his pipe and put his feet up.

302

'Some women, you see,' he explained, warming to his favourite subject, 'like a man to be weak — to be dependent on them. Betty's one of those. I was only a kid when I married — she's several years older than me, you know — and I think she wanted to mother me.' He laughed at the idea of his being mothered, and so did I. 'There are quite a few women like that,' he said ruminatively. 'Your little friend in Cornwall — she's one, you know.'

Oh, no she's not, I thought. What an extraordinary idea. I hadn't seen much sign of her mothering *me*. Harry was wrong about that. But then even the greatest experts can be wrong sometimes.

As the weeks slid by it seemed to me that all of us on the camp were experiencing a curious shift in our perception of ourselves in relation to the rest of the world. From an awareness that we were at the sharp end of a massive national effort to win the war, we were suddenly conscious of being on the periphery of the nation's life, of the new civilian life which was to be the beginning of the future. The talk was all of next week, next month, next year. The dreams of peacetime that had been little more than wishful fantasies, murmured from bed to bed in the billet after lights-out, now became practical plans, involving letter-writing, form-filling and circled dates on calendars.

Even Percy was inspired by the idea of new beginnings. He told us in his squeaky falsetto that Beryl had finally named the day; they were to be married in three weeks' time. The news travelled fast and the whole camp was agog. A collection was made and Percy was presented with a folding cake-stand, a gleaming monument of kitsch that rendered him speechless with pride. As well as the cake-stand he was inundated with practical advice about the wedding night. Percy took it all in good part, thrilled to be the centre of such attention, greeting each obscene suggestion with squeals of delighted outrage. On the great day the whole billet sent him a telegram (carefully worded to avoid embarrassment should it be read out at the reception), and that night at bedtime speculation was rife as to his progress. 'He'll be at it now!' someone cried. 'Good old Percy!' we all chorused. For the next week not a night went by without someone reminding us that at that very moment Percy was probably tasting the joys of matrimony.

We were scarcely out of our beds on the morning he returned. At first we didn't even notice the little figure shut the door and pad silently to his bed space. Then the shouts went up: 'Percy!', 'How was it?', 'Did you get much?', 'Think you're going to like it?'

He dropped his cardboard suitcase on his bed and sat beside it, his legs dangling. 'It weren't no go,' he said, shaking his head dolefully. 'The flag was up.'

Touring round the airfields with the new revue, I realized that everywhere we went people were preoccupied with the return to civilian life. Even some of Harry's dedicated cast were letting their minds stray to their future careers. Danny's agent came all the way from London to see a performance, causing Danny to reach new heights in his harmonica solo, leaping, spinning, grimacing and finishing on one knee with his arms outspread in a finale that would have made Al Jolson blush. His agent, a little bald man with moist, dark eyes and a powdered chin, came round to congratulate Harry afterwards, patting his bow tie and announcing to us that Danny's presentation was nothing short of masterly. He also told two of the cast that if ever they thought of turning pro he would be happy, as he put it, to handle them. He didn't offer to handle me, but did mention that if I could find a suitable comic partner there might be a future for me as a feed.

Being now a full-time theatrical I didn't see much of Alan; only occasionally we ran into one another in the NAAFI.

Like me he had to choose another job and was trying to get into Intelligence. Also like me he lived under the constant threat of a Far-Eastern posting. But he did have another plan; one that he said might interest me.

'I'm going to try for a place at a university,' he said, flushing to his ears at his own temerity. 'Apparently, if you've been accepted for a course of study you can get an early release.'

'Good Lord! Not easy to get a place though, is it?'

'Not very. But the Education Officer seems to think I stand a chance. He's arranged for me to sit the exams.'

'You crafty bugger. You must have been doing a lot of swotting.'

He smiled modestly. 'Quite a bit, yes. But it's been a piece of cake since Willoughby went.'

I had to admit I was pretty impressed. 'What university are you trying for?'

'Well . . . Oxford, really,' he said shyly.

'Blimey. Isn't that . . . I mean, won't that be a bit expensive?'

'Not if things go all right on the fifth.'

'The fifth?' I said. 'What happens on the fifth?'

Alan looked at me, aghast. 'The Election, you twit. The General Election.'

'Oh yes, of course.' I'd forgotten it was so soon. 'Will that make a difference?'

'Of course it will. University education will be free then – for everyone. If Labour get in.'

'Will they get in, though? I mean they never do, do they?'

'They've got to.' His eyes were alight with intensity in his pale face. 'They've got to, for all our sakes. We can't go back to all that poverty and unemployment and slums.'

His passion made me feel a little uneasy. 'Well, it's up to you, mate,' I said. 'You're the one who's voting.'

'Aren't you?'

305

'Too young,' I said. 'By three months. Come and ask me next time.'

Which I suppose was why I wasn't taking much interest in the whole business. I knew that a lot of people were. Feelings ran high in the billet: it seemed to be a straight choice there between Labour and out-and-out Communism. I suspected the arguments might be a bit different in the officers' mess: I couldn't imagine the Adjutant voting Labour. But then he himself was probably a good reason for everyone else to vote Labour. As I walked away from the NAAFI I wondered, if I had a vote, which way I'd use it. Somehow the pre-war world of bowlers and butlers and unearned privilege seemed like an outdated pantomime now: it would never come back. We'd all seen how the other half lived. We'd looked into each other's faces and realized we were all just people, and couldn't get far without each other. And free schools, free hospitals and no unemployment didn't sound a bad idea. Perhaps Alan was right; perhaps they would get in.

And four weeks later they did, with an unbelievable majority of 146. The whole camp seemed delirious with joy – joy and astonishment. Nothing like it had ever happened before. I saw Alan on the other side of the cookhouse, his freckles dancing with excitement. 'Wait and see!' he shouted to me over the clatter. 'You just wait and see!' Even Harry conceded gruffly that it was 'about time', so presumably he'd voted for them, too. Only Danny seemed unimpressed. 'They're so *drab*, dear,' he said, arching his eyebrows. 'No star quality. And that Attlee person. He looks as if he's come to measure the corpse.'

That weekend I got some leave, four whole days. There was plenty of it to be had now. I'd intended to spend most of the four days in trains, in the hope of getting at least one day with Pearl. But no reply had come to my letter and, realizing that it would be absurd to go that far on the off-chance, I decided to go home instead.

My mother had invited two aunts to tea: hardly an adequate substitute for what I was missing.

'Well,' said the tall one, putting down her cup with a firm hand, 'this is a nice business, isn't it.'

'What is?'

'This election result.'

'That poor Mr Churchill,' said the softer, rounder aunt. 'After all he's done for us. I simply don't understand it.'

My mother shook her head in agreement.

The tall one looked at me with candid brown eyes under unplucked brows. 'What do you think, Sam? What's happened?'

'I don't know,' I said. Which was true, I didn't. But even if I had, how could I have begun to explain to her what she obviously hadn't noticed, that the world had changed. If I told any of them how deeply distrusted Churchill was among the men I worked with, they wouldn't believe me. How could they understand how resentful so many servicemen were of the life they'd left behind? How four years of being Our Brave Lads and of the promises made to keep them brave had given them a taste for something better?

The tall aunt said, 'They'll ruin the country, you know.' She turned to my mother. 'The cloth-capped brigade, Jim calls them.' My mother giggled. The aunt's gaze swung back to me. 'You can't have people like that running things. And do you know who they're going to have as Foreign Secretary? A docker, if you please. What are people abroad going to *think* – after someone like Anthony Eden? And all this free-this and free-that: people don't really want it, you know . . .'

As she went on through what I had begun to recognize as the die-hards' litany – the destruction of the public schools, the demise of the old families who had made this country great, the coals kept in the bath – I had a sudden image of the black-eyed Glaswegian coughing his lungs away in the darkness of the pit; of Freddy Pearce's brother who'd been out of work for six years before the war; Percy's mum who'd died one freezing night in the outside privy (they'd had to take the door off to get her out); Nancy's stories of her brothers who had walked all night to find work in other villages; Pearl's aunt whose whole family, living in one damp room of a Wapping slum, had been wiped out by TB within a few years of one another; Pearl herself, skinny and huge-eyed, playing barefoot among the garbage in a treeless alley. I felt my throat constrict with pity at the unfairness of the world.

The aunt was still talking. 'And all that will happen in the end,' she was saying, 'is that we'll just be dragged down to their level, won't we?' She looked at me and seemed to expect a response.

My voice sounded husky. 'I think, actually,' I said lamely, 'it's meant to be the other way round.'

My mother looked at me sharply. 'Put the kettle on for us, would you, Sam?' she said.

I jumped up gratefully and hurried into the kitchen. I lit the gas under the kettle and stood, gripping the edge of the sink, struggling to control the trouble in my throat that was threatening to rise and swamp my eyes. The kitchen door closed quietly behind me. I rubbed a furtive hand across my face.

'Are you all right, Sam?' my mother said.

I nodded.

'You mustn't mind Edna, you know. She's always been a bit opinionated about things like that. I think she gets most of it from that dreadful Jim.'

I turned round and tried to give her a reassuring smile, avoiding her concerned look.

'Cheer up, dear.' She stood there silently until I was forced to look her in the face. She was studying me with the wry

308

expression I knew so well. 'It's not just politics that's upsetting you, is it,' she said.

Back in the camp I was aware of an irritation with the paraphernalia of war that surrounded me: stamping feet, echoing workshops, uniformed figures hurrying in and out of huts with files of documents, lorries swaying through the gates, tractors churning up clouds of dust; and all for no purpose, a chicken running round with its head off. Surprisingly, I also found myself impatient with the Entertainments Unit, as we now called ourselves. For all that we worked professional hours there was a self-congratulatory amateurishness about us that embarrassed me sometimes. Now that it was possible to consider such a thing, I began to yearn for a profession of my own. At home my mother had shown a long-suppressed interest in my future, inspired probably by the news that my father was on his way home. My life, I realized, was already drawing away from this irrelevant airfield.

I still waited daily for a letter from Pearl, but none came, and my excuses for her began to run out. In a confessional moment I'd shown her photograph to my mother who'd put on her glasses and examined it carefully. 'She's very pretty,' she'd said at last, with an inflection that left a large 'and . . . ?' hanging in the air.

About a week later, on a fine sunny evening, I walked down to the billet to clean up before we took the show off to yet another camp. When I banged the door behind me I was greeted with a fierce hush from half a dozen airmen grouped round the radio. They were like waxworks, all frozen in mid-action: one with his arm poised in the act of combing his hair, another sitting on a bed, one hand in a shoe the other holding a boot-brush, another wrapped in a towel, still wet from the ablutions.

'What's up?' I whispered.

309

One of them jerked his head mutely in the direction of the radio. The news had already begun and at first I found it hard to follow. It seemed that the Americans had dropped a bomb on Japan that had wiped out an entire city. Not a raid, apparently, just one plane and one bomb. The announcer said the bomb was thought to have two thousand times the power of the biggest one the RAF had ever dropped; something to do with the energy released by splitting the atom. Two thousand times. My mind grappled with the multiplication. I remembered the devastated heart of Hamburg, after years of relentless pounding and the destruction of hundreds of aircraft; and all of that could now be achieved by a single bomb in a single night. A tremor of deep, atavistic fear went through me; suddenly the world had become an awesomely unsafe place.

When the broadcast finished no one moved or spoke. There were none of the cheers and euphoria that usually greeted news of successes, like the first crossing of the Rhine or the fall of Berlin. With a wild surmise, was the only way to describe how we looked at one another, each man busy with his own thoughts. Thoughts like mine, no doubt: immense relief that the war must at last be really over, no need any more to face misery or starvation in the Burmese jungle (or a barbaric execution in a dusty prison compound), and at the same time a rising terror at the scale of what we could now do to ourselves. Eventually someone murmured, 'Fuckin' hell!'

And a voice from the other end of the hut expressed something else that was in all our minds: 'Lucky Hitler didn't 'ave the bleeding thing.'

That night, as warm and scented and caressing as an English summer can offer, the cast were entertained in an officers' mess in the garden of a manor house, but the atmosphere was as sober as it had been in the hut. There was endless speculation about the technicalities of the bomb, and all leading to the same chilling conclusion. As a wingless flight lieutenant put it to me from behind his pink gin, 'Atom's supposed to be the smallest thing on earth, isn't it? Well, I mean, if just one of 'em can blow a whole city to smithereens, where's it all going to end?'

There seemed to be little sympathy for the victims of the bomb; the liberation of the Japanese prisoner-of-war camps was too recent for that. 'Anyway,' someone said, 'if they surrender now, they'll save a bloody sight more people – their own included – than that bomb killed yesterday.'

Three days later another city was vaporized and the Japanese decided to give up the unequal struggle. The world war was over and we turned our faces towards the long-promised peace.

Very often now, at the weekends, the whole station would be stood down, leaving the place almost deserted. The irony being that the only people still working were usually the Entertainments Unit. Which was why I was alone in the billet on the afternoon when an exhausted airman staggered in, carrying respirator, greatcoat, kit-bag and a battered suitcase. I'd never seen him before, he was obviously a new arrival.

'Christ, it's hot,' he said. 'Empty bed space in here, is there?'

I pointed it out, at the other end of the hut, and got on with changing my shirt. I heard him tipping his kit-bag onto the springs of his bed and stacking things on his shelf. When I was dressed I walked down to be sociable.

'Long trip?' I said.

He sat on the bed among the debris of his life and looked up at me through horn-rimmed glasses. 'Since yesterday morning,' he said.

'Blimey. Where did you come from?'

'St Merryn.'

St Merryn. Yesterday morning he'd been in St Merryn. I couldn't believe it. 'St Merryn in Cornwall?'

'You wouldn't chuckle. Bloody miles away. Still, it's worth it. I'm a lot nearer home here.'

'Where do you live?'

'Manchester.'

If St Merryn was anything like this place the odds were pretty long, but it was worth a try. 'What section were you in?'

'W/T.'

W/T operators often worked around the operations room. 'Was there a WAAF there called Fairbanks? Pearl, her name is.'

He shook his head unhelpfully. 'What she look like?'

Oh, my new-found friend from St Merryn, how could I possibly tell you? How could I begin to describe her to you, in any terms that you could understand? 'Small,' I said, 'dark. Rather pretty.' Forgive me, Pearl, for that rather.

It was enough, though. 'Oh,' he said suddenly. 'The *pretty* one. In Operations. Oh, yes.' He nodded happily. 'She's gone.'

'Gone?'

'Left the service. To get married.'

It was my turn to sit down. 'Married? Are you sure? Who to?'

'I don't know. That bloke, I think. The one that came down to see her a couple of times.'

'What bloke?' I tried not to sound like an interrogator. 'What was he like?'

'Just a plonk. Tall and thin – very blond. And dark eyes,' he added. 'As a matter of fact . . .'

'Yes?'

'I think he might have been ex-aircrew. You could see the mark on his tunic where his wings had been. Been grounded, I suppose. Probably LMF, some of the lads reckoned.'

When I escaped from the hut, I walked slowly up through the empty camp towards The Wings. I'm not sure now what my emotions were. I do remember being surprised at a totally

312

unexpected feeling of relief that seemed to have invaded me, but I can't really swear to what I've always believed – that at that moment I already knew I would never hear of her again.

As I neared the big hangar, I heard the sound of the AOC's Spitfire running up at the end of the runway. A moment later it roared low over my head, its shadow flicking across me.

I didn't bother to look up.